We all held our breath and waited for the signal . . .

Suddenly Garoit screamed out the goddamnedest sound I ever heard and the gang went over and around the dunes. I ran over the top of mine and saw the column stretching to my left and right as the sheets began lifting their rifles. Some of them got off a shot or two before they were dragged from their mounts.

I ran down the face of the dune and leaped at the nearest rider. The sheet had his weapon pointed right at me, but the shot missed, and I crashed into the man's face with the top of my head.

All around me the brothers and sisters were grabbing those weapons, pulling and knocking those sheets off their mounts. They punched, clawed, stabbed, fired, and strangled. I threw my gun to a sister and got my fingers on another, a lever-action rifle.

I pumped and fired at anything white until the piece was empty.

BARRY B. LONGYEAR
INFINITY HOLD

POPULAR LIBRARY

An Imprint of Warner Books, Inc.

A Warner Communications Company

POPULAR LIBRARY EDITION

Popular Library®, the fanciful P design, and Questar® are
registered trademarks of Warner Books, Inc.

Cover illustration by Paul and Steve Youll

Popular Library books are published by
Warner Books, Inc.
666 Fifth Avenue
New York, N.Y. 10103

 Warner Communications Company

Printed in the United States of America

First Printing: December, 1989

10 9 8 7 6 5 4 3 2 1

To N.A.

and

Those who died along the way

GREENVILLE,

A.D. 2115

THERE'S a story every shark's heard. It's supposed to have come from a crowbar pit on one of the upper rim-side planets. Maybe it was from Jonomann Penal on Menes, or Vandys Correctional in the Killilian Wastes on Rashnu. For all I know, it could have happened right here on Earth. It's about old protomo—a new shark on his first day in the crowbars.

After proto gets his uniform issue, he walks onto the block, and the first thing that greets him is a fist in his face. When the birds stop chirping, the new shark sees that the guy who decked him was the same guy who had been standing in front of him in the issue line.

"Why'd you do that?" protomo demands.

"You're new," he answers, then the slugger walks off.

Old protomo goes into a blind rage about this treatment, and he looks around for something to smash. The first thing he sees is a face and he drives his fist into it. With his anger cooled a bit, the new shark sees that the guy he punched was the guy who had been standing in the issue line behind him.

The fellow on the floor holds his jaw and asks, "Why'd you do that?"

Sharky answers, "You're new."

Thus endeth the lesson.

* * *

It used to be a tickle watching the protos being led to their cells. The oh-seven thousand door slammed open, then in came the cherry following the lime green directional lights. He'd be all wide-eyed, dressed in stiff new crowbar blues, carrying a double armload of sheets, blankets, underwear, and his second uniform. You knew what those wide eyes were seeing. You knew what those new ears were hearing. You knew what proto was feeling because you been there once yourself.

Protomo was seeing cage after cage of trapped sharks—vicious, unpitying animals; his new peers. You picked up that word "peers" if you collected some breaks and worked the clock in one of those rehab hotels where all you did was put on the heads and put in your time. It's a soft clock and it's something to do. I was in one of them for a short stretch. Williamsburg Rehab. Then I got transferred to Old Miss; the joint with the view of the big runny; the Union of Terran Republics' Penal Center at Greenville. We called it the Crotch.

The proto who came to the Crotch faced the rock clock: hard time. And after his eyeballs soaked up all those bars and cruel faces, his ears got pounded numb by the combination of a thousand rads and vids all on different stations, each one going full-blast, trying to drown out the rest. Then the sharks shouting at the top of their lungs trying to talk and be heard over the racket. The constant rumble of bars moving, the dit-dit-dit of warning alarms, then the slam after slam of bars closing, the stains blowing orders and watch calls into their little hand rads.

Jeez, man, she was slinky-y-y...block twenty-seven secure...turn down that damned thing, man I...just a little-bitty powder, man, I'm sick...fool got over to the woman's side, and he...dit-dit-dit, rum-m-m-m-mble—SLAM...hey, and he said...open the oh-eight thousand gate...turn it down or I'll slice your ass'n the yard...you're dead if you ain't got the bread...once he got there, hell they was uglier'n you... dit-dit-dit, rum-m-m-m-mble, SLAM!

Then there's that whiff. A blend of locker room, hospital, discount drugstore, garage, mildew, and underground toilet. Stale sweat, dirty clothes, disinfectant, sixty different kinds of after-shave, perfume, and deodorant—all overpowered by the constant smell of machine oil. The stuff that keeps those bars rolling, the locks turning, all that steel from rusting.

They say that after they were finished building Hell, the Devil loaded up an illegal hauler with the construction clean-up trash, and the hauler nosed around until he found a deserted place that no one would ever want. He dumped Hell's trash there, and they called it Mississippi. Then they found a fever swamp on the flood plain, they built a cesspool right in the middle of it, and they called it Greenville. When it came time for the Union of Terran Republics to build its maximum security facility for recidivists, incorrigibles, and unrehabilitatables, it seemed the Minister of Corrections selected the site after accidentally getting knocked into a vat at the sewage treatment plant in the El Segundo Home for the Intestinally Gross.

Summer, Autumn, Winter, Spring, the air at Greenville was so heavy, every time a breeze blew, you could hear the splash. That's what proto was breathing when he took in the sights at Hell's Shitcan.

Protomo absorbed that atmosphere, his chin trembled, and his buns started getting tight. He had been dropped straight through the floor of the candy store right down into the heart of Hell. God but it made your guts twitch.

Proto wasn't thinking about that little thing he did on the block that bought him his room at the Crotch. He wasn't thinking about that little old lady he tapped but just happened to thin in the process, or that cute little teller he yellowed as he shoved that note across the counter and aimed that greasy, black gun muzzle between her breasts, or that jury of his "peers" that never had to grow up where you stole and killed just to work your way out from under the bottom of that mountain of bodies, despair, and garbage called "home." He wasn't even thinking about that judge—who sat there, man, like he had to explain away the five-to-ten rock he was dropping on you.

Hell, proto wasn't even thinking about that lawyer of his—that cockroach cash register in the money threads who had collecting maximum court fees by running you through the juicer with a minimum of effort down to a science. No, that's not what protomo was thinking. All that was over. Done past. Ancient history.

What the new boy did is what we all did. He stopped thinking. Kept a numb skull. You think, man, and there's only one thing to think about: time—time and where you're spending it. You think in Greenville—or in any other pit—and you buy yourself infinity in the white rubber room.

When protomo climbed those stairs and followed the lights down that gallery toward his cell, the sharks whistled at him, made smacking sounds with their lips, said things. You know what kind of things. A lot of them were kidding; a lot of them weren't. Then you knew what pro was feeling: chicken feathers. Running down the legs terror, man. Like, if proto can't get to a white throne in the next five seconds, his brand-new blues won't be brand new no mo'. If proto knew anything, he'd start counting up the colors on those sneering, smirking faces, then check his own leather and pray like hell that his skin resembled the sharks in power.

... bay-beeee, will you look at ol' protomo ... not a hair on that sweet thing ... close oh-eight thousand gate ... you turn down that damned thing, man ... I'll get the bread, man. You know I'll get the bread ... o-o-o-h, will you scan the buns on proto, there. I'm giving up trying the women's side, man ... Dit-dit-dit-dit, Rumble, rumble, rumble, SLAM, SLAM, SLAM!

Like I said: it was a tickle watching the protos come in. And I laughed. You had to laugh at something. It killed time, and killing time is where it was. But you laughed real quiet, man, because if you laughed too loud, you might never stop. Then it was back to the rubber room.

Sharks had ways of murdering the clock. Some fools studied like maybe someday they'd become tycoons, scientists, deep space navigators, or teachers instead of muckshuckers and deadheads. Some of the brothers killed time by talking about breaking out; others just talked; others just sat and stared at the walls. Some escaped by numbing their heads with loud music, religion, or happy powders. A few mentally left the crowbars by writing stories and books. Some of them were even published, too. Some killed time by killing each other.

Some thinned the timepiece by getting into group activities.

The chappies would suck around singing hymns, the perverts and deadheads would hold therapy meetings, and we even had a theater group. On the men's side they were producing *Brother Crowbar*, an in-house ripoff of someone else's play. On the women's side they were rehearsing *Mob Cinderella*, another ripoff of an even older work. There was a tap on the pipes that *Mob Cinderella* was a spoof written anonymously by a genuine goomba wiseguy, but it never paid to believe the taps. After all, a lot of sharks thinned the clock by sending out lies and rumors just to see how long they took to come back.

Whatever. It killed time.

Some—quite a few—killed the clock by killing themselves; taking a flyer off one of the upper galleries, a strip of trouser leg around the neck from the top of the bars, even drowning in a white porcelain throne. The young, pretty pros did that a lot. There used to be nets strung across the open spaces between the galleries to save the jumpers, but the nets were removed years ago. Anything but money to help ease the overcrowding problem.

When I wasn't prowling the library for something new to read, or listening to the yard gurus, I killed the clock by watching my fellow sharks at work, play, and destruction.

There were the yard monsters. They whittled on the clock by pumping iron for endless hours every day, cultivating the body grotesque. A black nationalist called Rhome Nazzar was their unofficial leader, and he wasn't just meat between the ears. I'd seen him at the library too many times to believe that. But Nazzar had killed a lot of angel cakes, and when the haystacks walked by, you could see them give Nazzar that I-just-wanted-to-make-certain-where-you-were look as they gave the home-made cutters in their pockets a little squeeze for comfort.

We had lots of political filberts, like the anarchist Martin Stays who foamed at the mouth for his first year at the hotel. When he arrived, no one got a chance to see what he looked like, he was dropped into the black hole that fast. And every time they'd let him out, he'd rip, tear, and foam at the mouth again. Then it was back in the black hole. Out of his first year in the Crotch, he couldn't of had more than a month in the yard. When he finally stopped foaming at the mouth and they let him out of the black hole for good, he hung out in the library some.

Most of the time, though, he spent the same as me: watching the zoo, but real quiet.

Another pistachio was Nkuma, and he only had the one name. He was a semi-yard monster who went around spreading "the truth." He had been a libertarian Communist who discovered Jesus and was doing infinity for thinning the entire family he had been holding hostage when the stains finally cornered him.

One strange character was Ice Fingers. The name he used in prison was Herb Ollick, but he was really a middle management goomba, head of his own small family, out of some Jersey rathole. Whether that was the truth or a let's-stir-up-some-trouble rumor was one of the hotly debated topics on slow news days. However, after all of the bets had been laid, Herb would never say one way or the other. He'd just smile, write in his cell a lot, and polish his diamonds. That's how he got the name Ice Fingers. He wore five diamond rings, two on his right hand, and three on his left. Sharks weren't allowed to wear rings, but Ice had some guard captain on the cob. The rings were very valuable, but no one made a try for them. After all, it was just possible that Ice really was a goomba.

We had a prizefighter staying with us. His name was Abner Pandro, but his fans knew him as Kid Scorpion. The wagering was that he could have captured the heavyweight title if he hadn't gotten offended by a vid reporter's question and turned the interviewer into roadkill the next day. The Kid probably could have gotten away with it, except that when the stains arrived on the scene of the crime an hour later, Kid Scorpion was still driving over and backing up over the flattened remains of the visual fourth estate.

We had some notables on the women's side, too, although it wasn't often there was an opportunity to observe. Bloody Sarah, the UTR commando officer who was working the clock for murdering one hundred and fifty-some Suryian villagers, was our most famous prisoner. The next most famous prisoner was Marantha Silver, the MJ agent who everybody knew was doing the clock on a bad rap.

The women had their own yard monsters, too. There was a bull croc named Nance Damas who pumped a bit of iron and was there for torturing to death a rapist who had done a close friend of hers, and for torturing to death the six witnesses to the event who didn't do anything because they didn't want to become involved.

It was quite a place. As big Dave used to say, in the crowbar hotel you get to see the best of everything at its worst, and the worst of everything at its best. There was the Whacker. She was an ax-murderer from Washington who used to be a social worker. We had a police captain who threw the law books out of the window and thinned the sleaze he was after. There was the Soprano-maker, a pepper bit who used to geld her male friends with a razor when they disappointed her, and she must've had quite a crowd of disappointments, if you listened to the stories. But stories always grow hair in the crowbars. To live up to the crowbar yarns of her exploits, the Soprano-maker would have had to have been running through rush-hour crowds with a chain saw.

Anyway, there were lots of interesting people to watch at Old Miss. Watching the sharks was entertainment, and it kept me on top of what was happening. I knew the gangs, who to steer clear of, who to do favors for, and the little pieces of information that filtered through the grapevine or down the pipe from the front office.

I survived by becoming as valuable as I could to as many brothers as possible, and by being no trouble to the rest. I knew the score, the drill, the ropes, like any old hand at the game. I was twenty-seven; eleven of those years in the crowbar stacks. Three years in Lancaster Juvenile Rehab (assault), two and six in Binghamton with another deuce and a half at Jordonsville (armed robbery), a deuce at Williamsburg Rehab with a move and another big one at Greenville (murder, aggravated assault, armed robbery, resisting arrest) with, maybe, ten more on good behavior. Sixteen if I was naughty. I figured on doing the time and walking through the door in the year 2125 at the age of thirty-seven. Then news of Tartaros came down the pipe. *Brother Crowbar* and *Mob Cinderella* were canceled.

WHEN YOU WISH

UPON A STAR

THE whole lodge had heard about Tartaros before—a planet where seventeen other planets dumped their worst sharks. It just had nothing to do with us. We'd heard Parliament blow wind at the subject, read the editorials against the penal colony, heard about the protests, saw the issue dropped time after time. Earth wasn't one of the planets belonging to the Tartaran con cartel, so who worried about that? There were always more important things to worry about, like scoring a powder, spreading some corn, staying alive and disease-free.

But there was a turn in the arguments: for every shark supported in the crowbars, eight new jobs could be created, twenty families could be fed, or another step toward finding that elusive cancer cure could be taken. That's what came down the pipes from the front office. Earth had joined the human landfill. There were too many humans in too little space to waste precious resources on the antisocial element. The bottom line was the bottom line.

We were all going to be protos. All of us were officially notified three weeks after we already knew. Anyone doing numbers on murder one, rape, child molesting, unclassified acts of terrorism, a felony involving more than ten thousand credits (including the cost of apprehension and prosecution), a second felony of any kind, the "unrehabilitatable," and anyone who they felt like sending, were to be dumped on the big T. Everyone in the Crotch had already been classified as "unrehabilitatable." That's why we were in Greenville. So, we were all notified. All of our sentences had been "commuted" to exile on Tartaros.

I went to the prison library and looked up Tartaros. The information on the planet, even its location, was classified. The information on the planet's name was not. According to the ancients, Tartaros was Hell's hell. What the Sibyl told Aeneas, as she took him on a guided tour of Hell, was that the gulf of Tartaros was so deep that its bottom was as far beneath their feet as Heaven was high above their heads. All in all, it did not sound as though being exiled to Tartaros had much chance of being a move for the better.

Exile. It sounded like something out of the days of feudal kings, knights, and all that yore.

We waited, while I watched and listened.

"I don't care where I put in my time, man. It's got to be better than this place."

"Bay-beee. You have obviously not gotten the *word*."

"What *word*?"

"Nobody is going to fetch you off that rock after your time is up, bay-beee. *No* way. Your sentence has been *commuted*, changed, you have been handed the sticky stick. Tartaros is for *ever*, bay-beee."

"What? *Man*, when my time is up, *I* go back on the *block*. *That's* what the smear in the black rags said. And, *my man*, that's just what I intend to do!"

"*Sor-r-r-r-y*, bay-beee. The man has *changed* the rules. Isn't that just like the little devil? Let me consult my crystal ball. I see in our futures a long voyage, and a long, *long* stay."

"You telling me, man, that we *don't* come back? No matter *what* our sentences are?"

"You got it, bay-bee."

"Don't we got some *rights* in this? What about appeals?"

"*Sor-r-r-ry*, bay-bee. No rights, no fights, no deals, no appeals. We are being put on infinity hold."

* * *

Watching.

The family men began putting on the ants early. Cut off, no more contact, no more mail, no more packages filled with goodies some stain was paid not to notice. The coldest monsters in the crowbars would begin weeping at odd moments for no apparent reason at all. I listened to more than one sob story about Sonny, Sis, Fido, and the Little Woman. Even the patriots started to come out of the closet, pissing and moaning about purple mountains' majesty and amber waves of silicon chips.

The vids even got into it when the matter of pregnant prisoners came up. Why should the offspring suffer the punishment of the parent? Didn't that make the sins of the parent the sins of the child? I suppose the two-for-one reduction in the population totals helped the argument some, but the clincher was what it had always been: the children have been suffering for the sins of their parents since man invented sin. Why change now? Pregnancy was no ticket off of Tartaros. The abortionists had a busy season.

I heard some of the don goomba kingpinners were talking about hiring private raiders to come and lift them off the big T, as some of them began calling the planet. But the mob chiefs usually found their money was all dried up. That number two suit in the brotherhood got real assertive when he found out that number one was on his way to infinity hold.

The yard monsters kept pumping iron, but there were lots of furtive conversations between Nazzar and some of the others like Ow Dao, Steel Jacket, and The Match. For a time, security at the Crotch was maxed. The front office expected the hotel to entropize after getting the streak, and the stains were powered up to where they probably could have taken on the army of a medium-size planet. I had no complaints. It kept the streets clean for a bit. But the man should have saved the taxpayers the change. The Crotch wasn't ready to rock.

Instead, we were stunned. Thinking about change did that. Straightmeats fear change; the unknown. But you sit in the crowbars long enough and change is something you pray for. Even a move to another pit looks like a holiday. The thing that made the T look good to the sharks at Greenville was that none of us knew anyone who had been there. Not even the stains knew anything. The only ones who knew the real story were on

Tartaros. There was no trouble, and, after a few days, the stains went back to business as usual.

Watching. It was a tickle the way the sharks packed up the few things they were allowed to bring. Rads and vids, photos of Mommy and Fido, feelthy peektures, some health pills packed with classified vitamins and minerals. The tobacco addicts were jamming as many nails as possible into those tiny metal boxes. They were jabbering away, grinning like they were going off to grandma's for a holiday. I wondered what would happen if the pills, the weed, and the little vials of alk, powder, and other stuff ran out.

There's something invigorating in thinking about being smack in the middle of fifteen thousand freaked-out sharks who are all fighting rats, bugs, snakes, and giant squids in their imaginations. But the deadhead puffs can always find a way to continue being a loser. Hell, you can grow alcohol anywhere. When they can't get anything else, some of the powder puffs even get high by cutting off the blood to their brains until they pass out.

Me? I found myself—for the first time in my life—staring at the concrete walls of my cell, wondering about me, my life, the things I had done, the people I had done them to, the things that had been done to me. What about that teacher I punched out in high school that bought me my trey in Lancaster? You punch out people that have a mouth on them, and that bundle of wimps had a mouth on him. I got my trey, but at least that smear got his mouth wired shut. I was told he quit teaching. I did some good, then.

Good. All my life I was good. Never thought of myself as bad, although there were a lot of opinions on the other side of that. It had something to do with the definitions used by the straightmeats against the ones used by the sharks.

The straightmeats told me I was no good, but good was living up to your buddies. Loyalty. Good was never growing feathers on a job, pulling out and leaving your partner to entertain the stains. Good was keeping your blowhole shut when the man wanted you to roll over on a brother to keep the numbers down when the clock was dumped in your lap. Good was stealing enough to keep your face fed and food on the table for your mother and kid sister. That was good. Good was walking down the street swinging, knowing no one would tangle with you because if you didn't stripe his ass, your gang would.

That five I did in Binghamton and Jordonsville for liberating that mom and pop grocery. I thought about that judge—wheezy old smear in the black rags—lecturing me on the 'right to property."

The right to property. The judge he said, young man, he said, I don't think you will learn about this any other way. Five to eight in the Binghamton Crowbar Hotel where you will be denied your "right to property." I never had any bloody damned property in the first place. Big deal.

Halfway through my nickle at Binghamton, Eddie "The Whisper" got a modified spoon slipped between his ribs because he couldn't keep his blowhole shut. The stains knew that I knew, so it was go to the juicer and sing or go to Jordonsville. Jordonsville it was. Good. I goddamned well knew what good was. I didn't need a spoon between my ribs because I couldn't keep the wind out of my hole.

But after I spent my nickle, the doors opened and I was back on the block. My mom was dead. My kid sister off with some deadhead. No job. The gang gone—jail, dead, or just plain out on juice or powder. Hell, even the tenement where I had grown up was gone. In its place was a big hole in the ground waiting for some agency and a lot of money nobody wanted to spend to fill it with another housing project designed to deal with over-population by vertical filing.

Nights I would go out to the plush quarters and do a little liberating to keep change in my pocket. I only did easy stuff. I learned to do locks in Jordonsville, along with a few other things like boxes and alarms. I learned all about the "right to property": if you leave it sitting around like a damned fool, *it's mine*. Half the time I didn't even have to do a lock. Doors left open, windows open, cellar doors open, fancy boxes on dressers shouting, "Hey, look in here! This is where the good stuff is!", picture frames with shiny brass hinges on one side saying, "Guess what's back here?" Then you open it up and find a "safe" that couldn't keep out a spastic with a hairpin.

Then my kid sister, Danine, was found dead in some dump. She had taken a bunch of pills because her old man had gotten bored with her and split. Before he left, he had turned Danine's

sweet face into an ad for a horror flick. His name was Kosta
something and he was a powder puff looking for a bit with
some ass left to sell. I found him and thinned his shadow. I was
a little crazy after that.

I still had the gun and I went into the first bank I saw and
pulled it out. I didn't even need the money. But I needed to tap
that bank guard, and that first stain with a badge that came
through the door. When they laid the stripes and thumps on me,
I guess I needed those too. The chaos, the broken bones, helped
to kill what I was feeling inside.

Then there was the rehab facility at Williamsburg where they
decided I was beyond hope. I couldn't see what was wrong with
thinning Danine's old man, and they figured that wasn't a plus.
I had been sorry about the two stains who got broken up, but
they shouldn't have gotten in the way of my pain. That was it
for the rehab.

Then they sent me to Greenville. But from there where? A
place called Tartaros. The big T. Exile. Permanent sentence.
Infinity hold.

There would be no mail, no vids, no phones, nothing but a
free, no-frills, one-way ride. That was all corners with me.
There wasn't a single body on Earth I wanted to write or call
me. I thought about that for a long time, then I bought permission for a call and punched in the number of a bit I knew. It was
the only number I could remember. She didn't remember me at
all, but she wished me luck.

When it came time to pack my belongings, I couldn't think
of anything special I wanted to bring. I didn't have a thing that
would be useful, and there wasn't anyone I wanted to remember.

I mentioned this to the yard guru in the cell next to mine. His
name was Big Dave Cole. To keep me sane he had lent me the
first book I had ever read all of the way through. Southey's *Life
of Nelson*. It kept me sane, and started me on reading. So when
Big Dave talked, I listened. He said to me that I should bring a
book. If I didn't enjoy it myself, I could always trade it to the
print addicts for what I did want.

"There won't be many books on the T, Bando, and readers
will pay almost anything to keep reading."

I spoke through my bars. "What book should I bring?"

He laughed. "Hell, anything. After a few days without reading, there'll be those who'll swap you mother, best bit, and cat for a seed catalog."

"I don't know." I sighed. "It's almost like a point of honor not to bring anything. Taking something is like saying that I'm going along. It's like I'm thumbing my nose at the stains one last time if I don't bring anything."

"That's like trying to get revenge on someone by punching yourself in the head. Real stupid." I heard Big Dave move around in his cell for a bit, then he laughed and said, "Here. Bring this one."

I saw the corner of an orange cover and I reached between my bars and pulled in the little pumpkin-colored book. Its title was *Yesterday's Tomorrow: Daily Meditations for Hard Cases*.

Moving day.

"Nicos, Bando, 3340792. Stand at the door." It was a couple of stains with screenboards with more stains behind them herding the processed sharks out of the block. I stood at the door, grabbed the top of the bars, and waited until the stain was finished feeling me up.

"Any belongings, Nicos?" asked the short skinny one.

"No."

"You're not coming back from this one, sharkie. You sure you don't want to bring something with you from Earth? Some pressed flowers? A vid of your old gray-haired granny?"

"I got my blues, a back full of scars, and all the shit I can carry from you assholes. I got all I want from Earth."

"Suit yourself, tough guy."

I always had.

TO GRANDMOTHER'S

HOUSE WE GO

THEY moved us in groups of fifty to the spaceport. It was another tickle to think about space, other worlds, stars. When you have your nose in the garbage, garbage is all you ever see or think about. Thinking about not being on Earth, about being out there in space somewhere, was a cruise.

I used to dream about flying among the stars when I was a kid and could still dream. I would eat up the stories of UTR deep space pilots and explorers, imagining myself zipping past pink gas clouds and huge red stars. At least I was going to get to see some of those things on the way to Tartaros.

On the bus I sat by the window. That way I got to see all those places I never saw in the daylight. Sure, I saw plush before when I used to do it for jewelry, cash, coats, coin and stamp collections. But that was work, and always at night. There were still neighborhoods like theirs, neighborhoods like mine; people like them, and people like us. All those big highways, glass office buildings, cozy little mansions saying bye-bye to old Bando Nicos. Can't use you, Bando. Time to put you away—far away from us good, good people.

Hell, no one noticed the bus. It was just another vehicle in another rush-hour parade whining down another road. Fifty human beings on their way to infinity hold, but the world, the city, not one soul paused to take notice.

Maybe, somewhere in one of those glass office buildings, some government accountant was patting his fat belly and nodding over his backlit spread sheet. It took the Union of Terran Republics sixteen thousand credits a year to keep Bando Nicos locked up in Greenville. Now Bando and the whole joint were on their way to the spaceport and a place called Tartaros. Cost: the no-frills price of the trip. He'd pat his belly and nod again. Check, check, enter column, delete; the Ministry of Corrections was moving into the black.

I turned from the window and went back to watching my fellow animals. Nkuma was seated next to me, and in the aisle seat across from him was a defrocked priest whose name I never knew. Everyone just called him Fodder, and he was rocking the clock for raping a young girl and killing two parishioners in an alcoholic rage. He was the most guilty shark I ever saw, constantly mumbling prayers that might, somehow, plea bargain his way out of the big toaster. Nkuma leaned over and said, "Pack it, Fodder. There ain't no way 'round the red suit." With his cuffed hand Nkuma touched a finger against his own knee. "Sssssssss!" He lifted his finger, shook it, and blew on it. "Hot. Hot!" Then he laughed while Fodder continued his mumbling.

We never got to see the outside of the prison ship. The waiting pen had no windows, and there was nothing but a guarded corridor to the hatch. At the hatch I caught the whiff. It smelled like any other pit.

"Nicos, Bando, 3340792."

I shuffled out of the pack and made my way down the bare-metal aisle between the drab-looking seats. Whoever built that ship had saved a bundle on interior decorating. In the back of my head was an itch that wondered if I could keep sane doing nothing but sitting in one of those minimalist flight couches for the days it would take to reach Tartaros. When I imagined the ship, I expected to see windows. I thought I could kill the clock watching the stars pass by. But there were no windows. I felt panic gnaw at my edges. Close places make it hard to breathe. I have to see the outside or I suffocate.

I stopped before a stain who was carrying a bad look and a

screenboard. After checking the number on my jacket against his board, he nodded toward a half-filled row of seats. "In there, Nicos."

I looked toward the rear of the compartment. Rows and rows of cons. They looked like galley slaves in one of those old Roman ships. I glanced at the stain. "When do we get issued oars?"

His eyes were covered by his cap's visor. The rest of his face was like brick. "Oars?"

I shrugged. "Forget it."

His cheek muscles twitched. "Don't make trouble, Nicos."

"What'll you do, stain? Put me in jail?"

The tiny mouth beneath the guard's visor cracked into a humorless grin. "No more jails for you, burr-head. But I might arrange for you to make the trip to Tartaros with a couple of broken knees. Maybe you'd like a little walk outside after we take off? Maybe I just won't let you use the white throne for the trip."

The man always has the power. I did what I should have done in the first place: shut my blowhole. Again the guard nodded toward the half-filled row of seats. "Put your striped ass in that chair and buckle up, tough guy."

I moved in, sat in the last empty seat, and buckled the metal mesh belt across my upper thighs. Just for the laughs I tried to release the buckle.

"No way."

I looked and saw that my left-hand companion was one of the yard monsters from Greenville. One of the black gang that broke arms for Snowflake. Freddy something. I had done him a couple of favors. "Never hurts to try."

Freddy something nodded once, then closed his eyes and rested his head against the back of his couch. I looked to my right as another yard monster, Dick Irish, dropped into the next seat and buckled up. I closed my eyes and swallowed. Dick Irish's arm was one of the many snapped by Freddy in the line of duty. Irish nudged me with his elbow, grinned, and talked in a low whisper. "Keep low, Nicos. I got a little present for that black bastard." He glanced at Freddy then opened his jacket just enough for me to see the handle of a homemade cutter.

My gut knotted as I contemplated those two sweetmeats

having a slash-and-snap contest in my lap. I glanced up at the compartment's overhead and whispered to Irish: "Up there, Dick."

He looked up. "What?"

"See those things that sort of look like air vents?"

Irish frowned and nodded. "Yeah? What about them?"

"Cameras. They're watching us every second."

He glared at the air vent for a moment, shrugged, and leaned back in his seat. "How long's it going to take for the stain to work his way down a row full of sharks? I can make ground round out of Freddy before anyone gets here. I'm on infinity hold. I ain't got nothin' to lose."

I moistened my lips and whispered again. "Don't be a jerk. They got comp-run light cutters tied in with the cameras. You'll be cut in half before you can get that edge all the way out of your jacket." I glanced at Freddy, but the monster still had his eyes closed. When I looked back at Irish, he was glowering at the overhead.

He rubbed his chin, then clasped his hands over his belly and turned his face in my direction. "You sure, Nicos?" I nodded emphatically. He looked back at the overhead, then closed his eyes. "Goddamn stains."

The knot in my gut eased just a bit. Cameras? Light-cutters? Computers? How long was it going to take for old sweetmeat on my right to figure out that those air vent-looking things were only air vents? I felt an elbow nudge my left arm and I looked into Freddy something's smiling face.

"Smart," he whispered. "Stay smart." He resumed his sleeping pose while that protomo feeling crawled all over me. Greenville was beginning to look a lot better.

UTRPSS 1364

IN the ship, we were stuck in rows sixteen across. A few sharks were cut loose long enough every now and then to hand out tasteless little box chows to the rest. You went to the white throne under escort, and when you stood up to make the trip, you got to see the whole compartment. It was a long trip, and I got to count the rows a lot of times. Fifty-four rows, and all were full. Eight hundred and sixty-four cons in that compartment. Twenty compartments in the ship. Seventeen thousand two hundred and eighty cons. Maybe. I never got to see the sizes of the other compartments.

When the stains took you to the white throne, you were put through a zatz thing that cleaned you, clothes and all. You didn't feel clean at all, but it sort of killed the smell. I knew some of the happy-powder boys that had hollowed out heels, had sewed sweet death into their seams, and had even dissolved their shit and soaked their blues in a saturated solution. None of the stuff made it through the zatz.

"Man, how can that thing clean out a sealed glass container?" The whine came from a powder puff three or four seats down from Dick Irish. He had his shoe off and was looking with great woe upon an empty vial that protruded from the back of his heel.

When the puffs began getting tense with the sweat-writhe-

and-heave thing, the guards and even some of the sharks thought it was funny. At least the sharks that weren't sitting near them thought it was funny. A lap puddled in puke does terrible things to one's sense of humor.

When the puffos started seeing tentacles and strangling their seat mates, prescription downs were issued. I didn't even want to think about what the puffs would be like after landing. After the downs had all done past.

You got to brush your own teeth with a recycled toothbrush dipped in a paste that tasted like frog-fungus frappé. Back in my seat, the metal mesh belt was locked in place, then it was back to staring at the insides of my eyelids.

What can you do when you can't do anything? At first I tried sleeping. That constant rumbling vibration from the ship's engines helped to drown out the noises around me, but it's tough to sleep for weeks if you're still alive.

I hummed songs, I thought of every piece of my past that I could remember, I tried figuring numbers in my head, which was a waste. I couldn't do much with numbers when I had a calc. Without a box, I was helpless.

It got so that I would have given my left leg, and a good bit of my right, to get Big Dave's book out of my box in the cargo hold. There were a few paperback books that had been carried on board, but they never seemed to travel my way. I began having fantasies about the wonderful time I would have when I could plant my feet on solid ground, open *Yesterday's Tomorrow*, and read until I went blind.

Finally Freddy got bored enough that he wanted to talk. What he wanted to talk about were the men, women, and children, in and out of hotels, that he had tortured, maimed, and killed. With surprising gracefulness he would gesture with his hands as he talked, and the stories frightened me so that it took quite a bit of mental effort to remember to blink every now and then.

Watching.

There was a shark sitting in front of me who carried a long face on a slender body. The stains would call him out when it was his turn to visit the throne, which is how I knew his name was Clark Antess. I thought I had remembered him from the vids. He was a former member of Parliament, had been appointed by the First Minister to head the UTR Defense Force's Office of Procurement, making him the number two man in the Ministry of Defense.

Clark Antess had been caught with his manicured fingers in the till to the sweet sound of three mills. What that long face had to have been pondering was this vaporous thing fools call justice. See, there was a bird in the Ministry of Defense who had done the very same thing Clark had done, except that he had done it two years earlier for eight times the change. That fellow had done eight months on a rehab farm and was on parole publishing his book by the time the nabs got Clark.

It was all in the timing. An election came rolling around and it was again time to interview a couple of bums, drag out the drug addicts, and just to show the folks that we're not just down on the little people, let's nail someone who wears a suit. Antess found himself wearing a suit at the wrong time.

So Clark found himself with a bag full of bad numbers and riding a rocket to Hell's hell thinking that if he had stolen thirty mill instead of three, he wouldn't be on his way to infinity hold. Instead he'd be in group nodding his head and telling some counselor how he'd seen the light and was bent on mending his ways just as soon as the movie and vid-serial rights from his life story were negotiated.

One time when he came back from the throne and was facing me before he sat down, I held up my right fist and said, "Justice!"

He looked at me with those sad eyes, turned around, and sat down without replying. Freddy jabbed me with his elbow and observed, "You're always lookin', Bando. Always lookin'."

"I don't mean anything by it. Just killing the clock, same as everyone else."

Freddy grinned and shook his head. "No, you watchin', but not like everybody else. See, when the other yard eagles look around they're tryin' to find somethin' to laugh or shout at. They're tryin' to fill the moment. When you look you see things maybe you shouldn't."

"I don't know what you're talking about."

"Sure you do." He sat up, faced me, and opened his big brown eyes. "I've seen you lookin' with all those gears turnin' in your head. Sometimes when I catch you lookin' at me or

Irish or some other shark, sometimes I get the feelin' you're takin' somethin' that don't belong to you."

"Like what?"

"If I believed in vampires, I'd say you were soul-stealin'."

"Freddy, do you believe in the big bats?"

"No. I don't believe in vampires." Freddy closed his eyes and rested his head against the back of his couch. "That's why I figure you're some kind of ghoul livin' off the rest of us somehow—eatin' us with your eyes."

PUSSYFACE

DICK Irish wanted to talk about the new world we were going to, how it was a fresh start for all of us, and that he would go straight and make himself into a new man just as soon as he had finished butchering Freddy and settling a few other old scores he had in mind. Between trying to sleep sitting up, my legs hurting from sitting so much, being locked up with no windows, and listening to the yard monsters' horror stories, I was a long way from getting rested. Above the sink in the throne room was a mirror, and every time I looked at it, the fellow who looked back had aged a year.

There was a game we played like twenty questions, except we only allowed eight questions. One of us would pick a shark and answer questions on the yard eagle's criminal record or crowbar history while the other two tried to guess the shark's name. Dick Irish was as thick as frog-foot fungus, but Freddy was sharp. Anyway, he knew a lot about the sharks.

"Male?" asked Freddy.

"Yes."

"White?"

"No."

"Murderer?"

"No."

"Political?"

"No."

Freddy looked up at the air vent. "Arson?"

"No."

Freddy squinted his eyes at me and asked, "Does he pump iron?"

I nodded and tried to keep a poker face. There were maybe two hundred yard monsters at Greenville. "He pumps iron. You got one more question."

"Swindler? Yirbe Vekk? Steel Jacket?"

"Yes, and now you pick one."

Freddy closed his eyes and flexed his fingers as though he were strangling a rhino. "I got one."

I blew my eight questions, and an additional eight questions that Freddy gave me out of the goodness of his heart. I couldn't guess who it was, and Freddy expanded on the game. He gave me a five-minute description of the shark, and the only thing I managed to figure out was that, whoever the yard eagle was, he was a real asshole. Then Freddy told me. The shark was Bando Nicos. I got tired of the game.

Watching. Maybe halfway through the trip the sharks stopped making like a trip to grandma's for the holidays. First quiet, then talk; pumping the stains for something on Tartaros. But none of them had been there either. One of the seventeen other planets using the big T had supplied the prison ships, but the UTR had supplied its own guards. The talk got angry, then the guards shuffled us around to different seats. I said good-bye to Irish and Freddy and let my guts unwind for the first time in days.

I wound up with a pussy-faced filbert from Lewisburg Max on my right. He was a terrorist who looked like a daisy with a beard and sideburns. On my left was the aisle. In the aisle seat across from mine was Big Dom from Greenville. Him I knew. He was a big Greek with a brain the size of a pea who killed his clock by lifting weights ten hours a day. I had done Dom a few favors back in the Crotch.

"Hey, Bando."

"Dom. How goes it?"

The giant grinned, half the teeth missing from his head. "Need my weights, Bando. Dom needs his weights."

"Can't be too long, now."

"All this energy in me's ready to explode. I can't find no way to work it off. You know this ship ain't got no windows?"

"I noticed."

"I want to look at the stars, Bando."

"Just cruise, Dom. Can't be too long now. Just cruise."

"What about my energy? How can I work it off?"

"Try isometrics. Like you push and pull against things." I put my hands on the back of the seat in front of me. "Like this, and push. It'll work your arms, back, and shoulders. Get your legs into it and you can even work those too."

Dom placed his hands on the back of the seat in front of him and pushed. There was a hellishly loud cracking sound and Dom just about folded the shark in that seat in half. Those seats weren't supposed to move, and when they replaced the back on that one, I saw the steel supports the big man had snapped in two. He looked at me, his hairless eyebrows raised, looking very guilty.

"It's okay, Dom," I said to him. "It can't be too long now. Just cruise."

Dom nodded. End of conversation. The hairy thing on my right opened his mouth for the first time and whispered. "That sweetmeat a friend of yours?"

"What's it to you?"

The hair nodded at Dom. "We're going to need friends like that where we're going."

I looked at the kid. "What do you know about where we're going, Pussyface?"

The kid grinned. Nice dental work peeked out of all that hair. "I'm not like the rest of you yard eagles. I got ways of finding out. Tartaros is going to be my place."

I laughed. *"You?"* Skinny little punk. I laughed again.

The kid nodded. "Me."

I shook my head. "Look, Pussyface—"

"My name is Garoit. Darrell Garoit."

"Okay, Darrell Garoit, you pussyface. For openers, it's sharks with think-goo, coin, and connections that run the pits. Next, you're a pussy-faced little punk. Punks don't run the crowbars; they get run by the powered-up sharks. Last, just what is it that you know about Tartaros?"

He sneered at me, leaned his head back against his seat, then closed his eyes. I wrapped the fingers of my right hand around his skinny wrist and squeezed. "Pussyface, I can bust this arm like a twig. Now, I asked a question."

"All right!" Darrell Garoit rubbed his released wrist, then gave me a bad look. "There's no hotel on Tartaros. No crowbars, no stains. Nothing but cons. My group, the Freedom Front, we fought against the UTR joining the con dump on Tartaros, so I've studied all about it. See, there's no jail, no government, no guards. A guy with political savvy can go a long way there, if he can stay alive long enough. I plan to stay alive."

"You're packed. What kind of system is that? How do they get any work done, or keep the sharks off each other's throats, without hightowers keeping watch?"

"No guards of any kind, Nicos. No stains, no front office. We'll be on our own."

"That doesn't make any sense. What is it, then?"

"It's a dump. But it's the raw stuff of political evolution. Anarchy of a kind waiting for Utopia."

I looked around for a face, but couldn't find it. "Look, Garoit, my bunch from Greenville has a terrorist in it ten times riper'n you. He's an anarchist, too." I chuckled. "He's bigger'n you, too. You get a chance, you find Martin Stays and tell him how you're going to run the place. If it's like you say, he'll be thinking the same thing you are. Watch out for him when he starts foaming at the mouth, though. He's about due."

The kid nodded and smiled. "It's true. You'll find out."

Tartaros makes sense, if you think about it. If you think about it like a budget-strapped prison system up to its high pockets in population, sharks, angry taxpayers, and anticrime pressure groups. Dump the cons. It gets rid of them, no maintenance costs, no crowded prisons, and who cares what happens? The cons are being all set free, so why should they complain?

Free. Why that word yellowed my guts confused more than just me. All cons want to be free, except for a few sickies who can't sleep without a pile of crowbars to hug. But most cons want to be free. If what the kid said was true, then I could go off in the mountains of forests, set up my own shack and be at peace with myself. Maybe I could find a woman. There had to be female exiles from Greenville on board the ship. Exile to Tartaros could be the best thing that ever happened to me.

I thought about it, and thought about it some more. With each thought my cabin in the woods dream faded a bit more. Cons had been dumped on Tartaros for over forty years. We wouldn't be dropping into an uninhabited paradise. Forty years is a lot of cons, and the more that cons run a place, the more deadly and unpredictable that place becomes. What's more, if it was paradise, the man would have his own cabin put up there. No one ever turned paradise over to sharks. Tartaros would be something else.

No walls, no bars, no guards—but what? The word spread, but that question "What?" kept things under control. We were all going to be free. But what is "free?" Take a shipload of dumb sharks and have them ponder their first philosophical question. A lot of frowns, a lot of head shaking, a lot of fear, but no trouble.

By the time the ship entered Tartaros's atmosphere, I made certain of two things: Big Dom was going to stick to me like a second skin, and Darrell Garoit, former crazy bomber for the Freedom Front—whatever the hell that was—would be with us. Maybe he'd run things for a while. There was a new set of ropes to be learned, and he talked like he knew a few knots.

FREE AT LAST,

FREE AT LAST

BEFORE the hatch opened each of us was issued a heavy parka, five days worth of those little box chows and a plastic bottle of water in a sack, and a kit bag containing the personal belongings each of us had been allowed to bring along. I checked and my kit bag had only Big Dave's book in it, so I put my box chows and water in the bag, as well.

The hatch opened, and there was nothing but blackness beyond the illuminated bay. An icy smell of sulfur and dust crept into the ship. As soon as I stood at the head of the ship's ramp, I slung my kit bag on my shoulder and that protomo feeling was on me like slime on slugs.

Outside it was the kind of cold that sticks the insides of your nostrils together when you inhale. The area around the ship was lit up with a huge umbrella of yellow light. You could see that the ground was loose sand with little clumps of round-bladed grass sticking out here and there. Paradise it was not.

The edge of the light umbrella seemed to steam the ground where it touched. "The ship puts out a force field to keep the old sharks on the planet from attacking it." I looked back and saw Garoit staring wide-eyed at the yellow lights. His eyes aimed at me and he gave one of those nervous grins.

"No question about it, Nicos. This is a one-way trip."

I looked around and saw the expressions on the faces of a few of the powder puffs. They were beginning to take in that whatever deals they might have made with the guards to obtain various valuable medicines were null and void. Once we stepped beyond the yellow umbrella, there would be no more contact with the stains. The expressions were of resignation and suppressed panic.

A few of them, as always, put aside their panic to become predators. Each one began doing an inventory on the remaining puffs, making a mental list of who was probably holding what. This data was collated against each puff's physical strength and speed, as well as against each deadhead's place in the disembarkation order. Sworn lifetime friendships and blood brotherhoods were evaporating as everyone reassessed his priorities.

I saw Freddy waving a finger at me as he shook his head and mouthed the words, "Watching, Bando? Still watching?"

I shrugged and waved a hand in return as I faced the hatch. The names were called and checked off a screenboard as a body admitting to each name exited. The guard reading the names was the same stain who had ranked me on that first day before I had even gotten to my seat. On the trip I had learned that his name was Crawford.

"Nicos, Bando, 3340792."

I held up my right hand and wiggled my fingers. "That's me."

Crawford looked up from his board, his gray eyes laughing at me. "Well, this is it, tough guy." He nodded toward the hatch. "How's it look?"

"At least it's got a big beach," I answered with my usual you-can't-touch-me-grin. The grin melted as I looked upon one of the last persons I would see who would make it back to Earth. "Crawford, have a good trip back." What the hell, it didn't cost anything.

The stain looked out of the hatch and back at me. "Good luck, Nicos." He held out his hand.

I nodded and shook hands with him. "Thanks. It looks like I can use some."

Before he let go of my hand he looked like he was trying to decide if I'd be worth the waste of a few words. I passed the test.

He said, "Anytime before you arrive at the gates of Hell, Nicos, you can change your own luck."

I gestured with my head toward the hatch. "Here?"

He gave my hand a final shake. "Even here. Give it a try." He released my hand and called out the next shark's name and number.

After we were all out, the ship closed its hatches, turned off the lights, then gave us a two-minute warning to stand clear. We stumbled off in the dark, away from the ship, then watched as it rose into the night and fired off with a blinding white streak of light. I watched it until the light disappeared over the horizon. Big Dom stood next to me. He pointed up at the sky.

"Bando, look. I don't see no stars."

I looked up. "Your eyes haven't adjusted to the dark yet. Maybe it's just cloudy."

My eyes were adjusted to the dark. I could make out a couple of faint stars, but the rest of the sky was blank. The sky wasn't overcast. It was just empty. I pointed the two stars out to Dom, but the big man was crying.

"Them stars's all I could see from my window in Greenville. I knew them stars, Bando. The names, stories, 'n' everything." He looked down and shook his head. Then that look came over him. It was the way the head hung and the shoulders slouched. It said, "It is the purpose of the universe to dump on me. So what's new?" That's how the shark makes it from one day to the next without taking it slam between the eyes. I squeezed Dom's shoulder and looked up at the sky.

I knew enough about stars to know that they could have stuck us all the way outside the galaxy and the sky would still be crowded with lights. There should be thousands of galaxies up there, each one looking like a star, unless we had been stuck on the outside edge of the universe. Then, I thought, maybe that's what they had done. God, it made my guts knot.

I pulled on Dom's arm. "What're you looking for? A post office? C'mon. We better find a place to hole up for the night. You seen Pussyface?"

Dom looked around, a head and a half above the crowd of sharks. Somewhere there was talking, then everyone talking at once. Dom pointed toward a bunch of dark figures huddled together in their parkas. "The beard's over there."

We slogged through the crowd, our shoes filling with sand, until we came up on Garoit and his group. Six men and four women. I thought I recognized a couple of them from Greenville. He looked around at us, then held his right hand out toward his ten listeners.

"Nicos, Dom, these are the other members of the Freedom Front." A few of them nodded at us. Garoit turned back to his buddies.

"Later we'll pool our chow. Then I'll distribute according to need." He looked back at us.

"You two understand that?"

I laughed. Whatever had Pussyface been smoking? Dom walked until he stood inches away from Garoit. Then the giant looked down at the fuzzy little man and poked Garoit in the chest. "What's mine is mine, hairball. You got a problem with that?"

Garoit licked his lips and backed away, rubbing his chest. "No, Dom. No problem." He pointed at two of his buddies as the crowd of sharks started talking louder.

"Shaw, Emil, hold me up."

The two lifted Garoit up into the dark until he was sitting on their shoulders. Then he held out his hands and shouted. The strength of his voice surprised me.

"Listen to me! All of you, listen!" The blowholes quieted down some. In the distance there were the sounds from the other gangs that were organizing, but they quieted down and listened.

"I don't think the old sharks on this planet know about us yet," said Garoit. "That's why the ship put us down on the night side. But, they'll find out about us soon enough, and we have things they want—new coats, clothes, food."

He sat silent for a long moment, then he said in a quiet voice, "The only way we're going to survive is if we stand united. Right now there are sixteen, seventeen thousand of us. Nobody is going to tangle with a united force our size—"

"Stick it!"

The voice stood out, and was joined by other voices. "You're packed . . . Goddamned politicals . . . punk . . . the blowhole on that beard . . . the overripe mushrooms do grow in the dark."

Then most of the cons turned away and gathered with gangs and around leaders that they knew; prison gangs from their former hotels. A lot of them moved off into the night. Some, about sixty, stayed to listen to Garoit.

Martin Stays, Greenville's answer to Pussyface, was one who stayed. I saw Freddy there, which meant that Dick Irish couldn't be far behind. I saw Steel Jacket, Nazzar, and a couple of other Yard monsters from the Crotch. Most I just couldn't see because of the dark, but I heard Ice Fingers's voice, Kid Scorpion's, and a few others.

Garoit slung the bull around for half an hour about Freedom, equality, and crapternity. About the only thing he said that did make any sense was that being part of a strong group was the only sure way to stay alive. It seemed to me that depended on the quality of the gang you joined, and seventy flabby or underfed filberts was a wimp-looking bunch compared to some of the other gangs out there on the sand.

I was about to jab Dom in the arm and find a healthier new society to join, when a huge mob began working its way toward Garoit. Fifteen hundred, maybe two thousand bodies. From what I could see and hear, they were mostly women. They surrounded Garoit and his tiny band, then one of them separated from the others and walked up to the beard as his two buddies lowered him to the ground.

Her hood was up, and she stood a half head taller than Garoit. "We want to know what you plan to do, and how you plan to do it. And don't stick your flag in my face, tiny. Just give me the facts."

Garoit stared at her for a moment, then pulled at his beard. "Let me ask you: what do you want?"

"We're women dropped in the middle of a pack of real hungry sharks. What in the hell do you think we want?"

Garoit nodded. "I see." He nodded some more, then looked at her. "What's your name?"

"Nance Damas."

I had heard about Nance Damas for years. Bull Croc, yard monster, torturer, murderer, and all-around graduate of Old

Miss's Finishing School. I squinted in the dark to see her face, but it was too dark.

"My name is Darrell Garoit." Old Garoit looked like he was busting a gut swallowing eight hundred political slogans, trying to find the words that would win over Nance Damas and her crowd rather than have her leave him flat or break him in two.

"We stick together. We protect each other. That's what we plan to do."

Nance looked around, then faced Garoit again. "Who's going to boss this gang?"

Garoit looked around at the electorate, and I could see him eating his own flag. "It's not a gang, and there's no boss. First we get out of here. Find a place to hole up. Then we talk about it. Then we vote."

"Majority rules?"

"That's right."

"What if you lose the vote, fuzzy? Do you take your ball and go home?"

"Grunt all you want in the women's yard, Damas," Garoit said under considerable steam. "Here I said we vote on it, and that's what I meant."

Nance stood quiet for a time, then she looked up as we all heard a fight here, a fight there, breaking out. The first long night was already in progress. She looked back at Garoit. "Okay. Let's hole up. Then we talk."

But there was some that wanted right then to talk. Who's going to run the thing—red, yellow, white, black, male, female, straight, gay, fried, clean—a couple of fights, a lot of serious threats, a cutter or two pulled, a few drips of blush on the sand. Between Nance and Pussyface we tabled everything. For the time being, we'd stick together and sort out the banners in the morning.

It was the biggest gang, so me and Dom went along. Maybe another couple of hundred other men joined as we left. Maybe it was because we were the biggest gang; maybe it was because we had most of the women. We walked a couple of hours until we came to an area with tall dunes capped by that grass. We put out guards and huddled down together for warmth and to try and get what sleep we could.

There were a few of the sharks, men and women together,

who began to talk, and they must have kept it up for an hour or more. I glanced up a couple of times, and they were talking out their troubles. I snuggled against Dom, and I saw him looking up at the night sky. I supposed it wouldn't have hurt anybody if they'd found a place with more stars. I turned over, got a mouthful of sand, and spat it out. The stuff tasted like sulfur and chalk. My body began shaking with chills as the wind picked up.

Free at last; free at last. Goddamn it all to hell, anyway. Free at last.

A PATCH

OF GREEN

THE false dawn began with the sky a deep purple that faded into black. After a few minutes, pale blue edged into the black, then there was this moment of beautiful blue that filled the sky and slicked you into believing the planet might be capable of offering a halfway reasonable day.

Tartaros, however, had an effective way of evaporating the illusions it created. While you could still see your own breath as it hit the freezing air, green would edge into the blue, then the sky would fill with the color of blood. Afterwards that brassy orange light would drive out the red and the sun would come up hot and orange.

As the light burned off the frost, a few of us clapped and cheered. But not long before the disc of the star cleared the horizon, the sweats began, the parkas and shirts began coming off, and soon you felt like every breath was a suck off a blowtorch.

You'd say to yourself, it can't get any worse than this, then the sun would move higher, the sky would go white with the light from that star, and we stopped kidding ourselves about being lucky only to get sentenced to Hell. We began getting the earnest heat.

You breathed in the hot air and your lungs would block.

They'd jam—act surprised, like don't you know this stuff is too hot to breathe? Humans have only a certain temperature range in which they can survive, and this is way outside operating spec's. Yeah, but there's nothing else to breathe, so we breathed it and our lungs felt like they were crisping and curling up out of our mouths.

A little way into the morning and we all had our parkas off. That grass we saw the night before was gone—retracted into the sand. Most of us took off our shirts and put them over our heads and shoulders for some shade. The women, too, after awhile. There wasn't any reason to worry about the men. As hot as it was on the sand, even the perverts were limp and past it.

When the soft ones started to fade, a few of the stronger ones crutched them along. I watched and wondered how long that would last. Back in the crowbars the sharks would help one another if it didn't cost anything. In fact, that was the surest way of putting someone else in your debt. Every now and then it's real important to have the right people owe you.

Always, when the helping started to cost, then it was later, some other time, and "Do I know you?" We were on Tartaros now, but a leopard still had spots no matter what zoo you stuck him in. I'd been watching the zoo for a long time. It's a hard habit to break.

At the top of one of the taller dunes, we could see tall green mountains off in the distance. Where there were green mountains, there had to be life, water, shade. Perhaps there might even be people there who could point us toward life. The image of the mountains shimmered in the heat like a dream.

Any kind of green looked good from the middle of all that parched yellow, and any fool could see that moving in that direction was number one on our things to do list. But, no, we weren't just any fool; we were a collection of very particular fools. First we had to sit in what shade we could find and decide who was going to boss the gang.

I never realized the number of political filberts a hotel collects. I mean, who cares what party grinds the bennies? You're either on the ins or the outs whatever flag the pol carries. But a bunch of those dune sharks cared. I mean, they went at it for an hour without a seam. Nance Damas, Garoit, that skinny guy

Nkuma, a bunch of others. Martin Stays kept his mouth shut, though, and only watched.

I wondered if he was planning something. I caught myself trying to mind somebody else's business, and I stopped it. Sure he was planning something. Sharks are always planning something, and the something is usually something no good.

It was none of my business. In fact, none of it was any of my business. The spec was only worth a mental moment. Me and Dom ended the mentment, got bored, wandered off, and went looking for some excitement. We found something that got our attention real fast.

We climbed up a tall dune and looked back toward where the ship had dumped us. Not all of the brothers and sisters had taken off for the dunes the night before. What I saw in the old landing area was a maggot convention. There were maybe two or three hundred bodies stretched out on the hot desert.

They were dead and stripped naked, guts, blush, and think-goo spread out all over the pretty yellow sand. There were little black flying things flitting about from departed to defunct chowing down on our old cell mates.

In addition to all those dead bodies, we saw a mob of white-sheeted live ones moving in our direction. They were riding strange-looking critters and following the tracks we had made the night before.

Dom looked at me with a puzzled expression. "Bando?"

"Old sharks. Scavengers. They live off the protos when they get dumped. They must've seen the ship when it came down."

There were around five hundred of them. They had what looked like guns and were mounted on beasts that looked like water buffalos with tusks and too many legs. The animals didn't move very fast in the sand, but they were moving a helluvalot faster than Pussyface and his goddamned blowhole society.

I smacked Dom on his shoulder. "Let's stroll."

We ran back and made it to the center of the group. Garoit was trying to shout down a couple of other pistachios, while Nance was out on her back, resting in the rapidly disappearing shade of a dune.

I slapped Garoit on his shoulder. "Time to wind it up, Washington. The old sharks know we're here. About five hundred of them, mounted and with weapons, are coming straight at us.

They look like they already thinned around two or three hundred of the brothers and sisters who came in with us."

The whole gang got to its feet, talking at once. Nance sprang up and shouted, "Hold it! How far away are they?"

"Hang around for a couple more minutes and you can talk to them."

The bull croc leveled a gaze on me that could air-condition Hell with enough chill left over to solidify Mauna Loa. "How much time?" she demanded.

"At the rate they're going, maybe ten or fifteen minutes, a little less."

Nance held up her hands. "Now we gotta move. Shut the blowholes and no more wind. Let's get moving!"

No. First, there had to be more talk: "Izzat gang there black or white . . . maybe they'll help us. Think of that . . . ? Where'd they get the guns . . . ? Why do they have guns if all they want to do is help us . . . ? What about all the dead brothers and sisters from our ship they helped . . . ?

Garoit pulled at his beard, then whispered to Nance as he pointed toward the mountains. She looked at him for a second, then nodded. He faced the gang. "Here's what we're going to do. . . ."

Well, old Garoit may have been straight from the rubber hotel, but he wasn't dumb. What we did was to form up a column and run toward the mountains for about fifteen minutes. That run might not sound like much to jogjocks, but it was murder on a bunch of people who had spent the previous months sitting in a cell, and the previous weeks stretched out in a flight couch.

At the end of the fifteen minutes, we split into two groups, went off to either side of the trail, and doubled back behind the dunes. I flatted out on the sand, my breath coming hard, and my eyes out of focus. Dom flopped next to me, but he was hardly breathing.

"You should stay in shape, Bando."

"Not now, Dom. Not now." I died and was almost resurrected several times.

We waited. What we were waiting for was the same thing you waited for in the yard back at the hotel when some shark was angling for your deal. It was what you waited for back on the block as you listened for those little sounds that a rival gang made as it stepped over the line and entered your territory. We were waiting to kill first—before the enemy had a chance to kill us.

Soon enough, the sharks in the white sheets came along, riding their strange animals. They were just loping along, joking among themselves, not paying any attention. The ones with the guns had their pieces across their thighs, and they all ran their blowholes like they were on a bird hunt where they didn't really care if they got any birds. After all, they were all pretty plush from their last kill. Behind each rider was a bundle made up of parkas, clothes, chow sacks, and kit bags.

They were plush all right. I knew the feeling. They owned the block. It wasn't just because they held the territory and had the guns. They owned the block deep inside their guts. They were the primo mokker in the neighborhood, and every one of them knew deep down that you'd have to be gibbering out of all orifices to attack them. Pussyface must've counted on that. That conviction of invincibility in the dune sharks was why our surprise should work.

Garoit's plan called for surprise, since we had nothing but knuckles, fingers, belts, and a few homemade cutters. So we all held our breaths and waited for the signal.

I could hear the blood crashing in my ears my heart was beating so hard. I looked at the backs of my hands as they rested against the sand. The history of each little scar flashed through my mind. Street fights, a couple of zealous interrogations by the precinct stains, a seemingly endless series of fights inside the walls proving myself, keeping the boybungers out of my ass, showing the stains that no matter how hard they thumped, I wasn't going to sing.

I collected the scars before I got smarted and learned how to protect and get protected. Except, here I was again, stuck with killing or being killed, and not even the stains who dumped us on Tartaros would notice.

That was the strange thing. Back on the block, or back in the crowbars, there was always the man. The fight would be going down, and back there in your head you knew that if the man found out, he would stop it. But the man wasn't on the sand.

All of us could have died in the next ten minutes and no one would know. No one would care. No investigations, no grave markers, no nothin'.

There was a very powerful feeling in my gut. This was wrong. It was all wrong. Tartaros was wrong, dumping us here was wrong, what those dune sharks had done back at the landing site was wrong, what we were about to do to stay alive was wrong, and I was wrong. Everything was wrong, and it was the first time I had ever felt like that.

Suddenly Garoit screamed out the goddamndest sound I ever heard and the gang went over and around the dunes. I dug into the dune with my feet, ran over the top, and saw the column stretching to my left and right. The sheets began lifting their rifles as we hit them. Some of them got off a shot or two before they were dragged from their mounts. The weapons made a loud cracking sound when they fired.

I ran down the face of the dune and leaped at the nearest rider. The sheet had his weapon pointed right at me, but the shot whizzed by my ear, and I crashed into the man's face with the top of my head. Once we were on the sand, I pulled the rifle from his grasp and was about to fire when his mount stepped on his chest and went straight through.

All around me the brothers and sisters were grabbing those weapons, pulling and knocking those sheets off their mounts. They punched, clawed, stabbed, fired, and strangled. I threw my gun to a sister, got my fingers on another, and pulled the sheet off his critter when he didn't want to let go. I stomped him in the jewels and he let go.

It was a lever-action rifle, and I pumped and fired at anything in white until the piece was empty. Then it became a club. I ducked a flying blade and swung the weapon's stock into the blade-slinger's surprised look. His face splashed like a ripe tomato. Those animals were rearing up, bellowing, and screaming, pawing at the dust and smoke in the air, while we fought it out in the dust around their razor-sharp hooves.

I had my rifle across the neck of one of them, pinning the sheet to the sand, when it started getting very quiet. The fight was over. I lifted the piece, but the one in the white sheet didn't get up. I pulled the sheet off and stared at her. It was a woman and she was dead. I sat on the sand, looked around, and stared at the maggot convention. From defunct to departed it was a whole lot of death.

I hate death. When it tugs at my sleeve like it always does in the crowbars, I can almost ignore it. Then it just becomes a stiff neck, a backache, a sour stomach, or a crabby attitude. But when death reaches up out of all those worms and rot with its stinking, wart-covered hand and rubs its shit straight in my face, I can't do anything but be scared.

For quite a while I wondered if I would toss my chow. I didn't lose it. Then I wondered what I must have become *not* to toss my chow. I still didn't lose it, which maybe made me a different kind of sick.

I saw some of the therapy-group perverts and deadheads hanging on to each other, and wished I had someone whose strength I could borrow. I heard a low snort and turned to look. One of those animals was giving me the eye, and I returned the favor. The creature was large, but built low to the ground like a rhino. It was covered with matted shag, had two huge horns that were more straight than curved, and red eyes like a cartoon bull with a bad attitude.

The hooves were curiously small and pointed, making it a priority not to have one of those critters step on your foot. Partway above the hoof, however, was a hair-covered joint that was easily six times wider than the hoof and acted like snow-shoes in the sand. Between the snowshoes and those sharp hooves pegging the critters into the sand, they had to be one of the most surefooted things in the desert.

As dry as it was, I couldn't accurately gauge the smell. What smell there was reminded me of the horse barn at Lancaster, which wasn't all that bad. The riders hadn't used saddles. The backs of the creatures were broad, flat, and amply upholstered with that shaggy fur. To climb up and to guide the mounts, the longer shag at the back of the neck had been braided into reins.

The animal gave another snort, it shuddered, and its legs collapsed. It gave off a weak cry of pain, and deep in the shag of its neck I saw that it had been wounded. I found a second wound in its side, and was standing there with my teeth in my mouth trying to figure out how to help the critter when a rifle barked at my right and the animal became still. I looked and someone with a gun turned away and was looking for more wounded animals.

Garoit and Nance supervised a body count. Between the sheets we had attacked and our own people, we left six hundred and some-odd maggot chows on the sand. We had some wounded, but if the heat didn't get them, I figured the cold at night would. We took around fifty of the white sheets prisoner and stripped the rest. We took with us the sheets, the weapons and ammunition, sleeping rolls, the food, and the four hundred or so animals that were still in good shape.

We didn't take time to vote that day. Darrell Garoit just fell into running things. He aimed us toward the mountains.

ALNA

W ITH a little bit of encouragement we got some of the prisoners to talk, and the shavings of information we got didn't bring the mountains any closer. According to the sheets, the animals were called lughs or lughoxen, all of the riders came from Boss Kegel's gang, and when Kegel found out what we had done, that would be the end of the universe. "But you keep headin' f' them mountains, chup," one of the sheets said to Garoit. He was grinning as he said it, too.

We put the sheets to walking and learned how to start, stop, and steer the simple-minded animals. Garoit chose four scout leaders from among our selection of yard monsters. They were Nazzar, Dao, Vekk, and Rojas. I had to admit that the four he had picked were probably the only four sweetmeats who still had working brains.

The yard monsters chose up teams; and the ones on the animals rode scout ahead, both sides, and behind while the rest of us in the middle walked. We kept the prisoners with the walking column.

The point of the column moved toward the shimmering patch of green ahead. Those mountains hovered before us like something from the story I had found when I had looked up the name Tartaros. The story was of Tantalus. He stood in water up to his chin, but every time he stooped down to drink, the water level would go down. He was dying of thirst. Above his head, hanging from branches over the pool, were luscious fruits: apples, figs, pears, and more, and every time he reached up to pick one, the wind would lift them out of his reach. He was dying of thirst and hunger, yet he would never die, because he was doing infinity hold in Hell.

I kept watching those green mountains, imagining the shade of those trees, the cool waters trickling down those mountainside brooks, the fat berries to be plucked from the bushes. Yet the mountains never seemed to get any closer. I had to think about something else before I rented the gibber suite at the rubber hotel.

I had one of those white sheets on to keep off the sun. It fit like a poncho with a wide hood, but it was made of some rough-spun stuff that made burlap look sheer. My shirt and parka were wrapped into a bundle and slung on my back. I also had one of the leather kit bags, a water skin, and two of the ammo belts, in addition to my own kit bag.

The ammo for the rifles was made from blue plastic with a lead slug fixed on one end. When I looked at the rifle, instead of a hammer, there was a sparking mechanism that ran a tiny metal wheel over a piece of flint like an antique nail lighter. As near as I could figure out, all of the blue stuff was ignited by the sparker firing out the slug. I looked down the muzzle of that piece to see how clean the ammo burned. There was only a slight haze on the smooth surface. There was also something else.

That barrel was grooved—rifled. I knew something about the old guns, and I'd seen rifling before. It was a good piece—accurate, hard-hitting, with a smooth operation. That put some questions in my head, because the only way those pieces could have come to be was to have been manufactured on Tartaros.

I was working on that one when I found myself walking next to a black sister wearing Greenville blues beneath one of those sheets. From the expression on her face, she was about to make reservations for the rubber hotel. She had a bad scrape on her left cheek that had opened up her skin, and she still had blood beneath her fingernails. Her eyes were wide, brown, and frightened.

"What's your name?"

She almost jumped at my question. Then she looked at the feet of the person walking in front of her. "Alna. Alna Moah."

"Do you know me?"

She closed her eyes and nodded once. "I've seen you around, back in the hotel. Nicos, right?"

"Bando Nicos."

"That a spic name?"

I gave her a good study, but she hadn't meant anything by it. "That's my name."

"I used to work the library in the Crotch. That's where I know you from. You read a lot."

"Yeah."

Her eyes darted in my direction, then back to the sand. "Those sheets we took prisoner. They say it's like this all over. It's like this all over the whole world. It's just like back in the Crotch. Find a big gang, crawl, kill, open your legs, bend over, and kiss ass to stay alive."

She looked back at me. "I won't be raped again. I can't live like that. No one ought to have to live like that."

"Maybe we won't have to."

"Says who?"

"We were the ones doing the rocking today, sister."

She looked at the sand, closed her eyes, and kept walking. "Nicos, you ever kill anyone before?"

I shrugged, then nodded. "Yeah."

"Murder one?"

"Yes. So I've killed." I sighed and shook my head. God, I felt awful. "Nothing like this."

"I got to one of those guns," she said as though she hadn't heard me: "It just fell on the sand in front of me. I picked it up and started crying. I didn't want to kill anyone. Someone fired at me, then I aimed and fired back. It was a sister. You know what I mean? A *black* sister! And it meant nothing to her. *Nothing!* She was aiming a gun to kill me so I fired. I saw her face when she knew she was dead. And it hurt! I could see that. I could see from her face that it hurt her horribly."

I nodded. "I imagine it hurts—"

"Then I brought down another one. And another. I was so scared." She held her hands over her face.

"God. I don't even know how many I've killed. How can you not remember how many men and women you've killed?"

"I don't know."

She was just standing there, iron despair filling her universe. I half raised my arm to put it around her shoulders, but lots of things brought it down again. She was black, and her gang from Greenville might think I was trying to pull a dip. The black gang from the men's side might mark me for all I knew. They didn't like chili peppers rubbing on the mau sisters. The women from all of the hotels on the ship made up one big gang, and who knew what some gibbering female might accuse me of. It hadn't been long since I'd seen the sisters in action.

The next thing I knew, her hands were grasping my arms and her face was buried in my chest, while sobs shook every inch of her body. I stood there like a totem pole for one of those century-long seconds, waiting to be thinned, then I just didn't care. I put my arms around her and buried my face in her neck.

It took a second, and I felt like a baby, but I could feel my own tears dribbling into my mouth, and I didn't even know what was making me cry. We stayed that way for a long time.

THE FOREVER SAND

AT sunset we didn't look any closer to that patch of green than when we started. We were some discouraged, and the mountains still looked like a day's walk away. As the light in the sky died, we broke up the prisoners into tiny groups so they couldn't start anything, and we settled down for another cold meal and frozen night's sleep.

Alna spread her sheet on the sand and we planned to use mine for a top cover. Don't conj up any ideas on that score, because dipping wasn't any part of it. Alna and I had cried together, which's a lot more intimate than dropping dip. Besides, she was half in shock still from the battle. Anyway, she was an old rape mark and finished with men. More than that, she was as tired as last year's parole argument.

As for me, I had spent the last few years making certain that the last thing I ever thought about was sex of any kind. Back in the Crotch it helped keep me out of the white rubber room. It also made it impossible for me to feel certain things. I was tired, too. Both of us had our parkas on.

Alna wasn't hungry, and she sat with her arms around her knees, staring at the small group of prisoners nearest us. I watched her for a while, thinking that she was very pretty, and that she hadn't said much of anything at all about herself. I didn't know her. I wondered what it had been that had paid for her reservation at Old Miss.

I began searching through the leather kit bag I'd liberated from one of the sheets during the battle. In the bag were thread and needles, a couple of pieces of cheap jewelry, a pair of dice, some cookies that weren't too bad, a really tough-chewing piece of cheese, some cooking and eating implements, and something that looked like hard candy. I unwrapped one of the candies and popped it into my mouth. It had no taste at all. I bit it and whatever it was tasted like the warden's toejam. I spat it out and noticed one of the tied-up prisoners giving me a big smirk.

"What's the tickle, sheet?" I demanded.

He just kept right on smirking as he looked away. I got up, tippied on over to him, and sat by his side. "You know, friend, it's real unfriendly not to share your joke, especially since I'm one who could use a good laugh right about now."

"Stiff off, chup." The rest of the prisoners chuckled at the comment.

I leaned over and unlaced one of the fellow's boots. With the long string in my hand, I doubled it, wrapped it around the sheet's neck, and pushed the ends through the loop. Then I pulled on the lace until his eyes bugged out.

"You're getting unfriendlier by the second, Oswald." I gave the lace another yank. "Now, I can sort of figure out what 'stiff off' means, and I'm pretty sure what you're telling me when you say 'chup.' But there's something I think you ought to know. It looks like a real long way to those mountains, and who knows what we'll find there. Now, the only reason I can think of to keep you alive is to eat up our food and drink our water. So pretty soon now someone is going to figure out that those reasons aren't anywhere near good enough and you're going to be eating one of those dunes. So if you got something you want to say that might make you a little more valuable, maybe you better blow now. Do you read me, Oswald?"

I gave the lace another tug. "Talk to me."

"The blues," he coughed. "You don't eat 'em. Make fire with 'em."

"Blues?"

"Dolt out, chup. The *blues!* The blue ice cubes? The fire

cubes. You tried to eat one. They're not for eatin', chup. Make a fire."

My tongue found a piece of that foul-tasting stuff stuck between my teeth. I reached into the kit bag and found another piece of the hard candy.

"How do I light it?"

The sheet looked up like I was beyond all hope. I yanked on that lace and about pulled the dune shark out of his boots. "Fire, Oswald. Tell me how to light this damned thing right now or start inhaling through your asshole."

"Rub it—" Oswald coughed, and I eased up on the lace. "Rub it on some metal. You rub it on metal."

I let go of the lace and rubbed the fire cube against the barrel of my rifle. It began sparkling on one corner and I dropped the cube on the sand when it became too hot to hold. It burned hot, but not very bright. Alna moved close to the light and washed her face in the warmth as she stared at the dull light.

"Thanks, Oswald. That was real helpful."

"My name's Suth, chup. Ondo Suth."

"Pleased to meet you. My name is Bando Nicos. I should tell you that if you call me 'chup' one more time, I'll slit open your belly and feed you your own guts."

"Term your hosties, fel." Ondo shook his head. "Chup don't mean nothin' in the sand. Nothin' bad. We just say chup like some say fel, buddy, or muthfuck."

"Just call me Bando and we'll be chill."

Alna looked up from the light at Ondo. "What are 'hosties'?"

"Again?"

"You said 'term your hosties.' What's it mean?"

The sheet nodded and grinned. "Luv, it figures 'don't be angry.'"

"Like in 'terminate your hostilities'?" I asked.

"You got it, chup."

I let the 'chup' remark pass, took out what looked like a little pot, emptied one of my box chows into it, and held it over the fire. The smell and the light drew attention from the brothers and sisters. We told them how to light the fire cubes, and soon the dunes were covered with tiny pricks of deep orange light. In a few minutes Darrell Garoit appeared, his face lit by the orange of my fire cube.

He pointed at the light. "It doesn't seem very smart to make light at night. It's like an invitation to every dune shark within twenty miles."

I glanced up at him. "You might just be right." I returned to watching my chow cook. "I don't see how you can stop them, though. Too many remember how cold it was last night."

"That's the way I see it. Anyway, maybe we're too big to attack, especially since we have weapons now. We're in between the dunes. That might hide us some." He pointed a finger at Ondo. "You."

"Ondo Suth, chup."

Garoit squatted in front of the prisoner and stared him in the eyes. "How many more of you are there out on the dunes?"

"More of me, chup? I'm all of me there is."

I nodded at the boot lace still wrapped around his throat. "Careful, Ondo. We can still reinstitute the oxygen conservation program."

The prisoner nodded and looked up at Darrell. "Well, chup, it's this way. My gang numbers close onto a hundred thousand—"

"Pack it, Suth," commanded one of the other prisoners sitting behind Ondo. I stood until I could see a large blond man with dark chin whiskers glaring up at Garoit.

"Give me your name," Darrell demanded of the blond sheet.

"Stiff off, and with your face, shouldn't be too tough."

"What?"

I grinned as I turned to Darrell. "He just told you to go fuck yourself."

"He did?"

"Uh huh. Said you were ugly, too."

Alna laughed, and her tickle was picked up by a few listeners. Garoit walked over to the blond prisoner, hauled back his boot, and kicked the sheet hard in his thigh. The thump and the prisoner's cry could be heard all over the camp.

"Give me your name, feather head, or I'll spread your cheese all over the desert and leave you for the sand bats."

"His name's Edge," said Ondo. "Jak Edge."

"Pack it, Suth, else Boss'll march you certain as death."

Garoit squatted in front of the one called Edge. "You don't look stupid, but you sure act that way. What's your boss going to do to you that I can't?"

Jak Edge looked away from Garoit. "He can term me family, chup. He can march them out on the sand until they've died of the thirst. That's what he can do."

Garoit studied Edge for a moment, stood, and called out the name of one of his followers from the Freedom Front. "Emil?"

A voice from the dark answered, "Listening."

"Herd these sheets together with our bunch." He pointed at Ondo Suth. "Leave me that one."

"Understood."

As Emil got them to their feet, the one called Edge said to Ondo, "Mind me words, Suth. There're some that you don't want out on the march yourself. Hear me?"

After the prisoners were gone, Garoit sat next to Ondo facing the burning blue. "Who's this boss?"

"Kegel. Boss Kegel. He'd put his own mother on the march, if he had a mother."

"March?"

"It's not complicated, chup. He faces you toward the sand and says march. You got no food or water and no one's lasted more'n four, five days. Course everyone puts in at least two, three days of pure hell before they term. Kegel usually has a pair of watchers on you to make certain you don't double back and no one helps you. The watchers drink water and spit it in your tracks, too. The way you're leadin' this gang, you'll find out about it soon enough."

"Find out what?"

"What dyin' of thirst means, chup. Know these mountains your makin' for?"

"About twenty miles west? What about them?"

"They was only twenty miles west yesterday too, true?"

"Say what you're going to say."

"What if I said them mountains aren't even there, chup? What then?"

"Not there? Are you saying the mountains are a mirage?"

"A couple of kinds of mirage, chup. Here's the ace. Those mountains are near two thousand miles west of where we sit tonight. The lughs can make five, six hundred miles without water, but they'll be long dead before you reach the mountains. But, no mind because you'll be dead long before the beasts."

He grinned. "Here's where it gets fun, chup. See, even if you was at them mountains, they be Hell's Divide, and nothin' lives there because nothin' can live there. It's so dead there it makes this place look good."

"Those mountains are green," I protested.

"Chup, you ever hear tell of a mineral called olivine?"

"No."

"No matter. All you have to remember about olivine is it's green, you can't eat it, and them mountains is made of the stuff. That's all that's green on the divide. Worse'n that, from the divide it's another eight hundred or thousand miles through West Hell before you get to any water."

It was silent around our tiny circle. I held out my hot box chow to Alna and was pleased when she took a bit. As I held it out to Garoit I asked Ondo, "Why're you telling us this?"

Ondo tore his gaze away from the food and looked at me. "I have me reasons."

"I can't trust 'em 'til I know what they are."

"Bando, you told me to become valuable, true?"

"Is that the only reason?"

"Bein' alive's not reason enough? And I be a sight more value to you than to Boss Kegel. Maybe you can see your way clear someday to treat me that way."

Garoit pursed his lips and nodded. "We'll see."

I asked the sheet, "What if we went north? How much desert is there that way?"

Ondo laughed, "Chup, you can pick it, sure." He quieted down and leaned forward, his hands still tied behind him. He glanced at Garoit, Alna, and then at me.

"I'm lettin' you know where you be. This stuff"—he nodded toward his feet—"is part of somethin' called the Forever Sand. The Forever is the biggest, hottest, meanest, dryest, dyin'est desert under Alsvid."

"Alsvid?" asked Garoit.

"The name of the sun, chup. It means scorchin' heat, and it was named after a horse."

"Out of Norse mythology," said Garoit. "One of the horses that drew the sun god's chariot."

Ondo shrugged. "Maybe. Anyways, like I said, west of here you got near three thousand miles to go before you be out of the sand. North you got a third again as much to go before you reach the Greenland Plains. If you want to try east, it's twenty-five hundred miles you got before you reach the Sunrise Mountains and water. There be only one way out of here, and that's south to the Big Grass. There's ways to keep goin' out here on sand grapes and such, but to stay alive, you got to get off the sand."

"How far?" asked Garoit.

"The grass begins mebbe three hundred miles on. I can show you on a map. But as soon as the grass begins, so does Boss Kegel. That's Kegel's territory from the grass down to the Sea of Stars and west to the Southern Divide. You have to go through Kegel. And he's not goin' to like it, and he's not goin' to like what you done. This mob's hit Kegel's pocket like stripes on a squeal."

"Isn't that what you are?" I interrupted. "You're a squeal, right?"

After a moment's pause, Ondo nodded. "Call it what you want, chup. I'm pure and that's why you can trust what I say. Too, I'm thin if Kegel brings me home for dinner." He glanced at Alna. "Kegel's short on women, and you got a plush gang of 'em."

I looked at Garoit and the beard was smiling and looking at the sand between his feet. "Share your tickle," I said.

He looked at me. "I was just wondering how long I'd be alive after suggesting Ondo's plan to Nance Damas."

I laughed. Alna didn't. Garoit turned toward Ondo. "Is there any other way through Kegel?"

Ondo nodded. "The same way you got through us. Fight." He turned his body to the left, which exposed his tied wrists to us. "Chup, could you kindly cut these? If I don't hit the dunes soon, I'll have but nothin' for comp'ny."

I frowned at Garoit, and the beard smiled and said, "Cut the man loose before he shits in his sheet."

After I cut him loose, Garoit escorted Ondo into the darkness. I held out the cooker to Alna, but she wasn't eating. Instead she was staring at the light from the fire cube. "Another fight?" she muttered. "Will we have to fight again?"

"We don't know that Ondo is on the level. He just might be playing it up for position, or just to make himself look big."

"Is that how you read it, Bando?"

I thought about it for a bit. "No. I think he's corners. I believe him, and I think we'll have to fight." I took a bit of the hot box chow and nibbled at it. "It probably won't be the last time, either."

She shook her head and mumbled something that sounded like, "I hope I die first."

I put out my hand to place it on her shoulder, but she pulled away from it. "What's the matter?"

"Bando, I've seen nothing but fighting my entire life. I've never seen anything but fighting, and I've lost everything I've ever had to fighting. I was fifteen the first time I was raped. I lost two brothers in the colors, and even my father when he couldn't stay away from his old gang. My mother and kid sister were killed in a street riot protesting . . . I forget what they were protesting." She looked into my face.

"I was married before, and that was one long fight. I used to sit and wait for him to come home at night and beat me and my child. Then he'd rape me. It was the only sex he enjoyed."

She looked at me as though she hated not only me, but all men, which was probably the case. "One time he had me in the hospital with a broken jaw and four broken ribs. That was when he beat my baby girl until she died. Five days later I got out of the hospital and shoved a butcher knife into his heart."

I nodded and said, "And because you waited the five days instead of thinning him right away, you bought the big one and the Crotch."

"Almost right. They gave me murder one, but sent me to Freeman Rehab where I became the guard's favorite rape. Then a bull croc at Freeman named Ilene tried to rape me." She looked up at the starless night sky of Tartaros.

"I shoved my thumbnails into her eyes, and when she was blind I took a hammer and a piece of table leg and showed her what it was like to be raped to death. Then I was sent to Greenville."

She shook her head and said in a whisper of pain, "I can't take it. I can't take it anymore. I don't want to fight. I can't fight." Her eyes closed, I reached out my hand, but she turned away and walked into the darkness.

THE PURE

I told myself that the universe is packed with people I can't help no matter how much I want to help. I dug my heel into the sand as I confirmed to myself that such a state of affairs was no comfort. Anyway, I couldn't think of anyone who needed more help than I did.

A shark, one of the haystack deadheads from the men's side, stopped by my fire cube and squatted next to me. He smiled at me and said, "I hear you have a copy of *Yesterday's Tomorrow.*"

"Who'd you hear that from?"

"Big Dave Cole back in the Crotch."

"I didn't know Big Dave hung out with the deadheads."

The man laughed, seemed just about to say something, then he put it to rest. "I'd like to borrow your copy."

"Why?"

"I'll bring it back in an hour or so. We just need it for the meeting."

"You want to buy it?"

Rus Gades nodded. "Yeah, but I'll have to talk to the group about coming up with a price. What do you want for it?"

I looked down as I rubbed the back of my neck. "I don't know. Let me think about it." I reached into my kit bag and pulled out the tiny pumpkin-colored book. I looked at the deadhead.

"You're not going to rip this up for papers or anything like that, are you?"

He shook his head as he smiled. "No. Those of us who used to drug don't do it anymore."

I still hung on to the book because I had never heard such a load of crap in my life. "Just what does your group do?"

"We help each other to recover. We usually start off a meeting with a reading from *Yesterday's*, but all our stuff was lost in the battle."

"By recover, you mean like from drugs?"

"And other things. Haven't you ever heard of CSA?"

I frowned. "The Confederate States of America?"

He chuckled again. "Compulsive Self-destructives Anonymous. We're made up of addicts of various kinds. Drugs, sex, work, gambling, emotions, overeating—"

"I know," I said as I held up my hand. "A platitude for every problem."

"Maybe you'd like to come to a meeting and see for yourself?"

"No thanks." I held out the book. "Take care of it, and you'll have it back in an hour?"

"Right, and thanks a lot."

As I released the tiny volume, I asked, "Did Big Dave belong to your bunch? I'm just curious."

"I can't say. Our traditions don't allow us to say who is a member."

"I don't see what difference it makes here on Tartaros. I can't exactly phone it in to the nearest vidwatch."

"The rule hasn't changed any." He nodded at me. "I'll bring this back in an hour."

He walked off into the dark and I pondered the prospect that Big Dave Cole might have been in CSA. That was scary to think about, because Big Dave never seemed to need anyone or anything. He always seemed to be happy and comfortable. In fact, that was why I used to talk with him. I used to like to be around him. He was strong, and I could almost draw strength from him to last out the Crotch for another day.

It was scary to imagine that the person I had drawn so much strength from was a deadhead, pervert, or some other kind of addict. But then, I didn't know for sure he was a deadhead.

I was stewing that around in my mind when Garoit returned with his prisoner. Pussyface wanted to get some sleep, so he left Ondo Suth with me and didn't order him tied. After the beard had gone, Ondo asked, "Does he trust me?"

I leaned on my elbow and stared at the tiny light. "Who can say? Pussyface is a political. Filberts think different than regular sharks."

"About you, then, Bando Nicos? You trust me?"

"Hell, no." I laughed.

"Why?"

"Why?" I shook my head and used some of the new lingo I'd picked up.

"Dolt out, chup. You're a squeal, right? There's only a couple of things to call a man who trusts a squeal, and that's either stupid or dead."

Ondo looked very hurt, and I laughed at him. "Man, what galaxy are you from? You act like you never seen crowbars before."

"Maybe if I showed you about the sand grapes?"

"Sure, you show me about the sand grapes."

Ondo found some of that retractable grass. He brushed the sand away from the blades until he could get a good grip on them. He pulled and came up with a bunch of roots that looked like tannish green grapes. He knocked the sand from the bulbs and popped one into his mouth.

"Water," he said as he chewed.

I took one and popped it into my mouth. When I crushed the bulb with my teeth a deliciously cool squirt of water shot into my mouth. Then came the taste. It began smelling and tasting like wet cardboard. Ondo laughed at my expression.

"It'll keep you alive, but you have to find your happiness someplace else." He waved a hand. "Don't swallow the pulp. It'll give you stomach cramps."

"Maybe you can trust me now?" He looked at me with wide brown eyes. He was about twenty, although right then he seemed much younger. He began talking in a low voice. "I'm not like you sharks, Bando. I did nothin' to get here."

I waved my hand in disgust. "Yeah, I know. The hotel's filled with the innocent. Tell it to the chappy." I spat on the sand. "Where're you from? What hotel?"

"I was born here, Bando. I'm native to Tartaros." My eyebrows went up, and Ondo nodded.

"Like I talked it, chup. I'm one of the no crime, nothin' but time, pure."

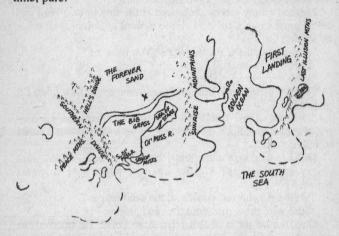

He pulled his sheet up over his head and spread it inside out on the sand. He pulled a metal pin from his boot and touched one end to the fire cube. The cube attached itself to the pin and Ondo held the light over the sheet.

"The best I can draw it, this is a map of the Big Land and what I can remember of First Landin'."

From his pocket he pulled a sliver of green wood and held one end in the flame from the fire cube. He marked an 'X' on the Forever Sand and said, "We're about here."

I studied it and said, "It doesn't look all that far to the grass."

"Hey, chup, looky here." Ondo pointed at the map. "There's no scale here, but see the lake called the Sea of Stars?"

I looked and found the large lake in the Big Grass halfway between the 'X' marked on the map and the range of mountains called the Sunrise. "Yeah, I see it. Pretty big, is it?"

"Kind of big, chup. From southwest to northeast it's almost two thousand miles."

If Ondo's map was anywhere near any kind of scale, the Forever Sand was large enough to swallow the North American continent. I began feeling very, very small.

IARGALON

I listened as Ondo talked late into the night, and I didn't notice when Alna returned. Just at some point I looked and she was there, igniting another blue. She sat next to me, but we didn't touch. While Ondo talked, he kept looking at the map.

"East of the Big Land is another continent we call First Landin'. That's where me mums and dads was put down. First Landin' is mostly a desert called the Graveyard. It's got a tricky range of mountains, too. From the eastern desert it looks all high and even more green than Hell's Divide. The range got the name Last Illusion Mountains, because if you ever fell for the trick, it'd be the last time you ever fell for a trick.

"The Illusion's cut right down the middle of the Graveyard, so if you manage to make it, there's no water and over a thousand miles of desert in whatever direction you pick.

"The stories are that the first twenty loads of exiles thinned at the Illusion before someone smarted and went south." A look of pride spread across Ondo's face.

"That someone was me dads, Arkin Suth. He was a geologist and swindler from Planet Duat. As he told the story to me, he knew the image was a mirage 'cause of the shimmy—a bit of distortion that made the edges move some. He'd seen 'em in deserts on Duat. Trouble was, he couldn't get the leaders to listen. They said the shimmy was just the heat.

"Dads backed off. He was set on stayin' alive along with some others. It took him a day or two to figure they'd been put down south of the equator, so it stood to reason if they kept on south, sooner or later they'd run out of sand.

"The next mornin', with a lot of bad feelin's, he broke off from the main group. About eleven hundred exiles went with him. It took near eight days, and the water was about all out, but they come upon a wide grassland. Then, at sunset, they come upon a beautiful huge freshwater lake they named Lake Real because so many of 'em thought it was a mirage when they first saw it. There was birds of a sort on the water, and plenty of lughoxen livin' wild. They could of made a nation there.

"Once they was there and didn't need me dads to guide 'em, though, the gangs chose up sides and began fightin' again. Me dads tried to cruise 'em, and soon a couple o' bosses, real hostie, wanted Dads thinned. So in the middle of the night me dads slides for the south. A sis named Hira, me mums, asked to go along. About fifty others, too. They slid out and went south down the five hundred miles that lake was long. They wanted to stop and set up homes lots of times, but Dads wanted to get clear of the gangs at the top of the lake.

"He led 'em south, away from the lake for near thirty days, until they ran into ocean. They just called it the ocean, but it's called South Sea now. They was near a thousand miles or so away from the gangs, but Dads didn't want to settle on flatlands backed by saltwater, so he gathered up some of the lughoxen and struck out for the west into the mountains. In the middle of the mountains, he found a tiny valley with fresh water, green grasses, and trees so big one of the things sawn into boards could build ten houses. Hira named the valley Our Place, and they started in to build houses."

Martin Stays walked up, put his hands in his pockets, and stood there listing as Ondo continued. "To hear Dads tell it, Our Place was Heaven, if a little dull. He used to say he missed workin' with money and numbers a bit. More'n that, Dads was always wonderin' what was under the edge of the sky. From the tops of the mountains we could see a huge lake on the western side of the mountains, and far beyond that, another ocean.

"One time up there lookin' at the sunset on the ocean, he told me about Iargalon. It's an old Earth name, and it means Land-Beyond-the-Sunset."

He smoothed the sand in front of his crossed legs and used his finger to draw in the sand. "This is how me dads said the old ones'd write it out. It's read from right to left." He leaned back and showed us the spelling.

"Me dads used to say that was the old Kelties name for a land called America on Earth. That's where me dads come from. It was a land that had unlimited promises. Dreams." Ondo leaned over and rubbed out the figure.

"Dreams thin, too."

He clasped his hands and closed his eyes. "They made a good life in the valley, and now and then they'd get a wanderer or fugitive from another gang that'd stay and join. Most everybody farmed or raised the lugs, but me dads and mums went into the iron business. As a boy, they showed me the rocks to look for, how to make a hot stack, and how to pound out the slag. That was where the nails, axes, saws, and knives came from. They used to settle their troubles among themselves, there was no gang, and no one was boss. They was just free.

"Me world was green mountains, crops in the fields, barns full o' lughoxen, a full table, friends to play with, and a peaceful bed at night. There was Mums and me dads. Mums'd gone to school and she taught me letters and numbers, and how to do what's right. Never did know what Mums did to be exiled off to Tartaros. I think she was real ashamed of it.

"Up in the mountains there'd be stories about Iargalon. Sometimes me dads would tell one; sometimes me mums. I even told one or two. There was a land beyond the sunset, and maybe someday . . . Well, that all ended when I was eight and one of the Lake Real gangs got pushed into us by another gang."

He became very quiet and Alna asked, "What happened?"

Her features were reflected in the light from the cube. I looked beyond her, and standing at the edge of the shadows, Stays was studying the map. I pointed at an empty spot near the burning cube. Stays nodded, walked over to the place, and sat down.

Ondo looked up at Alna, and without blinking he said, "In a couple of hours all we had built in Our Place was done past. Me dads tried to organize a fight, but they striped and thinned him. It was Rack Tanner's mob, and before me dads died, they raped me mums in front of him a dozen times."

Alna grabbed my arm and held on as Ondo continued. "I saw it happen from where I was hid. Then they killed m' mums by cuttin' her throat and sittin' her up so she could watch herself and Dads die. Next day the gang was gone and the valley was dead."

He sighed and the glisten in his eyes was very real. "I buried me mums and dads, then I buried the rest of me friends, the ones I could find. After that, I went to the furnace, stoked it up, and began makin' myself a brace of throwin' knives. Don't know how long it took. Don't know how long I practiced with the knives as I tracked down Tanner's gang, but I thinned him —him and every one of them what did me dads and mums. When I'd worked out me pain the rest of the gang was after me, so I strolled. I came to the west coast, made a log raft with a couple of other fugies like meself, and went to find out what the dream was beyond the sunset."

He shrugged and spat out the pulp from his sand grape. "When we landed, we got captured by the Hand, then we was thrown to Boss Kegel. He give us an offer to either ride and kill for him or die. I had knives, but his people had guns, so I rode. I been with Kegel since."

Martin Stays waited until he was certain that Ondo had finished. He pointed at the sand in front of his feet. "That figure you drew in the sand. Do it again."

Ondo shrugged and made the marks he had made before. As

he made them he said, "You're sittin' on the Land-Beyond-the-Sunset, chup. Don't waste time on it."

Stays studied the marks, and I could see he was memorizing them. When he was satisfied that he knew them, he erased the marks and drew them himself. "Like that?"

Ondo nodded. "That's how me dads drew it."

Martin Stays leaned his elbows on his knees and studied the marks some more. After awhile he said out loud something I think he meant only to say to himself. He said, "Wherever you are, there is a sunset and a land beyond it. It will always be invisible to those who quit looking for it."

Everyone else had begun turning in as I sat alone with my thoughts at the fire cube. As the size of the cube dwindled, I thought about what Stays had said about there being a land beyond every sunset. The possibility of hope was the core of the thought, and I hated the thought of having any kind of hope if the hope would turn out to be nothing more than another lie.

There was something else that stuck in my mind. It was something that guard on the ship had said to me on my way out the hatch. Something about being able to change my own luck.

In the middle of the Forever Sand at night was a strange place to be thinking about hope, changing my luck, and lands beyond the sunset. I heard a noise to my left and I looked up and saw the deadhead who had borrowed my book.

"Here it is, and thanks."

"It was nothing." I took the little book and flipped through the pages.

"I spoke to the group about it, and they'd like to buy the book from you. We have some tobacco, food, stuff we took off the sheets, some clothing, even some other books. What do you say?"

"Let me think about it, okay?"

"Sure. If we're still alive we'll be meeting tomorrow night. Can we borrow it again?"

"Yeah. Sure."

Rus Gades waved and nodded his thanks, then he walked off and was swallowed by the dark. I faced the open book toward the dying fire cube and continued to flip through the pages.

There was a pumpkin-colored ribbon marking a place. I began reading there.

> Do I find myself in despair with the words "It's hopeless" on my lips? Once again am I collecting evidence to confirm how pointless it is to try one more time?
>
> Ponder the arrogance it takes to declare a person, place, thing, or situation hopeless. Although hope and hopelessness exist in the present, they both find and make their lies or truths in the future. To have the certainty that something is hopeless, then, I would have to know everything about the future. If I know less than this, I cannot make a judgment that something is hopeless.
>
> I cannot see the future, which means there is nothing—no person, place, thing, or situation—that I can declare hopeless. In the absence of certain hopelessness, there is hope.
>
> Shall I have hope or despair?
>
> It is my choice.

"Back in the crowbars they would say that this guy is short on yard smarts," I muttered as I closed the little book and stuck it in my kit bag. I didn't feel as certain as my words sounded.

When I was finished putting away the book, I pulled my sheet around me, snuggled up against Alna, and thought about the stupe who had written all that treacle about hope and hopelessness. Whoever it was had to have been sitting in a plush chair in a plush room trying to overcome the despair he or she was feeling over the price of magnolias or something. Maybe his video heads needed cleaning. Maybe it was a vid star who broke a fingernail or woke up with the Zit From Hell on her nose.

Just to satisfy my curiosity, I opened my kit bag and took the book out again. I looked and there was no author listed. The brief introduction stated that the selections came from recovering addicts of various kinds.

"Leave it to a deadhead to believe in hope."

"Bando?" It was Alna's voice, thick and sleepy. "Are you all right?"

I shoved the book back into my kit bag. "I guess so." I smiled as I snuggled up against her. "I hope so."

A BEGINNING

IT didn't sound like much of a choice. At first light we gathered on the facing sides of a couple of dunes as Darrell explained about the mirage and why we had to head south where Boss Kegel and a hundred thousand armed cons were waiting for us. There were prisoners who said that Ondo Suth was lying and that if we didn't head for the mountains we would certainly die.

Ondo replied that the ones who wanted the gang to head for the mountains counted on the sheets knowing more about living in the desert than the newly arrived exiles. He insisted that only death would result from heading toward the mountains.

The filbert named Nkuma got into the middle and began calling Garoit a bunch of names in a couple of different languages. He pointed out that the lives of everyone hinged on whether we could trust Ondo Suth, and that he, for one, didn't trust him.

Garoit tried to shout Nkuma down, so Nkuma fed Pussyface a fist. Darrell went out, Nkuma headed west for the mountains, and around three hundred of the gang, fifty animals, and thirty rifles went with him. Democracy in action.

Dom was one of those who went with Nkuma. I tried to stop him, but there wasn't any point in trying to get physical with Dom. That would be like trying to arm wrestle an avalanche.

As best as I could, accompanied by finger-drawn maps in the sand, I explained where the Devil's Divide was, mirages, and the Big Grass south. Then Dom summed up for all eternity the central issue of the past several thousand years' discussion in religious philosophy.

"Bando, if it ain't real but I can see it, it's a lot realer than somethin' that's real I can't see."

I watched the big man tag on to the end of Nkuma's gang, and offered a little request to that which cannot be seen. Some night I hoped Dom would open his eyes and see the sky filled with stars.

"Bando?" I heard Alna's soft voice. I turned to look at her, and she was looking at Nkuma's herd.

She had a strange look on her face. "You're not going with them, are you?"

"Maybe," I answered.

"You're joking. Did you notice that the prisoners who said they wanted to go to the mountains didn't go with Nkuma? They're staying with us. Why they're staying with us is because they want to live. That filbert Nkuma is going to get his bunch thinned."

Her eyes looked down. "Are we something, Bando?"

"Something? What are you talking about, something?"

"Are we something? Anything? To each other?" She pointed toward Nkuma's gang. "Almost all the sisters I know—my friends—are with Nkuma. I want to be with them." She looked down for a moment.

"But if we're something, I'll stay with you."

"What'd I just tell you? Your friends and Nkuma are off to eat sand until death do them part."

"Answer me. What are we, Bando?"

It was no time to lecture her on being in command of her own life. If she went with Nkuma, she'd die. I didn't figure it was time to search my own heart for feelings that had been paralyzed for years. But I guess that helped put things into a grotesque kind of balance. I was impotent and she was terrified of sex. Perfect. A match made in Heaven.

And when, I asked myself, is the black gang going to stripe my ass for what they think is me dipping on one of their sisters? Besides, Bando Nicos always kept his options open. It would

be a cold day in Hell before this busy bee tied himself down to
one blossom, always assuming that I could get my stinger
working again. Anyway, I didn't really know her, and she
didn't really trust me. Of course, I didn't really know anybody,
and I didn't really trust anybody.

As such things usually went, I made my decision based on
cold reason and flawless logic: She had cried on me; I had cried
on her. It was a marriage made in Heaven and it was a cold day
in Hell.

"Yeah. I guess we're something."

With one hand she gave my arm a tiny squeeze, turned and
waited for Garoit's mob to begin moving south. This was going
to be some torrid romance. I wondered what peaks of passion
we would climb when she squeezed my arm with both hands.
The prospect fairly made me tremble with anticipation.

I spat in the sand as some noise drew my attention. There
was another argument raising the dust near Garoit, and I
worked my way through the sharks until I saw Pussyface spitting blood at a yard monster from Greenville.

The yard monster was the leader of the black gang, Rhome
Nazzar, and he made Freddy the leg-breaker look anorexic.
Considering who he had picked his fights with, I figured Pussy-
face must be dragging around a death wish the size of a hippo.

I guess he deserved a little credit. Right after his knuckle
entrée from Nkuma, Garoit was up to his ears in there flapping
his jaw at the monsters, asking for another helping. I wasn't
certain that what I was feeling for him was respect or pity, but it
didn't make any difference. If we lost Garoit, I couldn't even
guess at the pistachio that would slide into control.

I positioned myself between Darrell and the yard monster
and asked Nazzar, "What's the problem, friend?"

The yard monster's eyes went wide. "You're about to die, is
the problem now, greasy."

I grinned, which is what I do sometimes instead of raging off
into hysterical fits of temper. When I could see again, I spoke. I
tried to soften my observations with logic and sweet reason.

"Listen, Frankenstein," I began, "I don't swap taps with
sweetmeats 'cause I'm not stupid. If you want to work your jaw
on my socioeconomic heritage, I won't stop you. Not in the
daylight."

My grin went a little wider. "But what I will do is slide on you in the shadows. I'll glide out of the night like a phantom and, maybe, shove an ice pick in your ear. I think maybe I'll give the pick a couple of quick gorm arounds in there before I shove it all the way in and yank it out. What do you say, Frankenstein?"

The yard monster stared at me for ten of the longest seconds of my life. Then he nodded and said, "My name is Rhome Nazzar. I apologize for the 'greasy' thing. I was out of line."

"Bando Nicos. So pleased to meet you."

I turned to Garoit and almost fell flat on my face I was so light-headed from the sheer terror of certain doom averted. Pussyface was staring at me like I had a tentacle growing out of my forehead. "What's your problem?" I asked.

Garoit pointed at Nazzar. "He's the problem."

What the hell. Maybe I was immortal. I looked back at the yard monster. "Pussyface says you're a problem. How about it?"

Nazzar put his hands on his narrow hips and looked at his feet for a second. He lifted one of his massive arms and pointed over his shoulder with his thumb.

"It's the prisoners. Me and my point gang have been set to guard some of them. I'm no stain and I don't like it."

I shrugged. "No problem. We'll get someone else."

The big man shook his head. "That's not the way I see it."

I took a deep breath and let out a long, slow sigh. "Share your sight, Brother Crowbar, so that we can all see as you see."

"No guards, no prisoners, is the way I see it. Either the sheets join us, we cut them loose, or kill them. I just spent twenty-four years in crowbars with the stain grinding his foot in my face. I'm not going to let us build our own little walking penitentiary here on the sand. No guards; no prisoners." He looked around and shouted at the watchers.

"No prisoners!"

There were a lot of nods from the brothers and sisters. I was nodding myself. I looked at Garoit. "I agree with Nazzar. It looks like a lot of the sharks agree with him."

"It doesn't make sense," Garoit hissed through his torn lips. "It isn't safe." He looked at the brothers and sisters.

"We have something to protect here, and that means keeping down those who want to destroy us."

"No!" shouted Nazzar. "Kill them or cut them loose. Don't keep them down." He looked around at the brothers and sisters.

"From when we all cherried as protos, that's what the stains and smears have done all our lives: keep us down." He pointed at his heart. "We got to know better than that." He looked around until his gaze settled on Nance Damas. She was stretched out on the sand, her legs crossed, her hands clasped in back of her head.

"Damas, what about you? You speak for the sisters."

"No," she answered quietly as she sat up and got to her feet. "I only speak for me. The sisters speak for the sisters."

She pointed at the faces in the crowd. "The rest of you sharks do the same." She looked around, ending her scan with Nazzar's face. "We vote on it."

Garoit held up his hands. "Wait, there are things we have to discuss first. The issues aren't as simple as—"

"It looks pretty clear to me," answered Nance. "Either we can hold someone prisoner or we can't. Vote on it."

Nazzar shouted, "Vote on it!"

The call was picked up and repeated until Garoit nodded and held up his hands. When things were quiet, he said, "We resolve that this gang shall not have the power to take and hold prisoners. All those in favor, raise your hands."

Nearly all the brothers and sisters put up a hand.

"Opposed."

There were maybe twenty hands. Garoit faced Rhome Nazzar. "You win. We can't hold prisoners."

Nazzar grinned widely.

Garoit returned the grin. "So now it's time for you to keep 'em, kill 'em, or cut 'em loose."

The grin disappeared. "Me?"

"You started this shit, Nazzar!" Garoit exploded angrily. "You got it your way, so finish it!" He looked around at the voters.

"We're heading south. Since no one trusts anyone else to do a fair job at rationing, everyone is responsible for his or her own water and food. We have three hundred miles to make before we reach water. If we can make forty miles a day in this heat, it'll still take seven or eight days. If you run out before then, we'll show you how to get water from the sand grapes. If that isn't to your taste, that's tough."

A sharper edge of scorn slid into his voice. "So that we can put some distance between us and Nkuma and those of Kegel's gang Nazzar turns loose, we'll march today, take a brief rest this evening, then begin marching at night and sleeping during the heat of the day. We'll continue traveling at night from then on, unless there are any objections from the constituency."

He whirled his hand around his head and pointed south. "Scouts out." His face grimaced like he was trying to be gracious and swallow a slab of raw liver at the same time.

"Please."

Garoit and the others began moving south. I hung back wondering what Nazzar would do. "What're you lookin' at?" he demanded.

"Nothing," I answered. "Except maybe you might want some help?"

He averted his eyes and nodded. "Thanks. Come on." He turned and walked toward the space between two dunes where he was holding the prisoners. There were ten or so guards holding guns on the sheets. Nazzar stood before them, his rifle held across his chest.

"We just took a vote, people. It was about what to do with you." I watched as the faces lightened a shade.

"We don't hold prisoners from now on, so you have three choices. Either you can join up with us, we kill you dead right now, or we send you out into the sand with nothin' but your ugly faces."

"Hey," called Jak Edge. "If we join, what's that mean?"

"It means you're part of this gang, and if you sell us out to some other outfit, you're dead."

"We can just walk on out o' here if we don't join?"

Nazzar nodded. "That's right."

"I don't understand," said Edge. "You mean you're going to let us go, even if we end up fighting you again?"

"Yeah," said Rhome Nazzar, "but I can promise you one thing, sly. If you do fight us again and your ass gets captured again, you can count on a quick trip to cement city."

Jak looked around, but each one of the sheets was taking his own counsel. Nazzar held up his hand and shouted, "Everyone who wants to die, form a line right here."

There were no takers. The yard monster moved over a couple of paces and held up his hand again. "Everyone who wants to get cut loose out there in the sand, form a line right here." There were a lot of looks, but no one chose the sand.

Nazzar lowered his hand and said to the sheets, "Then you are now members of this gang. If you betray us, you die. Does everyone understand that?"

There were nods.

"Is there anyone in this group who does not feel comfortable with fighting only for this gang?" He looked over them all, one at a time. Finding no one who wanted to die, he began moving south. Ondo Suth and the new members of the gang followed him.

Years later I would look back upon what the brothers and sisters did that morning about the prisoners as the beginning. The beginning of what I'm still not certain, but that's what I called it. It had another name, but the name was a curse on Tartaros. No yard eagle could pronounce that name without spitting, cursing, or giving out with one of those real cynical laughs. Maybe we're still looking for another name, although "The Beginning" is good enough for me. Years ago, on another world, the straightmeats called it "justice."

THE LESSON

CLOSE to noon, the sun hammering us into the desert, I heard one of the sharks say, "Look at that. A three-hour difference. The days here are twenty-seven hours long."

I looked over, and a woman had a stick stuck in the sand. She was squatting next to the stick and looking at her wristwatch. I stopped by her side and asked, "How much?"

She pushed back the hood on her sheet and looked up at me. She was older. Maybe she was in her fifties. "How much what?"

"How much difference? You know, between Earth and here?"

She pointed at the stick. "Three hours, more or less. This is pretty crude for a noon indicator, but I'd say the days are about twenty-seven hours long. Maybe twenty-seven and a quarter. I'll know with a lot more accuracy after sunset when I take my next measurement."

I pointed a finger at her. "Astronomer?"

She stood up, pulled her stick out of the ground and shook her head. "Social worker."

I watched her back as she walked away, thinking about twenty-seven-plus-hour days. A twenty-four-hour-long day on Earth was bad enough. Twenty-seven on Tartaros was insane.

There was shouting coming from the front of the column. I picked up my pace and soon I got a good look at what the front walkers were shouting about. The spaces between the dunes were covered with a layer of naked, sun-blackened corpses. There were thousands of them.

Here and there I could see those black flying creatures flitting around. "Sand bats," said a voice from behind me. I looked and saw that the speaker was Ondo Suth.

I turned and grabbed the front of his sheet. "Did your bunch do this?"

"No. It couldn't of been us. There must be fifteen, twenty thousand down there." He pulled himself loose.

"Kegel's not the only gang that works the sand, Bando. Might be the Hand, or the Spanish gang. Even Boss Morret from over the Divide's been known to work the sand. It'd have to be a bigger bunch than mine to do that."

"There's all kinds of little free-lance gangs out here, too," Jak Edge threw in. He nodded toward the landscape of corpses.

"Anyway, it was short."

I looked away from him and back at the bodies. "How can you know that?"

"They're all together. Usually by the day after landin', they're divided up into little groups, like your shipload did. Look."

Jak moved forward and pointed at a place in the sand that was mostly clear of bodies. He squatted and pointed down at a discolored stripe that ran along the surface.

"See here?" He brushed away the loose sand to show the discolored portion to be made of fused-together granules.

"What's that?"

"This is where the edge of the ship's guard shield touched down." He pointed around at the corpses. "The ship must've just left. They couldn't've been down more'n a few minutes when they got hit."

"Jak," called Ondo. "None of the dead've been shot."

We both looked up and Ondo was working his way through the bodies. Jak Edge and I joined him, and it was true. Some of the bodies showed the effects of a well-honed razor or ice pick, but there were no bullet holes.

"So, what does that mean?"

"Let me see," said Jak as he climbed up the nearest dune. I accompanied him, and when we both had some altitude, Jak pointed toward the east where the bodies seemed to be the thickest.

"There. See the tracks?"

"Where?" I squinted my eyes against the sun.

"Beyond that wall of bodies, see the tracks going off to the east?"

"Yeah."

"That's where this shipload of protos met the attack." Jak pointed to where the bodies were few and scattered out. "Here they were runnin' away from the attack."

I nodded. "Okay. I see that."

Jak started walking down the dune toward the east, picking his way carefully between the corpses. "We'll follow the tracks."

I followed, checking each body as I passed. None of them showed any evidence of being shot, although most of them showed evidence of having had their eyes eaten out. The sand bats were responsible for the eyes, however.

I concentrated on Jak Edge's back and tried to keep from vomiting as I fought to make sense of the evidence. The sharks from this ship had been hit by a strong force, but a force that had no firearms. There were no droppings from the lughs or carcasses, so the attackers hadn't been mounted, either.

We could see from the tracks that the attackers had numbered many thousands, and had spread out to attack on a wide front. We followed the trail for about a mile, when we found another guard-shield oval. There weren't any piles of corpses littering the landing site, so it was easy to see where the ship had put down.

There were a couple of stripped corpses. Leftovers from an early power struggle, or maybe a couple of old scores settled. I said to Jak, "This ship put down first, didn't it?"

He nodded. "I'd say the second ship put down just as this one took off. These chups figured out their chances real quick, and banded together to improve their chances with the second bunch's supplies and clothes. I'd say they struck before the second ship'd even lifted off."

He spat on the sand and said, "Thus endeth the lesson."

"Lesson? What'd you mean by that?"

Jak's eyebrows went up. "If you don't know the joke about the new shark gettin' fed a fist on his first day in the crowbars, you must be the onlyest shark in the whole universe that hasn't heard it."

"Yeah. I remember. 'Why'd you do that?' 'you're new.'"

"Thus endeth the lesson," completed Jak.

We returned to the second landing site to find that the column had moved on. I looked at all of the corpses and it finally sank in. This load of exiles had just stepped out of the hatch, and the whole shipload had died—seventeen thousand of them.

I looked up to find Jak, just to have the sight of someone living before my eyes. He was walking toward the west. I picked my way around the stiffs and followed him until we found the trail of the departing sharks. After murdering and stripping their fellow sharks, the victors had headed west toward the mirage.

Only a mile or so from the scene of the massacre we found about a hundred and fifty more bodies feeding their eyes to the sand bats.

"The sharks stuck together for almost a mile," said Jak. "I'm impressed."

I saw a trail heading north, a second heading northwest, and a third continuing west. "So, now they're all going to die?" I asked.

"Now it begins. The mob divides in blood, each time its pieces becomin' smaller, weaker, more fearful. Follow these trails out and you'll find more branches with a little pile of bodies at each fork."

"When Nkuma split off, no one died."

Jak nodded slowly. "Very unusual. Your Nance Damas has good instincts." He took a breath and sighed as he turned to catch up with the column.

"Bando, you'll never see your friend Nkuma and his bunch again. They're bait for the sand bats."

I stood in the silence for a moment, letting the smell of death's fingers cuddle around me. I had a headache and something in me wanted to explode. I had to ask myself, didn't the UTR know what was going to happen when they dumped us here? Damn them!

Why had no one come down to Tartaros to see how the experiment was progressing? Every crowbar hotel in the system had half a billion sociologists and criminologists infesting the places like rat plagues. They were always doing little studies, having us answer questions, feeding their computers with tons of worthless data in order to generate grants, degrees, and more worthless data.

One of the corpses had an arm raised, its fingers outstretched toward the sky. Its empty eye sockets stared at me while something inside of me screamed that we did not deserve this. No one deserved this.

I looked and Jak was out of sight. I ran to catch up with the column. All I wanted to do right then was to surround myself with the living.

THE RETIRED MESSIAH

ALL that day we marched south, that green-looking mountain of a mirage always hanging there on the right, that flat white horizon to the south never seeming any closer, the image of that field of corpses always fresh in my mind. I would glance at the mirage—no. My eyes would be drawn toward the mirage almost as though I were under a spell of some kind. I would tear my gaze away from the mirage, but in minutes I'd find my eyes once more feasting upon the illusion.

From time to time I caught others taking surreptitious peeks at the mirage, and more than one of them fell back in the pack. When they reached the end they turned about to try and catch up with Nkuma. I mentioned it to Garoit, and he answered with just a touch of sarcasm, "It's a free country, isn't it?"

He stormed away toward the left of the column as I said to no one in particular, "Who yanked his chain?"

An amused voice came from behind me. "It's tough being a messiah."

I looked around and there was Martin Stays. He was wearing one of the desert sheets over his blues and did not carry a weapon. Judging from the way my face felt, I was gathering a hostie or two against Stays. "At least Garoit is doing something instead of sitting on his ass making smug comments."

Stays laughed and shook his head. "Don't get me wrong, Nicos. In my day I was a bigger asshole than Darrell Garoit can ever hope to become."

He adjusted his gait until he was walking beside me, both of us on the hard sand between the dunes. His face became serious. "I put in some time on the barricades waving a banner and shouting 'follow me!' to a bunch of children who wanted a better way and thought they could take a shortcut through me."

"Ah, you pols have an ego thing working. You always think you're better than everyone else in or out of the crowbars."

"You're right." As he turned his head and looked at me, his eyes narrowed. "My ego fed on that be-my-guru stuff until I was as salted as Charlie Manson and riper than July compost."

He looked down for a moment, nodded, and continued. "Bando, I could point my finger at a building and say 'disappear,' and it would entropize. I could point at a smear and say 'die' and the pol would drown in blush. My mission was pure, my motives righteous, my intellect tuned to reality, and I had a hundred sets of hands eager to place their lives in jeopardy to try to turn my fantasies into reality."

"How did you wind up in the Crotch?" I asked.

"You were already at Greenville, weren't you?"

"Yeah. I remember when you showed up after that big trial. Didn't your bunch get shot up trying to kidnap some pol?"

"Yes. It was one of the members of Parliament."

"Yeah, Stays. I remember when you showed up. I saw four stains trying to sit on you until they could drop you down the black hole. I thought you were the original foaming-at-the-mouth pistachio from Hell."

"I was."

"Was?" I snorted out a laugh. A con is a con is a con. "But you're all better now, right?"

"Not better. Different." He looked up at the southern horizon. "In that abortion of a kidnapping attempt, five of my people got wiped, four were wounded, two of the pol's security guards were killed, another stain was turned into a vegetable, and the pol got off without a scratch. That evening, just before the nabs arrived, I saw her on the vids. She was so far up in the polls at that moment she was having a public orgasm."

"What did you expect?"

"I thought like a child. I expected things to change simply because so many wanted change so badly, and were willing to die for it. But all I'd done was to make what was already in place more entrenched than ever. I got to think about that each time I was dropped into the black hole, and each time it made me crazy. When they would let me out, I was your basic mad dog. Then it was back in the hole.

"One time sitting in the hole, the anger finally dribbled out of me. I was left with nothing but failure, shame, and confusion. In the center of my being was a huge cavern that demanded to be filled with new answers. I've been looking for some of those answers since—something in which to believe."

"Answers." I laughed and held out my hands to indicate our companions in the white sheets and crowbar blues. "What good are your answers here?"

Martin Stays was quiet for a moment, then he pulled me to a halt and asked, "Don't you believe in anything?"

I pulled away from him. "Yeah, I believe in something. I believe I'm in it up to my ears, and have been in it since I can remember. As for politics, I believe in whatever the strongest goon next to me wants me to believe. If you belong to Yard Monsters for Jesus, then I'll hallelujah my ass right on down to the River Jordan and bubble my bum. If you can swing the sweetmeat and you like the Purple Puck Suckers, I like the Purple Puck Suckers, too. As they say back in the crowbars, it don't mean a thing."

He studied me for a moment, then averted his glance. "It means something. Nicos, what we're in right now will change someday. It has to. That change is going to take some kind of form, and the form is up to us."

"You sound like you have an itch to crawl up on those barricades again. Maybe you want Pussyface's job?"

He shook his head. "No. What I learned in the black hole was that what I need aren't followers; what I need are answers." He took a deep breath, looked off to the west, and sighed.

"Nicos, about Garoit."

"What about him?"

He pointed toward the mountains. "Just about all of his Freedom Front dips chose Nkuma and the mirage. Pussyface is taking it personally." He lowered his hand and smiled. "Give him time. Being a messiah is an educational process. The lessons come hard."

He dropped back and I walked by myself for a moment. I felt uncomfortable and looked around, but there was no one I knew near at hand. I was alone with my own head, and the head was asking, "What do I believe?" I didn't have any answers.

Back in Jordonsville there was this chappy who used to ask that during his sermons on Sundays. "What do you believe?" In the backseats we used to tickle around and sing, "I believe for every drop of rain that falls a spot gets wet," and other selections from the *I'm Too Smart to Believe in this Shit Songbook.*

I stood at the foot of a huge dune. I looked up and began climbing through the loose sand toward the top. Once on top, I looked around. Here we were, a bunch of killers, thieves, terrorists, perverts, and crazies, caught in a furnace between Hell and a mirage, heading south to do battle with an army that outnumbered us ten to one. Just for the laughs, I tried to think past Kegel's army. What if we lived through that? Where would we go? What would we become? What would become of us?

I thought about my reading from last night. "At least it's not hopeless." I laughed. I wondered if there would ever be a time when I could say that without laughing.

What do I believe? I saw the brothers and sisters below, strung out, rifles slung, stumbling along, half-asleep under the force of the sun. Alna was among them, and whether she lived or died was an issue with me. There was something I believed in. I couldn't call it love, but Alna and I had something.

Far ahead was our main force of armed riders, and to the left and right were somewhat smaller forces. I could see the flank riders on my side riding in exactly the same manner the sheets had been riding when we had surprised them. I had never seen Kegel before, but I believed in him, and in his army. Sure, I believed in lots of things.

One thing I believed in was that unless things changed soon, we might not live long enough to be massacred by Kegel's army. I could see the problem. We weren't an army, and we certainly couldn't fight one that was expecting us with any hopes of survival. But how to shift the odds?

I thought, maybe I should just cruise, mind my own business, and see who walked away with the chips. That was crowbar wisdom, yard smarts. That was the intelligent thing to do. Of course, no one ever accused me of being intelligent.

Tartaros, this gang, Garoit and Alna were in the hand that I had been dealt. I figured I better play that hand to the best of my ability. Anything less than that and I might as well fold. And if you stay in a hand, you may not be smart, but you must have hope, no matter how stupid that hope is.

There were lots of things to do, many changes that needed to be made. There wasn't any point in going to Garoit and Nance Damas until I knew what I wanted, and I wouldn't know what I wanted until I knew what I was talking about.

I sat down on the dune and watched the brothers and sisters as they passed. I was looking for a certain face—praying for a certain face. If I remembered it right, it was a very beautiful face. The face of a primo killer. She was called "Bloody Sarah," and I tried to remember her particulars.

Former Major Sarah Hovit was late of the UTR commandos, and held the Crotch record for the number of murders committed without receiving the death penalty. I had forgotten the exact number, but it was around a hundred and fifty. The story had traveled the pipes the year before last, just before Major Hovit transferred to the Crowbar Blues.

Sarah Hovit had been in command of a counterinsurgency field team of thirty soldiers on the planet Surya. By following orders and playing kissy-kissy with the locals, her command had been caught in an ambush and thoroughly mauled. Half her command had been killed, and a third of those who remained had wounds. The few weapons they had were out of ammunition, and she was ordered out of the area. She sent her troops back, but she stayed behind herself to tie up a loose end or two, counterinsurgencywise.

There was the village they had done the kissy-kissy in, and the people in that village had not only helped stage the ambush for the rebels, but also had participated in the actual fighting.

Sarah Hovit did a personal sweep of the village, and when the investigators assembled and divided up the remaining body parts, a hundred and fifty-odd Suryian men and women had gone to a better land. Now the planets of the Suryian Charter were in revolt, but Bloody Sarah had been long since stuck in the Crotch for disobeying orders and murdering innocent civilians.

She had been in Greenville, so she would have been sent to Tartaros with the rest of us. At the landing, did she join the gang with the rest of the women? If so, did she survive the battle? If she did survive, was she now with Nkuma trying to chase down a mirage? I studied the faces below me, and thought about what I believed. I believed that unless we managed to put together one hell of a fighting machine over the next few days, we would be eaten alive by Boss Kegel or some other gang.

I thought I saw her on the far side of the column. She was small and had modified one of the sun sheets to fit her tiny frame. As she walked along her attention was divided between searching for any kind of danger and her rifle. She had her weapon taken apart and it looked like she was cleaning it. As I watched her I realized I was a little afraid of her. Her story about why she thinned that village had been to neutralize a local rebel strong point. But I remembered the vids.

The vids had called her "Bloody Sarah" and the viewers saw a blood-crazed shark in feeding frenzy searching desperately for live bodies to make dead. They even had some bits of vid taken by a reporter that had been with the team and who had remained behind when he learned that Sarah Hovit was staying back in the vill to win over a few hearts and minds.

The reporter didn't live through the experience. The villagers, after all, were armed. But his tape was found during the investigation the next day, and the viewers were treated to scenes of Bloody Sarah darting from shadow to shadow, patiently seeking out and eliminating the maximum number of villagers with the minimum amount of effort. In the middle of her spree, she even stopped at one point and sharpened her knife. This is how we all learned that a standard issue UTR commando knife will hold an acceptable edge through seventy-five throats.

The one scene that the vids replayed thousands of times until Sarah was found guilty was the one where she ran past a villager as she was dashing from the right side of the main street to the left side. She passed by the armed villager in a blur, leaving the Suryian rebel with a surprised look on his face. The expression became more pronounced as the fellow reached to his throat to find that it had been slit from ear to ear. You could see it on his face as clearly as if he had said the words: "I'm dead." He turned and looked for his assassin, but by then, Sarah was long gone.

They would always follow the clip with a slow-mo replay showing Sarah flashing by the rebel. She would lift her arm as she came abreast of him, she'd position the knife in her hand, rip it across the man's throat, and continue past, all without even glancing at the mark. She had devoted less attention to slitting that guy's throat than you would spend swatting a mosquito. And he was left standing there with his teeth in his mouth, his blush gushing down his front, and that silly look on his face. It was that look more than anything else that had convicted Bloody Sarah. No one seemed to be able to remember that the guy was carrying a weapon he wasn't supposed to have. All anyone could remember was the look on his face when he knew he was dead.

Well, there she was. I had found our general. Now I had to chase down the administration to begin the process of placing the creation of an army before the voters. I got up, headed toward the front of the column, and began looking for Pussy-face.

A GATHERING OF
MONSTERS

AS the light in the sky faded to that deep purple, we sat around one of those burning ice cubes. There was Garoit, Nance Damas, Bloody Sarah, Alna, Martin Stays, Ondo Suth, and the four yard monsters who led the four groups of armed riders by virtue of being able to stripe any chup who challenged their leadership.

Rhome Nazzar was one of them. He had been bossing the point. The left flank leader was a golden mountain with an expressionless face named Tou Dao. He was a bandit chief who had been transferred to Greenville because the UTR facility at Shenyang was afraid of him. He looked like he could eat the crowbars out of a cell block and shit nails. He was called "Ow" Dao, but not to his face.

The right flank leader was a black nightmare from the yard named Yirbe Vekk. There was a story around the Crotch about an escape attempt that Yirbe engineered years ago. The attempt failed and Yirbe was cooked once in the lung and once in the gut with a beam weapon. He was supposed to have taken the weapon from the stain that did the shooting and beat it to pieces, on top of the stain. I couldn't vouch for the story, but in the light from the ice cube I could see Yirbe's chest scar. He was called "Steel Jacket" and, curiously enough, Yirbe Vekk was in for his third stock swindling scam.

The monster who bossed the rear guard was an Indian from Mexico. He was an arsonist who had been sent to the Crotch after he had burned down the UTR calaboose at Culiacan just to prove that he could do it. His name was Mig Rojas, and he was known as "the Match."

Pussyface was shaking his head. "Are you gibbering through your pores?" he asked me.

"No more than anyone else is around here. I take it you have some kind of objection to my proposal."

"As soon as you put an army together, Nicos, the army runs things, which means whoever's in charge of the army runs things. Is that what you want?"

I raised my eyebrows. "Garoit, if we don't put something together so we can get through Kegel, Kegel will be the one running whatever's left of us. That is, unless we get taken over by some other gang first."

"Just an observation," said Sarah Hovit. Close up she was compact in stature, and carried not a single ounce of fat. Her hair was bright red, and her eyes were black.

"If we are going to defeat Kegel," she began, "all of us will have to be in this thing you call an army. There won't be any civilians. We can't afford the dead weight."

"That's just great," said Garoit. "The first thing we do with whatever freedom we have left is to turn it into a bloody fascist dictatorship."

Nance Damas laughed. "No one elected you president, beard."

"Yeah, but I'm not about to put everyone in jackboots and paint swastikas on their arms."

"Pussyface, what are swastikas?" asked Vekk.

"Forget it."

I shook my head and looked at Garoit. "Either we put an army together or you come up with another answer, fast. Remember those seventeen thousand corpses we saw today? We can't stay in the sand, and the only way out is through Kegel. How about it? Do you have another answer?"

"Maybe Kegel won't push it to a fight. Maybe we can negotiate."

"After what we did to his buzzard brigade? Grab a piece of the real world, Pussyface."

Nance eyed Garoit and pointed at Ondo Suth. "This one's said it before, beard. The only thing we've got that Kegel wants is women."

Garoit rubbed his eyes. When he brought his hand down he looked at Martin Stays. "How about you?"

"To me it looks like a choice between all of us becoming soldiers or going into the slavery business."

Nance pointed a finger at the beard. "Don't forget that those 'slaves' outnumber the men in this gang five to one, and we have most of the guns, knives, and hatchets."

Garoit waved his hands back and forth. "Don't pop an artery. No one is going to sell anyone." He rubbed his eyes again. When he lowered his hand, he looked into the flame of the fire cube.

"We have to stick together, and if we can't get around Kegel peacefully—"

"Count on it," interrupted Ondo.

"—then we'll have to fight." He looked at Sarah Hovit.

"If we have to fight," she began, "we'll have to know how. To do that, we have to train. To do that we have to organize. To do that we have to be an army."

"I guess you've got the know-how, Hovit." Garoit stood and pointed first at Nazzar, and next at Ow Dao. "But how are you going to get these sweetmeats to carry your banner?"

He bent over, rested his hands on his knees, and spoke to Yirbe Vekk. "How 'bout it, Steel Jacket? When this little bit here tells you to jump, what're you going to do?"

"Nobody tells me to jump." He grinned as he glanced at Sarah. "But I've watched the vids. I've seen the major in action. If she suggests something to me, chances are I'll take the suggestion."

Bloody Sarah smiled at Vekk and Garoit looked at Rhome Nazzar. "What about you?"

Nazzar chuckled. "Man, Garoit, I've never seen someone fight so hard to lose in my whole life."

"What about it, sweetmeat? When this little white bit starts ordering you around, what are you going to tell her?"

The yard monster grinned widely. "I watched the vids too, Garoit. I've seen the white slice move through a dozen armed hogs and come out the other end with a string of sausages and a side of bacon. I guess I'd tell her, 'yes'm.'"

There was laughter around the circle. Garoit turned and looked down at Bloody Sarah. "What about you? If these four muscleheads can't do the job, do you have what it takes to fire them?"

Sarah Hovit climbed to her feet and pushed her sun sheet behind her shoulders. With her hands on her hips she smiled gently at Garoit. "First let's see if there's any need."

She turned and pointed a finger at Rhome Nazzar. "This is a little tactical test, Rhome. You're leading a group of fifty armed soldiers against an exposed uphill position held by two hundred of Kegel's best and I tell you to kill the enemy, what would you do?"

"Kill them."

She looked at Tou Dao. "You are in command of twenty worn-out unarmed soldiers and are facing a superior enemy force that holds the high ground and is heavily armed. I tell you to kill them. What would you do?"

"Kill them."

She looked at Yirbe Vekk. "I order you to sneak into a heavily armed enemy camp by yourself and kill everyone in it, what would you do?"

"Kill them."

She pointed her finger at Mig Rojas. "I'm dead, so is the beard, and so is everyone else in the gang. You're wounded, dying, and unarmed, and thousands of the enemy are closing on your position. What would you do?"

"Kill them."

Bloody Sarah paused as the circle became very quiet. She turned around and smiled at Garoit.

"I'll play these."

THE NEW ORDER

AFTER the night march and a brief nap, we gathered in the heat of the morning to become an army. Garoit explained what we had discussed the night before, and in a matter of seconds we had a fight on our hands. The main factions were divided between those who wanted the new organization and those who didn't, although there were a thousand variations.

A proposal was shouted into the middle of the brawl, and I heard Martin Stays say, with a touch of wonder in his voice, "I'll be damned. We're going to have an election."

There were three candidates. Garoit was already there, so he was up. A pro-army faction of the women put Nance Damas up, and the anti-army candidate was a shark named Neala Gates. We did the vote by raised hands, and it wasn't even close. Nance Damas came in first, followed by Neala Gates, with Darrell Garoit coming in a pitiful third.

There was some grumbling among a few of the men who objected to a woman bossing the gang, and there was more grumbling among a few of the women who objected to a bull-croc lizzie bossing the gang. There was no way of getting around the fact that the women were the majority, so those male grumblers were told to either like it or head for the dunes.

When it became clear that sexual preference had nothing to do with bossing a gang, the straights chilled out and put it to rest.

Later I saw Garoit. Pussyface looked really depressed. After the vote was settled and the talking was still loud, I overheard Nance Damas say to Garoit, "I need a number two. You interested?"

I'd seen Garoit swallow a few since the landing, and this one just about choked him. I could almost see the space behind his eyes trying on a foot-stamping temper tantrum for a reply. Instead, he looked at me.

I think he was remembering our ride together on the prison ship and his smug assurances that Darrell Garoit would be running things on Tartaros. I shrugged and felt embarrassed. I didn't know what to tell him. He turned his head and looked at Martin Stays.

Stays shook his head and looked Garoit in the eyes. He asked, "Do you think you have anything to contribute?"

Garoit flushed deep red. "Of course I do, but—"

"Then shut up and take Nance's offer. Quit taking everything so personally."

Garoit took the job and walked off into the dunes to eat worms, if he could find any. Nance held up her hands for quiet and explained to the constituents how it was.

"Sarah Hovit is in charge of the army, so she is in charge of you. You elected me, so you are in charge of me. I am in charge of Sarah. I have appointed Darrell Garoit my number two, and when I'm not around, he's in charge."

She looked at the sky for a moment, then back down at the faces. "We have a fight coming up, and we have to work like hell to prepare for it. You now belong to Sarah Hovit. Anyone who has a problem with that can leave now. We aren't going to hold anyone prisoner."

There was a lot of looking around, but no one walked. After another minute or two, Bloody Sarah stood in the center and began talking. She had a voice that could be heard throughout the camp. It was a special kind of voice that made you believe you could lift mountains. She ended with a strange speech.

"The God Razai is the desert death lizard of the planet Surya," she said. "It can run all day in the hot sun and not thirst; it can run all night in the freezing cold and not tire; it can go for a month without food and not hunger. It can do all this, take on three times its number, and kill quickly, quietly, efficiently, and without mercy. Even if you should manage to kill one of them, the Razai's single-minded determination is such that, three months later, its sun-dessicated corpse can still jump, bite, and poison the fool who comes too close. I name you all for the Razai, and will see that you live up to your name."

I was amazed to see the brothers and sisters raise a thundering cheer for their new commander. Even those who had voted against the army were cheering. As I remarked to Martin Stays later during the night march, "By definition those sharks can't take discipline. How is she going to get them to run all day and run all night? How is she going to get them to follow orders?"

Stays thought for a long time before he spoke. "It takes a kind of discipline to do your numbers in the crowbars and not go insane. Not only does the juicer want protomo to undergo eight different kinds of hell from rape to endless monotony while he does his numbers, the cherry is supposed to do it without complaint. Not everyone can do it, which is why so many die behind the crowbars. But all of us made it, one way or the other. We have discipline, at least the kind Bloody Sarah needs. We can endure."

"Can you see Rhome Nazzar following orders?"

"Maybe. Hovit is giving them the chance to bet it all for the right thing. She's giving them the chance to earn being good. Do you know what those sharks'd be willing to do to feel good about themselves? What would you do, Nicos, to feel good about Bando Nicos?"

I jabbed my thumb at my own chest. "I feel just fine about me."

"Not all of us are that lucky, Bando."

Alna took my left hand in hers and held it gently as Martin Stays walked ahead. I squeezed her hand and said, "Pretty soon Nazzar and the other monsters will choose up sides. Think we might be separated?"

"Would that bother you if we were?"

"Sure."

I looked at her as we walked, then I bent over and gave her a tiny kiss. She wrapped her hands around my left arm and rested her face against her hands.

"What about you and fighting, Alna? The way you feel about it. What'll you do?"

"I'm just going to trust Bloody Sarah. That's all." She continued to rest her head against my arm.

We were that way when Nance Damas fell in beside me and said, "Nicos, there's been a razor job toward the back of the walking column. Things look ugly and we can't fight each other and Kegel both. Check into it."

"Check into it?"

"That's right."

I stared at her for a moment because I was in shock. "What do you mean, check into it?"

"Check into it is what I mean when I say check into it. You're not stupid. Clean out your ears."

I pulled Alna to a halt and shouted at Nance, "Do you mean *investigate*?"

"Yeah."

My throat became very dry. "You mean, like a *cop*?"

"Nicos, you're acting like this is your first day out of the rubber room. I don't care how you check into it, just so you wind up with the truth and settle it."

She studied me for a bit as she rubbed her chin. "Maybe you should bring someone with you. The razor's name is Jobo Ramis, and he's a mountain looking for someone to fall on."

"What if I tell you to go to Hell?"

"You're not a special character, Nicos. Either do the job or hit the dunes."

She turned and left me standing there in shock. I heard a laugh and Martin Stays was holding his middle. "A cop! A *stain!* Bando Nicos, a *po-leece-man!*"

When he calmed down enough to listen, I appointed him my deputy.

HERE COMES
THE JUDGE

WE scared up a gun for Stays. The sky was just
growing light as we worked our way down the
column to the part that wasn't moving. There was
a crowd and in the center of the crowd was a
bleeder. The guy leaking all blush was white ex-prizefighter,
Kid Scorpion.

The name on his front office file was Abner Pandro. His
forearm had been sliced real nice, and he was holding his right
side in what looked to be a non-vital part. He was in the middle
of a group of about fifty sharks that seemed to be growing
larger.

The sharks loved a fight they could watch without having to
participate, and cutter fights were colorized. I could see what
Nance meant. With a choice between watching two gorillas
make hash out of each other or joining the army, not only might
the ranks wind up pretty thin, something violent could get
started here that might not be possible to stop. This had every
possibility of turning into one of those forks in the trail marked
with a heap of bodies.

Stays grabbed my arm and pointed toward one edge of the
crowd. "That's Ramis. The tall mokker with the shiny head. I
know him. Watch yourself."

Ramis was big and shaved bald, and the homemade cutter he

had in his hand looked as big as a sword. I glanced at Stays, and he shot me your basic wimped-off shit-eating grin. "How're *you* going to handle it, Chief?"

The first thing that came into my mind was unslinging my weapon and drilling Stays between the eyes.

"Let's get this mob moving."

I walked into the center of the crowd and stood between Ramis and Kid Scorpion. That was when I saw that the Kid had a cutter of his own balanced in his left hand.

Most of those in the crowd were drooling for a fight, and I wondered if there was such a thing as being addicted to violence. I noticed some addicts of another kind, too. In the crowd I could pick out two or three deadheads who were well into the sweat-writhe-and-heave thing. Sooner or later we would have to deal with the deadheads. That was a big problem coming up real soon. Right now they were substituting blood for the alk and other stuff.

There was a roar from the crowd. I turned and saw that Kid Scorpion was waving his cutter. It was time to stop worrying about the deadheads. One thing at a time. I held my rifle up at waist level and aimed it around at the crowd as I raised my voice.

"Now, these two razors have some rhubarb to eat, and they don't need anyone here except those who want to get into the cutting. If you stick around, you're going to have to fight."

"Sez who?" demanded a yard monster from the edge.

I fired my piece and kicked up the sand between his legs. He grabbed his balls with both hands, jumped backward, and landed on his ass in the sand. I waved the gun around some more.

"People, if you aren't going to fight, cruise." The crowd began moving off. There was a background mumble of threats and curses, but after a bit there was only Stays, me, Ramis, and Kid Scorpion. I waved my piece at the Kid.

"Let's move out into the dunes so we can settle this thing."

The Kid looked at Ramis, and Stays pointed his weapon at Ramis. "You heard the man."

Ramis spat on the sand. "The man," he said with scorn as he lifted his knife. "The *man* is forgettin' what we do with the *man*."

"Ramis," Stays said with a deadly quiet voice, "I'm not very good with this gun, but at this range I couldn't miss a microbe." He gestured with the weapon's muzzle.

"Start moving."

"You're dead meat, haystack. You and the spic both."

Stays aimed his weapon at the center of Jobo Ramis's face. "Then I got nothin' to lose."

Ramis bit at the skin inside his mouth, then turned and walked east with long strides. The Kid followed and Stays and I brought up the rear. I looked at Stays and he gave me another one of those grins. He was having the time of his life.

When we were well away from the others, I asked the Kid, "What happened?"

"None o' your business, asshole."

I looked at Ramis. The mokker waved his hand at me as though he were brushing away a fly. "This's nothin' to do with you, Nicos. Why don't you and your asshole-buddy go play po-leece-man someplace else?"

I nodded my head emphatically. "Oh yes it does have something to do with me, Ramis. I've been appointed by our esteemed leader to investigate and settle this caterpillar fight. Now, one way I can settle this is to thin both of you right now and say that you attacked me and Watson here. Unless someone wants to talk to me, that looks like the way to go. Right, Watson?"

"Elementary," said Stays, with only a foot or so of tongue in his cheek.

"Bah!" Ramis growled. "This is beef that goes back to the Crotch, Nicos. Let us settle it our own way."

I nodded. "If you'll settle it, that's all I want. What I don't want is you two trading these little taps and scratches while slinging around all of these big threats. It upsets things. If you both want to cut it up, get down to the earnest slicing. It'll save me a lot of trouble." I looked at Kid Scorpion.

"How about it? You want to get in there and yank out a few yards of guts?"

The Kid thought for a long time. He looked at the sand and threw down his cutter. "I'm no razor."

Stays jabbed me with an elbow. "What now, Chief?"

I glared at him and shook my weapon as I muttered, "I could

just as easily blow your balls off, Watson, or doesn't that make any difference to a retired anarchist?" I turned from Stays and looked at Jobo Ramis. "Why're you after the Kid?"

Ramis's eyes narrowed as he looked at Abner Pandro. "He came for me. He's worked on me with his fists back in the Crotch. I wasn't gonna let it happen again. I told him then I'd kill him the next time he hit me."

I looked at the Kid. "Well?"

The fighter grinned and nodded. "I whipped his ass, an' good. But he ain't sayin' why I done it. He stole somethin' from me. I found out about it and put the thump on him real good."

Ramis pointed a finger at the Kid. "That thing you say I stole was mine! The Bird gave me that before he died and you stole that from—"

"I didn't steal nothin'. I bought that from—"

"Enough!" I shouted. When they were quiet, I shook my head. "Look, you both know there's no way to sort out old crowbar beefs. They go on forever. You two forget this one. Forget everything that happened before we landed here. It's done past."

The Kid held out his right arm streaked with blood. "What about this?"

I raised my eyebrows. "Maybe you should get someone to bandage it up? With all the killers, thieves, and swindlers in the column, there ought to be a doctor or two."

The Kid's face became dark with anger. "I mean what're you goin' to do about him cuttin' me? This happened after the landin'."

I looked at Ramis. The big man looked down and shrugged his shoulders. "The Kid came at me with his fists. I'm no boxer. What was I supposed to do?"

I looked at the Kid as Stays said to him, "It's your ball."

Kid Scorpion held out a hand as he looked down. "Yeah, I went for him, but back in the Crotch he threatened—"

"Back in the Crotch is done past," I interrupted. "Back in the Crotch is ancient history. It's long gone, done past, dead, like it never was." I pointed at him.

"Kid, you went for him with your fists and got cut. You asked for it. Don't go for him again and you won't get cut again. Now bandage up, shut up, and put it to rest. If it happened before the landing, it's done past, dead." I waved the muzzle of the rifle around. "If you can't put it to rest, I'll put it to rest for you. Do we all understand me? Am I clear?"

The Kid looked as though he was trying to choke down a big one. Finally he nodded. I looked at Ramis and the mokker nodded once and headed back toward the column.

"Bando?"

"Yeah, Stays?"

"I have a question."

"What?"

"With all of the new friends you and I are making these days, don't you think it might be wise if we sort of stood watch over each other when it's time to sleep?"

I looked at the drips of the Kid's blush on the sand. "I don't suppose this is going to be the end of trouble."

Stays snickered and pointed toward the column. "Killers, crooks, mass murderers, torturers, bombers, thieves—just about the highest concentration of me-first mothers in the universe. Every single one of them has been judged an unrehabilitatable criminal. At least a third of them should be in rubber rooms, and the only thing that they hate more than each other is a cop." He lowered his hand.

"Should we live so long, I think we've found full-time work."

OLD ANARCHISTS

NEVER DIE

THAT evening as we sat around the fire waiting for the night march to begin, I had my arm around Alna's shoulders as I looked at the faces. Bloody Sarah was updating Nance about organizing and training the riders. Sarah had also appointed Ondo Suth as an adviser and training officer.

Sarah had kept the four riding groups and had added a walking group to back up each of the riding groups. The combination of each riding and walking group was called a guard, and Sarah had taken sharks from each of the guards to train herself. Most of them were retired military of one kind or another. Once they were trained, they would go back to their guards and train them. After that, sharks would be appointed to train the walking column.

The walking column itself was changed. Those with weapons walked on the sides, while the weak, wounded, and non-fighters walked in the center. A group of the non-fighters was assigned to keep track of the food and water situation, which was in pretty good shape right then.

A medical unit was being formed, as well as a sanitation team whose job it would be to dig latrines and fill them in when we left an area. A machinest who had ended a labor dispute by killing six union officials with a bomb, and a weapons fanatic who had supplied death to most of the galaxy, formed the core of an ordinance unit and were already busy collecting parts and repairing weapons. Stays and I were the po-leece. The silence that announcement drew was enough to convince me that, the very first chance I got, I was going to fade like a friend in need.

There were a lot of things we needed to learn about fighting on Tartaros and surviving in the Forever Sand. We weren't making forty miles a day and our water was nowhere near enough to last us until we reached the Big Grass. Besides the sand grapes, Ondo knew of some other things to do to get water and food.

Farther toward the south we would begin running into desert plants that could be recognized by a long stalk that supported a purple flower that looked like a thousand tiny little bells. The flower was edible and tasted like celery.

If you scooped away the sand and made it to the root, there was a white and lavender bulb that was anywhere from six to twenty inches across. The bulb could be cut up and chewed for water, or grated and the pulp squeezed. The water was sweet with sugar, and the pulp dried out and ground made a self-rising flour.

Ondo continued talking about edible lizards and insects, and I settled back to think about being a cop. Man, it made my skin crawl just thinking about it. How many times had I seen some arrogant stain in tailored grays and mirror-glasses, strutting a fat ass down the block, itching for a skull to crack to prove that the street belonged to the badges.

And what would a gang of cop-haters do with me and Stays? Just to ride the fantasy for a bit, what if everything worked out just fine, we whip Kegel and find the promised land? What then?

I nodded just a little. What they'd do with us is what's always done with cops. You flatter 'em, you call 'em names, you stroke 'em, you spit on 'em, and when nobody's looking, you kill 'em. Nobody but the cop-killers ever gets real with a cop because, underneath all of that hate, scorn, and ass-kissing is fear.

Everyone fears the cops, and the more honest the cop is, the more the stain's feared. A cop's husband told me that once. I was in a squad-room cage waiting to be pissed on, and I was sitting on the bench in a corner against the bars, my arms folded. There was a guy standing by the door to the squad room, and he was nodding and talking to the stains. A female cop breezed through, patted his cheek, and said it would be a few minutes more.

There was an empty chair next to the cage and he sat in it. After awhile he asked me, "Why are you here?"

I blasted at him, "None o' your fuckin' business, man!"

I faced away from him and he was silent for a long time. Then he said, "I'm afraid of them, too."

"Huh? Cops? You afraid of cops, man?"

"That's right."

I laughed. "Say, is that little stain you're waitin' for your old lady, or somethin'?"

"My wife."

"You afraid of her, man?"

I remembered he sat back in his chair, looked out at the squad room and said, "Just a little. But it's there."

As I remembered it, he was the guy who told me that cop was an abbreviation for "constable of the people."

I was afraid of cops and the law then, and I was afraid of them now. I was getting afraid of myself. If I couldn't corner out my head and get right, maybe I'd just have to leave the gang and continue on my own.

I brought my attention back to the present and looked at Pussyface. Garoit was on his side staring into the flame of the ice cube, and Nance was listening to everything that was being said. Every so often she would poke Garoit's shoulder and ask, "You hear that?"

At last she got to me. "Bando, that job I gave you?"

"Yeah?"

"Well?"

"Well, I settled it."

Garoit snorted out a laugh and said, "I think Nance would like you to expand on that a bit."

"Expand? What expand?"

Nance clasped her hands together and looked at me with unblinking eyes. "So what was the beef? How did you settle it?"

"Jobo Ramis and Kid Scorpion were working an old yes-I-did-no-you-didn't from back in the Crotch. I told 'em to knock it off."

Nance looked at Martin Stays. "Can you add anything?"

Stays nodded and said, "The chief here—" There was a round of laughter at my expense. I let him bathe in a glare for a bit, and when the laughing died, Stays continued with, "Bando laid a couple of rules on the mokkers. First, if it happened before the landing, it doesn't count."

"What was the other rule?"

"The other rule was, if two razors want to walk off into the dunes and slash it out, that's their business. It becomes his business"—Stays pointed at me—"when the fighting disrupts everybody else." He looked around at the circle. "As a matter of fact our little band is developing quite a body of policies and laws."

"What're you talking about?" asked Nance.

"I'm talking about our rules of operation. We have quite a bunch."

Garoit spat at the sand and said, "Some anarchist."

"I'm only your humble reporter, Garoit, not a judge." Stays reached into his parka pocket and pulled out a tiny black notebook. He opened it and said, "The first policy"—he grinned at Garoit—"was made the night of the landing." He read, "Each person is responsible for his or her own sustenance."

I nodded. "Yeah. After Garoit said something about redistributing the wealth, Dom grabbed him by his throat and said 'What's mine is mine.'"

There were some chuckles, Stays nodded and looked back at his notebook. "The second policy was put together on the third day when Nkuma split."

He read, "Each person is free to follow the leader he or she wants."

Nance held her hand out over the fire cube. "Let me see that."

Stays handed her his notebook, and as she read, I said, "Who're you supposed to be? Hammurabi? Moses?"

"No, I'm no lawgiver. As I said, I am only your humble reporter."

When she was finished looking at the notebook, Nance handed it to Garoit and looked at Stays. "Your handwriting really bites."

"Sue me."

"Why're you keeping a record? Why're you doing that?" She pointed at the notebook in Garoit's hands.

"I don't know. It's interesting seeing what a bunch of sharks come up with after they've been handed this special kind of freedom." Garoit handed the notebook to me. I opened it and began reading.

    1. Each person is responsible for his or her own sustenance (Dom's Decision). On the march, dl.

    2. Each person is free to follow whatever leader he or she wants (Nkuma splinter). On the march, d3.

    3. Policies can be changed by the leader and by majority vote (the vote on Nazzar's no prisoners proposal). On the march, d3.

    4. Policies changed or affirmed by majority vote become laws (no prisoners) changeable only by majority vote. On the march, d3.

    5. The leader of the gang is elected by plurality vote (the pro-army/anti-army contest between Nance Damas, Darrell Garoit, and Neala Gates where pro-army candidate Nance Damas won and everyone became a part of the army). On the march, d4.

    6. The leader has the power to appoint subordinate positions (Nance Damas appointed Darrell Garoit number two, Sarah Hovit head of the army, and Bando Nicos "investigator"). On the march, d4.

    7. Each appointed officer has the power to appoint subordinates (Sarah accepted her current choice of generals, Bando appointed Martin Stays "deputy"). On the march, d4.

    8. The "no prisoners" law includes not forcing anyone to serve in the army (Damas interpretation). On the march, d4.

    9. Not serving in the army is grounds for expulsion from the Razai. On the march, d4.

    10. Fighting to the death is allowed as long as the fighting is confined to the combatants (Ramis-Pandro rhubarb). On the march, d5.

    11. Any crimes or issues that originated before the landing are done past. Any kind of retribution based on such crimes is a new crime (Ramis-Pandro rhubarb). On the march, d5.

* * *

LAWS (voted on)

1. No Prisoners (either keep 'em, kill 'em, or cut 'em loose) proposed by Rhome Nazzar, voted in on the march, day 3.

When I finished reading, I handed the notebook to Alna and frowned at Stays. "Watson, you sure can find more damned silly ways to kill the clock."

Garoit rubbed his chin and held out his hands. "Stays, what's the point of trying to make some kind of constitution out of the choices we've made so far? Most of the things you have in that list were nothing more than the most expedient thing to do at the moment—what seemed like a good idea at the time."

"Garoit, you have just described most of the statutory laws in the universe."

"That's going to be the motto on our great seal? 'It seemed like a good idea at the time'?" He shook his head.

"You can't make a society out of stuff like that. It has no central plan, no principle, no coherent purpose or goal. That flaws it right from the beginning."

Stays pushed himself to his feet and looked down at Alna and smiled. "Make sure it gets back to me, okay?"

Alna nodded, but did not stop reading. "Sure."

Stays put his hands in his pockets and looked at the sky's fading light. "Garoit, you're right. Of course you're right. It is flawed." He looked down at Pussyface.

"Then, what's the point?"

"The point is, I'm not a sophomore any longer. I'm not looking for perfection." His eyes seemed to search his inner self for an instant, then he grinned. "Maybe you hadn't noticed, Garoit, but we aren't out to build a new society. The society is already here. The only thing we have to work with is the same thing that we had to work with back on Earth: change."

"Still, there are principles that—"

"To Hell with the principles," Stays interrupted. "And to Hell with the ivory-tower chair queens who dreamed them up." He pointed a finger at Garoit.

"Look, some academic with time heavy on his hands between classes sits down and says, 'How should things be?' For answers he doesn't go down on the block, or in the factories and schools, or in the fields or the barracks to find out anything about the men, women, and children who might have to live in his 'How should things be.' No. For answers he searches the insides of his own head, which is filled with the sludge of other academics who found time heavy on their hands between classes. And what's the result?"

Stays put his hands in his pockets. "Earth. Too many people, thousands of murders every day, billions going hungry, air so thick with shit you can paint your house with it, and a criminal justice system that is so swamped that the only thing it can do efficiently is sort out the privileged from the poor, and spring the privileged." Stays spat on the sand and smiled.

"I would like to end this lecture," he continued, "by saying that I don't give a dilly damned rat-fuck for philosophic first principles or all of the rarified atmospherics of legal scholars and political science majors individually or in congress. I've seen and lived in the results.

"Right here on Tartaros, on the Forever Sand, we are in the trenches, and right here is where we have to solve our problems and come up with solutions that work for us. They don't have to work for the universe. They only have to work for us. Perfection is the great deity of the adolescent mind, and I'm feeling mighty old and tired these days. I don't want to see the word 'Justice' above the courthouse door. Instead I'd like to see 'We try our best to sort out the shit, but sometimes we make mistakes.' To tell you the truth, Garoit, right now I'd settle for a system that worked half decently most of the time."

He turned and walked toward the darkening dunes. Those in the circle were stunned into silence. It was more than any of us had ever heard Martin Stays say at one time in years.

I watched his back as he faded into the shadows, realizing that Martin Stays was the person on Tartaros I trusted the most and trusted the least.

Alna looked up at me and asked, "Do you know what the Major has me doing in the army?"

I shook my head. I couldn't think of anything Bloody Sarah would assign Alna that wouldn't send Alna to the rubber Hilton in gibber city. Not being in the army would mean she was out. But if she did whack out—go crazy—what would our new society consider expedient? Alna had used her rifle in the battle, but she was still just on the edge because of it.

"No," I sighed. "What's she got you doing?"

"I'm learning to be a nurse."

"A nurse?"

"You know that doctor who was sent to Greenville for all of those mercy killings? Jane Sheene?"

"I remember. Four, five years ago?"

"Yes. She's teaching me how to treat wounds. I'm going to be a nurse."

As Alna talked about her first day of training, I nodded to myself because it made sense. You've got someone who doesn't want to fight. Make her a nurse. It makes a lot more sense than locking her up, exiling her out of the tribe, or forcing her to join some society of religious or political pistachios to somehow place a different color on the simple fact that she did not want to fight.

I saw Garoit looking at Alna. He was biting nervously at the skin on the insides of his mouth. I could almost hear him thinking, "What if everyone refused to fight?" and a hundred other old questions from the done past. But that was the point Stays had made. Those questions, and their answers, were done past. Here on the sand all we were concerned with was what worked. We weren't concerned with what would work under such-and-such conditions, or what would work ten years from now, or what tried to work in the distant past on a distant unworkable planet.

We were on Tartaros. We were on the Forever Sand. What worked right then and there was our concern. For me, Alna being a nurse worked just fine.

Just about then Rus Gades came up to us. Without being asked, I reached into my kit bag for my copy of *Yesterday's Tomorrow*. As I handed it to him, I asked, "What goes on in those meetings?"

"Why not come to a meeting and find out?"

I laughed. "Do I look like an addict?"

"No one looks like an addict."

"Look, I was just kidding, but do you think I'm a self-destructive compulsive, or whatever it is?"

Rus shook his head. "It's not a judgment I'm qualified to make. You're the only one who can figure that out. But there's something you might want to think about. If you do something that causes you big problems, and you keep on doing the same thing over and over again, you are dependent. You're an addict."

I shook my head. "I don't do anything like that."

"My guess is that no one except the natives got to Tartaros by accident. Were you born here?"

"You know I wasn't." I was getting a little angry. "What does being here have to do with being an addict?"

The man shrugged. "Maybe nothing if the Crotch was the first time you ever saw crowbars. I've never heard your story, Bando, but my guess is that you've seen the insides of jails and squad rooms lots and lots of times."

I pointed around at the dunes. "Most of these sharks've done the same thing. I'm not the only repeat customer in the hotel."

He smiled. "That's right." He turned and began walking as he said, "I'll be sure to get the book back to you before we move out."

I stewed in my sheet for a time, trying to get to sleep. Even though me being addicted to going to jail was the most salted thing I had ever heard, it gnawed at me. I couldn't put it to rest.

Alna turned over and said, "Bando? What's wrong?"

"Oh, that spud-nuts who said I was addicted to jails. Can't get it out of my head."

"I don't think he meant that you were addicted to jails. I think he meant you were addicted to the things that keep putting you in jail."

I began thinking about what she said, and that ended what chances I ever had for some sleep. Being a cop in the middle of two thousand sharks was all the problem I needed right then. I didn't need someone messing with my mind, too. I decided to tell Rus Gades to keep the damned book and to stay out of my face forever.

THE CHOPPER

THAT night during the march, Stays and I saw the beginning of the stars close to the southern horizon. We were at the head of the walking column, and at first I mistook the lights for a city. I said so to Stays, and before he could respond a woman's voice from behind me said, "They're stars."

I looked and saw a woman with graying hair. She wore a sheet, but she wasn't carrying one of those rifles. Instead there was a hand ax hanging at her waist. It was the same woman who had been measuring the length of the day before we discovered all of those dead sharks.

"This place doesn't have but two stars at night," I countered, "and who are you?"

"My name is Seraphine, young man, and those are stars. Tartaros's orbit is around a star that is located at the edge of a dark cloud known as the Spider Nebula. The northern pole of Tartaros points toward the center of the Spider, which is why we couldn't see but two stars until tonight. The farther south we go, the more stars will become visible."

"Are you some kind of astronomer?"

"Strictly amateur. By trade, I'm a social worker, as I said before."

Stays laughed at the sound of the filthy word. To sharks,

soshes were the hated underclass. They were made up of idealistic do-gooders without experience, skill, or sense dropped into fantastically complicated family and community situations to see what they could do to make the simple complicated and the serene frustrated. All of them started out with a desire to wallow in and feed off of the gratitude of the bleeding masses they attempted to band-aid. Once they discovered that they were little more than objects of hate or contempt, however, they dropped the "love me" bit and went for the long green and serene.

I remembered two years before when the case workers for the entire UTR went on strike for more corn and bennies. The prison newsletter in the Crotch carried a picture of a long-haired thing carrying a sign that demanded parity with other "professionals" like doctors, money threads, and such. The picture carried the caption "Soshes Get Honest." The yard gurus always said that trusting a sosh was more stupe than trusting a squeal, and the yard gurus never lied unless it could get them something.

"I don't trust a sosh's word about social work. Why should I believe you about black gas and Spider clouds?"

"Are you a biologist?" she asked me.

"No."

"Can you tell whether or not you have your dipper in your mitt?"

"My dip—you mean my dick in my hand?"

She grinned. "My, you are quick. Yes, that's what I meant."

"Yeah. So?"

"So, there you are. You're no more qualified to talk about your weenie than I am to talk about the stars."

"Lady, at least I got a dipper."

She grinned. "And I have the stars." She let the grin fade. "Once I heard about Tartaros, I looked up the information in my books. Take my word for it, Nicos." She pointed up toward the blackness. "That is the belly of the Spider." She pointed south toward the lights. "Those are stars."

"All of the stuff about Tartaros was classified. I tried to look it up myself."

"I was using my own books, not the censored stuff from the prison library."

Without moving, she kept staring at the lights. She glanced to her right, saw a dune that she liked, and climbed it. Once she was on top of the dune, she looked again. After a moment she called down to us.

"Those are stars, but you had best call Nance and Bloody Sarah. There are other lights below the stars, and I think they might be from a camp." She stayed very still for a long moment, her unblinking eyes studying the horizon.

"One of the lights just went off and then came back on again. It's a camp."

The word was passed, and I ran up the dune and stood next to Seraphine the sosh. I looked below the alleged stars and saw lights that were the same dull orange color given off by the fire cubes. In a matter of a couple of minutes Nance Damas and Rhome Nazzar had joined us, followed in a couple of more minutes by Sarah Hovit and Ondo Suth.

After a few seconds, Sarah nudged Ondo. "Well?"

Ondo's expression was worried. "I'm not sure, Gen'ral." He pointed toward the lights. "Must be Boss Kegel, but I can't figure why he's so far north."

"Maybe he's looking for his lost patrol," I offered.

"Ah, no. We weren't due for days." He scratched at his chin for a moment. "See here, he might be checkin' up on Jak Edge."

"What about him?" I asked.

Ondo turned toward me. "See, Jak's been a pain in Boss Kegel's side for a long time now."

"Why hasn't Kegel done him?" asked Stays.

Ondo gave a little shrug. "I think Kegel's afraid. I think he's afraid Jak's got too many followers and puttin' a move on Jak would pull hisself down."

"Does Jak Edge have that kind of power?" I asked.

Ondo shook his head. "I don't think he ever did, but if he did, that was before you killed most of his soldiers back at the dunes. Me thinkin' is that Kegel wants to catch Jak away from his soldiers and do him. I can't think of no other reason for Kegel to be here. Boss Kegel hates the sand worse'n locks." He held out his hands and let them fall to his sides. "It might not even be Kegel."

Sarah grabbed Nazzar's arm and pointed toward the lights. "Rhome, put together your ten best and scout out the position.

Scout it just like we talked about yesterday, and remember: leave no one behind who can talk."

"You want us to do it on foot?" he asked.

"That's right. Those animals stink and make too much noise. Ride halfway, then go on foot. Keep alert for their patrols and pickets. Before you go in, check your ten for noise. Then become as shadows, be the night, invisible."

Nazzar nodded and gestured with his thumb at Seraphine the Sosh. "Chopper. With me."

He skated down the dune and the sosh followed him into the darkness. I was damned if I was going to ask, but Stays didn't appear too proud.

"We're in big trouble." He looked at Bloody Sarah. "Is that old white woman one of Nazzar's ten best?"

"You're kidding," she said.

"No."

Sarah Hovit grinned. "That's the Chopper." When she saw that Stays's face remained blank, she said, "Seraphine Clay? You never heard of the D.C. Chopper?"

Then I remembered. How could I have ever forgotten the D.C. Chopper? As Blood Sarah followed Nazzar down the side of the dune, I looked into the shadows as a bitter taste in the back of my throat made my stomach strongly consider the possibility of issuing the most colorized belch of all time. I thought back to when even the Crotch recoiled in horror as it watched the story. The vids loved it, though.

She had been a caseworker in the Union of Terran Republics' national district capital until she had a breakdown trying to get the system to help some people. There were evils working upon a particular family.

There was a drug dealer who couldn't be persuaded to stay away. There was a judge who tied everything up with the letter of the law. There were a couple of cockroach lawyers who were squeezing the juicer and the family along with it. There were three gang toughs who thought it was funny to keep terrorizing the family. There was a hospital administrator who couldn't work his way through a paperwork blizzard in enough time to save a baby that had a deadly disease that an obstetrician at the same institution had failed to detect when the child was delivered. There was a supervisor in the social services department who seemed not to care about anything except where her next vacation was to be held. There was the steward of the local union who—

—It just seemed like everything in the universe had combined to frustrate Seraphine's attempts to help this particular family. Maybe, like a lot of us, Seraphine believed that if she only cared enough, if she only tried hard enough, if she only shouted loud enough, and worked long enough, if—

And none of it was enough. It was like trying to melt a granite mountain with a drip-drip of water. Reality reached its hand up out of the sewer and smacked the social worker in the face. That shitty handprint on her cheek said, "No matter how hard you try, no matter how strong your will, no matter how untiring your efforts, no matter how deep your love, this family will die that long, slow, horrible death slated for most of the world." That slap said, "There's nothing you can do about it, Seraphine."

Then something inside of Seraphine's head gave a loud snap, and she had said, "Oh yes there is."

There had been an antique butcher's ax mounted on the wall of her father's living room along with some other antique tools he had collected. She had always seen it hanging there, doing nothing, meaning nothing.

Suddenly the ax became to her a tool of social reform. She bought a new sharpening stone, and after putting a razor edge on the blade, she went forth to do the good work.

Anyway, that was the story her money threads put out. He tried to sell the juicer that Seraphine was the most salted pistachio that was ever meant to go directly to Gibber City. The juicer didn't see it that way, because Seraphine didn't look crazy, no matter how enthusiastically she had taken her revenge. There had been a total of sixteen men, in addition to three boys in their teens and five women, who had mysteriously disappeared over a nine-day period.

When they found the first body, it had been hit at least fifty times with a hatchet or ax. From dental examinations the police had determined that the open cases on drug kingpin Billy Aculos might as well be closed, since Billy Aculos was burger.

The next three bodies were members of the Fang. The Fang was a center city youth organization that specialized in drugs, murder, and mayhem for the hell of it. The parents of the Fang members never did have much confidence in the sorting job the morticians had done before burying the chopped remains of the three victims, but after watching the news on the vids there had been a lot of jokes in the Crotch about quarter-pounders, and burial by the quart. Does the Devil use a microwave, or does he still flame-broil?

After the remains of twenty-four bodies had been found, the stains still hadn't a clue to the identity of the D.C. Chopper, as the vids had named the social worker. The perpetrator of the now famous Burger Murders was still on the loose, and Washington was paralyzed.

That was when Seraphine had finally had enough. Whatever her monster was, it had become small enough for her to feel some remorse for what she had done. Seraphine Clay quit her job, went down to the local police station, and was made to wait almost four hours before the stains gave her a chance to turn herself in. Even then they didn't believe her. She just didn't look like a crazed ax murderer. As a matter of fact, she looked like a social worker.

It's too bad that some station's vid-jocky hadn't been in on Seraphine's interrogation, because I would have loved to have seen the expressions on the faces around that room when, frustrated one final time, Seraphine had reached into her oversize tote bag, pulled out her wide-bladed, short-handled butcher ax, and sunk the blade deep into the interrogation table—right across the fingers of Officer Lefty Bodeen. Since the digits on the table leaking all the blush were from Lefty's left hand, I had always wondered what Lefty Bodeen's friends had ended up calling him. Righty?

Anyway, if the Chopper had been sick, she should have been sent to the rubber hotel. If she was guilty of that scale of premeditated murder, by the man's own rules she should have been thinned by the application of lethal rays. Either she was sick or she wasn't, and the consensus in the Crotch at the time was that she was as salted as Manson, and she had done it without drugs.

But the man is always changing the rules when it suits. The Chopper was dropped into the Crotch because she fit somewhere in between: she was sick, and the smear in the black rag knew she was sick, but the jury, the public, and the press demanded a guilty body upon which to take out their fear and frustrations, much like the Chopper had done on them.

I suppose the point worth pondering about all of this is that it worked. The family she had tried to help was rescued from the sewer, and several important reforms were instituted to streamline the operation of the department. This improvement, and what had inspired it, had caused much debate in the Legislative Assembly, and even more windbreaking on the vids.

One of the vid commentators at the time had showed a still of Seraphine's supervisor all chopped up, many of the pieces on the desk next to a work basket overflowing with case reports. The commentator said about the new reforms, "Sometimes you just have to cut through the red tape." That got a real good laugh at the Crotch.

The Chopper had to be in her fifties, but she was one of Rhome Nazzar's best ten, which meant she was still a hand with an ax. I sort of wondered who her cellmate had been back at Ol' Miss, and how long it had taken before she managed to get a night's sleep doing bunkies with the Blade. On the men's side we called her the Blade or the Whacker, which is why Stays and I hadn't recognized her name.

It was while I was thinking about Seraphine Clay that I first realized that there are some very dangerous persons in a prison, and that they were all running loose on Tartaros. I wasn't thinking of the contract killers, leg-breakers, and yard monsters. The ones I was thinking about were the ments who kept a tentative hold on reality by reaching through a bucket of blood. I thought about that, and I thought about the incredible fact that the only law the Razai had was a prohibition against holding prisoners. Garoit's side of the issue didn't seem so silly right then.

When that itch at the back of my neck eased a bit, I faced Sarah. "Won't that leave Nazzar's bunch at the point short a few? Should Stays and I go up and fill in?"

"Sarah has it covered." Nance lifted a hand and rubbed the back of her neck.

"Anyways, you're not in the army, Mr. Po-leece-man. You got business someplace else."

"You got another yard monster snap-and-slash for me to referee?"

"Something like that."

That itch on the back of my neck returned. "Exactly what?"

"You know a yard monster named Dick Irish?"

"Yeah. I was locked in the seat next to him in the pit ship when we left Earth."

Nance lifted an arm and pointed. "Back at the end of the column. He just knifed and killed a mau named Freddy. It's turning into a salt-and-pepper thing real fast. Handle it."

PAYBACK

B Y the time Stays and I reached the rear of the walking
column, things were very ugly. The words were loud
and the threats were graphic. There must have been over
four hundred sharks milling around. Toward the center
of the mob, Dick Irish was in the clutches of two black yard
monsters, the three of them surrounded by a salt-and-pepper wall
of anger that had the maus and the haystacks getting ready to rock.

It was clear to me that everyone was using Freddy's killing
as an outlet for every frustration that had been accumulated for
the past ten years or more. The way the words were going, the
black-and-white stripe of this zebra was the one running the
animal.

I knew what I looked like, and Martin Stays was as white as
rice. I looked around quick and found someone with the proper
qualifications: big, black, armed, and quiet. I didn't recognize
him, but he was standing apart from the shouting and watching.
I jabbed Stays in the ribs.

"C'mon. It's time to integrate the po-leece."

"We are integrated," he answered with a smile, "you just
think we ought to darken the mix, noo?"

I ignored him and walked up next to the candidate I had spied.
Stays stood next to me as I asked him, "What's your name?"

A towering glower looked down upon me and studied me like an insect. "Marietta," came the response.

"Marietta?" I repeated.

"That's right. You're that little spic, Bando Nicos." She jabbed me in the chest with a finger about the size of a ham. "Why're you sniffin' around me, down an' brown?"

He was a she, but she was still big, black, armed, and not caught up in the spirit of the moment. Besides, with three-fifths of the gang composed of women, it made sense to have women in the cops. I glanced at Stays, but he had his back turned toward me. I looked back at Marietta.

"You know what I do?"

She nodded, that glower even deeper. "I sure do. You must be the onlyest po-leece-man in the whole world."

"Not really. I have Watson here." I pointed over my shoulder at Stays.

"Unh," replied my candidate. "Deppity Dawg. So, you wanna invite me up to your dune to polish your badge or what?"

"You see what's going on here?"

She nodded. "I got eyes."

"I need help. You want the job?"

That powerful glower melted into an equally powerful grin. "Why you sweet little thing. You want me in the po-leece?"

"We're going to call it something else, but that's right."

"I thought you were makin' a move on me, chili pepper!" She slapped my arm, and laughed loudly. "Man, Pancho, I thought you were after a ride on the magic mountain."

Despite myself, I blushed. "No. But I could use the help."

She nodded, then she gave out a huge sigh. "But maybe I was wrong about you, chili pepper. That might have been one sweet ride."

It was dark, but the heat from my face felt like it could be seen in the dark. I turned toward Stays, but he was kneeling on the sand, holding his guts, quaking. I thought he had been knifed, and I knelt beside him. I was not much relieved to find that he was only laughing and could not control himself.

I punched his arm and hissed, "Whenever you're finished, asshole, we have a killing to handle."

I stood up, checked the load on my rifle, made certain that Marietta was behind me, and waded into the crowd. Every now and then the sharks refused to part for me. Then a huge black arm would reach over my shoulder, tap the immovable object to get its attention, and suddenly the immovable object would stroll.

When I faced Dick Irish his expression changed from panic to hope. "Nicos!"

The crowd quieted a bit and I nodded at him. "Dick. What's going on here? What did you do?"

Dick Irish's eyes grew wide. "I did Freddy like I said I would. He broke my arm and I gave him the payback."

A voice from the salt said, "Spic, if you let the pepper do Irish, there'll be a war right here."

"Shut your face!" bellowed Marietta. "Pancho'll do what's right. The rest of you don't have no business here, so git!"

"Yes we do," shouted a voice. "This gang isn't bossed by a big gun; we vote! We got a right to see how this is handled."

I looked back at Marietta, closed my eyes, and nodded. "They do have that."

Marietta glowered as she scratched her chin with her rifle's front sight blade. "Okay." She lowered her weapon and faced the voice.

"You all can stay and watch, but no bad words—no threats. If you threaten somethin', what you say is exactly what you goin' to get. If you threaten to kill the chili pepper here, you'll be dead before your face hits the sand."

I remember standing in the middle of that nightmare thinking that Marietta's offering was an interesting policy. Threatening murder is the same as committing it. That would sure put a curb on most of the conversation that takes place among sharks, or thin the population considerably. However, it was not the time to discuss law. Right at the moment Marietta's rule was the only thing covering my ass, so I kept it—my ass and the rule both.

I looked at the black yard monsters holding Dick's arms. "We only got one law in the Razai, and that says no prisoners. Let him go."

"Is your gourd dribbling, Pancho?" asked the yard monster hanging on Dick's left arm. "What if he just strolls on out of here?"

I shrugged. "What about it? What we're going to do about him thinning Freddy can be decided if he's here or at the other end of the column. It makes no difference." I looked at Dick. "If you got something to say, though, you better stick around."

I pointed at the yard monsters holding Dick. "Well?"

I heard the word "Well?" boom out over my head. I silently applauded my instincts that had chosen Marietta from the crowd. The yard monsters released Irish. He shook out his arms, rubbed his wrists, and took a couple of steps toward me.

"Bando, I told you I was going to thin Freddy once we got out of the pit ship."

I moistened my lips. "Dick, will you stand by what I decide in this, or do you want us to put up someone as a black rag? Maybe you want a jury."

Dick Irish shook his head. "I'm not sayin' I didn't do it, Bando. I'm sayin' that it was somethin' that needed to be done. I don't want no judge. I know you'll do what's right by me."

I knew the answer before I asked the question, but this was for the record. "Dick, you thinned Freddy, right?"

"Right, but you know—everybody knows—he broke my arm back in the Crotch. I owed Snowflake a couple of decks, and—"

"Dick," I interrupted, "that was back in the Crotch. This is Tartaros."

"So?"

"So did you hear it when we made the rule? Did you hear when we said if it happened before the landing, it's done past?"

"Yeah, I heard it, but that don't make no difference to me. See, back in the Crotch he broke my arm. I don't—"

I lifted my rifle, aimed, and fired, striking Dick Irish in the heart. His face looked very confused as he went over backwards and turned his face up to the belly of the Spider. He dropped to the sand and was still. It was very quiet.

From behind me I heard Marietta whisper, "*Damn*, Pancho!"

I spoke to the crowd. "It's payback, just like in the yard. If you steal, payback is you return what you took plus a little. If you can't return what you took, then you return something worth as much. If you can't or won't return the stuff, or stuff worth as much, you get thinned. You lose it all."

I looked down at Dick's still form. "Dick Irish took a life. He couldn't return what he took, so his payback was to give up the life he had." I looked around at the crowd.

"If it happened before the landing, it didn't happen. Before the landing is done past. Tartaros is a new hand. Play it that way. The cards you were dealt last hand don't play here."

There was a moment of silence, then a voice asked, "What about Dick's stuff? Who gets it?"

"Yeah," said another voice. "And what about Freddy's stuff?"

I looked around at the faces. "Did Freddy have any relatives?"

A slender woman with night-black skin held up her hand. "We slept together." She looked up at me, her eyes filled with tears. "I loved him."

"What's your name?"

"Ginger."

I held out my hand. "Anyone else?"

One of the yard monsters who had been holding Dick said, "Freddy was my friend."

"Did you sleep with him?"

"What're you tryin' to say, you spic-ass little greaseball motherfucker?"

I grinned. "Nothing offensive, I assure you." I held my rifle across my chest.

"But here is the way I see it. Sleeping together here on the sand is as much of a marriage as anything we got. A wife gets the husband's stuff, unless he makes a will giving his stuff to someone else." I looked at the one who claimed to be Freddy's friend.

"If there's something particular you'd like, talk to Ginger about it."

"What about Dick's stuff?" came a voice.

I got angry. "What's with you people? Hard of hearing?" There were a few blank expressions, so I spelled it out.

"Payback. Dick took something from Freddy, and he can't pay it back. So he owes Freddy everything he's got. Ginger gets the lot."

"Hey chili pepper, who appointed you judge and jury?"

There was some laughter and a lot of angry grumbling. I walked over until I stood next to Dick Irish's body. I turned him over with my toe. I looked down at the dumb son of a bitch and said, "He did."

The rest of the scene faded from my awareness as I looked down at Dick's face. The big, dumb son of a bitch just couldn't let go of the past. I wondered if any of us could. Was the time before the landing really done past? Had I simply performed the final atrocity upon Dick Irish, and with his permission?

My rights and wrongs were very confused, and I began to

feel sick to my stomach as a wave of fear washed over me. I had just thinned one of the honker yard monsters, and the rest of the haystacks should be on me like white on winter. Taking Dick away from the black yard monsters should have had the maus all over me.

I looked around at the few remaining faces, for most of the crowd had rejoined the column. Why were they letting us get away with it? Marietta, Stays, and I were armed, but so were many of those in the crowd. Marietta was intimidating, and Stays and I could probably take care of ourselves against an equal number, but the three of us together were nothing against an angry armed mob.

I felt a hand on my shoulder, and I turned and saw Stays. I shook my head as I whispered to him. "I don't understand. Why're we still alive?"

Stays gave my shoulder a pat and said out loud, "The reason is simple, Chief. We aren't just a mob of con artists, thieves, and killers. Those sharks hate what you did, and probably hate you for doing it. But every one of them, deep down, knows it had to be done."

I spat on the sand. "It's a dirty job, but somebody's gotta do it." I turned my back on the pair and began walking toward the head of the column.

"That's right," Stays answered.

I turned and looked back. Stays was standing in the sand, looking up at the belly of the Spider. He paused for a moment and slowly began nodding his head.

"That's exactly right." He pointed a finger at me, and then at Marietta.

"We're not a gang like the others out here, brother and sister Crowbar. We aren't together because some big gun threatened us. We're together by choice for our own mutual interests. We are a tribe, a society, a civilization."

Marietta rumbled out a laugh and said to Stays, "Man, you have got more bull in you than Elsie's ass."

Martin Stays laughed. "That's why I get the big money."

They both laughed, and I didn't want to listen to them. I especially didn't want to listen to them laugh. All I wanted to do was to put down this anvil I was carrying and to get the picture of Dick Irish's face out of my head.

It was still night, but in the east the sky began turning purple. It was bed down time, and I wanted to find Alna. As Stays pulled out his notebook, I aimed my feet toward the front of the column.

In the half-light of dawn, the column halted. As I moved toward the front to find Alna, I saw Rus Gades in a group of about twenty sharks sitting in a circle off by themselves. They became silent as I walked up behind Rus. I pulled the book out of my kit bag and held it out to him. "Here."

He took the book, but kept looking at me. "What's bothering you, Bando?"

"Me?" Nine million things clashed inside of my head. "I don't know. I just killed somebody." I looked around the circle of faces. I knew most of the men from the Crotch. Deadheads, alkys, rapists, weenie wavers, child molesters, killers, and your choicer run of the Asshole All-stars.

"I just killed somebody I didn't want dead."

By the light of the dawn, Rus began paging through the little book. When he reached the page he wanted, he handed the book up to me and said, "Read that. It might help."

I looked down at the page marked with the pumpkin-colored ribbon and began skimming the lines. Blah, blah, blah, it ran with a few platitudes generally concerned with asking for help in letting go. It was about how to let go of fear, of pain, of guilt, of sadness, of all kinds of things.

I handed the book back to Rus. "That's cute. But my problem isn't me trying to let go of pain. My problem is trying to get pain to let go of me. Keep the book. I have no use for it."

I turned my back on them and continued toward the front of the column.

A POLICEMAN'S LOT

IT was light by the time I found Alna. She was wrapped in her sheet and was sleeping at the bottom of the western side of a dune. The air and the sand were still icy, but in minutes that would change.

I sat next to her and looked down at her face. She smiled when she slept. I wondered where she was in her dreams. Was she in a safe, beautiful place? Had she found a strong, handsome protector? Had she conjed up a magician that could fix her and fill all of those incredible needs she had?

I was surprised to feel a tear streak its way down my cheek. I reached up to brush it off and felt the week's worth of growth on my face. Pretty soon all of the men would be pussy-faced. I looked at the glisten of the tear on my finger with the detachment of a scientist observing a curious natural phenomenon. Maybe I was tired, or maybe it was the wind, or maybe I had gotten something in my eye. Things like that used to seem important to me at one time. *Macho* is, after all, the Spanish word for asshole.

Then everything that I could see became blurred, pain twisted my guts, and the tears could no longer be argued out of existence.

I climbed to the top of the dune and sat cross-legged on the sand as my guts writhed. I stifled the cries by burying my face in my hands, but the tears flowed and I choked on them.

The edge of Alsvid peeked over the horizon, filling the sky with brassy light. I didn't know why I was crying. Was it killing Dick Irish? Irish was an asshole, and the universe was a better place without him. In fact, Jesus could have done a lot more for the human race if, after love one another, he had said, "But first thin the Dick Irishes, the dumb sons of bitches." The death of Dick Irish was no loss.

Was it because I had been the executioner? I was no cherry. I had killed before. It was a litttle late in the game to be crying over a lost innocence that had never existed in the first place.

Maybe it was carrying everyone's hate for being Mr. Po-leece-man. That was part of it, although getting everyone in the world to love me never had been my thing. I never did want what was in your heart; I was after what you had in your pocket.

Still, it had been everyone's job to take out the soiled spot of Dick Irish, but I was the one who had done the laundry. I took out the spot and was hated for it. A few of the tears were for that.

From my past I remembered a bit of conversation I had overheard in a police squad room centuries ago in one of those monster piles of human shit that ringed Philly called King of Prussia. I was cuffed into a holding chair, and a stain that was old enough to be my father was tapping my current credits into his terminal while I was trying to look bad-assed to cover up the sick fear I felt. Even then I used to stink up my finger scratching my *macho*.

My contribution to the information updating exercise had been over for some time, so I was just a piece of furniture while I waited to be taken to Lancaster Juve. Every time that old stain would stretch, take a break, or look around the squad room to rest his eyes, he would look right through me. I was a piece of meat to be processed, and it was easy to see that and hate it. That way I gave my fear a hiding place.

While I was trying to kill the old stain with my eyes, a young cop, maybe only twenty-two or so, stopped in front of the old guy's desk. I noticed the tears of anger in the young cop's eyes and the garbage stains on his pretty blue shirt.

"What're you cryin' about?" asked the old stain, real sensitive like.

"They threw garbage at me! I took that bloody murdering bastard out of that building, and the people he was killing threw *garbage* at me!"

"What'd you expect? Flowers? Money? Gratitude?"

The young stain worked his mouth a bit, but he had no words. The old stain leaned back in his chair, clasped his hands over his belly, and studied the young officer for a moment. Then he looked me square in the eyes and said, "Listen up, Pancho."

"My name is Bando, pigshit."

The old stain nodded toward the young officer. "This is Patrolman Danner, Bando. Danner and his partner are big heroes today. They managed to track down and apprehend Henry Vicat, the Old Gulph Slasher. The Slasher murdered at least nineteen that we know about in the Gulph district, and now Henry Vicat's neighbors can sleep again at night. What do you think about that?"

I spat at the young stain, but I couldn't make the distance. It probably had something to do with a dry throat. The old stain smiled and looked at Patrolman Danner.

"There you have it, youngster. The civvies out there don't notice dog shit unless they step in it. Once they do step in it, however, they have all kinds of things to say about those whose responsibility it is to keep the dog shit off the sidewalk. That's what we are, Danner: turd pickers. We're society's poop scoops.

"If the civvies don't step in the shit, they never think about the thing that picks it up. Civvies look at us like garbage collectors, sewer workers, undertakers, and proctologists. They're really not comfortable about shaking your hand. Know what I mean?

"But we're a little worse than them in one respect. See, the civvies never identify with garbage, sewerage, the dead, or even with their own assholes. However, they do identify with the turds we scrape off the sidewalk. Every powder puff deadhead who murders nine bystanders on his way to get high that we stick in front of a jury has this going for him: Every juror has a piece of knowledge stuck in his gut that says, there but for the grace of the Great Juju go I, which is why they threw garbage at you when you arrested Henry Vicat."

"It's wrong," said young stain Danner. "It's not right."

The old stain went back to his terminal. As he typed he talked. "Danner, there are only two reasons a sane person can have for being a cop. The first reason is the cob, getting on some golden boy's corn dole and squeezing it down to the last drop. The other reason is because it's a job that needs to be done, and doing that job is a satisfaction. If your purpose is to get gratitude from the civvies you save, resign from the force and become a priest."

I thought long and hard about that conversation. Somehow I understood the young cop a bit, but I wished I could talk to the old stain. I had tried to spit on him, too, but the old guy was pretty nimble and had sidestepped the shot.

I picked up a handful of sand and let it trickle through my fingers. This was Tartaros. Was Earth really done past? It became warmer and beneath my sheet I removed my parka and shirt as the heat increased. I tied them into a bundle that I could sling and pulled the white hood over my head. I turned to my right to keep the sun out of my face as a piece of truth came to me.

It was the responsibility of being Mr. Po-leece-man that was weighing me down. I was sinking under it. I felt trapped, like I was being eaten alive. I didn't know what to do. I thought about what some of the stains and smears I had known on Earth had done with their responsibilities. Let them slide, and if you can grab a cob on your way out from under, do so.

What would happen if I eased out from under it like I'd seen and heard about so many times before? There were stains who took corn from the dealers and players. Black rags weren't above sucking a cob, either. Every day on the vids there had always been scandal after scandal about another tycoon, general, politican, judge, or vid star who had been caught with a dusty nose or sticky fingers, but only once every winter in Hell did you hear about one of those nibs going down to the crowbars.

No one had to take my word for it. All anyone had to do was ask former First Minister's appointee to the Office of Procurement, Clark Antess. No one could have been forced to believe that Antess would have gotten the idea to grab the three million on his own. His type doesn't even park in a crip zone unless everyone else is doing the same thing. Everyone had to know that there were others—lots of others. But, just for the sweet old record, no one ever pressed Clark Antess very hard for names, did they? That was the difference between stealing three million and thirty million. Thus endeth the lesson.

The ones hired to keep the rules dumped on them worse than anyone else ever dreamed of doing. It was written: A crook's only a crook, but to fuck over the law big time, you need a lawyer. That was one reason why dirty cops and black rags with sticky fingers never lasted long behind the crowbars. After being sent down, they would be thinned in a matter of hours after being released into the general pop.

I think the reason was because of this fantasy the sharks believed in. The fantasy went something like this: If all you cops, judges, and politicans were honest and did your jobs with integrity and courage, the world would be a much more livable place.

I think, deep down, sharks would like to believe in honesty and goodness—something better than themselves. No one dropped more scorn on a cop who can't be bought than a shark in the crowbars. But deep down in the guts was an admiration for the untouchable cop or judge that was just short of worhsip. Even when they cuffed you and dropped the rock in your lap, they were firm places—anchor posts—in an angry sea of slime.

And you could see it in their eyes when a crooked pol, cop, or judge made the news. They'd snicker, nod, and crack wise about them like, "No kidding? A crooked cop? Grow up." To show how wise and yard smart they were, the other sharks would laugh knowingly.

If you watched the way I watched, however, you could see that twitch in a jaw muscle, that downward glance, that nervous biting at the skin inside the lips, that symphony of impatient gestures that sharks do when they feel betrayed and don't want to let anyone else know. Every time it's like finding out for the first time that your father was flawed, your mother had a defect, that God left a few loose ends. The crooked cops hurt the killers. They hurt everyone in the pits.

They say one crooked cop hurts all cops, but no one ever suspected that a dirty stain hurts the sharks, too. But like any other Santa Claus thing that gets blown away, the there's a better way fantasy turns out to be just that: a fantasy. The dirty cop or judge, just by being there, confirms to the shark what the man with his face in the toilet always knew: This is as good as it gets.

The cops would always say to the vids that the cops who were sent to prison were killed just because they were cops. That was not exactly true. In fact I knew several ex-cops behind the crowbars who were just as liked, respected, and accepted as any murderer or thief in the place. Two or three of them were with the column. None of them, however, were in the pits for taking corn and looking the other way. The three ex-cops I was thinking of were all in the Crotch for murder.

One woman cop had gotten drunk and had thinned her husband. The other two, one male and the other female, both from different cities, were sent down for doing a little of what the Chopper had done big time.

The male cop was called Cap. He was a lanky, red-haired former police captain from Atlanta who had been trying to put the shutters on a local sleaze boss called Lou Imagia. The sharks used to call him Diaper Lou because his specialty was providing, for a price, little boys and little girls for sex and snuff parties.

Diaper Lou certainly didn't want to go to the crowbars. Not only would he be cut off from his kiddies, after we got hold of him his balls would have been cut off just prior to his being cut off from his supply of oxygen.

Maybe three out of every five sharks in the pits, male and female, had been sexually molested as children. That's why they always saved the slow strangle for child molesters. It gives you time to reflect upon your past life of misdeeds when it takes fifteen or sixteen mintues to die.

So, Diaper Lou couldn't afford the rent in the crowbar hotel, which was why he had sharp money threads and a couple of black rags and stains chewing on his cob. After Cap's third case against Diaper Lou blew up in his face, it became clear that the system was never going to get Lou Imagia, and the snuff-a-kid franchises would go on until the sickos found some other way to get rid of their money.

After he returned from court, Cap ordered his men to close the investigation on Diaper Lou. That night, behind a wall of security systems and guards that made it easier to get at the First Minister than at the kiddie-snuff boss, the captain closed Diaper Lou's file for good, along with his eyes.

Cap got away clean, too, and turned himself in the next morning. For *that*, not for being an ex-cop, the sharks used to give him a hard time. Anyway, the case turned into an election year rights and ethnic thing, so Cap found himself in Ol' Miss doing the rock clock. The way we thought of the captain, any shark who made a move at thinning Cap would have been committing suicide.

The female cop, Marantha Silver, had been a top inspector in the UTR Ministry of Justice. The MJs had a lot of respect in the hotel because when they were on the job instead of on the cob, they could put together your life story from the remains of your gerbil's three-week-old fart.

As the story went, agent Marantha had been assigned as part of an investigation by the MJ into drug moneys being used to purchase off-the-rack political candidates. The vids had uncovered the story first, and at Blackhall the First Minister reacted with a public protestation of his innocence and a proclamation of his support of the MJ's thorough and complete investigation of the matter. A clean sweep was the order of the day.

It was the public order, anyway. On the block and in the back rooms, it was business as usual. Maybe Marantha Silver was just too thick to understand what had been expected of her. Maybe she just hadn't gotten the word. Maybe she had gotten the word, and just didn't give a damn.

Anyway, she took the investigation right into the First Minister's office, and that was when the MJ started emptying sacks of marbles on the nice clean floor. Press secretaries started sending their own press secretaries out to talk to the reporters, platoons of ranking witnesses turned up to be too ill to testify in front of committees and at court, and "Marantha who?" became a whispered joke in the halls and craphouses of the Ministry of Justice.

Marantha was taken off the case, she was assigned to another station four thousand miles away from the First Minister's office, an investigation was begun on her background and finances, three hundred some-odd agents collected up and grilled old boyfriends and girlfriends, former classmates, teachers, employers, and supervisors and subordinates of hers at the MJ.

From her criminal past the MJs had turned up a student loan that she had repaid several months late, and there was someone who had once been a fellow student back in the eighth grade who was doing six to eight months for mugging the secretary of a law firm. For some reason the implications of this set of circumstances staggered the viddies. Sure, plenty of viddies had climbed on the cob, too. Being on the tube didn't keep you clean. There was serious talk of a special prosecutor.

When news of the special prosecutor cockroach leaked out in a flood, I rememberd a yard guru I liked a lot named Stogie Gomez remarking that, if she lived long enough, we would see Marantha Silver in the Crotch.

"There's no room in the MJ for a good cop this year," he had said. At the time I thought he was farting through his hairpiece, but fourteen months later agent Silver was dropped through the crowbars into the women's side for murdering another agent. Her plea of self-defense was considered preposterous. The idea that the MJ and Blackhall would stoop to having one of their own agents hit to cover up the First Minister's dirty fingers was not even considered, except in the crowbars.

Stogie Gomez had pointed out that Marantha's jury had consisted of too many angel-cake social uprights who were too inexperienced to be able to believe that anyone could get dirty, even a first minister. If the trial had been held inside the crowbars, the jury of sharks would have cut her loose in a second. Then they would have arrested and convicted her for her stupes.

Anytime during that whole thing, Marantha could have taken the smart way. She had been close enough to make Blackhall sweat, so there must have been plenty of cash offers. Right now she could have been rolling in the long green and serene instead of trying to stay alive upon Tartaros. She just hadn't been smart.

The same thing with Cap. He'd been to Disneyland; he knew the score. The smart door was right in front of him all the time, and he slammed it in their faces. Plain stupe, right?

Maybe it was something else. Maybe it was something that every shark would like to believe in, but can't. Maybe some people just don't feel comfortable on a cob, no matter how much corn they get. Maybe there is such a thing as an honest cop.

Okay, maybe Cap was just a little squeamish about taking money over the corpses of little kids who had been raped to death with a table leg. But the smart way was still there for him. He didn't have to take any corn. He could have just averted his head and let that horrible responsibility slide. If he'd kept his eyes shut he'd still be a police captain in Atlanta, maybe even chief of police, pretending to serve and protect.

Then I thought, maybe people like Marantha and the Cap don't like pretending about certain things. Maybe they hate it; hate it enough to rather die than do it. Trying to understand someone like that made me shake my head in despair. Me, I would have taken the money, shut my mouth, and considered myself both smart and lucky.

The more I thought about it, the more I realized what I was feeling. With Marantha and the Cap as reference points, it became clear to me why I had been crying. I remembered only too well my confident speech to Martin Stays about what I believed in. I had told him that what I believed in was the strongest goon standing next to me.

"If you can swing the sweetmeat and you like the Purple Puck Suckers, I like the Purple Puck Suckers, too."

I was crying because I had never felt so unworthy before in my entire life. Unworthy to do a job. Unworthy to do this job. Unworthy to do it correctly. Anybody could be a crooked cop. What would it take to be an honest one? A competent one?

I heard soft footsteps in the sand behind me. I turned, looked up, and saw Alna. She stood behind me, put her hands on my shoulders, and began rubbing them. "It's daylight, Bando. Why didn't you come to bed?"

"I had some thinking to do. You heard about last night?"

"Yes." She squatted next to me and rested her face on my shoulder. "You did what you had to do."

I stood up, brushed the sand from my blues, and looked down into Alna's eyes. "Lady, what do you say we get to a place where there's grass and trees, maybe a few mountains, a pond, a quiet little valley? What do you say about striking out on our own? Nobody to watch out for except you and me. What do you say?"

She stood as her face blossomed into smiles. She lifted her hands and fiddled with the drawstring of my hood. "I'd love that, Bando. Just you and me?"

"Just you and me."

"We could build a nice little house, couldn't we? Do you know anything about building?"

"I can learn, even if I have to teach myself." I held her chin in my hand. "Back in Lancaster Juve I once taught a rat to sit on its hind legs and sing."

"You didn't."

She pulled her head away and raised her eyebrows at me. "You never taught a rat to sing." She turned and began walking down the shady side of the dune. I followed.

"I thought it was singing," I said. "The other sharks thought it just sounded like eeee eeee eeee eeee eeeeeeee, but to me it sounded like 'The Russian Easter Overture.'"

I put my arm around her shoulders and she put her arm around my waist and said, "Bando Nicos and his singing rat. Give me a break." We both laughed, and I clung to the laughter.

"The rat was named Brunhilde!"

We laughed some more, and I hoped I wouldn't cry. Brunhilde was still at Lancaster for all I knew. God, I loved that rat. It was the only thing besides my sister that I had ever loved. My sister, a rat, and maybe one day soon I would trust myself and Alna enough to love her. Maybe today was the day.

Alna and I found a place alone and made love for the first time. I don't know about rocket ships flying and fireworks going off. Out in the sand it was enough just to feel a little tenderness.

A ROOM WITH
A VIEW

AS we slept in each other's arms, I dreamed about a tiny green valley with a clear running stream.

I was sitting on the bank of the stream looking up at the top of a wooded hill. That would be the place for our house, I thought. A nice view, plenty of trees for shade and firewood. The water was down where I was sitting, and I started thinking about digging a well.

I heard a voice and I looked down the stream and saw Alna standing in a meadow, her arms filled with wildflowers. She was wearing a bright yellow gown of material that caught every little breath of air and flowed with it. The meadow surrounding her, as beautiful as it was, seemed oddly familiar—somehow threatening.

I heard the voice again and opened my eyes.

I was back in the furnace on the sand in the middle of a bunch of sharks who hadn't had a shower in weeks. I couldn't figure out who smelled worse: me or Alna.

I sat up and remembered where I had seen the meadow from my dream before. That had been the view from my cell at Lancaster Juve. Every year we used to have to cut the hay out of that meadow and I would get sinus problems.

Nance, Garoit, and Ondo were standing over us.

"What?"

Nance pointed south toward the point scouts. "Rhome and his top ten are back. That camp belongs to a gang called the Hand, and Ondo says they shouldn't be here. He figures they're on their way to take on Kegel through the backdoor."

"What's that to us?" I asked as I disentangled myself from Alna.

Nance squatted in front of me and lowered her voice. "Maybe nothing. Maybe the Hand is our ticket through Kegel. Maybe we can join forces. Maybe we can thin them and take their food and water. What we took from Kegel's scavenger patrol won't last forever. Also, they have weapons, ammo, and riding critters. Almost enough to outfit the rest of the Razai. Anyway, we're heading on up to the point for a talk. I want you along."

I pushed myself to my feet and put my sheet over my head. When it was in place, I asked Nance, "You heard about Dick Irish?"

"Yeah, I heard."

"Well?"

"Well, what?" She folded her arms and shook her head. "It's a little late if you're asking for permission."

"I'm not asking for permission! I just wanted to know what you—I mean—" I stood there feeling very hot in the face. "Okay, I guess I was asking for permission. It is a little late."

"You did what you did, and it's done with, Bando. If you can find something useful out of it, keep that part. For the rest, if it moves, let it pass. If it doesn't move, piss on it."

As I fell in behind Nance, I tried to remember what the little pumpkin-colored book had said about letting go. In different words it was pretty much what Nance had said. It was something about accepting the things I can't change, and me killing Dick Irish was one thing that no one in the universe could change.

I wondered how you accept such a thing, and I sort of wished I had stayed for the CSA meeting.

THE HAND

UP at the point camp, Nazzar's best ten were a short distance away resting. Sarah and her generals, Nance, Garoit, Stays, and I were in a circle around Ondo as he smoothed the sand and drew his map on the smoothed portion with fine black sand from a pouch at his belt. He would hold some of the black sand in his fist and pass it above his map, quickly sketching in terrain features, dotting in some boundary lines, and lettering in the gang names. The last mark he made was the "X" showing our position.

When he was finished he reattached the pouch of black sand to his belt, rested his elbows on his knees, and looked around at the faces. "You know already about Boss Kegel. His territory runs from where the Big Grass starts down to the northwest shore of the Sea of Stars." He reached out his arm and pointed with his stick. If the Sea of Stars was almost two thousand miles long, Boss Kegel's territory was as wide as the North American continent. If he only had a hundred and fifty thousand in his gang, there might be some big gaps through which to sneak. We all watched and listened as Ondo pointed and talked.

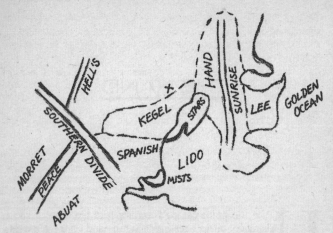

"Here at the east shore of the Sea of Stars is where the Hand's territory begins. The Hand's bossed by a sewer slug from Planet Ghitan who calls hisself Carlo T. He thinks he's some kind of criminal royalty, and he hates Kegel's guts worse'n locks. You know the camp down there is the Hand because of the painted hands on the rumps of the lughs. You'll see different colors and they belong to the different military units."

He pointed. "The Hand runs the east shore of the Sea of Stars, and all of the Sunrise Mountains. When I came over from First Landin', I fell in with the Hand."

"How'd you wind up with Kegel?" asked Stays.

"The Hand won't take just anyone. You need to be born into it, or have a certain kind of name. Since Carlo had a message he wanted to send to Kegel anyway, he had his guard run me over the mountains to the Sea of Stars. They took me in a boat and dumped me on Kegel's shore."

"What's this gang called Spanish between Kegel and the Southern Divide?" I asked.

Ondo looked from me to Nance and the others. "I'll run down what I know." He pointed at the territory called Spanish. "It's named after Boss Tommy Spanish. The bloodiest battle I was ever in was with the Spanish gang. I don't know where Tommy comes from, but nobody messes with the Spanish gang.

He has ways of killin' that make parchin' to death in the Forever Sand look fun. The word is he's talkin' to the shadows."
Ondo tapped the side of his head, then pointed at the territory
south of the Sea of Stars marked Lido.

"The boss of this gang is Quana Lido, a woman. I don't
know much about 'em except that they make the fire cubes and
the blue goo for the ammo. Once I was on a boat trip to the
south shore where we traded some wild grain for t' blue stuff."

He pointed at the west. "Morret and Abuat, I just know their
names. We never tangled or traded with 'em."

He moved back to the edge of the circle, squatted down, and
wrapped his arms around his knees. Nance nodded at Sarah.
"Let's hear it."

Bloody Sarah nodded. "It was easy to get into the camp."
She thought for a second. "Maybe it was too easy." Whatever
feeling it was, she shrugged it off and continued.

"From what Ondo and the others overheard and saw, it looks
as though the Hand is making a raid on Kegel's territory.
They're camped in one big clump of about eight hundred men. I
only saw a very few women. The men are armed, but not alert.
The way we read it, they don't expect anyone else to be in the
desert. Their mounts are away and downwind from the camp
under light guard. The camp guards they did put out don't know
what they're doing, and are in all the wrong places if they do
know."

"What are you saying?" asked Nance.

"I think we can take them, if that's what we decide to do."

I spat on the sand and asked, "Is that what we're going to
be? Like all of the other animals out on the dunes, killing and
grabbing? I just had to take a life to meet payback on a murder.
Isn't what applies on the small scale going to apply to the Razai
as a group?"

Nazzar growled at me, "Hey, chili pepper, why don't you go
out and start a flowers and love movement? You can call it
Pussies for Peace."

I started getting up, but Stays's hand on my shoulder kept
my ass in the sand. "Attacking the Hand is an option, Chief,"
he said. "There are other options. We'll consider them all."

I simmered down, trying to remember that the only things I
would be accomplishing by a fight with Nazzar would be hiding

how I felt about thinning Dick Irish and a premature trip to the Big Toaster. Nazzar's yard monster work back at the Crotch wasn't just for show, although he had a well-built body as a result of all the time with the irons. The point general was also quick on his feet, and deadly fast with his fists. I'd seen him mince a mokker or three over the years. Me tangling with Nazzar was just suicide under an alias.

I quit my struggle against Stays's hand. As I shrugged I nodded at Stays. "Okay."

Garoit stood up. "What about making up a delegation to go and feel them out about helping us, or maybe letting us join up with them?"

"The second you walk into their camp," said Sarah, "there goes your surprise, and we can't take them unless we have the element of surprise."

"We have them outnumbered," said Nance.

Sarah nodded. "Yes, we have more bodies than they do, but only a few of them are armed or have enough training to be fighters. We've got around four hundred and seventy rifles that work, and enough ammo for eight or ten shots per rifle. If we hit them in camp there won't be more than fifty of them that can get it together and be armed in time to defend themselves. If we announce ourselves first, we'll be facing eight hundred rifles, and every one of those jokers was carrying double belts of ammo."

"If y' join up with the Hand," cautioned Ondo, "Kegel'll eat y' alive. The Hand's big, but it's no match f' Kegel. At least they's no match f' Kegel on Kegel's own ground."

Ow Dao chuckled. When he spoke his voice rumbled out, "Ondo, you said that Boss Kegel won't like us anyway. Remember, we thinned his raiding party? You also said, whatever else we do, we have to go through Kegel to get out of the sand. In the balance, eight hundred more rifles aimed at what Kegel throws at us does seem attractive."

While the discussion continued, I heard someone come up behind me and I turned to look. It was Marietta. Behind her was a tall man with red hair that was going to gray. His beard was gray streaked with dark gray.

Marietta squatted behind me and said, "Chief, we got a bit of trouble."

I shook my head. "Man, I don't know what's going to happen to us when we no longer have the desert and all of those killers out there to keep us together. If we ever do get the fear of war and the threat of thirst and starvation off our backs, we're going to wind up killing each other just to keep up the chaos level."

"We still have some trouble, Chief."

Stays looked back at her. "What is it?"

"Back in the middle of the column. Mojo Tenbene says Herb Ollick tried to kill him."

"Ice Fingers?"

"Right. Herb says he didn't, and the salt-'n'-pepper thing is heatin' up fast."

"I guess we don't have to worry about the mob doing anything to us here. Were there any witnesses?" I asked.

"Haw!" she exploded. "Nobody's seen or heard nothin' since eighteen an' ninety-two."

I got to my feet and tapped Stays on his shoulder. "Hang in here and let me know what they decide." Stays nodded back and I faced Marietta. There was a different look to her face.

"What is it?"

"I could of handled it if it was just what I told you."

"Yeah?" I could almost see it coming.

"See, there's a guy down in the walkin' column who's confusin' everythin'. That's why I came to get you."

"Who is he?"

"His name's Pendril. Jason Pendril."

"I never heard of him."

Marietta's eyebrows went up. "Well, you know when I said Ice Fingers said he didn't do it?"

"Yeah."

"Well, Jason Pendril is Ice's lawyer, and he says that we have to give Herb Ollick a trial."

"A cash register? He wants a trial? Here in the sand?" A rotten taste crawled into my mouth as I watched Marietta's head nod.

How had a money threads managed to stay alive in the Crotch? He probably had kept a low profile, had done favors for the yard monsters, the way I had. He probably had so many markers out for free legal work, the best thing that ever happened to him was Tartaros. If he had a connection with Herb Ollick, maybe he had a wire in to goomba central. That would've kept him alive.

All I needed was some slippery cockroach cash register with a mouthful of Latin, the scruples of Attila the Hun, and the angles of a snake to intimidate the hell out of me. Whenever I saw one of those smug, indulgent smiles followed by one of those pat little mouthfuls like, "Let me handle it," "I know what I'm doing," and "Trust me," I know some lawyer is going to get rich and Bando Nicos is headed for the crowbars with empty pockets and a new asshole.

"Damn. Not a lawyer." I looked at Marietta. "I can't get a break."

"If it don't get any worse'n that, Chief, we can handle it." She grinned with menace. "You can always thin the cockroach." Marietta turned and headed north toward the column.

I thought about Marietta's remark, and it was true. I could always kill the lawyer. I wouldn't have to be crooked to do that. There wasn't a lawyer in the universe who had gone more than an hour without doing something that deserved killing, not that I have anything personal against cockroaches.

"Stays, give me your notebook."

"Why?"

"Don't lay that why stuff in my face, Hammurabi. Just give me the damned notebook."

Stays gave me that big grin. "Why?"

Why? Why did I want the notebook? I held out my hand. "Because it's all we got for rules right now, chup."

Martin Stays pulled out his notebook, handed it up to me, and nodded. "Just so you understand. Don't lose it."

I grabbed the notebook and began running to catch up with Marietta. Stays called out from behind me. "Chief, there're some additions since you read it last."

As I followed the rookie, I suspected that I was already losing whatever it was that I had in the way of confidence. When two razors start going after each other, any fool whose blood isn't up can see how to work it out. Courts with black rags and money threads blowing smoke and angling mirrors were no-man's-land.

It wasn't that the juicers were all rigged, and the rags and cash registers all crooked. Every now and then I had come across a lawyer or judge who was really trying his best to do the job, serve justice, and all that crap. They were the poorest and most depressed people I ever met this side of Skid Row.

I remembered that sad-eyed jerk with the trembling smile saying to me one time, "The judge, he really likes you, Bando. He's giving you sixteen to twenty years."

The funny thing was that the judge really did like me and my attorney wasn't making a joke. After I thinned my sister's live-in dealer, everybody understood and wanted to help me. Sixteen to twenty years. All I could figure was that it wasn't assholes who made the system; it was the system that turned everybody into assholes.

I glanced at Stays's notebook, wondering if what we were doing was constructing another asshole factory. The tall man with the gray and red hair fell in beside me.

I looked at him. "Was there something you wanted?"

He pointed toward my newest rookie. "Marietta said you might be able to use me."

"What's your name?"

"Brady. John Brady."

"Why'd the rookie grab you, Brady? Did you get lonely for Hell, or did you just look too happy to suit her?"

He smiled. "She knows I've done some police work."

"Oh?" I paused and considered the man standing before me. He looked like a cop, or an airline pilot, maybe a priest or a vid player who does fathers on the sitcoms. It would be more luck than Bando Nicos had ever seen in a bunch of years to get someone in the Razai Cops who knew what he was doing.

"Where did you do stains, Brady?"

"I was on the force in Atlanta."

"Atlanta?" I skidded to a halt, which is no mean trick on sand. "Like, In Georgia, North America?"

"The same."

"Cap? You're Cap?"

"I was a police captain, yes."

I held out my hands. "You're the one who thinned Diaper Lou!"

The man's smile vanished. He nodded, looked down, and shook his head. "I really don't know what I'm doing here. I guess Marietta thought I might be able to answer some questions for you. Anything I can do, just let me know." He shook his head.

"I'm sorry." He began walking away.

"Hold it!" I grabbed his arm. "Don't go. I'm sorry if I seemed a little stunned. It's just that I've been in it over my head for days, and I was just thinking about you not so long ago." I held out my hand. "Man, am I glad to see you!"

Cap Brady looked down at my hand, his face looking very somber. "Bando, the day I killed Lou Imagia I became what I was fighting against. I broke the law."

"Hey, Cap, none of us got here because of a great résumé." I gestured with my hand again, and Brady took it. He had an iron grip and a strong smile.

"Thanks, Bando. This means a lot to me."

I placed my free hand on his shoulder and said, "I'm the one rolling sevens." We ended the shake and continued following Marietta. "Cap, as long as I'm rolling winners, have you ever heard of an ex-MJ cop named Marantha Silver?"

"Sure. You'd have to have lived under a rock not to have heard of her."

"She was in the Crotch, I know. But is she with the column? If she is, we could sure use her."

Cap nodded. "Yes, she's with us. Would you like me to ask her?"

"Yeah. Great."

Cap stopped and said, "I'll catch up with you. I have to go back to the point."

"Why?"

"Marantha's there. She's probably sleeping now. She's one of Nazzar's ten best, and they were real busy last night." He waved a hand. "I'll get back to you as soon as I can."

I watched his back for a moment, suddenly feeling like maybe what I was doing was not entirely a lost cause. I thought for a second, then opened Stays's notebook and did a quick scan of the pages. The murder of Freddy had added a few provisions to the policies of the Razai.

12. The Razai have the right to observe the judicial process (Freddy–Dick Irish murder). On the march, d5.

13. A threat is a crime, and it carries as a penalty the performance of the threat upon the threatener (Freddy–Dick Irish murder). Issued by Marietta Jackson, On the march, d5.

14. If the parties to a dispute agree to it, the dispute may be settled by the investigating cop (Freddy–Dick Irish murder). On the march, d5.

15. The penalty for all crimes is payback, and payback for taking a life is everything plus a little (Freddy–Dick Irish murder). On the march, d5.

16. As part of payback, the murder victim inherits all from the murderer (Freddy–Dick Irish murder). On the march, d5.

17. Without a will, the spouse inherits. Without a spouse on record, sleeping together constitutes spousehood (Freddy's estate to Ginger). On the march, d5.

My eyebrows went up as I read the final entry. According to policy number seventeen, Alna and I were married. I wondered what Alna would have to say about that when I told her.

A niggle of something else was bothering me. It was about the whole policy-making thing. It seemed like every time anyone made a decision, a new poicy was made. So far it hadn't run us into trouble, but we had a couple of real crazy rules on the books. Thirteen and seventeen came to mind real fast. A threat being the same as the action threatened promised to get half the gang thinned for just working their blowholes the way sharks've done since the invention of crowbars.

Sleeping together constituting some kind of marriage status promised to make for a lot of lonely nights. Either that, or it would make marriage into nothing. Then, I thought, what was marriage? It was a contract. And what did I know about contracts? They had super cash registers on Earth who did nothing but contracts.

Anytime I had ever brushed up against a contract, particularly if it involved black rags or money threads, it was like splitting fly hairs in the dark with a dull ax. Also, every time a money threads came at me with a contract and one of those smug "You don't have to worry about that provision," or "This item doesn't really mean anything," or "No one ever enforces those provisions," I know some lawyer is going to get rich and Bando Nicos is going to wind up with empty pockets and a brand-new asshole.

I shook my head and decided to take things just as they came. One shovelful of shit at a time was all I could handle. Trying to deal with the whole mountain at once was overwhelming.

I looked again at number seventeen. Someday, I thought, someone is going to demand that these things get voted up or down, and I just might be the one who does the demanding.

I looked up from the notebook and turned to follow Marietta, but she was out of sight. All of the dunes looked the same, and there were so many different trails and footmarks going off in all directions, I couldn't possibly figure out which trail was hers.

For a second I felt lost—frightened. Then I realized that all I had to do was climb one of the dunes to see where I was. I was about to climb the nearest one when Marietta's voice rumbled behind me. "This way, Chief."

I turned and saw her standing between two dunes, her rifle slung, her hands upon her massive hips. "Why didn't you follow my trail, chump?"

"How was I supposed to tell which trail was yours? A footprint is a footprint."

"A footprint is a footprint? Check it out, Sherlock." She shook her head. "Listen, chump—"

"I believe they pronounce it 'chup'—"

"Listen, *chump*, I spent a month in court listenin' to lectures on footprints, complete with movies and plastic models. A footprint is what got me my numbers, *chump*, and sent my sorry ass to Tartaros. Don't tell me a footprint is a footprint! And don't tell me how to say 'chump,' chump!"

"Okay, I can follow the trail now."

She shook her head. "You couldn't track a three-legged rhino through wet sand on a sunny day." She presented me her back and continued toward the column.

Mighty touchy on the subject of footprints, she was. I mentally noted this particular area of Marietta's expertise in the unlikely event that the Razai Cops should someday find themselves in a land with enough water to make footprints possible.

TENBENE V. OLLICK

THE sides of three dunes faced each other, and there were, perhaps, five hundred spectators there availing themselves of the amusement benefits of policy number twelve (The Razai have the right to observe the judicial process). When I arrived there was even a tiny round of applause. We were entertainment.

The vids and rads didn't work on Tartaros because there were no broadcasting stations. Batteries had just about all run out on the vid players, and the solar-powered outfits were just about burnt. Very few sharks had brought books along, and the few decks of cards there were could not be bought, borrowed, or stolen. For something to do, then, this left conversation and watching Bando Nicos make a fool out of himself.

There was a clear place between the three dunes, and I slung my rifle and stood in the center. When the chatter eased off, I said, "Mojo? Mojo Tenbene, do you have a charge to make?"

A tall dark man standing at the bottom of the dune to my left raised his hand. "I am Mojo Tenbene." He lowered his hand and pointed toward the dune to my right. Ice Fingers sat there, his face impassive, his fingers glittering. "This man, here, he took a blade and tried to thin your brother, Mojo."

There were angry support noises coming from the crowd. Many of the comments suggested ill happenings upon my person should the trial not go to the threatener's liking. I pretended not to hear the threats. Instead I unslung my rifle and looked around at the spectators.

"We have a rule. It's number thirteen. It says that a threat is a crime and that a threat carries as its penalty the performance of the threat upon the threatener. In other words, anyone who threatens to bust up my face is going to wind up with a busted face. If you threaten to kill me in the hopes that it will make this thing turn out the way you want, you die." I glanced back at Marietta. She held up her weapon, looked around, and the crowd got real quiet.

"I think they got rule thirteen, Chief."

I looked back at Mojo Tenbene. "Who do you say did it?"

"Him! Herb Ollick! Ice Fingers! The big goomba from Block Nine!" Mojo walked half of the way over to the right-hand dune and pointed at Ice Fingers. Herb Ollick didn't seem to be the least bit worried. It was almost as though he were still connected and all he had to do was wiggle his finger to fill the dunes with goons. I vaguely remembered him from the Crotch. Sometimes I'd catch a peek at him in the yard or on the galleries. I wondered if he really had been in the mob. Anyway, he was used to having others do his work for him. The cockroach was just his current garbage man.

"What do you say, Ollick?"

Herb Ollick held the stub of a cigar between his fingers and nodded at another man.

The third man got to his feet, and I'll be best man at a lughox's wedding if his hair wasn't styled. This had to be Jason Pendril, the money threads for Ollick. In the middle of that desert, without any kind of a shower for weeks, the cash register managed to show up at "court" with styled hair.

"Damn, will you look at the hair," I whispered.

Marietta mumbled something. "What did you say?" I asked without taking my eyes off of Pendril.

Without lifting her gaze from the crowd or lowering her weapon, she bent over and whispered into my ear, "It's a rug."

"A what?"

Marietta sood up and pulled at her own hair. "A rug. A hairpiece." She pointed at Ollick.

"Oh." I nodded toward Pendril. "Your name?"

"Jason Pendril for the defense."

The man had an expression on his face that was very frustrating. It wasn't quite contempt, and it wasn't quite smirking. It was close, though.

"So, how does Herb answer the charge?"

Jason Pendril turned and spoke to the crowd, rather than to me. "As the unfortunate demise of Dick Irish has shown, Nicos, entering a plea with you may not be the healthiest thing we could do."

There was laughter, and I felt an imaginary knife blade turn in my gut. When the laughter died down I looked at the smug expression on the cash register's face for a long time, realizing as I did so that I was seeing every cockroach meatwagon barnacle that had ever put on a lawyer suit to juice me and drop me into the black hole.

It was important to me, as well as to Herb Ollick, that I not try to take out my entire revenge on the whole gang of money threads by crushing this one little cockroach and his client. Still, this little fantasy popped into my head. It wasn't anything complicated or subtle. Pendril would raise his hand, he would open his smirking mouth, and say to me, "I object." Then I would lift my rifle and blow off his face.

I tried to shake the thought from my head as I whispered to Marietta. "Where are we?"

"The roach doesn't want to enter a plea," she whispered back.

I said to Pendril, "If your client refuses to say if he did it, I'll assume he tried to kill Mojo."

"That is not how it is done in a court of law, Nicos."

I really did feel like lifting my rifle. Aim. Boom. No face on the cockroach and Bando Nicos gallops over the dunes leaving nothing but a cloud of dust and a shrill cackle. I wrestled myself into the present moment.

"Maybe it's not how it's done in the juicer, Pendril, but it is how it's done in the yard. You've been in the crowbars awhile. Silence is a plea of guilty there. Silence is a plea of guilty here."

The money threads threw up his hands to indicate his helplessness before such a stupe. "In that case, of course he enters a plea of not guilty."

Pendril showed no reaction to the hisses and boos of a few of the watchers. Marietta began walking around the clear area between the dunes, aiming her rifle and her face up into the crowds. They quieted down.

I checked Stays's notebook, found what I wanted, and said, "Mojo, Herb, according to rule number fourteen, if both of you agree to me settling this, I can take care of it. How about it?"

Mojo nodded. "That is just dandy with me." There were murmurs of approval and disapproval from the crowd.

I looked at Ollick, then at Pendril. The money threads was giving me his best patronizing smile. I wondered what rule I would create by running over, sticking my foot in Jason Pendril's face, and turning his kisser into tomato soup.

Pendril again addressed the crowd instead of me. "My client chooses to have a jury of his peers decide his guilt or innocence."

There were more murmurs of approval and disapproval, and then there was a voice that spoke up from the dune face behind me. "Bando, I'm not makin' a threat, understand? I'm just askin' a question."

I turned around and looked. There was a wiry little bastard Mexican sonofabitch from the Crotch named Hector Diaz. For reasons I never understood, Hector and I hated each other at first sight.

"So?"

Hector grinned as he held his rifle in his arms like a baby. He stroked the weapon and asked, "What would happen if we just smoked you and the big sister crowbar there?" There were ugly chuckles and hisses from the spectators.

"What if we just got tired of you playing little tin god and just thinned your brown-sugar ass?"

The ugly sounds from the spectators were cut short by the sounds of three rifles levering fresh rounds into their firing chambers. I looked and saw Martin Stays standing at the top of Hector's dune. I turned and saw Cap Brady at the top of the dune behind Mojo, and a woman that had to be Marantha Silver standing at the top of the dune behind Herb Ollick. I nodded at her and she smiled back.

I turned toward Hector Diaz and said, "My guess is that you'd be dead before your face hit the sand."

Hector grinned and held out his hands. "Just asking," he said as he sat down to the laughs and jeers of the others.

I knew I looked good right then, in front of the others. But I was grateful that no one could see the yellow feathers lining the inside of my stomach. As things quieted I looked at Ollick and Pendril. "How many do you and your cockroach want on the jury? Pick an odd number."

Pendril fowned. "Odd number?"

I nodded. "Majority rules here, and we don't want any ties." I looked around and called out to the crowd. "Anyone who wants to be on the jury, line up right here." I held my hand out indicating the space between Ollick's dune and the dune behind me. Perhaps fifty sharks began moving down to the jury line.

Jason Pendril put on his most outraged is-this-what-you-call-justice voice. "Do you propose that verdicts be handed down on the basis of a majority vote?"

"No," I answered. "I do not propose it. Majority vote is the way we do things in the Razai." I glanced at Stays's notebook. "Numbers three, four, and five."

Pendril pointed at the notebook. "What is that?"

I held up the open notebook and faced it around at the crowd. "This is a record of the votes and other decisions that have been made by us so far." I looked at the money threads. "For what it's worth, it's the law here."

"May I see that?"

"Pick a number, first, then while we're putting together the jury, you can go back to law school." My comment drew another chuckle from the crowd.

Herb Ollick got to his feet and whispered into Pendril's ear. Pendril whispered back, then they seemed to fight in whispers for a bit before Ollick sat down and Pendril said, "Most of the men and women in that jury line aren't white."

I stepped to one side, glanced down the line at the faces, and looked up at Marietta. She looked down the line and nodded. "He's right."

I looked at Pendril and said, "You're right. And when you're right you're right. Pick a number."

As we spoke a few haystacks got up to join the line, followed immediately by a few more maus, hows, and a chop or two. Everyone was getting civic-minded.

"The point is," said Pendril, "how can my client receive a fair trial if most of the jurors are, say, of another ethnic persuasion?"

After the hoots and catcalls died down, I looked at the jury line. The salts and the peppers were at it, jabbing and grab-assing around, the whole thing a joke to them. But there was a life and a few other important issues at stake. One of those issues involved a possible fight the Razai was facing with the Hand. We had to prepare, and we couldn't afford to waste the whole day settling the Tenbene–Ollick hash.

I said to the jury line, "I want you all to understand why we are here." I turned from the line, looked around at the crowd, and looked at Pendril, Ollick, and Tenbene.

"We are all here for the same reason. That reason is to make certain that Mojo and Herb get exactly what's coming to them." I looked back at the jury line. "Herb is up for attempted murder. If you get to be part of this jury, your job will be to see to it that Herb gets what's coming to him."

A number of black hands traded fives to the cruel laughter of a few sharks in the jury line and up on the dunes. Something occurred to me, and I continued, "Remember, if you say Herb is guilty, and we find out later that he isn't guilty, then all of you in the jury who voted for guilty will suffer the fate that Herb suffered."

There was a rumble of exclamations from the crowd, and a few of the men and women in the jury line became less civic-minded and headed back to their seats on the dunes. "And it goes the same if you vote him innocent and he turns out to be guilty. You will stand the punishment he should have stood."

"Nicos," said Pendril, his voice loaded with scorn, "are you just making this up as you go along?"

Since that was exactly what I was doing, I grimaced a bit as I sorted among my possible answers. I settled for one I must have heard a million times in front of some black rag's bench. "If you don't like the rules, change them." I turned to the crowd.

"You elected Nance Damas, and Nance appointed me. If you aren't happy with the way I handle things, talk to Nance about it. If you aren't happy with the way she handles me, hold another election." I pointed at the jury line.

"Now, let's get on with it."

The jury line was pared down to about twenty-five or so who were prepared to back up their judgment with their lives. Maybe there might have been one or two who didn't think I was serious. There were a few salts, a few peppers, but mostly chili peppers, chops, and hows. I turned to Jason and Herb. They were still blowing hot whispers in each other's ears.

"You two come up with a number yet?"

"Not quite yet," answered Pendril.

"Do thirteen!" came a shout from the dune behind Mojo. "That fits a jury of sharks! Thirteen!"

The call went up, and a jury of thirteen appealed to the sharks. Since Pendril and his charge either couldn't or wouldn't come up with a number, thirteen it was. I held up my hands for quiet. "I make it thirteen," I called out.

I looked around and found a pair of specs. They were on an old woman who might have been black pepper, might have been chili pepper. It was hard to tell when they got that old. I pointed at her and asked, "Can you read and write?"

"Yes." She stood and walked over to me. I handed her Stays's notebook. "Pick a fresh page and write down the names of the ones picked for the jury, understand?"

"I understand." She pulled a writing instrument, perhaps a pen, out from under her sheet. She turned to the next page in the notebook, and waited. "Yes?"

"What's your name?"

"Ila Toussant."

"Write your name in there, too, and thanks."

Turning to the jury line I said, "Everybody get down and pick up some sand."

I squatted over and picked up a handful. "When it's your turn, stand beside me and I'll hold both my fists out like this." I stood and held my arms to the front parallel to the ground.

"Hold your fists out the same and we'll open our fists at the same time. I might have sand in both hands, only my left hand, only my right hand, or sand in neither hand. If your hands match mine, you are out. If your hands do not match mine, you are in."

I pulled my hands in beneath my sheet and dumped my sand into my left hand. "First one. Let's go."

The first one was a skinny female chili pepper. She stood to my right, we held out our fists, and opened up. She had sand in both hands. "You're in," I said. "Give your name to Ila. Next."

In nineteen tries we had selected a thirteen-shark jury. There were nine women and four men. I had them stand where the jury line had been and looked up at the sun. It was getting to the point where we could begin expecting small metal objects to turn to liquid.

"Okay, Mojo, let's have your story. Don't take all day."

"One second," interrupted Pendril. "Don't I get the opportunity to question the jurors?"

"Nope."

Pendril went red in the face. "Do you call that justice?"

"Nope."

"What do you call it, then?"

"I call it a jury, and I call it getting on with it." I pointed at the jurors. "Those men and women are backing up the decision they make with their lives. Is grilling them about their political beliefs, ethnic backgrounds, or tastes in music going to move things along any faster or fairer than that?"

"You just can't pick due process out of the air, Nicos. There are time-tested rules that have—"

"I think all of us have had some experience with your time-tested rules, Pendril. So, we're going to do it this way mainly because we can't afford to fart away the next six months to two years playing around with a trial the way they do it back on Earth."

"Speed does not make justice!"

I sighed and shook my head. "Neither does dragging it out forever make justice, whatever that is." I scratched my chin and thought for a moment. Every shark had thought about the justice thing at one time or another. You can't sit through the middle of a jury trial with all of that grandstand blowholing by the cockroaches going on without trying to come up with an answer that was more efficient than the current definitions. Of course, the sharks never come up with very good suggestions in this department, because anything that would be an improvement on the current mess meant that sharkie would be dropping through the crowbars all that much sooner. But we were serving something a little different in Tenbene v. Ollick.

"Okay, Pendril, here's a definition of justice as it works in the Razai on this desert today. Justice is everybody getting exactly what they deserve as fast as possible." I held my hands out indicating the jury, myself, Mojo, and Herb. "That is why we are all here." I nodded at Mojo. "Let's have your story."

Mojo stood up and said, "Man, last night I was walkin' by these haystacks, see? Not a mau or chocolate brow in sight, do you see what it is?"

"I understand," I confirmed.

"Yeah, well, see, I was movin' up to the front of the column to get out of the dust. My lungs can't take all the shit in the air, catch it?" Mojo pointed toward Ollick.

"This fishbelly angel-cake haystack, he doesn't want me walkin' up with the white folks, see—"

"Objection," called out Pendril. "The witness is drawing conclusions."

Immediately that fantasy of blowing off Pendril's face leaped to mind. With an effort, I wrestled it back into the dark. "So what?" I asked.

"Mojo had no way of knowing what my client thought, therefore him saying that Herb Ollick didn't want him walking with—"

"I know that. So does everybody else."

Pendril folded his arms and began, with elaborate patience, "The rules of evidence—"

"Bite it off, Pendril. Those rules aren't our rules."

"The rules of evidence are designed to keep improper, incomplete, or illegal evidence from being presented to the jury. Tenbene concluding that—"

I held up my hands. "Enough." I turned to the jury. "Are any of you people having trouble understanding Mojo?"

They all shook their heads. I looked at Pendril. "Let Mojo say it the way he wants to say it. The jury isn't stupid. It can sort out the chicken from the fricassee."

I faced Mojo. "Go on."

"Man, I forget where I was."

"He didn't want you walking with the white folks," prompted Ila Toussant. I looked at her and she showed me the pad. She was keeping a transcript of the entire thing. I nodded at her and faced Mojo.

"Yeah, well this ugly, white, faggot, motherfucker, he—"

"Objection!" Jason Pendril was on his feet. "Nicos, you cannot allow this inflammatory language to go on—"

"You'll get your chance, Pendril. Now, shut up!" I looked at Herb Ollick.

"Ice, you better tell your cockroach to quit slowing things down. You've been around awhile. You ought to know by now that the lawyer gets all the money and glory, while you get the bill and the crowbars. It's your ass that's on the block, not his. See, you are responsible for whatever Pendril does. So, if he slows things down to where we have to give the trial to Mojo by default, you are the one who pays. Understand?"

Herb Ollick nodded, he grabbed Pendril by the seat of his trousers and pulled him down into a sitting position. Then Ollick put a bug in his ear while we listened to the end of Mojo's story.

There wasn't anything unusual in Mojo's tale. Every shark had seen the same thing a hundred or a thousand times. One guy operates his blowhole, another guy blows back, the years of frustration dump into the temper of the moment, a cutter gets pulled, and it's slash-and-snap time at the zoo.

When he was all done, I asked him, "Mojo, you got any witnesses?"

Mojo nodded. "I gots lots o' witnesses. Trouble is, man, all of 'em are mighty pale, if you get my meanin'."

Pendril got to his feet and said in a very quiet voice, "May I cross-examine now?"

I held up my hand. "Just a minute."

"He has no witnesses. My client has half a dozen—"

"I said, just a minute, Pendril. I have to explain something before any witnesses are called." I looked over to the Ollick dune. "Are any of you planning on being a witness for Herb?"

Seven haystacks got on their feet. They were laughing and jabbing each other around. "You people who want to be witnesses, listen up. When you give testimony here, what you say can decide whether a man lives or dies. So, if you lie, and later we find out that you lied, the maximum payback that this trial is considering will happen to you, whatever happens to Herb Ollick. In this case, that means death. Understand?"

One by one the witnesses declared themselves non-witnesses by sitting down. A haystack and a mau seated behind Mojo stood up. The haystack waved his hand once. "I want to testify."

I held up my hand. "Let's always take the short road. The most important witnesses first. Then if the jury needs more, we'll get more." Lowering my hand, I turned to Pendril.

"Is your client guilty or innocent?"

Jason Pendril frowned and looked at me as though I had just spoken to him in Suryianese. "He entered a plea of not guilty."

"I heard that. What I want to know is something different. What did Herb Ollick tell you? Did he do it?"

"I'm not a witness here, Nicos."

"Everybody is a potential witness, including you."

"I can't be made to testify against my own client. The attorney-client privilege forbids any such—"

"That doesn't exist here," I interrupted. "Let me run a streak by you, counselor. This is Tartaros, the big T. This is not Earth. Your job here is the same as the jury's, and it is the same as mine. We are all here to make sure that everybody gets exactly what's coming to them."

"No." Pendril addressed the crowd. "My job is to give my client the best possible defense I can, regardless of his guilt or innocence." He faced me.

"That's my job!"

I shook my head. "Nope. You're just like everybody else, Pendril. If you know Ollick's guilty, and you keep it from us, then you are just as guilty as he is. And in the Razai, that means you suffer the same punishment."

"Don't be juvenile, Nicos. What's that going to do to the attorney-client relationship? You wouldn't be able to tell your attorney anything. What kind of effect do you think that would have?"

I considered it for a moment and answered, "I think it would make someone who was guilty real nervous. That's what I think." I pointed my finger at him. "So let's have your statement, Pendril. Is this guy guilty or not."

"I have to think about this—"

"There's nothing to think about. If he's guilty, either you know or you don't know. If he's guilty and you know, either you tell us or you don't. If you don't tell us, and we find out that you knew he was guilty, you'll suffer the same punishment that he suffers. Understand?"

"I understand." Pendril shaded his eyes against the sun, glanced at Herb Ollick, and looked again at me. He pushed his hands into his pockets and shrugged.

"In that case, he's guilty as hell." Jason Pendril sat down to the combined gasps, cheers, and jeers of the spectators.

One of the jurors called out, "I think we've got enough."

I turned to the jury. "Is there anybody who needs something more?"

They looked at each other, shaking their heads. "We've got enough," repeated the juror, a chop chop female who couldn't have been more than eighteen years old.

"So, what's it going to be?"

Altogether they called out, "Guilty!"

I turned to Mojo. "That's it. He's all yours."

"What?" Mojo Tenbene stood in front of me, his hands on his hips. "Chili pepper, you're supposed to waste his white ass."

I shook my head. "There's no need. You're still alive. He didn't try to kill me. He tried to kill you."

"You wasted Dick Irish."

"That I did. And the one I did it for was Freddy, since Freddy wasn't there to do Irish himself. Since that was the case, Dick Irish got the max. You're still here, so you can collect your price for what Herb Ollick did to you. I only do contract killing for the dead."

Mojo's face looked frightened, then it looked sly. "I can do anything I want with him?"

I thought about it some. "You can't violate the law. You can waste him, take all he owns, or send him out of the Razai. Everything he owns, including his life, belongs to you if you demand it. But you can't torture him, make him a servant or slave, or anything like that because that would make him a prisoner and break the only law we have."

I pointed at Herb Ollick. "Make up your mind what you're going to do. We can't hold him prisoner either. So smoke him or do whatever it is that you're going to do."

Ice Fingers stood in the same place where he had been when the jury had found him guilty. He looked up at Mojo as the black man approached. Mojo stopped a couple of paces from Ollick and unslung his rifle. Herb Ollick closed his eyes and tensed all over. When the expected shot did not hit, Herb opened his eyes. The muzzle of Mojo's weapon was lowered to the ground. Mojo was looking at the tips of his own shoes. Slowly he lifted his gaze until he was looking at the haystack.

"Ollick," called Mojo.

"Yes?" Herb's voice sounded awful dry.

"Ollick, you been rubbin' your white trash goomba shit in my face ever since you got dropped in the Crotch, and now you tried to waste me. I can mow your white ravioli ass right now!" The muzzle of Mojo's weapon came up again.

"Man, I can trigger off this gun and thin your fat ass in a split second. I own you."

Ollick nodded and closed his eyes again. I thought I saw a tear fall off of Herb's face, but I couldn't have sworn to it.

Mojo stood like a statue for a long time. Taking a deep breath, he let out a sigh and lowered his rifle. "Ollick, I want an apology."

Herb looked up, his eyes wide with surprise. "An apology?"

"That's right. I want you to say you're sorry for callin' me a nigger. I want it just like that. And for pullin' a cutter on me. I want to hear you say that."

Herb Ollick rubbed his eyes, and I thought I saw his knees shake. "Mojo, I'm sorry. I was way out of line. I'm sorry for calling you a nigger, and I'm sorry for pulling a cutter on you. Any excuses I got aren't any good. Not here. I'm sorry."

He glanced at me and held out his hands. "I really am."

I asked Mojo, "Is that it?"

"Yeah." Mojo turned and walked off.

I turned to Herb and said, "You're free to go." I looked at the jury and the crowd.

"It's all over."

Herb glanced once at Jason Pendril, then he turned and walked away in the direction opposite from Mojo's. Jason Pendril walked past the jury and headed for the front of the column.

A single person behind me started clapping. I looked up and saw Martin Stays, his rifle slung, slapping his hands together, a big grin on his face. Marietta and Ila took it up, then Cap Brady and Marantha Silver started applauding. A few of the sharks even joined in.

Maybe it was a compliment. I didn't know. Maybe I was just too tired to figure out what had gone on and what was going on. All I wanted to do was make it to the head of the column and get back to Alna and some sleep before the night march.

Stays came sliding down the dune toward me. "Hey, Chief. Nance wants you up at the point."

"Why?"

"We're going to send a delegation to the Hand. She wants you to go along."

THE DELEGATES

IT was late, and the shadows were filling the valleys between the dunes. We were about two miles west of where the bunch from the Hand had made camp for the night. Two hundred armed Razai under Nazzar's command were taking positions around the Hand camp, and the walking column would be moving up during the night, guarded by the remains of the armed sharks under the command of Yirbe Vekk.

Twelve of us sat in the shade. There was Nance, Garoit, Bloody Sarah and two of her generals, Ow Dao, and Rhome Nazzar. Stays sat to my left, Marantha Silver to my right, and to Marantha's right were the Chopper and two more from Nazzar's best ten.

One of them was Slicker Toan. Slicker was a clumsy-looking haystack with half-closed eyes that made him look like he had the smarts of an eggplant. He was very strong, very smart, as nimble as an athlete, and one of the best pickpockets in the universe.

The other was a woman, a tiny pepper named Minnie McDavis. She used to run marathons, she was absolutely ruthless with either a knife or a gun, and she was one of those persons who never seem to be noticed. In broad daylight she was almost invisible. She was the one who used to geld her men with a razor when they disappointed her. It sort of shriveled me up to think about it, if you get my drift.

After reading the notes Ila Toussant had written on the trial, Nance tossed the notebook back to Martin Stays. Turning from Stays she glanced at me. "You boys made a lot of law today."

Her legs were crossed and she leaned forward, her arms folded, her elbows resting on her knees. "I wonder where all of this is going," she said to no one in particular. She shrugged and sat up. "In another day, we might all be dead, so why wonder?"

She looked at me. "Bando, you put Stays in charge of the cops, right?"

"Right." When I had told Stays that Nance wanted me to appoint a number two, he said Cap Brady would be a better choice, but Cap turned down the job. If I was captured or killed, Stays would be chief.

Nance looked at Sarah. "Sarah, you're with the delegation, too. Nazzar's in command in your absence, and if Nazzar drops, it goes to Ow Dao, right?"

Bloody Sarah smiled. "Yes, but General Dao would prefer to be called Tau Dao."

"Sorry. I forgot."

Tau Dao nodded his forgiveness. Nance looked at Garoit. "If I drop, Pussyface, you get your old job back, at least until the next election."

"Why don't you send me, instead, Nance? You don't know what's out there, and anything could happen."

Nance smiled. "You know, Pussyface, I almost think you're afraid something might happen to me."

"I am!" he said loudly, then repeated himself more quietly, "I am. So send me as your representative. I don't serve any other function around here. Look, I won't make any deals or commit us to anything without your approval. How about it?"

Nance looked around the circle for a moment. She looked down at the sand in front of her feet, picked up a handful, and began letting the sand trickle through her fingers. "I thought about it, Garoit, and I'm going to tell you why I'm not sending you." She brushed off her hands and folded her arms again.

"Listen, all of you. My name is Nance Damas. I was given life as the mistake of a stupid Juarez hooker. I have been molested, raped, almost killed, and left to die in the sewers and garbagbe cans of Earth. The only person whose love I could ever accept was a woman, and she was raped and murdered. I did the rapist and the six witnesses who let it happen because they didn't want to get involved. That put me in the Crotch when I was seventeen. I've lived in Hell ever since. I don't know anything but filth, cruelty, the backs of hands, and the shitty end of the stick." She unfolded her arms and held them out.

"I'm smart enough to know that we—the Razai—we got something here. I think it's something that might be important." She burst out with a quiet laugh. "That's all I know."

She pointed at Garoit. "Pussyface knows a lot more. He's smart and he's read and thought about a lot of things. I know, because the two of us have talked a lot. I think we need Pussyface. He's valuable for the future."

She held her hand to her breast. "If I die, it's no great loss. That's the way I feel about it"—she looked at Garoit—"and that's why I'm going instead of you."

We all tried to speak at once, but Nance held up her hands and ordered us to silence. "Shut the goddamned hell up! We're right next to the damned Hand, and we can't afford to have them hear us with you working your blowholes at full pressure!" She put her hands down.

"Now, I don't want any we-love-you-and-need-you testimonials from you assholes. I told you why I'm doing what I'm doing, and that's the end of it. Understand?" She got to her feet. "Does everybody understand?" There were a few nods around the circle.

Nance pointed to my right. "Seraphine, I want you, Marantha, Slicker, and Minnie to be our guard. If things start happening, you have to keep the Hand off us long enough for us to signal Nazzar and Dao."

The Chopper nodded and Nance held out her hands. "What are we waiting for? It's time to let the rest of this planet know we're here and in business."

We all got to our feet and Nance led off, heading east. I looked at Stays and started unbundling my shirt and parka. It would be getting cold soon. "Stays, maybe you ought to make up another copy of the rules."

"Okay."

"See if you can find some more paper. Somebody's got to have some."

"Okay." Stays held out his hand. "Take care of yourself, Sherlock."

I shook hands with him. "Same to you, asshole. When you can, let Alna know what's happened to me."

"Okay. And here's something someone left for you." He held out the tiny pumpkin-colored book.

I took it and looked at it for a long time. I had told Rus and his bunch to keep the book. Him returning it made me a little angry. I was glad he returned it, because I was afraid. That made me a whole lot more angry. I reached under my sheet and shoved the book into my pocket.

"You can't ever tell. It might just be so boring that I'll be grateful to have something to read."

"You can't ever tell," Stays repeated.

I turned and fell in behind the Chopper. I felt that it was going to be another long night.

THE IRISH GOOMBA

ON the way to the Hand camp, Nance wanted us to talk. Bloody Sarah had said that, although it had been no difficulty getting past their guards, it might be something of a difficulty getting a guard's attention, without making the clown look bad.

We didn't want to embarrass either the guard or the leader of the camp. Sharks that think they look bad don't think straight, and the first thing they do is look for someone to blame. Since people with guns tend to do their blaming in the loudest and most destructive manner available, and since we had no doubt that the someones taking the blame would be us, Nance figured it would be best to walk in making as much noise as a marching band and let the guard discover us on his own.

While I walked, I listened a bit to the others, but I had something that was gnawing at the back of my mind. I took the opportunity to ask Nance, "If you left Garoit behind because he's so valuable, why did you bring me?"

She laughed and put her arm across my shoulders. She was about four inches taller than me. "*Pobrecito*," she taunted with a grin, "did big old nasty Nance hurt the little copper's feelings?"

I felt my face get red, then I laughed. "Okay, okay."

Nance's voice became serious. "You know, Bando, that

number two of yours is real smart. Maybe smarter than all of us put together."

"Stays? He's an old bomb thrower. I've seen him foaming at the mouth wearing a rubber jacket."

"Bando, did you get here because of your deep respect for government institutions, or because you were so well adjusted?"

I shrugged and put in a ment. After the mental moment had expired, I said, "Yeah, he's smart, but it's different than with Garoit. Pussyface got all his stuff out of books. Stays did some of that, but he's got something else. He watches people and I think he learns from them."

"How so?" Nance removed her arm and pushed her hands into her pockets. With the last of the red and purple light in the sky, it was getting chilly.

"Like when I look at us, Nance, I see a bunch of sand sharks kicking and biting to stay alive. Martin Stays sees principles, institutions, trends. This business with writing down the laws and policies. I never would've thought of that."

Nance nodded. "It was a smart move."

"I don't know. That list of rules is sort of developing a life of its own. Like that rule thirteen that makes a threat the same as the crime being threatened."

"What about it?"

"I thought it was a dumb rule. I guess I still do, but when the sharks were making bad-ass at the trial, I pulled old thirteen out of the hat to shut 'em up and save my buns. Just by doing that, I pumped life into that rule." I faced her.

"I'd sure feel better about this law business if we weren't making it up as we go along. Don't you think we ought to get the whole gang to vote on some of those things?"

She heaved her shoulders slightly and cocked her head to one side. "Maybe. You know, this little gang of ours is less'n a week old? If we make it through another week, maybe we can start wading through votes, rules, laws, and such. Right now there's more important things to do, like getting out of the Forever Sand. Maybe this bunch we're going to see can help."

"Maybe."

She reached out a hand and squeezed my shoulder. "Don't worry about how the law's going in the Razai, Bando. There's nothin' in the universe that's been jawed over, tested, and voted on more than the law back on Earth, and d'you remember what that was all about?"

"Yeah," I answered. "The juicer."

"It's a mess that no one understands 'cause it doesn't mean anything. It's just a machine for keeping the cockroach money threads rich, keeping the ins in, the outs out, and the downs down."

Nance stopped and turned around. I turned to see why. Bloody Sarah was tugging on Nance's sheet. After we had stopped, Sarah pointed to the top of the dune to our left. Standing on top of the dune, admiring the fading rays of the sunset, oblivious to all but the desert's beauty, was a guard. Although his hood was off, exposing his red hair, his rifle was slung and his arms were folded beneath his sheet for warmth. A ten-year-old nearsighted cripple with a wooden leg and a bad wheeze could have crept up on him and taken him out with a rubber chicken.

If we called to him we'd make him look bad. We also didn't want to startle him. Bloody Sarah held up a hand and said, "Look at that haircut. He's from Surya."

I looked, but I didn't see anything particularly special about the haircut. The sideburns were pointed, maybe the center brushed forward some. Anyway, it was a sign to Sarah. She cupped her hands, turned her back on the guard, and made a strange bird sound, like "Call-all-all-alllll."

I watched the guard and a smile spread itself across his face as he listened to the sounds of the early night.

"Call-all-all-alllll," Sarah repeated, and the smile faded as a frown creased the fellow's forehead. He looked to his left, to his right, then unslung his rifle.

"Call-all-all-alllll," cooed Sarah, and the guard looked down at us.

The man studied our party for a moment, then said, "That's the call of a beautiful bird, but the nearest one of those birds is forty light years away from here, *nohomiht?*"

"*Ahviht,*" replied Sarah, and the guard came down from the dune, his rifle carried across his breast.

He stopped several feet from us. After examining our faces, he asked, "And who is the Suryian night dove?"

"I am," answered Sarah.

The guard squinted in the fading light, then his eyebrows climbed up his forehead. "Bloody Sarah, as I live and breathe!"

"And you?"

"Vin Otelli." He smiled. "The UTR stains sent me here for serving the other side of the rebellion."

"Yet we are both here, *nohomiht*, Vin Otelli?"

He nodded. "*Ahviht*. All of us had assumed that when you were taken to Earth that it was to receive a slap on the wrist and a fat pension. Instead we are both here, which makes me wonder just what the point of the war was."

"What is the point of any war, Vin Otelli?"

"Freedom, justice, rights, and other meaningless mouthfuls." He smiled and nodded. "You do the night dove call very well."

"Thank you."

"It made me wonder, just a bit, if I was losing my mind." We all laughed, and Vin Otelli asked, "Who are these others?"

"We are a delegation of peace from the Razai."

"Razai?" He frowned. "This is the word for the desert death lizard on Surya."

"We are named after the lizard. It seemed appropriate since we were born in the desert."

His face seemed to light with hope. "Is your gang from Surya?"

"Ah, you are homesick." She shook her head. "We are not from Surya. We are from Earth." Sarah nodded toward Nance. "This is our leader, Nance Damas." She held a hand out toward me. "Bando Nicos, one of our subchiefs, and our guards, Clay, Silver, Toan, and McDavies."

Vin Otelli studied us for a few seconds. "I've never heard of the Razai before. There is supposed to be nothing between the Hand and the Southern Divide but Kegel."

"You have heard of us now," said Nance. "We've come to parlay with your boss."

Vin Otelli studied Nance. "You boss the Razai?" asked the guard.

"That's right."

"I've heard about Quana Lido, but you're the first woman gang boss I've ever seen." He grinned. "Is this because there are a lot of women in the Razai?"

"Why?"

"Women are in short supply in the Hand. They are in short supply everywhere."

"Vin Otelli," Sarah interrupted, "shouldn't you notify someone of our presence?"

The guard's face became serious. "Look, if I should do that, the two men would be put to death." He thought for a moment, then shook his head.

"I was about to say that you women might be able to find husbands and protection in the Hand, but this one"—he indicated the Chopper—"is too old."

He nodded toward Nance. "You've been a boss, and that might be too much of a temptation for you. Carlo would want you thinned just as a safety measure. Besides, you're a little brown for Carlo."

He faced Sarah. "And you, you're just plain too dangerous to let stay alive. Everybody in this galaxy must've seen those vids of you back in that village."

He pointed at Marantha. "You might be acceptable."

Marantha said quietly, "I am so relieved. For what might I be acceptable?"

"Marriage. Marriage in the Hand. You look like just what Carlo has been after."

"Indeed?"

Vin Otelli frowned as he looked us over once again. "Where's the little black one?"

"Behind you," Sarah answered.

The guard's frown deepened as he turned and saw Minnie McDavies standing behind him. I could tell from his expression that he really wanted to know how Minnie had managed to get from in front of him to behind him in full view without being noticed.

"Don't creep around like that, sister Crowbar. You make me nervous."

"I make a lot of people nervous, friend." Minnie grinned. "You were about to say about the little black one?"

"Yes." Otelli looked back at Nance. "The little black one would be killed on the spot. No maus, no chops, hows, or chilis."

I snorted out an angry laugh and pointed a finger at the

guard. "Well, brother Crowbar, just what in Hell do you have to be to get into this exclusive club?"

Vin Otelli slung his rifle and held out his hands. "Look, I'm not trying to start a war. I'm just telling you how it is in the Hand. If you can't scare up a Sicilian or two in your family tree, or an Italian with a bad attitude, or at least a goomba phantom that smells like pepperoni, forget it."

Nance poked Vin Otelli's chest with her finger. "I'm from Earth, Hand job, and I've seen enough genuine goombas in and out of crowbars to populate this planet ten times over. One thing I know about 'em is that they keep their mouths shut. You work your mouth like every backyard gossip I've ever met. The other thing I know is that none of them ever looked like you. With that red hair, teeny nose, blue eyes, and whitey-white hide, you're about as Sicilian as sauerkraut."

"Vin Otelli," said Bloody Sarah to herself as she smiled and nodded thoughtfully.

The guard's face was very angry. "I'm not from Sicily myself, but my family came from Sicily, and that makes me Sicilian."

Sarah laughed and nodded. "Vin Otelli." She pointed at him. "I know you, but if your family came from Sicily it was by way of Belfast." She faced Nance.

"When I knew of him, Vin Otelli pronounced his name Galvin O'Dell. Back on Surya, Galvin O'Dell used to make quite a point of mentioning coming from a long line of Irish revolutionaries." She looked again at the guard.

"Have you been giving us a wee little kiss off the old Blarney Stone, goomba? Sure and you must be the fastest of the world's fast talkers to convince Olive Oil and the rest of the gooms that you come from a long line of pepperonis."

All humor left the guard's face as his finger moved into his rifle's trigger guard. "I am descended from Sicilians—"

The guard arched his back and looked strange for a moment. That was when I realized that Minnie had somehow gotten behind him again. We heard her quiet voice.

"With me right now, O'Goomba, I have the sharpest razor the universe has ever seen. Ease that finger off that trigger, brother Crowbar, or what I have in my hand right now goes home with me."

He quickly removed his finger from the trigger and held the rifle by its muzzle at his side. "Okay?" he asked with a note of panic in his voice. "Okay?"

We heard a very girlish giggle, and then Minnie said, "Finestkind." She moved to his side and looked up at him with an enormous grin.

"Hey, goomba," said Marantha Silver. *"Parla italiano?"*

"What?"

"Non capisco, Vin Otelli," said Marantha. "What is going on with the Hand? Do any of you know anything about Sicily? Do you people know anything about our thing?"

"Our thing?"

"Cosa nostra?"

"I don't understand."

Marantha Silver smiled and nodded. Looking at Nance she said, "This is amazing. Somewhere along the line some boss began living a fantasy about being a mob don. Using whatever he had in his head for guidance, he's got the whole bunch living the same fantasy." She pointed at the guard. "Or in the case of our goomba shamrock here, living a lie to stay alive."

"That's not true." He pointed a finger at her. "Who are you to judge these things, anyway?"

"Mi chiamo Maranta Argento."

She looked at Nance and repeated, "My name is Maranta Argento. I had it legally changed to Marantha Silver when I joined the MJ."

Nance's eyebrows went up. "Argento? Are you any relation to Red Pete Argento? The Argento family of Philadelphia?"

"He was my father."

Nance shook her head in wonder for all of us. The story behind a genuine Mafia princess winding up as a top MJ cop must be a trim little tale, indeed. It would have to wait until several urgent crises had their turns.

Nance walked up to the Irish goomba and poked him in his chest with her forefinger. "Look, ratbait, it appears that the only real Sicilian around here belongs to the Razai. We have your lie, as well as the Hand's lie, all sewn up in a little sack. Is my message coming through?"

"I think so."

"I'm going to be straight with you, Mick O'Goomba. The

Razai needs help, and we're hoping to get it from your bunch here. But don't ever get the idea that we're helpless. Right now our legions surround this place and are ready to land on the Hand like sixty tons of cement."

She folded her arms. "We're a peaceful bunch, and all we want to do is ask for help. The Hand is free to help us or not. But if that group of bogus goombas wants to make trouble, we'll leave nothing but your bones and mustaches for the sand bats. Is any of this getting through to you, O'Goomba?"

"Yes. I'll do whatever you want."

"I want you to help us, understand?"

"I understand."

"If you're helpful to us, Galvin, we'll take you into the Razai." Nance grinned. "And we do have lots and lots of women."

Galvin O'Dell started as Minnie McDavies put her arm around his waist, leered at him, and said, "Lots and lots of women."

In moments O'Goomba was leading us through the dunes to the camp. Just before we reached the lights of the Hand's camp, Nance and I were at the rear walking together. When she could see my face, I raised my eyebrows and mouthed the word "legions?"

She pulled back one corner of her mouth in to a tiny little grin and walked ahead. It was funny, because Nance never struck me as being any kind of operator. She always seemed to be straight up with everyone, her thoughts and feelings right on the tip of her boot for anybody. There was all of that I'm no good and that's why I'm leaving Garoit behind stuff for just one example.

Of course, she might have been the best confidence operator ever to grace my experience. If that's what she was, she was more than good. She was beyond art.

I looked at her back as we hiked through the sand. She was a big, bull-croc lizzie who had survived the universe's endless series of harsh judgments with her fists and her will. The longer she lived was how she measured her revenge against life.

Sure, she had done a neat little con on O'Goomba, with the mighty legions of the Razai surrounding the Hand, awaiting only the slightest signal to roll down and tamp the camp. Why shouldn't she know how to do the con? She went to college at Ol' Miss in Greenville, and the Crotch was the best place to learn such skills.

I shook my head as I trudged along, my heart filling my throat. Conning others was never a problem for me. It's second nature to anyone coming off the block. It's conning myself I was no good at. As the first lights of the camp appeared, I was afraid and that protomo feeling was all over me.

I found myself walking next to Minnie McDavies, and I whispered to her, "Just what was it of O'Goomba's you had in your hand?"

I know she was a mau and it was night, but I swear she blushed.

THE PRINCE

FROM the outside it looked like something from the vids, maybe the *Arabian Nights* with a bad cast. Huge tents filled the camp area. They were made of the same material as the sheets we wore, but they carried bright colors in several designs, including handprints.

The colors and designs were repeated on some of the sheets on the soldiers I saw. They seemed to be the military markings Ondo mentioned. There were a couple wearing red markings, and bunches who wore blue, black, green, and white.

After being challenged, O'Goomba informed the guard commander of the great and powerful Razai gang's desire to parlay with the Hand. He added that, should this parlay not transpire, or should it turn out badly, there were the many legions of the Razai straining at their leashes, waiting to tear out the throats of the Hand.

It sounded a bit overdone to me, but the guard commander seemed to buy it. He sped off, and returned in a few minutes and said, "Please follow me."

The biggest tent looked huge enough to parade elephants inside. With Galvin O'Goomba and his guard commander leading, and flanked by an armed guard of about eighteen or twenty men, we were led inside as the iciness of the night spread across the sand. No one had searched us, and no one had asked for our weapons.

Once inside the huge tent, we were led through a corridor illuminated with oil lamps. There were more guards lining the corridor, and even if they didn't impress Nance or Bloody Sarah, they sure as hell impressed me.

The corridor opened onto a huge central room that was comfortably warm because of all of the oil lamps lighting the area, and from the four metal pots that contained the burning blue ice. The air in the tent smelled a bit smoky, but sweet, like flowers.

The room was crowded, and when we entered the crowd spread to the sides giving us a view of the opposite side. O'Goomba faced away from us, held out his hand, and said, "Pau Avanti, I present the boss of the Razai, Nance Damas."

O'Goomba faced Nance. "Boss of the Razai, this is Pau Avanti, Prince of the Hand, Son of Carlo T., Don of the Eastern Shore and the Sunrise Mountains."

Pau Avanti sat high upon a genuine golden throne inside his huge palace of a tent. He was a tall, powerfully built man with a dark, scowling face and shifty, suspicious eyes. His robes were of some fine light blue cloth that shimmered as it moved. On his fingers he sported golden rings set with large, garish gems that seemed not only to reflect light, but to give off a light of their own.

Standing to his right and left were more guards, and before the throne was an audience like old-time kings had in the vids. They were mostly men, and the few women who were there looked like court professionals. Our delegation stood in front of Pau Avanti, with Nance in front, Galvin O'Goomba and Bloody Sarah to her left, and Marantha Silver to her right. I was in the rear comfortably situated between Minnie McDavies and the Chopper.

Pau Avanti crossed his legs, leaned his right elbow upon an armrest, and gestured with his hand. "You are here before me, woman, with tales of a great gang that comes in peace, yet is ready to have its many legions crush the Hand like so many insects."

He grinned. "Why do I not believe you?"

"It's your choice," Nance answered. "But you might want to think real hard on which way you pick."

She turned around and pointed with her arm, indicating the entire camp. "Our trusty spies have seen the best you have here, Pau Avanti. Shall I tell you?"

"Please do."

"You have some real pretty tents, but you can only put up eight hundred rifles. Isn't that true?"

The man on the throne looked uncomfortable as he recrossed his legs. "Perhaps. Perhaps not."

Nance laughed out loud, and we laughed with her. My laughter might have been just a shade shrill. I checked and made certain that my right side was covered by the Chopper. When I looked to make certain that Minnie was protecting my left, I noticed she had vanished. I did a quick scan of the room, but could not find her.

"Pau Avanti," said Nance, "we have no desire to harm you or your people. Although we have more than ten thousand to throw against you, we are here strictly in peace. However, we do have a battle in mind."

"What battle might that be?"

"The Razai are heading south out of the desert. To do that we need to get through Boss Kegel. We think you're moving against Kegel. Perhaps we could join forces."

The prince rubbed his upper lip. "What makes you think we're moving against Kegel?"

Nance held out her hands. "Are you out in the desert taking a vacation?"

The entire population in the tent erupted with laughter, which quickly quieted as Avanti waved his hand. "Why we are here is only our business." He pointed with his finger at Nance. "Why you are here, chili pepper, is the question."

Although she hid it pretty well, I could almost see the hairs on the back of Nance's head stand straight out. She took a step toward the prince, and six of the goombas standing around the throne moved in to protect their boss.

Nance held out her hands in a gesture of defeat and said, "Perhaps we can discuss this better alone, Pau Avanti."

Pau Avanti and some of his toughs laughed at this, then the prince's laughter was cut short. In a moment the laughter of the others died as they saw Minnie McDavies holding a razor at the left side of the prince's throat.

The toughs who had moved away from the throne to intercept Nance took a step back, but Minnie grinned and touched the edge of the blade against the skin of Avanti's throat.

"Don't come any closer, you handsome boys. In my hand is the sharpest razor in the universe. I can take his neck down to the spine in less than an eyeblink."

One of the toughs said, "Say the word, Pau, and she's done past."

Minnie whispered into the prince's ear. "Don't you want your head? If for nothing else, you need it for this," she said as she stuck her tongue in his ear.

"Get out!" shouted Avanti as a blush covered his face. "All of you get out!" He nervously moistened his lips. "I have things to discuss with our friends."

Grudgingly the court emptied and stationed itself just outside the room. Minnie released the prince and smiled at him as he rubbed his neck, stared at her, and wiggled his finger in his ear.

Nance looked back and motioned with her head at Marantha Silver. Our own Mafia princess walked up and grinned at the prince. "Pau Avanti," she said, *"parla italiano?"*

"What?"

"Tell me about *omerta*, Prince. What do you say when the fire is placed in your hands?"

"What fire? I don't know what you're talking about." He pointed a finger. "Do you?"

"Yes, I do." She folded her arms and smiled. "How would you like to boss the Hand?"

He studied her for a moment, then closed his eyes as he leaned back in his throne. As he opened his eyes again, he said, "I am Carlo's most loyal and devoted son."

"There is no question about that, Pau Avanti," said Marantha. "The question is, do you want to take his place as boss of the Hand?"

The prince sat up. "Say what you have come to say."

"Very well." Marantha looked at the man on the throne. "Pau Avanti, you are not Mafia, you are not Sicilian, you know next to nothing about either, and the only reason you hold the position you have is because this Carlo T. is just as ignorant."

"I suppose you think you know more than Carlo, more than me?"

"I am the daughter of a don. My father was Red Pete Argento, head of the Argento family in Philadelphia." She smiled again. "That's on Earth."

"I know where Philadelphia is," he answered. He placed his elbows on the throne's armrests and began rubbing his temples with his fingertips. He continued for a few moments, and clasped his hands when he was finished. He gave his throne room a careful scan to make certain none of his own gang was present.

"If I was interested, which I'm not, what do you think you could do to change things?"

"I could show you things, teach you things." She held her hand out toward us. "But not in front of the others. After all, *omerta*."

He pointed at Minnie McDavies. "Will you need her here?"

"No, but Minnie will be here. She is here, she is there, she is everywhere."

He sat up and nodded. "I will listen to at least a little of this nonsense, just to be polite." He held out a hand toward the corridor. "May I call my chief adviser?"

"Consigliori," she corrected.

"Yes, my *consiggalorry*, is it?"

"Close. And, certainly, it's permitted."

The prince held up his hand. "Voam! Come here."

A slender man in dark blue fine cloth robes entered and stopped at the right side of the throne. "Yes, Pau?"

The prince held out his hand indicating the rest of us. "Take our guests and entertain them." He pointed at me. "What's your name?"

"Bando Nicos."

"Be sure to offer him the hospitality of the Men's Hall." He gestured back toward Toan. "Him, too."

Pau Avanti looked around the room, his brow growing heavy with frown. "Where is the little black one?"

Minnie was gone. Nance shrugged and answered, "She's probably out there somewhere keeping watch on us. If anything should happen to us, she's the one who will signal our legions."

The prince stared at Nance for a moment. "She has a rather disturbing way of getting about, doesn't she?"

"She disturbs some persons. I find her quite comforting."

"Indeed."

The prince nodded at Voam and the *consiggalorry* held out his hands, indicating that all of us, except Marantha, should exit. Nance and I walked together, and as we came out of the entrance there was something bothering me. I spoke to Nance beneath my breath.

"Doesn't it strike you as just too good to be true that we have our very own Mafia princess right here in the Razai to run interference for us?"

"That does seem too good to be true," Nance confirmed.

"Yeah, especially since she's a cop for the MJ."

We were led to a place where what looked like a banquet had been laid out. There was a large circle of men sitting and eating, with the few women that there were waiting on them. The food looked very good, but my appetite died as my conversation with Nance continued.

"You know, Bando," she whispered, "Marantha's no Mafia princess."

"What?"

"She was the lead in our production of *Mob Cinderella* back in the Crotch. Everything she's said so far is straight out of the script." Nance grinned. "I played the part of Red Pete Argento."

I felt sick to my stomach. "But the Italian. She spoke the language."

"Right out of the script, Bando. She's really quick on her toes. Now that you mention it, I think she's Jewish. Keep your fingers crossed that she doesn't run out of lines."

A BIRD IN
THE HAND

NANCE and the Chopper were seated at the banquet and greeted with what appeared to be great enthusiasm. Atan Voam took Slicker and me to another tent. A guard on either side of the entrance lifted up double flaps and we walked into wonderland.

There was a rich scarlet carpet beneath our feet, a table heaped with hot meats, golden pastries, and beautiful fruit. There were even what looked to be wines and candies. There were six men seated on cushions around the table with four beautiful women clad in next to nothing waiting on them. Almost in shock I took a step backward and bumped into Slicker.

"Steady," cautioned the pickpocket.

One of the six men, a young-looking fellow with a closely trimmed dark gray beard, got to his feet and looked inquiringly at Atan Voam. "My friends," began Atan, "Pau has asked that you entertain these two representatives of the Razai." He held out a hand toward me. "This is subchief Bando Nicos and his guard."

Slicker simply stood there looking like a side of beef, and I said, "His name is Slicker Toam."

Pau Avanti's number two glanced at Slicker as though he were trying to attach the name to the physical being and was getting a bad fit. Shrugging it off, he addressed the men at the table. "I count on you to show them the full courtesy of the Men's Hall."

"It would be my pleasure," said the man, standing. His clothes were of a fine material, and his trousers and pullover were deep maroon. He had very rich-looking soft leather boots of gray on his feet. He nodded toward me. "My name is Padra Amitis. I command the Loyal Reds."

He held out his hand and introduced the other five men at the table. As each one was introduced, he stood and gave a friendly little smile and bow.

There was a squat bull of a man named Dagi Preit. He was the commander of the Mighty Blacks, and from the way Padra Amitis handed out the strokes, I gathered that Dagi Preit also ranked everybody else.

Yal Donat, a tall, blond, intelligent-looking sort who ought to have been off someplace painting flowers, was the commander of the Swift Whites. Mano Leaf, who had more chili pepper in him than goomba, was the commander of the Courageous Golds. A yard monster named Dono Vicar commanded the Faithful Blues, while a weasel-looking thing with burns on his face named Hach Imis commanded the Steadfast Greens.

There was a moment when I felt like introducing myself as Bando Nicos, commander of the Chicken Yellows, but my attention was drawn to a silver-looking cabinet on the far side of the tent. The Commander of the Reds noticed where I was looking and smiled at me. "Ah, can I offer you a bath?"

"A bath?"

"Certainly. I apologize for not thinking of it."

"With water?" I asked.

They all laughed and Padra Amitis led me next to the cabinet. It turned out to be a high-backed bathtub. He snapped his fingers and two women appeared almost out of nowhere. "Prepare our guest for a bath."

"Immediately," answered one of them.

I felt a sharp jab in my back and I turned around to see Slicker staring off into the distance as though he were dead from the neck up. "And my guard," I said. "He could use a bath, too."

"Of course," said Padra Amitis, and he snapped his fingers again. The two women who showed up were ordered to bring in another tub, and all four of the women were ordered to bring in hot water. A curtain was drawn between us and the dining area, and two more women arrived and began undressing us.

"When you're finished," said the commander of the Loyal Reds, "join us at the table."

After so much deprivation, my wishes and desires were being swamped with fulfillment. The undressing was sensual, but effective. I was helped into the tub, and as I sank down into the steaming water, I hoped that the dirt wasn't the only thing holding me together.

I closed my eyes, leaned back, and sank as deep into the water as I could. Perfume reached my nostrils, and it made my head swim. Soapy hands began gently rubbing my chest, stomach, legs, and all intermediate stops.

Later, feeling quite spent for several reasons, more hot water was added to the tub and Slicker and I were left alone to relax. It certainly beat slogging through the sand with Nance and the Razai Cops. I never believed it could be this good. I never believed I would ever feel this relaxed and safe again.

Another hand rubbed my chest and slid down my stomach where it came to rest among the jewels. I was so relaxed I didn't know if I was up for another round, but I was certainly willing to allow my bath-nymph to try. The hand fondled me, and as I was just beginning to grow hard, the hand gathered up my penis and scrotum together.

It felt just a little uncomfortable, and I opened one eye just a crack. I saw two very dark arms in the water as a husky voice whispered in my ear, "With me right now I have the sharpest razor in the universe. If you don't stop enjoying yourself so much and get back to work, what I have in my hand now will go home with me."

After a moment of paralysis, I nodded. The hands slithered out of the water, I looked around, and Minnie McDavies was gone.

"Slicker?"

"Huh?"

I looked over at the pickpocket, and if he had been any more relaxed he would have been liquid. "Did you see anything?"

"See what?"

I looked around again, almost doubting my senses, yet feeling awfully vulnerable. I stood up in my God-issue and grabbed a towel. "Let's get to work."

"Bando, can't we just lounge around a little longer?"

"You want to sing soprano for the rest of your life?" I demanded angrily. "Let's go!"

THE OTHER SIDE

IF I had a brick for every time I had wasted time dreaming about how things should be for Bando Nicos, I would be able to build four New Yorks. Behind the crowbars, the dreams were always about the other side of the bars. Outside, on the block, the dreams were always about another planet, another country, the other side of town, the other side of a security wall, the other side of a lock.

Sometimes I would get into primo deep wallow with my fantasies and wouldn't come out for days. I don't mean that I was gibbers or anything. It's just that I would have either the picture or the feeling of what things should be with me all the time.

It made it easier to pick up that piece of jewelry when no one was looking. After all, when you think about where I was, and then looked at where I should have been, things needed to be evened out. I had a right to even them. The diamonds were mine. The juicer never saw it like that, but it helped to keep a troublesome conscience quiet.

In the men's hall at the edge of the Forever Sand, with a full belly, a glass or two of wine buzzing my head, and the richness of the tent and the beautiful girls filling my eyes, I thought about all of the different fantasies that had ruled my life. I wondered if any of them could ever live up to the reality I was wallowing in right then. I even heard music coming from the banquet circle outside the tent. It was a snappy tune that almost forced you to move your feet.

"To brotherhood and honor!" toasted the commander of the Blues, Domo Vicar.

"To brotherhood and honor!" we all toasted back. I only touched the heady wine to my lips, and did not drink anymore. I could just imagine the alks back in the walking column dragging their tongues in the sand for just a wee drop of what I wasn't drinking, but I had to keep my head screwed on straight if I didn't want Minnie McDavies to get beneath my sheet with the universe's most honed gelding edge.

There was another reason for keeping straight. Sharks are sharks the whole galaxy over, and none of the brothers of the Crowbar would put on an extravagant show such as that without wanting something in return. What did they want? That was the question.

The one obvious thing they wanted was women. The few that Slicker and I had seen in camp were nice looking, but they were very few and seemed to be nothing more than servants or slaves.

A bare arm reached over my shoulder and filled my wine cup to the brim. I looked up to see one of the lovely servants, and she did have a pleasant smile on her face. I examined the face for as long as I could, and when I turned back to my meal and the conversation, something nagged at the back of my head. The woman smiled only with her mouth, and there was something about the eyes that bothered me. The eyes looked almost frightened.

Mano Leaf, the commander of the Courageous Golds, struggled to his feet to give a toast. As he did so, something slipped off of his cushion onto the floor. I leaned over, picked it up, and saw that it was a book. It had a leather cover that was so old the title stamped on the spine was unreadable.

Sickness gnawed at my guts. That particular cover was very familiar to me. I almost cried to see it. Robert Southey's *Life of Nelson*. Inside on the crumbly pages there would be a beautiful old engraving titled "Nelson's Conflict with a Spanish Launch." It would show the old-time British sailor, with all of his arms, getting ready to shove three feet of steel through a sad-eyed

Spaniard. Opposite the engraving would be the title page, and at the bottom of the title page it would say "London. Bickers and Son, Leicester Square, 1883." It had been Big Dave Cole who had told me that Leicester was pronounced "Lester."

After my quarantine at Greenville, I had been sitting on my bunk in my new cell splitting my skull with suppressed rage, trying not to blow up. I couldn't bear the thought of being dropped into the black hole, or into a rubber room, so I just sat there, my arms wrapped around my guts, trying not to make a sound, knowing that if I kept too quiet, that could end in the rubber room, too.

I had heard tapping on my bars. I moved to the barred end of my cell, crouched next to the left wall and whispered, "What?"

"Quick," a voice had answered. "Read this. It'll save your life."

I had reached through the bars to my left and felt the end of a book. After I had it in my possession, I opened it. It had been Southey's *Life of Nelson*, but I quickly flipped past the front stuff and began reading.

I had been well into Nelson's time on the *Agamemnon* before I had rapped on the bars and had asked the shark in the next pen his name.

"Dave Cole. In the yard they call me Big Dave."

"Big Dave, how is reading this going to save my life?"

He had laughed. "You're still alive, aren't you?"

"So?"

"It's working just fine."

That book had saved my life, and it had started me on a reading binge that had never ended. And now it looked as though the book was about to save my life a second time.

I opened the book as Mano Leaf wrapped up his toast, and inside the cover was the sheet Big Dave had cemented in to repair where the front cover had split off. On the second blank page in the front, Big Dave's name and number were lightly penciled in above a pen-written inscription to a fellow named Harold Drewitt dated July 1889. I had never been much of a mathematician, but no matter how I added up the numbers, the Razai was in big trouble.

I looked around at the faces and thought back to the routine Pau Avanti had put on in his tent. Whatever their other claims to

fame, the members of the Hand were certainly a slick bunch of
con artists. The secret of the con is always to give the mark
what he wants. We wanted the Hand to be a militarily weak and
careless bunch of half-wits, and that's just what they gave us. I
blushed at how we had been taken in, and covered it up by
laughing with the others at a joke that made no sense to me at
all. Somehow I had to warn the others.

Mano Leaf seated himself on his cushion as I replaced the
book on the carpet. Acting drunk, I struggled to my feet and
said, "Good friends, I know it is your custom to dine without
female companionship, but I am having such a good time, and
the music outside is so inviting, I must share a dance with my
wife."

"Oh, a wife!" said Padra Amitis.

"And a dance," added Yal Donat. "Perhaps we could all
have a dance?"

"Perhaps," I answered, "although she is very shy. But, come
along. She may want to dance the night away."

The six commanders cheered. I glanced at Slicker, and his
jaw seemed jammed in mid-glut. He got to his feet, however,
and brought up the rear of our happy procession.

When we approached the banquet area, several of the men
were dancing with each other to the clapping hands of their
comrades. Nance and the Chopper were clapping along, and
suddenly the music ended. There was much applause, and while
it was at its height, I came up behind Nance, bent over, and
whispered in her ear.

"I told them we're married, so let's dance and don't give me
any shit. We're in big trouble."

She turned her head, kissed my cheek, and whispered into
my ear. "You sure do smell pretty, Bando. I can't dance. Can
you?"

"How tough can it be?" I answered. "We just need something slow and huggy so we can cheek it up and I can fill your
ear with sweet somethings."

"You can't dance either?" She stood up, and never did her
six foot something look so tall. She turned to the small band
that had been plucking and blowing out the tunes.

"Something slow and dreamy." She looked at me with the
biggest brown eyes I had ever seen. "My man wants to dance."

I glanced at the Chopper and Bloody Sarah to dare them to laugh, but they were looking elsewhere.

A chorus of howls began and it ended with a round of applause and the band playing. The song was a slow folk melody of some kind that seemed very familiar to me. I put my right arm around Nance's waist, and was surprised to find her waist at waist height. Somehow she was squatting down, her bent knees hidden by her sheet, so that her head could rest on my shoulder.

"What is it?" she asked.

"The Hand must've hit at least one of the other gangs from our ship. Maybe more. I found something that belonged to a friend of mine. There's only one way he could have been separated from it, and that means he's dead. The Hand must've learned about the Razai from the others. I don't think the prince is here in the desert going after Kegel. I think he's after us—after the women."

She wriggled around, put her arms around my neck, put her cheek against mine, and snuggled her lips into my ear. If she hadn't smelled so damned bad, it might've been a considerable thrill.

"I don't get it," she whispered. "What about the guards, the sloppy discipline?"

"Just pin a cowpie on my nose, *querida*. Like a couple of marks with hay in our ears, I think we've been sucked in here real good, is what I think."

"O'Goomba? You think that mick wop red-haired Sicilian was doing a number?"

"That's what I think."

She was quiet for a moment. "Man, I would hate to think I believed he was that stupid because he was that smart."

"That's how you set up the mark, Nance."

Again she was quiet. I could feel her head shake slightly as she thought. "Bando, there's more to this. Have you seen any women in camp?"

"A few. They use a couple of angel cakes over in the Men's Hall for servants and—" I searched my failing memory for a term. "Bath attendants."

"Did you get your whistle cleaned, Bando?" I searched for a

response, but the heat from my face appeared to be response enough for Nance Damas.

"Bando, pick your feet up and put 'em down. When you slide around like that you're digging yourself into a hole. If you get any shorter I'll have to dance on my knees."

We shuffled around a bit more, and she whispered, "What about the column? Are they going after the column right now?"

"My guess is no. I think they want to seduce us. It costs less. If they wanted to fight we would've heard something by now."

We moved around a bit more and Nance whispered, "There's something more to this. We've got to get out of here. Keep alert."

I whispered back, "What's the name of that song they're playing?"

"*La Paloma*," she answered. "There's a lot of chili pepper in that goomba band."

The tune came to an end, Nance leaned back, gave me a big kiss on the lips, and turned to the crowd as she held out her hands. "I am having a wonderful time!"

The crowd cheered, and one of the men stood. "Then bring your whole gang in! We'll have a party!"

Another cheer. Nance grinned at the two-faced little bastards, gave me another kiss, and held out her hands again. "Before we can do anything like that, we'll have to get Pau Avanti's permission."

"I don't think there will be any problem with that," said Padra Amitis with a tiny bow. He held out his hand to Nance and spoke to me. "With your permission?"

I held out my hands and said, "Of course."

The all-Sicilian jug band started up with a rousing Italian *ranchero* titled *"La Noche e Tu,"* Nance stood up to her full height, and whirled the amazed commander of the Loyal Reds off into the night.

In turn, I danced with the D.C. Chopper and Bloody Sarah to let them know what was happening. Sarah couldn't dance any better than I could, but Seraphine knew some steps, and even taught some to me. It was hard to concentrate on dancing, though, with the threat of the Hand hovering over us, not to mention the ax the Chopper had hanging at her waist bumping into my arm.

Minnie McDavies even popped out of nowhere and got in a
dance. It was when I put my arm around her waist I found out
that, beneath her sheet, she wore God-issue.

As I removed my hand and placed it on top of her sheet, I
said to her, "You know, Minnie, you are about the oddest combination of intimacy and terror I have ever known."

She grinned at me and said, "Exciting, isn't it?"

LET'S PARTY

BACK in the palace tent, Marantha sat upon a cushion at Pau Avanti's feet. "A party is an excellent thought," said the prince. His eyebrows went up a notch as he looked at Nance.

"Was there a question?"

"Yes. I think more of our women would come to the party if there was some way they could freshen up. We've been in the desert a week—"

"—and sugar and spice only makes up for so much," said the prince. "I understand you completely." He placed a hand on Marantha's shoulder. "Please take one of our water sleds, with the compliments of the Hand."

"We are very grateful."

"Yes," said the prince. "Should those attending the party wish to continue on with the Hand, as your friend Marantha has done, this will not offend, will it? I understand that, according to your custom, the members of the Razai are free to join whatever gang they wish."

I was gaping at Marantha, and Nance poked me in the arm, snapping me out of it. "How about it, lawman?"

"Yeah," I answered. "Rule two says that each person is free to follow whatever leader he or she wants."

"Excellent," said the prince with a broad grin. "I fear that your gang will be a good deal smaller when we part company, Nance Damas."

"Perhaps some of your men will choose to join us?" she offered.

The prince's face was devoid of any softness or humor as he slowly shook his head. "No. That is not allowed." He squeezed Marantha's shoulder.

"Tell them, princess."

"Once a member of the Hand," she said, "always a member of the Hand." She smiled at me. "Bando, when you return tomorrow for the party, could you bring my things?"

"Sure."

Marantha looked at Bloody Sarah. "Sarah, ease army Rhome carefully home. Ease army steel, too."

Sarah nodded and answered with downcast eyes. "Your ease, sunrise."

HOME AND THE LAW

AS we marched through the night to our own camp, leading the six-lugh team water sled, I was glad I was me and not Nance Damas. The responsibility I toted by being a Razai Cop was nothing compared to her load. It wasn't just that the Hand was probably preparing to take us over. There were some other matters, as well. Not only would that takeover involve placing the women they decided to take into some kind of slavery, I guessed it would also involve killing off just about all of the men.

Just so it would be thick enough to patch a fusion reactor, there was Razai rule number two: Each person is free to follow whatever leader he or she wants.

In other words, in exchange for the food, drink, baths, fine clothes, and the rest of what the Hand could offer, it was just possible that some of the women might be willing to give up wandering in the desert, counting drops of water, and smelling like Hell with the Razai. They just might be talked into selling their asses for money, food, and a little security.

There were bits in the Razai who had been doing that all their lives. It was the way things were because it was the way things had always been. Any way you looked at it, we were going to get hit hard.

That was Nance's problem, not mine. As soon as we were

out of sight of the Hand's guard escort, Bloody Sarah pulled the sled team to a halt and said, "Minnie, Seraphine, Slicker, let's go."

They vanished into the shadows, and I looked at Nance as she got the sled team moving again. "What's going on?"

She looked from the lead critter to me. "Didn't you hear what Marantha said to Sarah?"

"What? You mean that stuff about easing Rhome's Army on home?"

A note of exasperation crept into her voice. "Obviously you haven't been attending your training classes."

"No kidding, Sherlock! Maybe I've been a little busy with the job you stuck on me!"

She touched her fingertips to my lips. "I was just joking." She removed her hand, clucked at the lugh team, and continued. "It's a real simple first letter code. She said, 'Sarah, ease army Rhome carefully home.'"

"Search," I said. "And then there was something else, 'Ease army Steel, too'—east. Search east. And Sarah answered 'yes.'"

"I think he's got it," said Nance with a smile that quickly faded as she pulled on the lugh critter's harness. "Let's get this water back, and be quiet for a bit, I'm trying to think."

I shut up. There was plenty to think about. What do we tell our own people? How do we keep the majority of the gang from going over to the Hand? How do we get Marantha back? And just what was east of the Hand's camp?

By the time we got back to the point camp, I figured whatever could be done about the military situation was in better hands than mine. The problem of getting back Marantha and of defending ourselves against the Hand concerned me very little because I had something else to occupy my attention.

My problem was Victor Myerson and Jim Bennet. When Nance and I returned to the point camp, Stays and Cap Brady were waiting for us. I followed the pair back to the column as Martin Stays filled me in.

"It's a rape case. Considering what our population contains, it's amazing it's taken this long for one to happen."

"Oh, I don't know," I answered with a touch of rancor. "We do pretty well for a town of two thousand. In less than a week we've managed a war, a murder, an execution, an attempted murder, and a rape." I spat in the sand.

"Let's have the rest of it."

"Jim Bennet, a shark from Lewisburg Max, claims that Victor Myerson, also from Lewisburg, boybunged him against his will. Myerson says he didn't rape anyone. Between the number of rapists and rape victims we have in the column, it's a real tense situation."

I nodded. "This is the nightmare I saw when Nance shoved this job at me. This is just the thing I never wanted to see. What are we supposed to do?"

Stays handed me several sheets of folded paper. "Just like always, Chief: What isn't in the rules, we make up. Here's your own copy of the *Law of the Razai*."

"That sounds real impressive."

"I thought so."

As we approached the walking column, I asked, "Is there any doubt about the facts? Did Myerson do it?"

"Myerson did it. He admits they had sex, but he says it wasn't rape. He says it was sex between consenting adults."

"Are there any witnesses?"

He nodded. "There are plenty who are willing to scream at each other, but I don't know if they're willing to back it up according to rule thirty-two."

I started opening the papers and Stays said, "Thirty-two is the rule that gives false witnesses the maximum penalty under consideration."

"That's a thought," I said. "What's the max payback for rape? What's the penalty? Do we let the victim rape the rapist back?"

"In this case," Stays answered, "I think this Myerson would regard that less like a penalty and more like a treat."

"Maybe that depends on what we rape him with."

"For rape, Jim Bennet is talking the big payback: death," said Cap Brady. "There's a lot of support for his position in the crowd. But there's something else." He glanced at Stays. "Tell him about the complication."

"A complication?" I said as I came to a halt. "You mean what you've been telling me is the simple part?" I rubbed my eyes as the lack of sleep made my skin tingle.

"Tell me about the complication."

Stays rubbed the back of his neck. I got the impression that he hadn't been getting enough sleep either. "The complication is one of the rapists from the Crotch. His name is Abe Lyles. He was in one of those therapy groups, and I think he meets with that bunch that keeps borrowing your book."

"CSA," I said.

"Yeah. Well, the complication is this. He says even if Myerson did rape the kid, it's not his fault. He says that Myerson's got an illness that makes him do those things." He lowered his hand. "And there's something else."

"There had to be." I rubbed my eyes again and took a deep breath. I guessed that just about one more thing piled on top of this crapheap would have me looking for a rubber room. "What is it? Is Pendril Myerson's cockroach?"

"No. In fact, Pendril is working for Bennet. Myerson has found his own money threads. It's a roach named Lane Rossiter."

"*Two* lawyers?"

Stays tapped the folded papers in my hands. "And both of them have copies of the rules."

"Anything else?"

Stays grinned. "Yeah. Welcome home, Chief."

BENNET V. MYERSON:

THE WARMUP

THE sky was beginning to lighten as I took in the scene. The crowd was divided between the facing sides of two large dunes. Since the column wasn't moving, and since it was an issue in which everyone had an interest, there were close to fifteen or sixteen hundred spectators. The only thing limiting attendance to that level was the fact that the organized guards had their troops elsewhere trying to prepare to meet the Hand.

I stood between the dunes with Marietta covering my back and keeping order. Stays covered the crowd from on top of the left dune while Cap Brady took the right. I counted the number of spectators who were carrying guns, decided the Razai Cops were understaffed, and a brand-new rule began to germinate within.

Pendril and who I guessed was Jim Bennet were off to the left discussing things. To the right I couldn't pick out Victor Myerson or his cockroach through any obvious means. I looked at the sheets of paper and raced through the rules from what's mine is mine down to rule forty-five, which said that one found guilty of attempted murder may be expelled from the Razai.

It wasn't so much the rules. I could remember them. It was the implications of the rules and how they fit together, and it was how the cockroaches could see those implications that had me with an acid stomach.

"You ready, Chief?" asked Marietta.

I nodded. "Okay."

"You can handle it, Chief," she said, giving me a wink. She turned around and bellowed at the dunes.

"Shut up!"

The dunes got real silent real fast. I glanced up at the sky, noticed that the light was entering that deep blue, deceptive, oh-what-a-beautiful-planet-this-is phase. Beneath my sheet I began removing my parka and shirt. It would be Hell in a hibachi.

I saw one of the women seated behind Bennet stroking her rifle and moving her lips in silent mutterings as she searched the opposite dune for someone. The odds were that she was a former rape victim. What I didn't need right then was an armed mob filled with righteous rage looking for an outlet. It was time for the new rule.

"Okay," I said as I undressed, "let's stack our rifles neatly right down here." I pointed to the area in front of me.

"Emotions run high in certain kinds of situations, and this is one of those kinds of situations. We don't want to turn this thing into a war crimes trial, so everybody who is armed and who wants to stay for the trial, bring your weapons down here. Anyone who doesn't want to give up his or her weapons, get away from here."

The scene before me could have been a painting. Nothing moved. Then Marietta nodded at the crowd and said quietly, "Do it soon."

Her request was underscored by Stays, Cap, and Marantha levering fresh rounds into their weapons and lowering their muzzles until they pointed at the crowd. One by one a few spectators left, but most came down and piled up their weapons.

Marietta asked me in a whisper, "What if the Hand attacks in the middle of the trial?"

I shrugged. "We have guards out to warn us. Besides," I added with some sincerity, "the court is not as worried about the Hand attacking it as it is worried about the Razai attacking it."

I noticed with some surprise that Herb Ollick was one of the ones who had come forward to supervise the stacking of the weapons. Ila Toussant came from the rifle stacks and grinned at me as she pulled out her own paper supply.

"Chief, am I still court clerk?"

I nodded. "Yes. Where's your rifle?"

"In the stacks."

"Go get it back. You're an officer of the court and you can't tell when you might have to dot somebody's eye."

While she returned to the stacks, I rolled my parka and shirt into a bundle and contemplated how fearful I was. I was afraid of so many things right then. There was the Hand ready to do whatever it was going to do to us, there were all of the angry faces up on the dunes who hated me for what I was doing and how I was doing it, and all of this was on top of my fear of the planet Tartaros and the Forever Sand. More than that, I was afraid of making a mistake.

More than anything else, I was afraid of having another Dick Irish haunting my dreams.

That little pumpkin-colored book was in my parka pocket, and I pulled it out. Once my bundle was rolled and slung, I took my copy of Stays's rules and opened the little book to tuck them inside. The first line on the left page caught my attention.

"With a foot in the past, and a foot in the future, all I can do with the present is piss on it."

I closed the book and stuffed it and the rules into my hip pocket as I remembered something Big Dave had said. He had once told me, "Right now is when you're alive, Bando. Don't waste now feeling afraid of the future because of what's happened in the past. Do your best, and things will work out."

"All the guns are stacked."

I looked up and noticed Herb Ollick standing in front of me. "Thanks."

He did a quick sweep of the area with his gaze. "Where's Marantha Silver? She's still in the RC, isn't she?"

"Yes. She's over at the Hand camp."

"Is she all right?"

"Sure," I lied. "She's just making some arrangements for us with them. Don't worry about a thing."

He nodded. "If you need any help, Bando, just let me know."

"Thanks again." The man started to turn away, but I called him back. "Herb?"

"Yeah?"

"If I keep it a secret, will you answer me a question?"

Herb smiled and flashed his ice fingers. "You want to know am I a *pezzonovante* in the organization, the *Capo di Capi* of the 'friends,' as we say in polite society, true?"

He had just said more words in a row than I had ever heard him say during the past two years. "You got it, Herb. How about it?"

He held up an ice-cluttered hand and whispered into my ear. "I am Herbert Ollick from Dayton, Ohio. In a certain sense, I am an illusionist. However, the court chose to call my illusions embezzlement, fraud, criminal conspiracy, and a few other things. I give people's eyes and ears what they want to see and hear."

I looked at his smiling face. "No mob?"

He shook his head. "No mob, although I did do a bit of newspaper writing years ago. I did an inside info column for a financial paper and made a bundle selling worthless stock tips prior to publication."

"What about the diamonds?"

He flashed his rocks. "Phony."

"But back in the yard once I saw you scratch glass with them."

His eyebrows rose as he said, "Quartz scratches glass too, didn't you know?" He reached into his ration bag and pulled out a roll of papers. "Here's something I've written that you might enjoy. When you're finished with it, make sure it gets back to me."

"Okay. Thanks."

He smiled and headed back to his dune. I felt a little disappointed. After all, it had been something of a minor brag point to be locked up in the same pit as a genuine goomba big shot. To find out he was just a fat little con artist was kind of a letdown.

The faces quieted down as the now weaponless sharks returned to their respective dunes. The air was very still as I thought about Big Dave and how I wished I could wrap this whole thing up and dump it in his lap.

Out of the corner of my eye I saw Nance seat herself among the spectators. Silently I nodded to myself, remembering what Nance had said about her lover's death. Nance certainly had an interest in how this one came out.

I stuffed Herb's papers into my ration bag and turned toward Ila Toussant. "Let's begin." I thought for a moment and then said, "This is the seventh day."

A strange look came over Ila's face. "On the seventh day," she said, "God rested."

"Yeah. But he wasn't chief of the Razai Cops. Maybe this is a case of 'eternal vigilance is the price of freedom.'"

She laughed. "I was thinking more along the lines of 'no rest for the wicked.'"

As tired as I was, that joke hit just a little close to home. That would be a slice of Hell, I thought, dragging my sleep-deprived corpse from one trial to the next as chief of the RCs.

I held up my hands and waited until something resembling silence was achieved. I looked left and right at the crowd seated on the dunes, and began to speak.

"Here, justice is everybody getting exactly what they deserve as fast as possible. All of us who are here, that is our purpose. Anyone here who interferes with that purpose will pull down the maximum payback this investigation will consider, whatever happens to Victor Myerson."

I looked at Jason Pendril. "Let's have your charge."

Bennet's cockroach got to his feet and stood between the dunes. I noticed that his hair was blond and very thin. His rug was not in evidence.

"Before we get started . . ." Pendril held out his hands and asked, "What do I call you?"

"What do you mean?"

"Should I call you 'judge,' 'your honor,' 'officer,' 'inspector,' 'investigator,' 'generalissimo,' or what?"

All of the selections, with the possible exception of generalissimo really bit it. "Just call me Bando."

"Very well, Bando. Before we can get started, there is a bit of housekeeping we have to do. It has to do with the penalty—the payback—for rape according to the Razai."

"Excuse me."

At the foot of the dune to my right, a well-padded fellow

with an olive complexion and wavy black hair stood up. This had to be Lane Rossiter, roach-at-law.

Next to where Rossiter sat on the dune was a large man who joked with a couple of nearby buddies. Victor Myerson was strong-looking, but he didn't look like he had done much iron time with the yard monsters. He was just naturally big. His hair was cut short, and he had a substantial beer gut.

I raised my eyebrows at Rossiter. "What is it?"

"Couldn't we put off the matter of penalties until such time as we determine that a crime has been committed? Tying the noose before we determine that there is a neck that should be in it seems to go against the presumption of innocence."

"No one is presumed innocent here," I answered, "and no one who ever was dragged in front of a court was presumed innocent. Let's end the games."

I looked at Pendril. "Did you have something to throw into this?"

Bennet's roach nodded. "Bando, rules twenty-four and twenty-five inflicting the max payback on jurors for bad calls, as well as rule thirty-two, inflicting the max on false witnesses, make it necessary to know right now what the max will be. Are we talking about a slap on the wrist or death? A witness who might be willing to perjure himself if he only risks a trivial penalty might not be willing to lie if, by lying, he risks death."

Lane Rossiter clasped his hands behind his back and said, "My brother seems bent on achieving a capital penalty for a noncapital offense. Rape, if such a crime has indeed been committed, did not take the life of the alleged victim. If how we define justice is to have a meaning other than hysterical vengeance, there must be a difference between the paybacks for crimes that leave live victims and those that leave dead ones."

I took my bundled parka, dropped it on the sand, and sat on it. I didn't have any answers, so I guessed I needed more input. I looked at the roaches and nodded. "Thanks." I looked up at the dunes.

"Abe Lyles?"

A man seated at the foot of the dune to the right stood up, walked until he stood between the dunes, and faced me. "I'm Abe Lyles." He was a slender, pleasant-looking man with brown hair and blue eyes. He was tall and stooped a little as if to apologize for his height.

"Abe," I began, "I was told that you think what we're talking about here is a disease, not a crime."

An uncomfortably angry sound rose from the dunes. As it quieted, Abe looked down and selected his words with care. "I am a recovering compulsive rapist—a sex addict." There was laughter and a batch of catcalls from the crowd. There were also a few muttered threats that almost caused me to invoke rule thirteen.

I stood up and shouted. "This isn't a football game!" The dunes quieted down and I continued.

"You are not here to root for your side. You have the right to observe. You have the right to volunteer as a juror. You have the right to testify as a witness. But your purpose here is the same as ours. Your purpose is to see that everyone here gets exactly what's coming to them, as quickly as possible.

"I'm going to repeat what I said at the beginning. Anyone who obstructs justice, that is, anyone who interferes with these people getting what they deserve as quickly as possible, will suffer the max payback under consideration, whatever happens to the guy charged. That means if you slow things down with these demonstrations and otherwise continue acting like assholes, you will catch the max."

I pointed around at the crowd. "So listen and pay attention, because what we are talking about right now is a possible death penalty for you. Now, shut your blowholes and let this man say his piece."

I sat down again and Abe Lyles rubbed the back of his neck, waiting for the emotional echoes of my speech to die out. Whatever he was there for, I had to admit that the guy had guts. Maybe a third of the men and probably three quarters of the women in that crowd had been victims of rape, and here was Abe Lyles standing in front of them all, not only identifying himself as a rapist, but preparing to support the position that rape wasn't a crime but was, instead, the symptom of a disease. Like I said, a gutsy fellow. Either that or he was rubber room bait.

On both sides of the witness, the cockroaches were

crouched, ready to pounce in an attempt at forcing Abe's testimony to serve their own positions.

"I remind both Jason Pendril and Lane Rossiter of rule twenty-nine that allows this witness to say his piece his way and in his own words. When he's finished, I'll allow you to question him if anything needs to be cleared up."

I looked around at the crowd. "Do we all understand why we're here?" I accepted the ensuing silence as an affirmative response.

I nodded at Abe. "Sorry for interrupting."

It became very quiet.

THE PRICE

OF RAPE

"I'M not sure why I'm here," Abe began, "except that I've had some experience with this, and there's something we all ought to know about rape."

He put his hands in his pockets, looked around at the crowd, and finished by looking at me. "And there's something we ought to know about rapists." He looked down and his voice grew quieter, but stronger.

"I am a rapist. Some of you know my record. For those who don't, I was dropped in the Crotch on my third rape conviction with no hope of parole. The record doesn't even begin to say what I really was. I don't know how many women I've raped, there were that many. I don't even remember them all, although as part of my recovery I have tried to remember."

He looked up at the spectators and said, "I'm not here to tell you that I'm proud of what I did. I'm here to tell you that I was insane with an addiction that caused me to hurt a lot of people. It's a clawing obsession that, once I translated it into action, became a compulsion that I couldn't stop." He shook his head slightly.

"Not only couldn't I stop it, I really didn't think I had a problem. I denied the whole thing to myself, through two trials, and to I don't know how many headshrinkers.

"I was in a constant state of hating myself. I had terrible and vast needs, and the only way I knew to meet those needs was with sex, and the only sex I knew was forced and violent." He looked at the sharks and pointed. "You junkeys know what I'm saying. Just to stay alive, just to keep from screaming, you had to have your stuff. You don't have your stuff right now, and look at you. But I bet most of you are still telling yourselves that you don't have a problem.

"That was the way it was with me. But for over six years, now—five of them on the outside—I haven't had to act out any of my rape fantasies. I got help, and the same help is available to anyone who needs it, even here in the sand. It's a disease that made me do terrible things. But it's a disease that can be halted."

He rubbed his chin, shrugged, and said, "I guess the only thing I have left to say is that there's no way to recover from this disease if you're dead." He looked at me.

"That's all."

Both of the cockroaches were practically pawing the sand. They were that eager to get at Abe. I was about to call on Pendril when a shout came from the dune on my left.

"I want to say something!"

I recognized the voice. It was Alna. I nodded and pointed to where Abe Lyles had stood. "Go ahead." I looked toward Ila.

"Her name's Alna Moah." I turned back to see Alna. She returned my look with nails. She appeared like she was back to hating all men again.

Her eyes were narrowed, her hands clenched into fists, as she spoke. Her voice trembled with pain and anger. "Bando, I can't believe you had that man speak! Are you saying that rape's just a disease, nothing but a head cold?"

The rumbles from the crowd got loud and then eased quickly. "I'm not saying anything, Alna," I answered. "Right now I'm only listening. Were you going to say something?"

She faced Myerson and pointed her finger at him. "I was raped by a husband, I was raped by four different guards, even a sister tried to rape me, and now she's done past for it."

She lowered her hand and looked around at the crowd. "But I'm just going to tell you about one time—the first time I was raped. We're looking for the payback for rape. To know that we need to know what was taken from the victim. For murder, life is taken from the victim, so max payback is to take the life from the murderer." She faced me. "Like Dick Irish."

She glanced once at Victor Myerson, and back at me. "When I was fifteen years old someone whose face I never saw dragged me into an alley, raped me, then beat me with a length of pipe and left me for dead. When I came to in the hospital, I couldn't remember what'd happened. I couldn't bear to think about it, so I just didn't think about anything. I was numb. I was trapped in my horror like that for months. So the first thing he took from me was my freedom."

She looked up at the brassy orange sky, the tears on her cheeks. "Once I started thinking about it, I couldn't stop think-ing about it. I just relived the nightmare over and over again. I couldn't eat, I couldn't do anything, I couldn't sleep. All I could do was cry, rage, curse, cry, and rage some more. So the next thing he took from me was my sanity."

Her voice grew quiet. "Everyone began treating me like I was different—something less. They treated me like I was spoiled goods, like somehow getting raped had been my fault." She placed her hand over her heart.

"I started to believe that it was my fault. Sometimes I used to stand naked in front of a mirror and scratch myself bloody with my nails. I didn't know why, and I couldn't stop. So the next thing he took from me was my self-respect."

She lowered her hand as she looked at me. "He took many things from me. Since that night I cannot trust, I am afraid to love, I am afraid to be loved. And in a world where this horrible thing could happen to a young, innocent girl, there could be no god. That faceless bastard took that from me, too. If he had only taken my life—if he had just killed me—he would have done me a favor."

She dried the tears from her cheeks with the heel of her hand and looked at Abe Lyles. "I don't know about any disease. Maybe Dick Irish was just sick and had to kill Freddy, but that won't warm Freddy's body up any. Maybe you are recovering, and if you are, I can be happy for you. But I'm not one of the woman you raped. If I was I'd probably be hoping for what I hope for the monster who raped me. I'd probably pray that you burn in Hell forever." She folded her arms and kept looking at Abe Lyles.

"Right now I am thinking that if they had thinned you after the first time you were caught and convicted of rape, there would be a lot fewer raped women in the universe." She looked at me. "Rape demands a bigger payback than murder. Death is nowhere near enough of a payback for rape, but it's all we can get."

She walked back to her place among the spectators. Everyone was looking at me. I stood up and walked until I was standing where Alna had been. The cockroaches were looking very frustrated. I spoke to them. "Pendril, Rossiter, since we don't have a jury yet, that leaves me as the only person who might change his mind by whatever points you might bring up or muddy up through cross-examination. But there's only one thing I really need to know right now." I looked up at Abe Lyles.

"As far as you know, is everyone who rapes a compulsive sex addict?"

He was silent for a long time. Finally he held out his hands and said, "I don't know. That'd be like asking if everyone who takes a drink is an alcoholic. For taking a drink, I don't think every drinker is an alcoholic. But rape is something sick in itself. To do it at all you have to be bent some." He shook his head. "But I don't know."

I scratched my head and faced Lane Rossiter. "How about your pigeon? Does he claim to be insane?"

Lane Rossiter got to his feet. "Our position is that no rape was committed. If it is the judgment of this investigation that a rape was committed, however, we'll keep our options open."

There were snickers from the dunes. I said, "You mean to say my client isn't guilty, but if he is guilty, it wasn't his fault because he was crazy."

"As I said, it's an option."

I laughed. "Not in this investigation, buddy. You pull that kind of shit with the paperwork and rule wizards back on Earth. This is no debating match. Your job here isn't to see what you can get away with. Your responsibility here is to plead *the truth* as you see it. Either he raped the guy or he didn't. If he did, maybe he was crazy. Don't come at us here with any of that down-home 'he didn't do it, but if he did do it, he didn't mean it,' smoke."

Rossiter and Myerson whispered among themselves for a moment, then the roach faced me. "Innocent. We hold that no rape was committed."

I nodded and leveled my gaze at both of them. "Then to you it really doesn't matter what the payback for rape is, correct?"

Rossiter sat down without answering. There was just one more thing I had to bring up. I faced Abe Lyles again. "Abe, for someone in the middle of this disease, you hold that it's like for any other kind of addict—there is no choice. Without help the compulsion must be acted upon. Did I understand you right?"

"Pretty much so."

The dunes seemed to wobble a bit and I got very light-headed. I needed sleep and lots of it. When Tartaros resumed its normal spin, I asked Abe, "Can the sufferer of this disease choose to get help?"

"Sure."

"Then by choosing not to get the help, you could say the rapist chose his disease and its consequences."

Lyles thought for a long time, and then he nodded. His voice sounded very rough. "Yes. I think you're right."

I bit at the skin on the inside of my lips as I faced Pendril. "Is there anything you want to add?"

"No, but I certainly want to underscore Alna M—"

"Underscore on your own time, Pendril. All we need right now are new points. Keeping in mind rule number thirty-one, which says 'Trials that are unnecessarily delayed by one party will be decided by default in favor of the other party,' do you have anything new to add?"

Pendril sat down and I turned around and faced Nance. "I want to vote on it. Up or down, death is the max payback for rape."

"Right now?" she asked.

"Right now. We have almost everyone here. If the vote is so close that the others would make a difference, we can send out runners."

"Can't you just make a decision? You know I'll back you."

"Nance, I've never been raped. I don't think I'm qualified to decide what a rapist takes from a victim."

She frowned as she got to her feet and stood between the

dunes. "Okay. The max payback for rape is death. All those in favor, stand up." I was one of the ones who were standing. It was an effort to find the ones who weren't standing.

"All those against." Everyone sat down and about forty sharks got to their feet. To his credit, Abe Lyles was one of them. Right then I made up my mind to go to one of those CSA meetings to see what was going on there.

Nance faced me. "There's your second law, Bando. The max payback for rape is death." She went back to her place on the dune.

I glanced first at Bennet and then at Myerson. "Are you both agreeable to me settling this matter?"

They both wanted a jury trial. I faced the crowd. "The penalty for being a false witness, an errant juror, or delaying the proceedings in this case, is death." I pointed to the area between the dunes. "All those who want to be jurors, grab some sand and line up there."

As I squatted down to pick up some sand for the choosing, Garoit came from behind the dune on my right, went over to Nance, and began whispering to her.

She began leaving, and I asked, "What's happening?"

"Later," she said, and they were gone.

Were we being attacked? Had Bloody Sarah and the scouts uncovered the Hand's hidden armies? What was going on?

I looked at the first applicant for the jury. It was Minnie McDavies back from her scouting mission. She was holding her face up with a big grin on it, and both of her fists out, knuckles down. I held out my hands and we both opened up at the same time. I had sand in both of my hands, she had none in hers.

"You're in. Next."

BENNET V. MYERSON

ET AL.

JIM Bennet was his own first witness. "Last night when the column was halted, I wrapped up in my sheet to get some sleep. Vic Myerson and his two goons got me up, and Vic said to me, 'Get your clothes off, sweet thing. It's time for love.'" Bennet spat on the sand and looked at Myerson, who was smiling.

"I told him no. I told him I didn't want to and to leave me alone. Then Huey held me and Lacy began pulling—"

"Just a second," I interrupted. "Who are Huey and Lacy?"

"Huey Garret and Lacy Moore."

I looked at Pendril. "How come you're not charging Garret and Moore as accomplices?"

Jason Pendril glanced at Jim Bennet and faced me. "Vic Myerson is the only one who actually achieved penetration. We thought—I thought going after Myerson would be a surer thing."

"Are you being paid by the victory?"

The roach flushed scarlet. "Of course not."

I faced Bennet. "Jim, how do you feel about these two: Garret and Moore?"

"I don't know what you mean."

"An accomplice is just as guilty as the perp. Do you want to charge them?"

Jim Bennet glanced at Pendril, at Myerson, and looked at me. "Will it affect my chances of nailing Myerson?"

"I don't know," I answered. "But they either did what you said or they didn't. So, do you want to charge them?"

Jim Bennet's face was twisted into an expression of anger, fear, anxiety. In a quiet voice he asked, "What about witnesses who saw what was happening and didn't do anything to stop it? Aren't they accomplices? Even more than that, the ones who saw what happened and won't testify because they don't want to get involved. Aren't they accomplices?"

"Accomplices are accomplices," I answered. "Do you want them charged?"

"Yes."

"Let's have some names."

Bennet closed his eyes and attached names to the faces in his mind. "Haman Surus and Claudine Lowe. I called for help. I begged them to help, to get someone. They just walked off. Barth Lazar was there, too. I begged him for help and he said there wasn't anything he could do. Then he left. None of them are willing to testify."

"Where are they?"

Bennet looked toward Myerson and pointed. "Right there next to Vic. The fat goon with the bald head. That's Huey Garret."

The fat goon grinned, cocked his thumb, and pantomimed shooting Jim Bennet. Bennet looked and pointed toward the top of the dune behind Myerson.

"Up there. The yard monster with the short black beard. That's Lacy. And Lazar is up there, too. And on the other side near the top are Claudine Lowe and Haman Surus."

I stood up and motioned with my arm. "Lacy Moore, Claudine Lowe, Barth Lazar, and Haman Surus, come on down!" There was some nervous laughter, then Lacy stood up.

"Why?"

"I think you might want to get in on this. You're facing the death penalty."

"My ass."

I grinned. "Yessir, that's what you might pay with. I want you all to come on down and enter a plea to the charges."

"I ain't enterin' no fuckin' plea," said Lacy Moore.

I pulled out the *Law of the Razai*. "Rule nineteen: 'In a trial, not entering a plea is a plea of guilty.'"

Lacy Moore took a step down from the dune and shouted, "How 'bout I come on down there an' feed you your own fuckin' foot, you goddamned cop sonofa—"

Cap Brady stuck his rifle muzzle into Lacy's left ear. "You don't have to enter a plea, sonny, but if you threaten the chief, we'll have to invoke rule thirteen and snuff your candle."

Lacy Moore's dark eyes darted back and forth in his head, making him look like what he was: a trapped animal. "I thought we couldn't hold no prisoners."

"Why, you're not a prisoner, bucko. If you want to leave, leave. But if you start making threats again, I'll have to stick this in your ear again." He pulled his rifle out of Lacy's ear.

Lacy looked down at me. "You tellin' me if I just walk, that's a plea of guilty?"

"That's right."

I looked at Lane Rossiter. "We already have a jury, and as soon as they make up their minds, the trial's over. The jury has seen and heard all of this. Don't you think you ought to nip on up there and talk to Lacy Moore? Right now he's doing his best to hang himself and the rest of you."

A man and a woman came down from the left dune, and the woman spoke first, the tears in her eyes. "I'm Claudine Lowe, and I'm so sorry, but what could I have done? All I've ever been told in the crowbars was to mind my own business, and that's all I did. All I did was mind my own business. I was afraid and—"

"We aren't in the crowbars anymore," I interrupted. "Are you entering a plea of guilty?"

"No!" answered Haman Surus. "We are not guilty of anything!"

I looked at the woman. "Does he speak for you?"

"Yes!" the man repeated.

I looked at the woman. "Claudine? Does this guy speak for you?"

She nodded. "Yes he does."

"Very well." I looked and saw Barth Lazar come down the dune and walk to the center. He looked as though he carried the sins of the world upon his back.

"I'm guilty," he said.

The silence following Barth's plea could have crushed solid steel it was so intense. You didn't have to be a cockroach to figure out if any one of the ones charged as accomplices were guilty, all of them had to be guilty.

"Bando," called Minnie from where the jurors were squatting in the sand. "May the jurors ask questions?"

"Sure."

Minnie stood up and asked Barth, "You said you were guilty. Of what?"

"Just what Jim Bennet said. Lacy and Huey were forcing Jim into position so Vic Myerson could rape him, and Jim asked me for help. I said I couldn't do anything." He folded his arms beneath his sheet. "I could've done something, but I was afraid." He glanced at Jim. "I'm sorry." He looked back at the sand.

Minnie looked around at the jurors and back at me. "I think we're ready."

"Wait!" Lane Rossiter was on like a shot. "You haven't even heard from the defendant yet, and there are still two pleas that haven't been heard."

I looked at Huey Garret and up at Lacy Moore. "How about it? Guilty or not guilty?"

"Not guilty," answered Lacy. He turned around and walked over the top of the dune, toward the point camp.

"Huey, what about you?"

"Not guilty." Huey remained seated. In his heart of hearts I don't think he believed that anything would happen.

I glanced at Minnie. "We're still ready," she said.

I scratched the back of my neck and looked at Rossiter. "Is there anything your client can say that might add to the jury's information?"

"Of course." He gestured with his head and Victor Myerson stood up. "Just tell them what you told me."

Myerson looked around, thrust his fingers behind his belt, and grinned. "You folks've been really taken in. What's going on here is nothin' new. I didn't just jump Jimmy's bones out here in the sand. Jimmy and me have been gettin' it on for almost a year. The guys back in the crowbars at Lewisburg Max know. And it's always the same thing with Jimmy. It's part of the game. I grab him, Jimmy cries a little and says 'no, no,' and I rough him up a little. Huey and Lacy just add some to the excitement when they pretend to hold him down. They don't do any harm. It's all part of the sex play. Huey and Lacy can tell you. Lots of the guys from Lewisburg can tell you."

I looked at Bennet, and he was so stone-cold steady with rage, I don't even think he was breathing.

"Did you want to say something, Jimmy?" I asked.

He bunched up the sides of his sheet, exposing his arms. He turned around once so that everyone could see the terrible bruises on his arms. So much for Lacy and Huey pretending to hold Jimmy down.

"Vic," he began, "there were dozens of times back at Lewisburg when you wanted sex, and just as many times that I told you no, and just as many times that you and your goons forced me to have sex. I think you just confessed to raping me dozens and dozens of times."

I glanced at Minnie. She turned and huddled with the twelve other jurors. When they were done, she faced me.

"There's something the jury thinks needs to be said. If a person shows that he or she is unwilling to do sex, and you go ahead and force that person to have sex, that is rape. It doesn't matter if you've had sex with that person before, or if you're married. Rape is rape." She pointed her finger. "And you, Victor Myerson, and you, Huey Garret, and Lacy Moore, wherever you are, are guilty."

She looked at Claudine Lowe and Haman Surus. "We find you two guilty, as well as Barth Lazar." Minnie turned toward me. "We don't know if we're allowed to recommend anything, but we think Barth should get some slack." She sat down.

Rossiter looked like he was going to burst a blood vessel. I suppose that was understandable. In a Razai court all of his best material was unusable.

"Jimmy," I said to the victim, "they are all guilty, and the max payback is death. What you do is up to you."

Bennet went to the stacks and picked up a rifle. As he did so Haman Surus and Huey Garret took off in opposite directions. With two clean, unhurried shots, Jimmy drilled them both. As he was bringing down his weapon, he popped Claudine Lowe right between the eyes, then faced Victor Myerson.

Myerson was crying and begging on his knees as the bullet went through his heart. As Myerson fell over, Jim Bennet faced Barth Lazar.

Tears began streaming down the boy's face. "You should've helped me! You knew better! Damn you, you should have helped me!" He pulled the trigger and Barth Lazar fell dead to the sand.

I stumbled off into the dunes and puked until my nuts ached.

THE MEETING

IT was something that I had to do, going to the CSA meeting. After the executions I had to face them. I didn't know if I could justify myself to them, I didn't know if I should justify myself to them. I didn't know if I would have to.

I sat on the sand next to Rus Gades. The pair of us formed part of a circle of close to sixty or seventy sharks with more coming. They began with a prayer, and I was preoccupied getting acquainted with my new platoon of ghosts, so the words didn't register. I saw Abe Lyles there, as well as Marietta and Cap Brady.

While they were reading some things out loud, I motioned for Marietta and Cap to come over. When they were next to me they stooped over and I whispered, "You two don't have to nurse me. I can take care of myself, so beat it."

"Speakin' just for myself, chump," began Marietta, "this here is my club. I belong here. If I make you nervous, maybe you ought to leave."

I looked at Cap and he nodded back. "I belong here too."

I waved them off and wondered what I was doing there. I didn't have long to wait, because there were some others wondering the same thing. After the readings, Rus Gades said, "I'm an addict, my name's Rus."

"Hi, Rus!" answered the crowd. The introductions worked

their way around to the left, and by then they had to go in and out of the ring several times there were so many there. I guessed a hundred or more.

They introduced themselves as addicts, alcoholics, co-dependents, children of addicts, sex addicts, overeaters, workaholics, rageaholics, and so on. Marietta called herself an adult child of an addict. Cap said he was a rageaholic.

After all of the introductions were done, everyone was looking at me. "My name's Bando," I said, and left it at that. There were a few greetings of "Hi, Bando," but since the four who had said that were Cap, Rus, Abe, and Marietta, that left a hundred plus who didn't want me there. I wasn't really sure why I was there myself. I rubbed my temples as someone called out, "How did he get in here?"

There was a muffled roar of agreement, and Rus Gades stood up. Into the following quiet he said, "Bando got in here the same way all of us did. Something pointed in this direction, and his feet brought him here." Rus looked down at me. "You don't have to speak, but do you want to say why you're here?"

I nodded. Rus sat down and I spoke from where I sat. "I've heard of CSA for a long time. I don't know if I have your kind of problem. Of course, it's been pointed out to me that if I do have a compulsive problem, not knowing about it is one of the big symptoms."

Taking a deep breath, I continued. "But I'm here for another reason. I'm here to face you people and to take whatever it is you have to dish out. I listened to Abe, yet Vic Myerson, and a number of others, are dead right now. I don't know about explaining it or justifying it. That's the way it is." I crossed my legs and rested my elbows on my knees.

"I heard Abe, I saw how he behaved and what he tried to do. I liked what I saw. That's why I'm here."

There was a long silence, as though everyone was afraid to speak. Finally, from the side of the circle across from me, a woman stood up and said, "I'm Ella. I'm an addict."

She was met with a round of "Hi, Ella!"

She looked down at the sand, then around at the faces. "There have been lots of times when I cursed the lack of justice in the world. Every time I did it, I confirmed for myself that things were just as rotten as I imagined them to be. That gave me a great excuse to go pick up and use. Every time I did that, of course, I'd get into trouble and then complain about the lack of justice in the world. The thing that never got through my thick skull was if there had been any justice in the world, I would have been dead fifteen years ago."

Some of the listeners chuckled, some of them laughed out loud. Ella continued.

"I hurt a lot of people serving my addiction. I hurt myself, too. But let me tell you what finally got me into CSA and recovery. It was a cop and a judge. I was caught holding, and I wasn't anything big. If it had been any other cop, I would have been able to cry or buy my way out. I've sold my ass to stay sick lots of times, but this stain wasn't buying. An honest cop, I couldn't believe it. And that ran me into an honest judge. I whined for justice all my life, and then I got it. They took my two little boys from me and dropped me into the crowbars."

She looked at me and smiled. "I called that cop and that judge a million names and damned them to Hell a billion times over. But the truth of the matter is that the first chance I got in the crowbars, I showed up at a CSA meeting because it had finally gotten through to me that I had a problem. That cop and that judge saved my life, and probably the lives of those who I might have killed if I had kept on using."

Ella looked around at the faces. "I've hit every meeting we've had since the landing. There were twenty-four of us at the largest meeting. There were six at the smallest. I haven't counted them, but it looks like there are way over a hundred here tonight." She looked at me. "I think you and Jim Bennet saved a lot of lives this morning."

She sat down. Others got up and talked, but I didn't hear them. The universe can get to be a mighty complicated place at times, and it is very confusing to get patted on the back when you expect to be beaten to a pulp. That is especially true when what you wanted was the beating.

Cap Brady got up at one point and talked about being a rageaholic. He was addicted to rage, and it was while he was in the middle of one of his rages that he had thinned Diaper Lou. I think he made a point that finally got through to me. It wasn't whether or not Diaper Lou should've been snuffed; it was what had it done to Cap.

I nodded. They could give me a medal and show me that I had cured everything from rape to spoiled milk by the death of Vic Myerson and his accomplices, intentional and unintentional. But what was adding their corpses to my collection doing to me?

By the time Cap was finished, however, I knew what I was. I was addicted to rage. That was what had dropped me into the crowbars each time. I didn't get in trouble every time I went off into a tear, but every time I had gotten in trouble, somewhere along the line I had been in a rage. That teacher I punched out. That wasn't a fight. At the time I had been insane with rage. I could have just as easily killed him.

My sister's powder puff old man, the bank afterwards, trying to pistol-whip a squad of cops by myself. Rages. I hadn't had one of those rages since the landing. What I heard at the meeting was that, if I kept coming back, I'd never have to do it by myself again.

PRECEDENT

I didn't think I had energy enough to dream.

I was wrong.

They were all there. Dick Irish was leading a delegation of corpses. Barth Lazar, Huey Garret, Haman Surus, Claudine Lowe, Victor Myerson. They zombied along, their arms stretched out toward me, their faces drawn and pale.

I heard Jimmy cry out.

"You should've helped me! Damn you, you should have helped me!"

His voice shredded my mind.

I heard the shot.

I saw Barth Lazar fall to the sand. I saw him fall again. And again and again.

It was like something from a repeating video image. Jimmy would cry out, there would be a shot, Barth would grab his chest and fall to the sand, Jimmy would cry out, *"You should've helped me! Damn you, you should have helped me!"*

The shot would slam against my ears—

None of the corpses could understand why they were dead. They had grown up with the court game on Earth, the land of pleas, tricks, stalls, appeals, deals. They would have walked in minutes. If by some fluke they had been held, just the five of them could have tied up the court system for years.

No one goes for the death penalty anymore because it's too expensive, what with all the appeals, news conferences, candle-carrying sobbers, and other idiots. Only the very poor, the very stupid, and the very repentant get the death penalty. The rich, the clever, and the vicious have the ability to drag it out for too long. That's why the juicer made the death penalty a bargaining chip.

Plead guilty and we'll give you life. This offer not available to the poor, the stupid, or those who really do feel bad about what they did.

So, it didn't make any sense. Why were they dead?

They weren't poor.

They weren't stupid.

They weren't repentant. In fact, as far as they were concerned, they hadn't done anything!

In a universe of sharks, you minded your own business, did your own thing, and went into frenzy with everyone else. If you want to get along, you go along. That's what they had done, that's what they had always done, so why were they dead?

Vic Myerson was the most confused. Jim Bennet was a faggot, wasn't he? The gay dude is always put down and he always goes down, right? That's the first slogan above the Crowbar Museum of Unnatural History, isn't it?

"Why am I dead, Bando? Why?" Inquiring ghosts want to know.

The frito fagitos; the guards spit on them, the sharks either ignore, fuck, or kill them, and everyone looks the other way. It's not like they were human beings, or anything.

I mean, look at the numbs who write letters, sign petitions, carry signs, and raise hell to keep lab rats from getting cut up in laboratories. Did you ever see them standing up for a crowbar fag's right not to get raped and cut to pieces? Of course not.

Those were the rules, man, and Vic had lived by those rules for his whole life.

"Bando," asked his ghost, "why am I dead?"

I tried to defend myself, to defend the RC, to defend Jim Bennet, to explain to Vic—to all of them—the reasons.

—We aren't on Earth.

—We're out of the crowbars.

—The cockroaches and the stains don't operate the justice machine anymore. The juicer is dead.

—We don't rape in the Razai; it's not right.

—We don't stand by while another is raped; it's not right.

—We are no longer tiny frightened little islands floating in a sea of law-made shit. We are involved with each other.

—If I stand by and let you bung Jimmy Bennet, you have every right to my asshole as well.

—Jim Bennet is a human being.

—One person's freedom is the freedom of us all.

—One person's slavery means we are all enslaved.

The reasons sounded made up and phony. The corpses looked at each other, shook their heads, and held out their hands as they asked, "But why are we dead?"

Two huge crows flew into a cornfield and began tearing at the ears of corn. They pecked, filled their bellies, and pecked some more. They grew bloated and fat, yet the pecking never stopped, and there was never any less corn. In fact, the more they pecked, the more corn there was.

I looked at the crows closely and recognized them. Cockroaches. Money threads. One of them was Pendril and the other was Rossiter. They began speaking.

The two crows filled the air with fine-sounding words like justice, rights, certainty, due process, mercy, motivation, the spirit and the letter of ninety million conflicting laws, all of which said that the dead should be alive and the alive should be dead, but in either case the process should decide these matters with all deliberate speed, which meant very very slowly, the attorneys should be very very well paid, and the cornfield should go on forever.

"What about the scarecrow?" I screamed.

The two crows laughed, flew over to the suit and hat hanging from a pole, and pulled the stuffings out of the scarecrow. The pieces of the stuffings fell on the dirt: constitutions, courts, oaths, codes.

While the crows covered the straw man's hat with droppings, I went before the Razai. I had it put to a vote, and the vote was unanimous: The max payback for being a lawyer from now on would be death. Guilty of cockroachery in the first degree.

The two crows, their feathers plucked, were sent walking into a barren, scorching desert.

"There are no cornfields on Tartaros!" I screamed.

I opened my eyes to see that Alsvid was high in the sky and the shadow I had curled up in had disappeared. Alna was not next to me. It was still a long time until the cool of the evening and the exhausting cold of night.

I was on my side. My hood was propped up with a flat green stick making a tiny tent out of my hood and forming a tiny spot of shade for my head. My eyes were filled with grit and I had a two-hundred-pound death grip on my rifle.

I relaxed my grip on the weapon, flexed my fingers, wiped the sleep from my eyes, and looked again at the stick. I didn't own any stick, so someone must have put it there. Bloody Sarah, Rhome Nazzar, Ondo, Nance, Garoit, Stays, and Minnie McDavies were seated in a circle staring at me.

"What?"

"You yelled something about cornfields," answered Nance. "Are you all right?"

My mouth tasted like I'd slept all night sucking on the warden's toes. I opened my water bottle, and what water I had in my ration bag smelled even worse than my mouth tasted. "Yeah. I'm terrific."

"Bando," said Nance, "about the way those trials finish up—"

"Trials?" I struggled into a sitting position, my legs crossed in front of me. "What about them?"

"There was a lot of shooting."

"That explains all the noise." I shook my head as I rummaged in my bag for something to eat.

Stays scratched the week's growth of hair on his chin. "We've been kicking around the shootings at trials, Bando."

I kept looking in my bag, wishing that they would change the subject. "That's the law for you. When you have to kill a lot of people, there tends to be a lot of shooting, and strangely enough a lot of people get shot."

"What if Jimmy hadn't been such a good shot?" asked Sarah. "He might have drilled a few innocent bystanders."

"Then the law would have come down on Jimmy with the max. Another shooting. All accounts paid."

"What about the innocent bystanders?"

"We don't have innocent bystanders. Not on Tartaros." I found a wrapped bar of something grim and took a bite. As I chewed I looked at the horizon and talked.

"I suppose we could hang them, except that we don't have any trees and the law says we can't hold any prisoners. Before you can hang 'em, you've got to hold 'em, and we aren't allowed to hold 'em. So, we do it the way we have to do it. We can't take prisoners, which means we can't separate potential targets from the rest of the Razai and hold them. So, it has to be done the way it has to be done."

I looked at Nance. "Ever since the Dick Irish execution, everybody's known how it's done at court, so anyone who wants to watch does so at his or her own risk." I took another bite of the thing-bar.

"Man, Bando," said Nance as she shook her head, "I didn't see the shootings, but I saw the blood splashed on some of the sharks. They were plenty upset."

I gave it a ment, trying to measure my feelings against what seemed to be real. For once they were the same. "When we splash blood for the Law of the Razai, Nance, the more people who are spattered with it, the better. The law, the things it protects, the deaths of those who break it, all belong to us—the Razai. I think they might remember it better if they have to wipe Vic's blood off their boots rather than if they just watch him taken off in the desert out of sight someplace to disappear."

Deeper feelings opened for me, and things I had never known about myself surfaced. "Nance, if it was up to me, I'd rub all their noses in the blood. See, Jimmy didn't kill those people. They killed themselves by what they did and what they didn't do. That's not all of it, either."

I clasped my hands and looked around at the faces. "I wonder how many of us own just a little piece of those executions."

Garoit shook his head. "No, man, I'm not taking on anyone's load of original sin. Sell that one someplace else."

"Pussyface, I can't figure out any way to stick it in the law, but I wonder how many times Vic and his two goons went on a pansy hunt, and everybody looked the other way. How many times've you laughed at one of those, you-mah-little-honey-now, Bubba-bungs-his-cellmate jokes?"

"It's not my job to keep the boybungers off the pansies," said Garoit. "That's why we hire cops."

I nodded. "In other words, it is our job but we hire somebody else to do it. Then we laugh at the rape-a-pansy jokes, keep our mouths shut when Vic or some other boybunger turns a human being into a piece of meat, and otherwise tell the cops we hired to forget about it." I spat on the sand.

"Risking a wounded or dead spectator and splashing their sheets with some blood, maybe that brings it home where it belongs just a little bit."

I felt sick to my stomach and tossed the remainder of the bar into my ration bag. "Anyway, that's how I feel about it. You want something different, make another law."

They were all quiet. I noticed the papers Herb had given me and pulled them out of my bag as I looked back at Nance. "Have you seen Alna?"

"No. Not since I left the trial."

I stood up and pulled the stick out of the sand. "Who do I owe for this?"

"I gave it to you, chup," answered Ondo. "You don't owe me."

"Thanks." I added the stick to my pack and shaded my head from the angry sun with my hood. I unrolled the papers Herb had given me and read the title: *Mob Cinderella* by H.O. I was surprised out of my depression. Herb Ollick was the author of *Mob Cinderella*. My picture of the man kept changing. I stuffed the papers back into my bag and went to join the others.

Once I was comfortably seated in the circle, I took a sip of that grim water, and let the vision of that meal in the Men's Hall pass through my mind as I swallowed.

The circle was silent and I looked around at the faces. "You all look like your pet rat died. What is it? What's going on?"

Nance nodded toward Sarah. "When they went scouting last night, they found something."

"Found what?" I looked at Bloody Sarah.

"When we were at the banquet, I noticed that most of the markings on the sheets were black, green, gold, white, and blue. Only three of the sheets I saw carried the mark of Padra Amitis's Loyal Reds. Thanks to Marantha's lead, we found them. They're about ten kilometers back toward the east. They have about two hundred rifles, and they're guarding something."

I wrapped my arms around my knees. "What are they guarding?"

Sarah looked at Minnie, and Minnie looked at me. "Prisoners," answered Minnie.

"They have women prisoners they captured from our ship. They don't look like they're holding any men. They have maybe four hundred women prisoner." Minnie glanced down for a moment. "I never knew there were so many lily-white haystack bits in the crowbars."

She looked up at me. "No maus, no chili peppers, no chops, no hows. Angel cakes, all of 'em."

I could see Minnie's cheek muscles twitch. "Man, they kept what they wanted and killed the rest."

Sarah spoke to Minnie. "Tell Bando how you know."

"I slipped in there and talked with them. They were taken the day after the landing." She waved a tiny hand in a graceful arc. "That's their pussy supply, Bando. When one of those phony goomba macho muthafuckers wants to rock off, he picks one and just does it. If the bit doesn't go along, the goomba beats her until she does go along. A lot of them don't survive the beating. Some who do survive don't look so good anymore, so they get thinned."

Minnie wiped the tears from her eyes with the back of her hand. "Bando, all of those women are from our ship. The Hand's own women, except for the few slaves in camp, are back in the Sunrise Mountains."

I rubbed my eyes as I tried to ignore the size and nearness of the crime. "So, among other things, we're facing a thousand rifles instead of eight hundred?"

Minnie leaned toward me. "Bando, those women are being raped and murdered."

I could see Bennet v. Myerson hovering above me like a great predatory bird. "And they asked us for help?"

"Yes."

"And we are the Razai. We don't stand by and do nothing

when someone is being raped. It's not right." I looked at Nance and the others.

"What have you yard eagles been discussing? What to do, or whether or not to do it?"

Garoit spoke. "It's terrible what they're doing, but the Hand has more than double the guns we have. We have to save ourselves." He held out his hands.

"Those prisoners aren't even in the Razai. They had the choice to join up back at the landing, and they chose another group. We don't owe them a thing." He let his hands drop between his knees. "We can't save the whole bloody world."

"Some revolutionary," I snorted and faced Sarah. "How about it? How do we stack up against the Hand?"

"They have us outgunned, but we have them outnumbered. With the two hundred guns they have guarding the women, their forces are split in two. That means we can bring a superior force against the two hundred rifles, equip another two hundred of our people with the captured weapons, and then we would have six hundred rifles against their eight hundred."

My mouth was dry. "What about our chances?"

"If you pray, remember to invoke your gods." She smiled and ended by saying, "It's possible that we could win a head-on fight, but I doubt it."

I looked at Stays. His lips were compressed into a narrow line. He looked down for a moment, then returned my gaze. "You said it first, Chief. We don't stand by and do nothing when someone cries rape. It's not right." He smiled and looked down. "After all, we just made that rule today."

I looked at Nance. "I just want to know. Is that rule worth the death of the whole Razai? The yard smarts would be to do what Garoit said. We can't save the world."

"Maybe. Maybe not." Nance folded her arms and let her head hang forward. "I'm thinking that we're not in the yard now." She smiled and looked up at Garoit. "And we'll never know about saving the world until we try."

Garoit faced her and held out his hands. "What if all we do is get wiped out? Remember, because of this stupid law against holding prisoners, Lacy Moore is over there right now filling Pau Avanti's ear with how many men and women we have, and how many guns we have. There's no surprise working for us, nothing. What about our right to live?"

Nance got to her feet, pushed back her hood, and scratched her scalp with both hands. After she fluffed up her hair, she placed her hands on her hips and looked toward the Hand's camp for a long time. When she was finished, she turned, looked down at Garoit, and asked, "Have you ever risked your life before?"

From Garoit's blush, I could see that Nance had tickled his macho. "Of course."

"That's right. You were a terrorist, weren't you?"

"Yes."

"When you risked your life, terrorist, was it always with a sure chance of winning and getting out alive?"

"No, but that was different. We weren't trying to conquer anyone; we were usually just making a statement."

"You mean you weren't out to overthrow a government or two?"

Garoit shook his head. "I'm not buying into this, Nance. Twist things around any way you want. The situations are different."

"Tell me, Garoit, you were willing to die for a statement?"

"Yes, but it was a statement of high principle. I was willing to die for the right of the people. I was willing to die for freedom."

Nance waved the front of her sheet in and out to circulate the air next to her body. "Maybe all we can do here is make a statement, Garoit. Maybe all we can do is die for that statement. Maybe it isn't high principle or sacred politics to you, but the statement goes like this: Every woman has the right not to be raped. Every *man* and woman has the right not to be raped. If all the Razai ever amounts to is to kill and die for that statement, my ghost'll be happy."

She looked around at the circle of faces. "I'm going to put it to the sharks, and if it goes my way, we are going to rock with the Hand." She faced Garoit. "We do have one big hunk of surprise left. The Razai is made up mostly of women, and the Hand knows that." Nance nodded. "But what is a woman? Macho-macho never did figure out that one."

As Nance spoke, I saw a vision. I cannot call it anything

less. As soon as Nance said that macho-macho remark, and that she was going to put the rescue to a vote, a complete plan dropped into my mind. It was so simple that it had to work. Or, if it didn't work, I could be certain of not living long enough to call myself a failure.

"Chief," said Stays, "I hear gears turning."

I nodded and looked up at Nance. "Either I've got a plan or I'm crazy." I looked at Stays. "Sort out all the angel cakes and anyone who can pass. With the water we brought back, get the cakes bathed and their hair washed. Their clothes, too. But just the angel cakes."

"What are you trying to do, start a race riot?"

"Nance'll explain everything when she puts it to the vote. Get 'em washed up, and find out if anyone has any perfume. And combs. Combs and brushes, and we need someone who knows about fixing hair."

"You won't believe this," said Martin Stays, "but Jim Bennet is a hairdresser."

"Great. Find out if he knows anyone else who does hairdressing. There's going to be a lot of hair to fix. And see if you can find Herb Ollick. I need to talk to him right away."

Stays glanced at Nance, Nance nodded back at him, and he moved off as I rubbed my chin and looked around at the faces. "Does anyone know how much sleep I've had?"

"Almost five hours," answered Nance.

"In that case," I said, "it must be a plan. I've had too much sleep to be crazy."

THE SECRET OF

GUIDO ABALONE

THE point, flank, and rear guards were called in, as well as Nazzar's newly organized mobile force. A few listeners were left out to raise the alarm in case of attack. It was a big risk, but Nance wanted as many in on this vote as was possible.

Stays had gotten the angel cake project moving in good order. Besides Jimmy, he had found one other man and six women who had experience hairdressing. While they tried to turn sand-and-sun-scoured straw piles into high fashion, others washed and dried the clothing, while still others attacked the clothing with razors and homemade cutters attempting to turn crowbar blues into playtime rompers.

A few lipsticks, compacts, and nail polishes were tracked down along with three bottles of perfume. Their brand names were: *I'm Yours*, *Enchantment*, and *Night Fever*. They all smelled the same to me.

There were four hundred and twenty-two angel cakes, and an additional fifty-seven who could pass, if the light wasn't too bright. By the time we had our town meeting, the chops, hows, chili peppers, and maus were a little microwaved, but once Nance explained the plan to everyone, however, tempers cooled.

Before she explained the plan, there was a security matter

that needed to be covered. The first thing Nance put to the vote was the Law of Silence. She told the assembled Razai that those who stayed to listen to what she had to say must be sworn to secrecy.

Everyone knew the word *omerta* and knew what it meant. Anyone who broke the law of silence and betrayed what she said would draw max payback on the spot. Anyone who could not keep the silence was told to leave the meeting before it started. There was plenty of looking around, but no one left.

Nance then told them about the women prisoners held by the Hand, what was happening to them, and that they had asked us for help. Nance wanted helping them put to the vote.

That was the day when why the witnesses were found guilty and thinned in Bennet *v.* Myerson was made our third law. What applied to us as individual members of the Razai applied to the Razai as a whole. If a crime is being committed, and the victim asks the Razai for help, the Razai must either help or be as guilty as the perp.

Garoit said his piece, and I could see his side of it. Every gang on Tartaros was probably committing crimes of some kind, and for each of those crimes there would be victims calling for help at some point. What was a tiny gang of two thousand that had only been in existence for a week supposed to do about the whole world?

However, at the moment, it wasn't the whole world we had to fight. It wasn't our tiny gang against all of the gangs of Tartaros. It was only this one spot in the Forever Sand, and it was the Razai against a small expedition from the Hand.

I've heard it a hundred times: In the pits you get to see the best of everything at its worst, and the worst of everything at its best. The sharks at that meeting were told everything, and there was a hot debate. The two cockroaches climbed into the argument with "Listen to me, I know what I'm talking about" attitudes, but they were on opposing sides, so there wasn't much point in listening to either of them.

The discussion continued, and fighting the Hand, which seemed probable, might mean the end of the Razai. We could all wind up dead or slaves. The chances of us coming out on top really chewed. Were we going to fight and maybe die for the right not to be raped and killed, or were we going to play it smart. In the end, Nance got her vote, and it was unanimous, including the cockroaches.

She then explained the plan and assigned parts and tasks to the members. Several of the professional street women in our bunch were either assigned parts or served as technical consultants. My part was to play a pimp and go in to the main camp with the angel cakes, each one polished, perfumed, painted, powdered, and puffed for the event. Each bit was armed with a point or an edge of some kind, razors, cutters, ice picks. For my own edge, Nance lent me her personal clandestine blade. It was a wicked-looking eight-inch blade with the point of a needle and the edges of a razor.

After much persuasion, Minnie McDavies got me down on the ground and gave me a shave. She shaved my face, which I guessed was a real stretch for Minnie. With a clean face and slicked down hair, I assumed my role as Don Guido Abalone's number one pimp 'n' sleaze, Fidel Midol.

The part of Don Guido, of course, went to Herb Ollick. In the play *Mob Cinderella*, Guido Abalone is the youthful suitor of Red Pete Argento's beautiful daughter, Maranta.

As the sun touched the horizon, the cooling shadows filled the valleys between the dunes. Soon it would be colder than ratbait in the black hole. When I thought about the coming cold of night, I wondered at the wisdom of my plan. It depended on the angel cakes looking sexy to macho goomba, which meant their outfits would be somewhat abbreviated. However, if all they were going to do was sniffle, chatter their teeth, and turn blue all over, maybe all they would do is turn off everybody.

I thought about it some, and I remembered vids of girls and women wearing those skimpy little skating outfits in subzero conditions on Earth. Then I remembered the hookers in Philly, the Apple, and up in the Combat Zone. The weather would be cold enough to geld every brass monkey in the northern hemisphere, and there would be the hookers on the sidewalks wearing high heels, short shorts, and a beauty spot. Then old Pepe Pimpo would come rolling up to collect his slice. He'd be wheeling a heated chrome machine with thermopane windows and be dressed in ear flaps and furs like Nanookie of the North.

There was something a bit once told me. She said that women have to be tougher than men just to survive. She said men only have to put up with women and other men. Women have to put up with how men treat women. She made her point.

I pondered these things and let go of them as Minnie finished shaving Herb. After his rinse, he stood before me with his hair oiled down, wearing a cut-down sheet tossed over his shoulders like a cape. It didn't matter what you did to Herb, he simply looked more and more like a loyal son of the Great Goomba. Shaved and caped he looked like Don Macho Di Capo himself.

He was Herb Ollick, petty con artist from Dayton, author of *Mob Cinderella*, holder of the Tartaros world supply of quartz rings. I remembered him asking about Marantha, and I asked him about the curious coincidence of how, back in the Crotch, the part of Maranta had been played by a woman named Marantha.

Herb smiled sadly and looked down. "The coincidence is even stranger than you think."

"How's that?"

"Did you know that *argento* is Italian for silver?"

"Maranta Argento *is* Marantha Silver? You mean—"

He nodded. "I've admired her ever since I saw the first of those stories about her on the vids. She is beautiful, of course, but courageous, too. And she has the integrity of a saint—an honest saint, of course."

"I understand."

"I watched every moment of those hearings, and watched as the MJs and the vid reporters and commentators shoveled mud on her, and she didn't flinch. Not once. She did her honest best, took the cards she was dealt, and played them without complaint. When she was condemned to Greenville, I thought up *Mob Cinderella* and wrote the part of Maranta Argento just for her. The saddest day of my life was when the stains told me that women would have to play all the male parts in *Cinderella*, which meant I was out. The happiest day of my life was when I found out that Marantha had tried out for the part."

I studied the overweight pseudo-mafioso. "Hell, Ice Fingers, you've got yourself a crush on a cop!"

He held out his hands and shrugged. "It seemed like a good idea at the time."

"Does she know? Have you told her?"

Herb shook his head and held his finger before his lips.

"*Omerta.*" He smiled that sad smile again, and asked, "Is she really all right, Bando?"

I frowned and spent a useless second or two checking my loaner blade from Nance. "I don't know, Herb. She's a hostage, except nobody's calling her a hostage. I figure she's safe until we either deliver the merchandise or Pau Avanti figures out what's going on."

"Is there much chance of that?"

"Herb, they've been two steps ahead of us since before we first ran into them." I placed my hand on his shoulder. "But as my little meditation book pointed out to me, don't waste time thinking about what might be or what might have been. Live in the present moment. Right now you are Don Guido Abalone on his way to see his true love, Maranta Argento, and I am Fidel Midol, your trusty pimp."

"What are you doing with a meditation book?"

"It was a gift from Big Dave Cole."

"You know, Bando, back in the Crotch my first cellmate used to meditate a lot. He'd sit cross-legged on the top bunk, close his eyes, and be like that for hours at a stretch. It used to spook me at first, but he was quiet, and it gave me plenty of time for reading. He also had some good things to teach me about serenity and acquiring peace of mind." Herb looked at the sun, a third of it now behind the western edge.

"One time he was meditating right after evening chow, and was still at it when I went to sleep. When I woke up the next morning, he was still meditating, and when I tried to snap him out of it so he could eat breakfast, I found he was dead. He was only twenty-two years old."

"Gee, Herb, thanks for sharing that. Got any more little up messages before we climb into the lion's mouth?"

"Sorry. I didn't mean to bring you down. He just popped into my head for some reason."

Herb looked at where Minnie had Garoit down on the sand, shaving off his beard. "I wonder what Pussyface will look like without his beard. I guess it can't be helped." He looked back at me.

"I, Don Guido Abalone, can't have my *consigliori* looking like an Old Testament prophet, can I?" He laughed a little. As his laughter faded, his face became very serious. He thought for a moment and frowned as he said, "This might be it."

"This might be what?" I asked.

"You, me, Garoit, Marantha, all of us. We all might be dead by this time tomorrow."

"Don Guido, that's true for everyone in the universe. What's also true is that, this time tomorrow, any or all of us might still be alive." I scratched the back of my neck for a moment because there was something about Herb Ollick that puzzled me.

"Herb, you're in love with a Jew cop, you're working closely with all kinds of maus and other types right now, and you just don't seem to be the type who'd sling around the 'N' word or pull a cutter on someone without a good reason. What was with you and Mojo Tenbene?"

"Bando, you've seen me. I'm not a very muscular fellow. However, I do have an imagination. When I was sent to the Crotch, there was no way that I could keep myself from getting bullied and boybunged by force. So I used my imagination. With a little hint here, a knowing nod there, I conned the whole Crotch into thinking I was connected. As long as they thought I was connected, they left me alone."

He shook his head and grimaced. "I'd been playing the role of a mobster for so long, I guess I lost myself in the part. I just got carried away."

"That's some dangerous role-playing. You're real lucky that I came up with the victim performing his own payback when I did."

"Yes." His eyebrows went up as he expressed a chilling thought. "Do you think it might happen to me again as Don Guido? Do you think I could lose myself in the part?"

I stared at him for a few seconds. "Just keep in mind what we're trying to do. We want the prisoners, we want to stay alive, and if there is any kind of a fight, we want the Razai to come out on top. As long as that's what Don Guido Abalone wants, I don't care if you lose yourself in the part or not."

Herb frowned as a thought seemed to darken the doorway of his mind. "Bando, what are you going to do about afterward?"

"About what?"

"You haven't thought about it yet?"

"Thought about what?"

Don Guido Abalone pointed a quartz-encrusted finger toward the Hand. "You've got hundreds—maybe thousands—of rape and murder cases to deal with out there. What're you going to do about them?"

What he had said was true. And what was I ever going to do about them? I rubbed my eyes and shook my head in despair. Right then the best-sounding answer I could think of centered around either surrendering to Pau Avanti or wiping out the entire Hand.

"Bando!"

I could hear Marietta's voice calling me, and I hoped it wasn't any more trouble. Just what I needed right then was another trial. That was when it got through to me that I wasn't the only RC in the Razai. Stays, Cap, Marietta, Marantha, they could all act as investigators. In fact, right now I could tell Marietta to run her own trial.

"Bando!" she repeated.

"Over here!"

She came around a dune and as soon as she saw me, she frowned. She nodded at Herb and came to a stop in front of me. "I've been lookin' all over for you."

"So, you found me."

She shook her head. "I don't know any other way but to let you have it right between the eyes. I found Alna—"

"Where? Is she dead?"

"No, she's alive. I found her tracks going back the way we came. I chased her down and talked to her. She's lookin' for Nkuma and his bunch."

"Why? Because I let Abe Lyles say his piece?"

Marietta shrugged as she nodded. "Maybe that. Mostly I think she misses her friends. Bein' lonely can make you do strange things."

"Lonely? She has me, doesn't she?"

Marietta looked at me in silence as she waited for me to answer my own question. It was true. She didn't have me. No one had me. I hadn't been available for anyone since before I could remember. I couldn't allow myself to get too close to anyone because if they don't get close, they can't hurt you. The thing that was screaming at me right then was, if I hadn't allowed Alna to get close to me, why did her trying to leave hurt so damned much?

"Well, where is she? I want to talk to her."

"She's still headin' for Nkuma and the mirage."

I was stunned. "Why didn't you stop her?"

"Rule number two, Chief. She's got the right to go wherever she wants."

"What? To kill herself?" I demanded.

Marietta placed her hand on my shoulder. "We all got that right, Chief."

Stays came around a dune leading a party of twelve scantily clad angel cakes. They were made up, and looked beautiful. They wore their sheets pulled up in front and thrown back over their shoulders. Their cut-down trousers were very short shorts and what was left of their shirts was hardly enough to qualify for a brassiere. If you concentrated on it, the only thing that looked silly was that they were still wearing their crowbar issue boots. It took me several looks before I recognized Bloody Sarah. She was perfection, and her image all but wiped out those memories of her ripping out the throats of those Suryian villagers.

I closed my eyes, feeling guilty as how I felt about Alna collided with how I felt about what I was seeing. Seconds after hearing my true love had taken off into the dunes, my tongue was in the sand panting after the angel cakes.

No wonder Alna had left. She must've known about the rub-down bath in the Men's Hall. Maybe she didn't know, but could see inside of me and saw that I had the morals of a goat, and not half the good taste. Maybe it was because Alna couldn't see inside of me because I was afraid to let her know me.

"The rest of them should be finished soon." Stays looked like he was presenting his first big school project as he faced me with a big grin.

"What?"

Stays waved toward the angel cakes. "What do you think, Chief?"

"Good," I answered. "They should do fine." I turned away as tears seemed to catch in my throat. Marietta squeezed my shoulder again and whispered in my ear.

"You can't fix everything and everybody, Pancho. You're

only a man. But right now you're an RC and you can't take out time for a broke heart. You got things to do."

"Fidel?" called Herb as Marietta removed her hand from my shoulder.

"What?"

"What did you answer?" demanded Don Guido Abalone in an angry voice.

I wrestled down my temper. It was true. There were too many important things that needed doing to waste time on blind rage. Besides, as they showed me at the CSA meeting, rage never did anything for me except get me in trouble. I still hadn't learned what to do with the rage I had bottled up in me. Maybe I needed to focus my rage on something, the annihilation of which would serve the cause.

I bowed and said, "Forgive me, Don Guido. How may I serve you?"

Don Guido held out his hand toward the angel cakes. "The girls are almost ready and I don't want us to be late for the party."

"Yes, Don Guido." I turned away and called, "Ondo!"

In a moment Ondo Suth and Nance led three lughoxen to where we stood. The critters had been brushed, their horns polished, and their hair braided and ribboned. On the back of one of the animals was the rat-faced glower of Don Guido's *consigliori*, Salvatore Capon, alias Darrell Garoit.

"Here are our steeds, Godfather," I announced.

"Excellent. Excellent."

Don Guido mounted the steed next to Salvatore's, and I mounted the remaining animal. Stays walked over and stopped next to my lugh. He held up some papers to me.

"Take care, Chief, and here's your additions to the *Law of the Razai*."

"Who is making all the copies?"

"Ila Toussant."

"She's very handy."

Stays laughed, but said with sincerity, "She's a gift from the gods. Again, take care."

"I'll do my best. By the way, here's something to think about that Herb mentioned." I stuffed the papers in my copy of the *Law*, and nodded toward the Hand camp.

"If the Razai still exists after all this is over, we've got a lot of rape and murder charges we're going to have to handle."

"Great Mother Crowbar," said Stays, putting a hand to his head. "I see what you mean."

"Here's something else to think about. I'm not the only investigator in the RC. Get my drift?"

"You want us to run trial investigations too?"

"You got it."

Stays rubbed his chin. "I don't know."

"Are you scared?"

"No, it's not that." He grinned. "Well, it is that, but there's something else, too."

"What is it?"

Stays looked up at me. "With the investigations going on at the same time, independent from each other, with the way we make up the rules as we go along, separate investigations might come up with conflicting rules."

"So figure out some way to take care of it. Like I said, if we're alive after this, we're going to have a lot of cases to process." I reached out my arm and patted his shoulder.

"I'll be as careful as I can."

Stays reached beneath his sheet and took something from an inside pocket. He held up his arm and handed it to me. "Here. I made you something."

I took it from his fingers and turned it over in my hand. It was a silver-colored five-pointed star with the words: "Chief— Razai Police" carved into its center. On the other side, the top point of the star had been shaped into a needle and bent back so that the star could be pinned on. I bounced it in my hand. "You really have a lot of idle time on your hands, don't you?"

"Do you like it?"

I reached under my sheet and stuck it inside my shirt pocket. "What'd you make it out of?"

"I cut it out of the lid of one of those personal belongings boxes. Do you like it?"

"Yeah. Make one for yourself, and make 'em for the rest of the RC. Maybe it'll be a good joke on Nance, if we live long enough."

Stays moved back, and as more girls arrived, Nance looked

them over and nodded her approval. Finally she examined Don Guido, Salvatore, and me as the last of the girls assembled.

"I have to admit," she said to Don Guido, "you are beautiful, you macho goomba thing you." She mouthed the words "You too" at Garoit. Salvatore Capon blushed.

Nance climbed halfway up the side of a dune so she could see all of us. "All of you look really..." She grinned and shook her head. "All of you look really silly."

Everyone laughed, and Nance held out her hands for quiet. "Keep it down!" When it was quiet enough for her to be heard, Nance continued. "Okay, now you know how to turn on macho man: Puff up your glands, dress like a little girl, paint up like a Commanche, make yourself smell like a drugstore, act stupid, and tell him you're a virgin."

They laughed again, and in a way I felt like they were laughing at me. In a way they were laughing at me.

Nance's voice became serious. "You all know the ready signal and the do it signal. We're counting on you to tie up and take out at least half of their force in the main camp." She was silent for a long time. "I'm counting on you to do your jobs without getting killed yourselves."

She looked us over one more time and said, "The rest of the army is in position." She smiled at me and looked at Don Guido.

"So go break a leg. Go break a lot of legs."

Don Guido saluted in farewell and urged his mount forward. Salvatore Capon rode beside him, and I headed the train of beautiful women, dividing my thoughts between what I had to do and wondering where Alna was and how she was doing alone in the desert.

THE SHORT BUT HAPPY

LIFE OF *EL FUGITIVO*

THE angel cakes were held under close guard by at least two hundred rifles while, in the palace tent, Pau Avanti and Don Guido tied up a few loose ends.

"Don Guido," said Pau Avanti from his throne, "there are several things I do not understand. I hope you can clarify them."

From his chair facing the prince, Don Guido waved his hand in a careless gesture. "I will try my best, Don Pau." We could all see how Pau Avanti preened at the use of the "Don" before his name.

"Very well. First, what was this business last night?"

"Business?"

Pau Avanti nodded. "Yes. The big woman, Damas, who bossed your gang. The poorly dressed attendants she had."

Standing behind the don's chair, Salvatore Capon was looking very nervous. For a brief moment I thought Nance's choice of Garoit for the part of Salvatore had been foolish, but the more I thought about it, the better the choice seemed. A *consigliori* standing in the center of an enemy's camp, his don's life in his hands, should be nervous.

Guido Abalone shrugged and held out his hands. "You cannot blame me, Don Pau, for being cautious. We knew nothing of you." He smiled knowingly.

"I mean to give no offense, but so many of the gangs are headed by maus or chili peppers. We even heard of a gang of chops. It is not wise to take chances."

"That is true," said Pau Avanti.

"It is good that you understand. You will understand as well, then, why we could not reveal the true nature of the Razai until we could satisfy ourselves that you were genuine. Hence, we could not trust you completely until the daughter of Red Pete Argento said that our two families could meet together in trust and mutual respect."

"Is that what that mysterious thing she said—that 'Ease army Rome' something—meant?"

"Of course."

Don Guido raised an eyebrow as he looked around the tent. "I trust Maranta is well?"

"Very well. She is getting dressed for the party, always providing that there is to be a party." From the tone of Pau's voice, it was clear that we were selling, but that the prince wasn't buying.

"I certainly hope there is no shadow between us to spoil the party." Don Guido waved his hand. "After all, we have gone to considerable expense to prepare for it. I have brought my best girls."

"In any case, Don Guido, Maranta is late." He held out a hand. "You know how women are."

"Yes, of course," answered Don Guido.

I was grateful that no one looked at me right then. Either I would have laughed or fled from the tent. Neither course would have aided our cause in the slightest.

There was a slight commotion at the rear of the tent, and I turned to see Marantha Silver, clad in a filmy macho glandthumper if I ever saw one. The prince held out his hand. "Ah, there she is now. Isn't she lovely?"

Don Guido stood, turned, and bowed until Marantha was seated on the cushions at Pau Avanti's feet. She looked surprised for an instant, then a light of understanding filled her eyes. She smiled warmly and said, "Don Guido, I am honored."

"Maranta." Herb passed off the comment like it was only to be expected and resumed his seat. Two things teased at my mind right then. First, I was wondering how Herb was keeping off his heart attack, because Maranta Argento was some lovely picture right then. The other thing was, how did Marantha know that Herb was playing the part of Don Guido? All I could figure was that Minnie McDavies had snuck in to the Hand camp to clue Marantha, but Minnie was supposed to be on her way east to sit on top of the prisoners until we finished at the main camp.

Pau Avanti placed his fingertips together as he turned from Marantha and studied Herb Ollick. "As I am to understand it, Don Guido, you are the boss of the Razai gang?"

Don Guido winced as he held up his hand. "Please, Don Pau. I am the head of the Razai family. We don't use words such as 'boss' and 'gang' because of the press. You understand."

"Press? What press?"

"Of course, of course," said Guido Abalone as he laughed. "But it is the tradition that is important, is it not?"

"I don't see."

Don Guido held out his hands and turned down the corners of his mouth. "So we are in the middle of a desert on a primitive planet. Big deal. The family has seen lean times before, has seen troubled times before."

He pointed his jeweled finger up into the air. "Always we maintained our traditions. *Omerta*, the oath of initiation, making your bones, everything wrapped in Valachi papers, *comprende lei?* You see that, don't you?"

"Yes. Of course." The prince's brow was heavy with furrow. He didn't look like he understood much. I certainly hoped that the one thing he did understand wasn't that he was getting his leg pulled.

Don Guido nodded. "Perhaps someday my family will find itself on another planet that has vids, reporters, and other forms of mass communication. Perhaps one day the press might come to Tartaros to see how we are all doing here, living off of the Union's terrible charity."

He intertwined his fingers and raised his eyebrows. "Perhaps one day Tartaros itself will even develop its own news media." He waved his hand back and forth.

"Whatever happens, if our traditions have been maintained,

we will be prepared. This is how it has been since the days of the Romans. Always the family must be protected."

"I understand, Don Guido."

"I was certain you would, Don Pau."

The prince nodded slowly and looked as though he were pretending to have difficulty saying something that might risk being regarded as disrespectful.

"With respect, Don Guido, what if I suggested that you have no legions out on the dunes? What if I said you only have four or five hundred captured weapons and a lot of weak, starving women? What would you say then?"

Don Guido flashed his phony diamonds as he grinned, and I swore that either Herb Ollick was the world's greatest con man, or he had completely lost himself in the part of Guido Abalone. "One thing I would say, Don Pau, is that perhaps you need your contacts cleaned. I think you might want to let your eyes caress the angel cakes I brought with me one more time before you conclude that they are starving."

Herb rolled his eyes a bit to the laughter in the tent, then waved his hand at the prince. "Please finish your thought, Don Pau."

"Very well, I will." Pau Avanti leaned forward, his elbows on his throne's armrests. He pointed a finger at Don Guido.

"You do not look strong enough or ruthless enough to be a don. What if I said that you are a nobody? What if I said your gang is bossed by that big bull croc lesbian chili pepper who was here last night with her little mau razor Minnie? What if I said I think I can attack the Razai right now, capture your women, and put the rest of you to death? What would you say to that?"

I could see Garoit sweating, and I knew I was, but Don Guido began laughing. When he was finished laughing, he leaned back in his chair, dried his eyes, crossed his legs, and said, "In answer to your questions, I would say that I think you have been listening to Lacy Moore."

"It's no crime," said the prince.

"No," agreed Don Guido, "but believing him could be very foolish, and quite hazardous to your health."

"Foolish? Foolish how?"

"Don Pau, did Lacy Moore also tell you that he is under a sentence of death by the Razai?"

The prince shrugged. "I assumed as much, since he had broken your law of silence."

"Since he has told you nothing but lies, Don Pau, he has not violated *omerta*."

"So?"

Don Guido paused, a mischievous smile spread across his face, and he asked, "Have you ever seen a man with painted lips, Don Pau?"

The prince's face grew dark with anger. "Explain yourself!"

Don Guido nodded and drummed his fingers on his knee. "I take it Lacy Moore hasn't told you that he is under sentence of death for trying to make love to a boy."

There was a gasp in the tent, and Don Guido inspected his fingernails and buffed off an imaginary smudge. "He and two other strange ones tried to force themselves upon a boy. The other two have already been executed." He shook his head at the evils of the universe.

"Of course, Don Pau, I have no idea how the Hand stands on this particular issue. I assume you all to be men, but I have noticed very few women in your camp."

Don Guido raised his eyebrows, nodded, and continued with a shake of his finger, "*Very* few women. Perhaps where you come from the brotherhood has adopted new ways—modernized. Among you it may even be called the brother and sisterhood—or, perhaps, the personhood?"

Herb chuckled merrily at his little joke. The silence in the palace tent could have consumed an exploding star.

"Perhaps Lacy Moore's evil," continued Don Guido, "is only considered a mere peccadillo, or even simple sexual preference, in the Hand—"

"No!" shouted Pau Avanti as he stood abruptly. "Make no more of these slurs upon the honorable name of the Hand, Don Guido!" He lifted his hand and snapped his fingers. "Bring Moore to me! Bring him to me *now!*"

Atan Voam, Don Pau's *consiggalorry*, ran from the prince's presence. Pau Avanti glared down at Don Guido. "You walk the thin ice, my friend. We are all *real* men here, and I, Pau Avanti, do not take kindly to your snide comments."

"I meant no disrespect, Don Pau. I had assumed you all to be real men. That was why I was confused by this reliance you seem to have placed on the words of the deviate Lacy Moore." Don Guido hung a limp wrist and let it flop. "I mean, my good friend, the name Lacy says it all, doesn't it?"

Don Guido held out his hands and looked around the room. "Lacy? *Lacy?* Makes you just a little sick to the stomach, eh?" Don Guido said this with a smile still upon his lips. At that point I was willing to wager, just before they shot us, Herb Ollick would take a bow.

Lacy Moore came into the room flanked by six soldiers of the Mighty Blacks. The procession stopped before Pau Avanti. Lacy looked nervously at us, then faced the prince. "What is it? Did they say I was a liar? I told you they'd say I was a liar."

"No." Pau Avanti pursed his lips and clasped his hands in front of him. "There is something else that has been said, and I want to know if it is true. This is important, so listen carefully. They say that you are under a sentence of death." He nailed Lacy with a down-home, East River, dead-fish stare.

"Lacy Moore, they say that you are the kind of man who makes do with boys. Are you?"

Lacy's face flushed bright scarlet and the prince looked away, ashamed. "You have answered my question."

"Wait, I—"

"You have answered my question!"

Pau Avanti nodded toward Herb. "My sincerest apologies to you and to the Razai. May this Lacy Moore meet the same fate as his two strange accomplices. He is yours, Don Guido, and—"

"*Don Guido!*" Lacy shouted. "Just a second, Pau Avanti. You've got this all wrong!" Lacy turned toward Herb. "There's a play. It's called *Mob C*—"

Herb Ollick leaped to his feet, reached into his sleeve, and before anyone could see what was happening, the handle of a cutter was sticking out of the left-center of Lacy's chest. The man looked down at the handle, wide-eyed, almost as though he didn't believe his own senses. He opened his mouth, but no sound emerged.

"Lacy," said Don Guido as cool as Jackson on Pluto, "that's a little payback from Jim Bennet." Then Herb blew Lacy a kiss.

Lacy clutched one hand to his chest and reached the other out toward Don Guido. The big man fell on his face, his hand still outstretched. He twitched for a bit as Don Guido stepped over him.

"Don Pau," he called over his shoulder, "I apologize for the stains on your carpet. I think we may begin the party now, don't you?"

"Quite," answered the prince. Pau Avanti faced Atan Voam. "Have this mess cleaned up." He turned back to Don Guido. "And you will please ignore my unthinking remark about not being ruthless enough to boss a gang."

"Of course." Don Guido bowed, held out his elbow toward Marantha Silver and said, "May I escort you to the tarantella, Maranta?"

She blushed and averted her eyes as she took Herb's arm. "Oh, Don Guido, I would love to."

Herb glanced at me and pointed at Lacy's still-warm corpse. "Fidel, be a good fellow and get my knife, will you?"

"Yes, Don Guido," I croaked. I watched the happy couple leave the tent arm in arm followed by a less than pleased Pau Avanti. It was time to party.

BOOGIE 'TIL YOU DIE

THE sounds from the all-Sicilian mariachi jug band reached levels of enthusiasm not even imagined the night before. Suspicions dampened things at the start, but between Don Guido's assurances and the picture of the angel cakes, Don Pau and his commanders must have decided that they didn't have to trust us as long as they guarded us very closely.

I didn't think the plan would work at first. The double number of guards surrounding us held their weapons at the ready, and kept their eyes on the dunes surrounding the camp. As the curiously Latin rhythms of the jug band filled the wide area between the dunes, however, the laughter and cheers filled the night air. Bit by bit the attention of the guards was drawn to the hundreds of dancing couples.

Despite the frosty air, the women had taken off their sheets to dance, and most of them were dancing barefoot as well. As the air got colder, the more animated they became, and the more green with envy became the guards and reserve soldiers. Don Guido was dancing with Maranta, and Pau Avanti's attention never wavered an inch from her the entire time, which was the point.

The plan had been a simple one based upon an awareness of a few of my own character defects. Thanks to Big Dave, CSA, and a lot of reading, I understood macho man very well. Take one insecure male who is terrified of women, teach him to compensate by treating women like pieces of meat, and you have created a curious kind of addict.

I made a mental note to remember that should I ever live long enough to make it back to another CSA meeting.

Anyway, to keep down his fear of women, the more women macho man must have. Of course, the more women macho man has, the more he is frightened of them.

This isn't how macho man sees, feels, or thinks, however. Macho man sees other men as threats and sees women as either spare mules or possible sexual partners. Macho man feels nothing except terror and deprivation, which he frequently interprets as horniness. Macho man thinks with his dick.

I knew all that, and I knew that there was a big slice of macho man left in me. I watched the angel cakes dance, and there is something about a woman's buns the sight of which ought to be listed as a controlled drug. I can watch them move and bounce around for just so long, then I feel compelled to leap out there and sink my teeth into some young thing's bottom—

—or, at least, that's the way I used to think before I became enlightened and got better.

The primary motivating force behind macho man is not sex. It is envy. Right then I felt envy. If I felt deprived, I could just imagine what the guards and the soldiers on reserve were feeling.

I tore my gaze away from the beautiful bouncing bottoms and began checking out the guard. We couldn't be lucky enough to have nothing but macho types carrying the weapons. There had to be a few dedicated types who actually were standing guard, but I couldn't find them.

At the edge of the dancing area, there were couples on spread sheets who were doing some numbers. I listened as one woman cooed in her macho man's ear.

"Not just yet, honey. We don't want to end the night just yet, do we? Be patient. Take it easy." All of the time she was saying those things, she was kissing the guy's ear and stroking his scrotum. The steam was practically shrieking out of his ears.

There was a pause in the music. Every girl had the physical

attention of one or two soldiers from the Hand, and close observations of the guards and reserves. I found Bloody Sarah lying
on a sheet, looking in my direction. The Hand commander of
the Loyal Reds, Padra Amatis, was up to his ears in her breasts.
I nodded at her, and she bent over and whispered something to
Padra. He pulled out his face, took a few gulps of air, and
shouted toward the band, "Play 'My Old Kentucky Home'!"

As the uppermost edges of the dunes surrounding us seemed
to undulate with the passage of mysterious dark shapes, each
one of the women whispered at her partner, filling his ear with
the provisions of the first law of the Razai. Along with the
whisper there was a sharp instrument that had been positioned
in a tender place. The members of the Hand were being given
the choice to either join, or die.

The strains of the ancient song filled the night as the women
whispered and the dark shapes slithered down the faces of the
dunes toward the guards. I positioned myself next to Atan
Voam while Garoit stood behind Pau Avanti. On the first note of
the repeat, I threw my arm around Atan's throat, held the point
of my cutter against his jugular vein, and hissed in his ear, "Join
the Razai or die! Choose!"

"No! I—"

I plunged in my blade and let him fall. As Pau Avanti
slumped back with an ice pick thrust into his temple, I assumed
that Garoit's selling job had been no more successful than my
own. I went for the guards who were at Garoit's back. One of
them tried to bring up a rifle. I blocked the rifle with my arm
and shoved my knife into his chest. His scream joined the
hundreds that tore at the night air.

I picked up his weapon and began shooting as the Razai
surrounding the perimeter killed the guards and rushed in
against the reserves, who immediately began scrambling for
their weapons. Before they got to them, two of the angel cakes
playing grope-grope in the shadow of the tents thinned their
escorts and ran along the rifle stacks, knocking them over into a
tangle of weapons.

A rifle went off next to my ear, I could feel my hair being
blown to the other side of my head, and I turned to my right to
see Galvin O'Goomba fighting with a jammed weapon.

"Galvin," I shouted, "don't be a fool! Join us and stay alive!"

"There's only two thousand of you," he said as he lifted his rifle for another try. "In the mountains the Hand has over half a million mounted warriors!"

I fired at his chest, drilling him through the heart. After he buried his face in the sand I said, "You did the smart thing, Galvin. There's no doubt about that." I knew a little about Galvin O'Goomba, and I would have liked to have spent some time over his cooling corpse, but there was no time.

I saw Marietta with Rhome Nazzar's group as they charged into the center of the Hand's reserve force. She had one goomba by the throat and a second by his hair. I saw Mano Leaf, commander of the Golds, catch a familiar hatchet in his back as the living stepped over Padra Amitis's blood-drained body. I couldn't find Sarah anywhere, but I knew the white slice would be out there thinning the crop.

Ow Dao and his troops put down a base of fire against the eastern guards, and Mig Rojas and his gang burst through and crumbled that half of the camp.

Perhaps only a hundred and fifty men of the Hand managed to get to their weapons, load them, and form into a defensive circle under the command of Dagi Preit of the Mighty Blacks. Nance called to them and read them the first law while the Hand's weapons and ammo was distributed among the Razai. To a man, the macho goomba remains refused to join. It took less than a minute of firing to silence their weapons. In minutes the dead were stripped of their weapons, ammo, and clothes.

I stopped to take a breath and look around. At the place of honor, Marantha was bandaging up Don Guido's arm and giving him all kinds of teary kisses. I felt a stab of that envy, and it confused me. I shook it out of my head and looked around.

In the center of the dance area I could see that at least two-thirds of the Hand's men had come up with the wrong answer when they were quizzed about joining the Razai. There were several dead women among them. I moved among the dead, feeling guilty because I didn't know the names of the dead Razai.

Then I saw one I knew, and I took a sheet to her side. I held the sheet as I knelt down on the sand and looked at Seraphine

Clay, the D.C. Chopper, one of the Nazzar's ten best. I would've thought that she was too old to bounce buns with the num-nums, but she was looking good. She had pushed an ice pick into the eye of her partner, but someone had gotten to her from behind.

I saw droplets of water splash on her bare middle and realized that I was crying. I removed her hand from the ice pick, arranged her arms, and covered her with a sheet. I felt a hand on my shoulder and looked behind me. Marietta was standing there and Nance was behind her.

"It worked, Bando," said Nance, "but it's not over. We still have to convince the Loyal Reds in the east camp who are back there guarding the women that it's over. We have over a thousand rifles now. That'll make convincing them a lot easier."

Marietta squeezed my shoulder. "There's plenty time for tears after the battle, Chief."

"What about Stays, Marantha, and Cap?"

"Stays got his scalp creased, but other'n that the RCs are fine. What about you?"

I looked back down at Seraphine. "Did you know the Chopper knew astronomy?" I lowered the sheet on Seraphine's face and turned toward Nance. "When we have the place surrounded, let me go in to talk to the Reds."

"That wasn't the plan. I'm supposed to read them the first law."

"So I'm making a new plan." I dried my face with my palms. "Let me do it, Nance. Please."

Bloody Sarah, her playtime rompers soaked with someone else's blood, walked up to us as she pulled on a parka and a sheet against the cold. "Nance, it's Garoit. He's been hurt. Jane Sheene did what she could, but she says he won't make it."

Sarah had something in her hand. She lifted her arm and held it toward me. It was a book. As soon as I touched the cover, I recognized Southey's *Life of Nelson*.

A CANDLE FOR
PUSSYFACE

WHILE they gathered up and assigned the weapons, and collected tents, sleds, animals, and anything else that wasn't on fire, I knelt next to Darrell Garoit. Nance was seated on the sand and Garoit's head was resting on her lap. His belly was all bandaged up, but the bandages hadn't slowed the bleeding down at all.

Nance brushed the sand from Garoit's face and smoothed his hair back from his forehead. I held his hand, and he squeezed back with more strength than I thought he had.

"Bando, you remember the ship?"

"I remember."

"Remember me saying how I was going to run things, take over, make a new world?"

"Yeah."

"You must've thought I was incredibly stupid—" He tensed with the pain and sweat broke out on his face. "God, I feel sick." He looked up at me.

"I feel so bloody useless, like I'm a mistake—some grotesque kind of joke God played on the universe. There's nothing I ever did right. Nothing that ever worked out. I failed on Earth,

I failed here. I couldn't even thin Pau Avanti without getting my guts ripped out."

He closed his eyes then opened them. He looked up at the belly of the Spider. "Bando, I always aimed so high and every time missed the mark so wide I kept shooting myself in the foot. I'm going to die, Bando, right here in the middle of a wasteland on a planet that's a human garbage dump. I'm going to die, and I don't have a single candle to bring with me. I don't have anything to show but a worthless heap of good intentions."

I squeezed his hand back. "Listen, Pussyface, if it wasn't for you, there wouldn't be any Razai."

"Play it in Paducah."

"I mean it. We're not a gang run by whoever's the toughest or meanest. We're not a gang at all, we're a democracy. When it came time to change leaders or policy, it was you who said, 'We vote on it.' The big fist doesn't command here. You put the people in charge of the Razai. That's why we're going to go and rescue those women instead of raping them ourselves. You did that—"

His hand was still. There was no strength left in it. I held his hand for a few moments more, then placed his arm at his side and looked at his face.

"He heard you," said Nance. "I'm sure he heard you."

I looked at her and there were tears in her eyes. "Damn you, Pussyface," she said. "Damn you for leaving me alone."

I stood up and turned away. It wasn't something for me to see or hear. After a few moments I heard Nance stand up. I turned around and Garoit was covered with a sheet. Nance picked up her rifle and handed me one.

"Okay, chili pepper. Right now I'm all the Razai has for a boss. You go in and talk to the Reds. If you can talk them out of a fight, I suppose that would be okay. To tell you the honest truth, though, I feel like butchering the lot."

I checked the load on the rifle she gave me, and nodded. "Let's go." We found the column, a thousand rifles strong, and joined it.

LOVE LETTERS

IN THE SAND

As we marched through the night, I thought of Alna. I felt I should go and chase her down, but I was heading in the wrong direction for that. My head was filled with what ifs. What if she was already dead? What if when she catches up with Nkuma she doesn't want me anymore? But why worry about that, I thought to myself, when the Reds might thin me on the spot?

I had the same sickness that had filled me after the first battle. It was a peculiar bone in my body that kept saying someday the killing has got to stop. But it was all confused with hurting over Alna, hurting over Garoit and the Chopper. I didn't know who else had been killed, and right then I didn't want to know.

I saw Marantha, now wearing a sheet. Her rifle was slung and she was walking a little farther back in the column. I slowed until I was walking next to her. "How's Herb?" I asked.

She looked puzzled for a moment, then laughed. "You mean Don Guido?"

"Yes."

"His name is Herb?"

"You remember him. Herb Ollick from *Tenbene v. Ollick*?"

"No kidding?" She held her hand to her head. "Of course!

H.O. Herb Ollick. He wrote *Mob Cinderella*." Marantha shook her head.

"I never recognized him. Brother Crowbar, does that ever explain a lot of things." She glanced at me. "He's okay. He took a round through his upper arm, but it didn't break the bone." Her lips pulled into a grin. "He did quite a job as Don Guido, didn't he?"

"Yes, he did. Tell me, how did you know he was playing the part of Don Guido? Did Minnie fill you in?"

Marantha laughed and shook her head. "No. No one told me. No one had to tell me."

"Then how did you know?"

"Did you ever get a love letter, Bando?"

"Love letter? No. I never got a love letter."

"I did. It was in the form of a prison play called *Mob Cinderella*. It was my fourth month in the Crotch and one of the stains hand-delivered a copy of the script to my cell. On the cover was written Nance Damas's name in case I wanted to try out for one of the parts in the play."

She shrugged her shoulders and looked down. "I was in Hell right then. I don't know how you feel about what happened to me—"

"Everyone inside the crowbars knew you weren't guilty, Marantha."

"Thanks. Thanks for that, Bando." She brought her head up. "So I was almost dissolved in self-pity when the script was delivered. I started reading it, and I wasn't two pages into the thing when I realized that Maranta Argento was me, and that *Mob Cinderella* was a love letter to me." She smiled.

"How did you figure it out? Do you speak Italian?"

"No, but *argentum* is Latin for silver. So Maranta Argento, Marantha Silver—"

"You speak Latin?"

"A little. I needed it for my law degree."

I stopped dead in the sand and pulled her to a stop next to me. "You're a cockroach?"

"I never practiced law, Bando. I needed the degree to become an agent in the MJ." She began walking again and I fell in beside her. "So Maranta Argento fell in love with Guido Abalone a long time ago. That's how I knew who he was. No one else could look or act like that." She glanced at me. "So, Guido Abalone is Herb Ollick?"

"Yes."

"He isn't connected at all, is he?"

"He's an illusionist from Dayton, Ohio."

"He's also very brave, and very much in love with me." She thought for a second and nodded. "I am very much in love with him." She grinned as she turned toward me. "Give us your blessing, Chief?"

I nodded and increased the length of my stride. "I have to get up at the head of the column." I left her behind in the dark.

Love. The word was an accusation, a curse.

Where was I about Alna? Why should I give a damn? Why was Bando Nicos crippled inside because some little mau bit took off into the night?

If there's one thing the Razai had plenty of, it was women, and all shades, too. Some of them were chili peppers and spoke the brown sugar. So who cared if Alna took off? Who needed her? Who cared if a couple of haystacks—a terrorist and a hatchet-killer—thinned out? I got along my whole life without Seraphine Clay and Darrell Garoit. I could again.

So a Jew cop gets a love letter from some fat bastard who can't tell if he's in the real world or flying through dreamland. Why should Bando Nicos get all teary-eyed about that, or about anything else?

What was it that guard had said to me on the way out the hatch? Something about anytime before I arrive at the gates of Hell, I can change my own luck. His name had been Crawford.

I spat on the sand. What did Crawford know about me, about Tartaros, about anything? I looked up at the belly of the Spider. Wasn't there a committee up there somewhere that measured out and dispensed the shit that landed on the universe? Hadn't that committee, time after time, taken the same vote? Dump it all on Bando Nicos and then see if there's any left over?

Change my luck, my ass. You don't just start things and move them. Events snag you and drag you along, and the only thing you can do is look out for the bumps and wriggle around to try and miss them. Tartaros was a fine example of that.

The Razai flew in the teeth of that, however. We were different. Events were dragging us all around down here on the sand, but Garoit had thrown in a spike, stopped it, and said, "We vote on it." The direction had changed, and he had changed it.

There were more spikes. Kegel's gang hadn't flattened and stripped us, leaving our bones to the sand bats. We had turned our luck around and had taken them out. We owed Garoit for that; too.

Nazzar and the no-prisoners vote made us over into something completely different again. And with the unanimous vote of the Razai behind us, we had beaten the Hand and were off to stop a crime. We were on a mission of rescue, and the only thing we could be sure of was that we were doing the right thing. Not the smart thing—the right thing.

I thought of the thing the powder puff Ella had said at the CSA meeting about justice. I couldn't remember it exactly, but it had to do with the best thing that had ever happened to her.

I was confused, which I guess was okay. From experience I knew that every time I thought I had all the answers, I was in big trouble.

"Bando, up here!" I heard Nance whisper, and I scanned the tops of the dunes until I saw her silhouette against the night sky. I climbed up until I was next to her.

"There."

I looked toward the little patch of stars in the south, then down at my feet. The camp was right below us.

"I'll start surrounding the place now," said Nance.

"When they get in place, have everybody light up one of those fire cubes."

"That'll make it easy for them to see us."

"Seeing is believing. We have them outnumbered and outgunned five to one. I want them to see that."

AN OFFER THEY
COULDN'T REFUSE

ONCE the Razai troops had the Reds surrounded, Nance gave me the high sign. I had my rifle over my shoulder and my hand on the pistol grip as I walked down the dune into the Reds' camp. There was a peculiar war going on inside my head. One side wanted to stay alive, to find Alna, to have peace, to live happily ever after. The other side wanted to die, and to take as many Reds with me as I could. It made me reckless and impatient.

A guard standing in front of me called "Halt!" I didn't stop, and he raised his weapon and fired, missing me by a yard. I pulled my weapon down and said, "Join the Razai or die."

He fired again, and I felt the slug whiz through the cloth covering my right shoulder. In a second it started to sting.

I pulled the trigger to my weapon and shot a round through the guard's chest. Another guard, twenty yards away, lifted his weapon to bring me down, and a flash in the dark from outside the perimeter thinned him flat.

Voice alarms went up all over the camp, and I kept walking until I was near some large tents. "Where's the commander of this camp?" I hollered.

A youngish man with a surprised face emerged from what I imagined was their smaller version of the Men's Hall. He was followed by a man with an older face framed by a black beard.

The one with the black beard said, "I am Novi Abennis. Temporary commander of t—"

Nance and the Razai touched off the lights, and it was impressive. From the dunes surrounding the camp came the sinister gleams of a monster with a thousand eyes. Novi Abennis's eyebrows mated with his hairline and I could almost see the digits adding in his head as he scanned our troops.

"What is this?"

"This is a once-in-a-lifetime offer," I said. I placed my rifle over my shoulder again. "Novi Abennis, I want the surrender of your camp. Have your men stack up their weapons and file out."

"You are from the Razai?"

"Yes."

A crafty look came into the fellow's eyes. "We have prisoners. Hostages from your ship. Women. We have over four hundred of them."

"I know. That's why we're here."

"Can we make a deal?"

"Sure, we can make a deal, Novi Abennis. You do what I say, surrender and have your men stack their weapons, and I'll let you stay alive."

His eyes darted back and forth in his head, desperately trying to find a route of escape.

"I must talk with Pau Avanti, with my staff."

"No talk. Just surrender. You don't have much time. Avanti is dead, and so is the Hand in this part of the desert."

"Razai," said the man, "if I give the word, my men will kill the hostages. Wouldn't it be smarter for you to deal?"

"I'm pretending that I didn't hear that. Abennis, we have a rule that holds that a threat is the same as performing the deed, so if you threaten murder, you get punished for murder, whatever happened to the victim. So, instead of slaying you here on the spot for threatening mass murder, I'm going to let you surrender."

He smirked at me and said, "If I give the word—"

I leaned forward and stuck my words right in his face. "First, at top speed with an automatic weapon, it would take your goomba jerkoffs minutes to kill all of the hostages. Second, you don't have any automatic weapons. Third, it will only take us seconds to kill all of you. Fourth, we figure there're worse things than dying, and being a slave is one of them. If you want to shoot, shoot, if being dead is what you're aiming at."

"I don't know!" Abennis held out his hands. "I have to think. What would happen to me and my men if we should be captured by Carlo T.?"

"Don't let that happen."

"I have to think."

I moistened my lips and pointed my rifle at his face. I could feel the advancing wall of rage coming over me. "You know something? I asked to talk to you because I was sick of all the killing and I wanted it to stop. I thought maybe I could do a little toward stopping it. But, you know, after one minute of talking with you, I feel like killing all over again!"

He raised his hands. "Take it easy. What will happen to us if I do as you say?"

I took a deep breath and let it out again. "We can't hold prisoners. So if we don't kill you, you can either join the Razai or go off on your own. You leave the prisoners and the weapons behind."

"Who gets killed?"

"That's up to your prisoners, although if you start killing them, I can guarantee that all of you will die." I aimed the rifle at his nose. "Your time's up. Five, four, three, t—"

"All right! I'm surrendering!" He turned around and shouted, "Men, we are surrendering. Stack your rifles and come out here." He looked up at the perimeter. "You men on guard, lay down your weapons. Everyone, stack arms and come out into the open!"

A PURE ROOKIE

AN hour later I found Stays beginning the job of processing the charges of the prisoners. His head was bandaged and he was talking to one of the bath attendants from the Men's Hall. Her brief bath costume was covered by a sheet, and her name was Margo Hoyt. She was reading his copy of the *Law of the Razai*. She nodded and faced the booklet toward him. "That's what it says right there. If a crime is being committed, and the Razai is asked for help, the Razai cannot refuse."

"I know, but—"

"In the Sunrise Mountains the Hand holds thousands of slaves, men and women, just like us."

"The prisoners we rescued were from our own ship."

She waved the booklet in Stays's face. "It doesn't say anything in here about a ship."

"They haven't asked us for help."

"I'm one of those slaves, copper, and I'm asking you for help." I saw Stays's face blanch at the name "copper."

"Excuse me," I said. "Stays, I'm taking a couple of critters and going off to find Alna. Is your head all right?"

"I'm fine. Bando, what am I supposed to do about this one? She says that—"

I held up my hand. "I heard." I smiled a little as I fed him back one of his own wisecracks. "What we don't have covered, we make up as we go along." I faced the woman.

"Keep at him. I think you have a case."

Margo looked at me through narrowed eyes. "I gave you a bath."

I felt the heat in my face. "Yes."

"What's your name?"

"Bando Nicos."

She nodded. "You are the chief of the Razai Cops?"

"Yes."

"I want to join."

I glanced at Stays, Stays held out his hands, and I looked back at Margo. "Why do you want to be an RC?"

"The Razai is down on slavery and rape, the RCs enforce the law, and before you can free my people, you have a lot of cases your investigators have to decide."

"What about all the other cases?" Stays interrupted.

"Here's some help for you."

Stays held his hand to his bandaged head. "What was the name of your hotel, Margo?"

"Prison?" She spat on the sand. "I'm pure, ratbait. I was born here."

Margo Hoyt was no crime, nothin' but time, pure. Her story would have to wait. I looked at Stays. "I'll be back as soon as I can. For now, you, Marantha, Marietta, and Cap sort out the crimes, charges, and executions. I'm taking a few days off."

"What about me?" asked Margo.

"And Margo," I said, thinking that Marantha, Marietta, and Margo sounded like a weird law firm.

"Have you figured out some way to avoid coming up with conflicting rules?"

"Yeah. The investigators all drop everything, huddle, and take a vote. It's clumsy, but it's all we could agree on."

"Sounds fine. *Adios.*"

Stays eyed the beautiful bath attendant with the mean expression. "The way things are going right now, Bando, by the time you return we might be heading east against the Hand instead of south against Kegel."

"Stick a light on top of a tall dune at night, and I'll find you."

"Hey, look at this." Stays reached beneath his sheet and pulled out a sawed-down version of a rifle, except this one had a very large caliber barrel. He held it above his head, aimed at the belly of the spider, and pulled the trigger. A shower of white sparks streaked into the night sky. We were too close to see how high it went.

"A signal gun," said Stays. "How about I send one of these up every hour or so at night?"

"Have you got enough ammo for that?"

"Cases of it."

I nodded. "Okay. That'd be great."

Stays reached out a hand and placed it on my arm. "Take care, Chief. And about Alna, good luck."

I turned to accept a good-bye from Margo Hoyt, but she was busy studying the *Law of the Razai*. What with Cap Brady being a cop, Marantha being a cop and having a law degree, Stays crawling with education, and now with Margo Hoyt zealously absorbing the words, I figured it wouldn't hurt if I studied the law a little myself if I should ever get a spare moment.

I grabbed a lughox for myself and another for Alna. In addition I took a load of extra water bottles, some rations, and a huge sack of those fire cubes. Instead of retracing our steps, I headed northwest into the darkness to try to cut Alna's trail. After an hour of riding, I began lighting fire cubes and throwing them out in front of me to see if I could find tracks.

Why was I there? It was because I couldn't get the image of Herb and Marantha kissing out of my mind. The feelings I had weren't feelings I had ever felt before, so I didn't have any words for them. All I could think of every time that picture of Marantha crying and kissing Herb came into my mind was, I want some of that, I *need* some of that. There was that look in her eyes, that note in her voice, when she talked about Herb.

Maybe Alna didn't want me anymore, but I wanted to make certain she knew that I wanted her. Maybe Alna needed some of that, too. Maybe that was why she had left.

After three or four hours of riding, I saw the tracks the column had made as it had moved south. I turned the critter north to follow the trail back, and I checked four more times with the fire cubes, and each time the lugh was still on the trail. Satisfied that the critter could find his own way, I folded my arms and tried to doze as I rode. The dreams came and I slept in the shadow of the Spider.

THE EIGHTH DAY

THE sun woke me up. Half of its disk was above the horizon, and I was already uncomfortably warm. The lughox wasn't moving. I dismounted and looked at its face, but it didn't seem any more tired than the other one. Still, I figured it wouldn't hurt to rest them a bit. They had been going all night. I took one of the water bottles and poured half of it down the critter's upraised mouth. I emptied the rest into the other critter that I had been leading.

As I removed my parka and shirt beneath my sheet, I looked at the tracks made by a thousand plus people. Individual trails by the dozens went off to the sides. If you wanted any privacy, that was where you had to go. I looked at my own tracks in the soft sand and couldn't tell the difference between them and the others. The only way I could try and find Alna was to try and find Nkuma. That meant riding until I reached where Nkuma had split off, then heading west toward the mirage.

I thought for a moment that by heading northwest, I could cut Nkuma's trail and shorten the time by a couple of days, but I might miss Alna. I wouldn't know whether she was in front of me or behind me. I scratched my head when I realized that that was already my problem. I could have passed her during the night and not have known.

I muttered a curse or two as I climbed to the top of the

nearest dune and strained my eyes to see. It was nothing but what it had always been, a vast ocean of sand. It was the Union of Terran Republics' litter box. I faced north and squatted on top of the dune as I tried to piece together some kind of plan.

Right then the only thing that seemed to make any sense was heading back to the camp and starting over with the search, but I couldn't bring myself to do it. I saw a flash of reflected light coming from the north. I held my breath and waited for another, but saw nothing. Was it my imagination? Was it Alna? Was it someone else?

Suddenly I felt very vulnerable about being alone on the Forever Sand. There were a lot of sharks on Tartaros, and lots of them were taught to swim in the desert.

I saw it again! The flash!

I slid, tumbled down the slope, and mounted my critter. "Let's go, animal!"

It started off at a walk, but at my urging, it began to do something between a trot and a gallop. Whatever it was, we were moving. I kept up the trollop, always heading north, and when the critter began slowing down, I switched critters, let them walk for an hour or so, then moved them into a trollop again.

Twice I stopped to climb a dune and examined the north for more flashes of reflected light, but saw nothing. As my initial excitement wore off and the day wore on, I took out my copy of the *Law of the Razai* and read the additions since Tenbene *v.* Ollick.

46. During trials spectators will not be armed (Bennet v. Myerson). On the march, d7.

47. Officers of the court will be armed during trials (Bennet v. Myerson). On the march, d7.

I nodded as I thought that there were a couple of sensible provisions. I noticed that we had not mentioned if the cockroaches were officers of the court. I made a mental note to make certain that cockroaches were *not* officers of the court, should the subject ever arise.

48. The infliction of the maximum payback under consideration for obstructing justice applies to everyone, including the spectators (Bennet v. Myerson). On the march, d7.

49. The first thing to be determined in a trial is the maximum payback under consideration (Bennet v. Myerson). On the march, d7.

If a bunch of spectators did get out of hand, I wondered if thinning the lot would be supported or end the Razai. There wasn't any room for slack left in the wording, unless the execution of the payback is left to the victim. But who is the victim when "justice is obstructed"? In such cases it would be up to the investigator to decide whether the victim of the obstruction was the victim in the case or the perp.

For a thin second, I envied Pendril, Rossiter, and Marantha their training in the law. The more I looked at it, and the more I thought about it, the more it seemed as though I was way out of my depth.

But then I thought about the law we did have and how it had worked. If we had been using juicer law from Earth, we'd still be fighting about who would be on the jury in Freddy v. Dick Irish.

I turned the page.

50. Friends of the court may testify (Bennet v. Myerson). On the march, d7.

51. Compulsion, addiction, or otherwise suffering the symptoms of a compulsive disease are no defense if the perp could have sought help prior to the commission of the crime. (Bennet v. Myerson). On the march, d7.

Fifty-one seemed to go against some universal truth or racial memory. How many times had the perps said, "I was drunk, Judge," and the black rags tapped their wrists and said, "Don't do it again." Then the perp goes and does it again, and the black rag gives him another tap on the wrist because, well, after all, he was drunk. He wasn't in his right mind. He didn't know what he was doing.

On Tartaros the argument played a little differently. "I was drunk, I didn't know what I was doing."

"Then you should have stopped drinking."

"I couldn't stop."

"Then you should have gotten some help."

"Well, I wasn't ready for that. After all, I wasn't that bad—"

Bang. You're dead. The price of not getting help has just gone through the roof.

Would it make a difference? The CSA meeting seemed to tell me that it would make a difference. Time would tell, and one thing we had lots of on Tartaros was time.

> 52. Truth is the only acceptable plea (Bennet v. Myerson). On the march, d7.
>
> 53. Forcing sex upon someone who has refused the advance, is rape (Bennet v. Myerson). On the march, d7.
>
> 54. Accomplices are as guilty as the perp (Bennet v. Myerson). On the march, d7.
>
> 55. Witnesses to a crime who take no action to prevent the crime are as guilty as the perp (Bennet v. Myerson). On the march, d7.
>
> 56. The jury may make nonbinding recommendations regarding payback to the victim (Bennet v. Myerson). On the march, d7.
>
> 57. The Law of Silence, if agreed to, is a binding contract. Violating the contract draws the max payback (Nance Damas in the vote on the third law). On the march, d7.

I folded up the papers and stuck them back in my pocket. I felt torn between two extremes. The first was this sense that, with this law, the Razai was bound into something special—something clean and honorable. I felt the law lifted us above the groin-thumpers and leg-breakers on Tartaros.

The other extreme was this feeling that we were a bunch of children playing with something about which we didn't know nearly enough. I hoped it wouldn't all blow up in our faces.

* * *

As evening began filling the valleys between the dunes with shadows, I realized that I must be ahead of Alna. I couldn't imagine her being able to go fast enough that I hadn't overtaken her by now.

I pulled up the critter and began getting into my shirt and parka as I dismounted and climbed a dune. Once on top I looked all around and saw only the sunset. I watched it, and thought of the many times I had cursed that star. While I watched, the sky turned from yellow to that brassy orange, and then to the richest gold. For some reason it seemed to fill my heart with a kind of peace. It's easy to see how the ancients picked on suns for gods. If things had been different, Alsvid could have been such a god. The great blackness of the Spider could have been another god. The ancients on Tartaros could have worked up a top-level mythology.

I turned and looked at the north. There were no lights or any other signs of life. I turned around as the last of Alsvid slipped behind the horizon and studied the south. I had told Stays to put out a light for me, but I wondered if I had gone so far that the Razai camp was below the horizon. Suddenly there was a white streak in the south that reached from the ground up toward the sky. The image of the streak burned into my eye long after it had faded from the sky.

It was Stays and his signal gun. I took it as a good omen, and began to climb down the dune. Another light in the west caught my eye, and I squinted and searched patiently for another glimpse. Slowly retracing my steps up the dune, I kept my gaze fixed on the spot where I thought I had seen the light.

And there it was. The steady dull orange of fire cubes. There was another gang of scavengers out there about four or five miles away. At least one more gang. Other gangs might be more disciplined about how they make their fires.

What if that fire was Nkuma's group coming back? But, then why would they be off the trail? I was pretty certain they were scavengers and not Nkuma's people, but I began worrying about the signals Stays kept zipping up into the night sky. They might attract all kinds of unfriendly sorts.

I decided to continue north. Once I ran into Nkuma, if I hadn't found Alna by then, I could turn around and go back the way I had come. I mounted one of the critters and went north at a relaxed walk. I reached into my ration bag and munched on a thing-bar as I rode.

I opened my eyes and saw that it was late at night. I had dozed, and something had awakened me. With a shiver I realized it was the bone-cracking cold that had awakened me. There was just the hint of a breeze, but it was enough to make the cold colder, and began the process of covering up the tracks. My first thoughts were to hole up in the lee of a big dune and start warming myself and my two animals with the fire cubes. My next thought had me riding north for all I was worth. Those tracks were disappearing quickly, and I did not want to lose them.

Every now and then I threw a fire cube far out in front, and we seemed to be keeping to the trail. As the critters trolloped, and I tried to take a gulp out of one of my water bottles, something hit the back of my hand, which in turn drove the water bottles into my face, knocking me out.

I could hear myself falling, I could even hear the critters bellowing in fear, but I never felt my body hit the sand. My last thought was that I was captured and would soon be dead.

SOMEONE TO WATCH
OVER ME

I HEARD crying, and soon after, I felt warm lips kissing my face. All I could think about was Vic Myerson, Lacy Moore, and a bunch of boybungers had grabbed me. I opened my eyes and looked up. By the light of a fire cube I could see a face. The face was right above mine.

"Alna?"

"Oh, Bando," she cried as she held my head and kissed me. 'I thought we'd killed you. I thought the Razai had lost and you were from the Hand trying to chase us down."

There was a salty taste in my mouth, and I realized that Alna was crying. There Bando Nicos was, getting the same teary kisses that Herb Ollick had gotten. My head was on Alna's lap. I reached up my hand, put it behind her neck, and pulled her head down into a very long and very overdue kiss. When we finally came up for air, we hugged there on the sand until something I'd heard finally gnawed its way into my awareness.

"We?"

She nodded. "Nkuma and a few others. They gave up on the mirage and have been trying to reach us ever since."

I sat up and looked around. "How few? When he left he had over three hundred men and women with him."

"There are seventeen left. Look over there."

I looked and at another fire cube I saw four men and two women sitting in a circle. The rest were huddled together under sheets sleeping. I could see Nkuma's face, and he looked different. He looked different the way Martin Stays had looked different when he had finally ended his time ratbaiting in the black hole.

Nkuma had been through something, and it had crushed him and made him into something new. Whether the new thing was stronger or weaker wasn't clear. One of the men at the fire had his back toward me, but there was not much chance of mistaking that lump. "That's Dom."

"Yes."

"Dom!" I called out. The big man pushed himself up to his feet and walked over. He squatted in front of me.

"Bando. You alive, you dumb chili pepper. I love your face, Bando."

"It's good to see you, sweetmeat. Dom, I found you some stars. In the south. The farther south we go, the more stars we'll see."

"Alna said."

I grabbed his hand and squeezed it for all I was worth. "It's good to see you again. I'm glad you didn't die."

Dom nodded and sniffed. "Lots of us died, Bando. We had fights, murders, thirst, some just dropped from being wore out." He grinned. "I hear Nance Damas is the boss and Pussy-face is number two."

"Nance is still boss. Garoit was killed in the fight, though. He did good. We all did good, but we lost a few friends."

"What was the fight about?"

I rested my head against Alna's lap. What was the fight with the Hand about? "I guess it was about slavery."

"Were we for it or against it?" asked Nkuma.

"Against it," I answered.

Nkuma stood up and came over, stopping next to Dom. "I hear you're a cop now."

I shrugged and raised my eyebrows. There wasn't any point in lying about it. "Yes I am."

The man nodded and looked back at the ones seated around he fire cube. His expression was haunted. Several times I thought he might cry, but each time he shook it off. He seemed ike he was about to split right down the middle.

He lowered himself until he was seated cross-legged before Alna's fire cube. "I have a cancer in me, Bando. It is a huge thing that is eating me alive, and I can't cut it out."

"Talk about it," I said. "The CSAs say you can cut your ache n half if you tell it to someone."

He looked at the glow from the fire cube and began talking, his words quiet. "I never thought so much could change in just a week. It's not just the deaths, but who I am, what I am.

"We took off that first day, me knowing more than anyone else in the world. I could see the mountains, couldn't I? What that Ondo was talking about, the Big Grass, was nothing but words. I did the smart thing, and everyone who went with me did the smart thing, too. And we died.

"Before that first day was over, eleven men and women were dead. They had disputes over food, clothes, colors, who gets to ride, who has to walk, and ages of ancient beefs from back in the crowbars. After that first night I tried to boss them the way any boss would do it. I told them to do it my way, or I'd waste 'em.

"That worked for almost a day. Then there was a minor scuffle that turned into a salt-'n'-pepper thing. Before I knew it, they were laying cutters across each other's throats. To try and stop it, I sent my goons in with cutters and—" He shook his head as he looked down. There were tears on his face.

"I don't know. Maybe twenty-five, thirty dead. We kept walking, and each time we looked those mountains never came any closer. Some of them wanted to break off and catch up with you people, but I wouldn't let them. I thought our best chance was to stick together. The next morning when we woke up, three-quarters of the plastic water bottles had been slashed. Some maniac had destroyed our water supply.

"Then the killings really went wild. I tried to stop them, but the only thing I could threaten them with was more killing." He took a deep breath and let it out slowly. "But I kept on. Despite everything, I kept on. I studied those mountains until I damned near hallucinated myself into believing they were walking away from us. I saw we were almost out of water, I knew that we should go back, yet I kept going on until it was even clear to me. We had to get back to you people or die.

"When we decided to go back, there were a hundred of us. We were all riding by then because none of the lughs had died. When the water ran out, we killed one of the lughs and took out its water storage bladder. We all drank from it." He nodded his head, indicating the survivors. "We were the only ones the water didn't kill. That was two days ago."

He looked at me, and it was as though his look was a plea for forgiveness. I couldn't meet his look for long because I had my own herd of ghosts to tend.

"Nkuma, you're in a bad place if you're looking for someone who never made a mistake. You did your best."

"But my best wasn't good enough!"

I sat up and looked him in the eye. "Sometimes that happens."

"All of those people are dead because I split off for the mountains."

Alna reached out a hand and touched Nkuma's arm. "Who is to say that if you didn't split, those same people wouldn't have been killed fighting the Hand, or in one of Bando's trials."

"Trials?"

I nodded. "And executions. Even among thieves and killers there are behaviors that cannot be tolerated." I grinned. "I read that in a book back in the Crotch." I reached out a hand and placed it on his shoulder. "The law doesn't mean that there isn't killing anymore. The law just gives you some rules to stay alive by, and makes it so that if someone does thin you, he gets his payback."

Nkuma dried his eyes and looked up at the belly of the Spider. "I just keep crying. I can't control it. It just pops out whenever it wants."

"So let it come."

He turned his face away, then suddenly he jumped up. I turned my head to look in the same direction, but Alna's body blocked my view. "What is it?"

"A bright streak of light."

"That's Stays. He's found a way of signaling me to let me know where the—"

A loud roar rolled over us. It was such a powerful roar that the air seemed to slap my face a thousand times. Dom stood up followed by Alna and me. "That was a ship landing," said Dom. "Up ahead. Close."

"What'll we do?" asked Dom.

I turned to Alna and held her hands. "I came up here to find you and tell you I love you and want you to be with me. That's the only reason why I'm here. Will you come back with me?"

She nodded, smiled, nodded again, and cried as she hugged me. I buried my face in her neck and hugged her back. After a moment she leaned back and looked me in the face. "You know what I would like to do, Bando?"

"What?"

"Up there at the landing. I'd like to tell the sharks they're kicking out of the hatch right now about the facts of life here. I want to tell them about the Forever Sand and the gangs."

"And about the mountains—the mirage," added Nkuma.

I nodded. "Maybe I have a thing or two to tell 'em." I looked at the giant. "Dom, I'm going to give you and the others all of my water and rations."

"Okay."

"Move at night. I want you to keep looking. Every so often there'll be a streak of light. You keep heading for that light, understand?"

"I understand. What about him?" He pointed at Nkuma.

Nkuma studied my face for a moment. "Could you use another policeman?"

I grinned. "Sure. But we call ourselves cops. The Razai Cops, or RCs." I looked at Dom.

"I think Nkuma wants to come with Alna and me."

Nkuma took Dom by the arm. "I'm going with them. Take care of the people and do like Bando says. Head for that light at night, and go south during the day." His voice caught a bit.

"Don't lose any."

"When should I go?"

I caught sight of Stays's fireworks. He had fired off two close together. "Dom, see it?"

"Yeah. I can follow that."

"Good," I said. "Get everyone fed then get going. You should be there in a day or two."

Nkuma, Alna, and I walked over to the critters. Nkuma mounted one, I mounted the other and pulled Alna up behind me. We urged the beasts north and heard Dom call after us.

"You'll see, Bando. I'll get them home."

A NEW LESSON

THE bright yellow force field lit up the sky for miles around, making it easy to find the ship. Shortly after we sighted the vessel, the force field went off, the sharks were ordered out of the area, and once they were clear, the ship lifted off the ground and roared into the night sky riding the tip of a blinding white streak. As the rumble of its engines died, I watched that little white streak grow smaller and smaller until it vanished over the horizon.

We urged our mounts forward, and a half hour later we came upon the first group of sharks. They were already fighting, arguing, and dividing themselves up into gangs.

"Haamisit!" cried someone to a god who was too far away to hear. "This is a nightmare!"

I nodded at Nkuma and he fired three shots into the air. I began lighting fire cubes and throwing them around the two lughs until we were circled with light.

We both held our rifles at the ready as the sharks gathered around. "Where are you people from?" I called out.

One small dark man at the edge of the circle said, "Mihviht. We come from the planet Mihviht. Who are you?"

"My name is Bando Nicos. I am a member of the Razai. We are all from Earth. I have come to invite you all to join us—"

"Join you?" bellowed a loud voice. Some giant pushed his

way to the edge and stood in the light. I don't care what planet they come from, a yard monster is a yard monster.

"Certainly. Join us."

"My name is Jotehba Mokk," declared the yard monster. "I boss the Steel Glove. The Glove is the biggest, meanest, most powerful gang that ever saw the inside of the crowbars. I eat mountains, shit nails, piss acid, and if you're real sweet to me, I might just let your bunch apply to join mine. Every hairless ass from that ship belongs to me, so you better go back and tell your boss to watch out, 'cause his ass belongs to me, too!"

There was some laughter, some more catcalls, and a little stretch of silence.

"Jotehba Mokk," I began, "have you ever killed anyone?"

The yard monster laughed. "Many times, little chili pepper. In fact I have just dealt with one fool who thought that being here on this planet somehow ended my power."

He turned around in a complete circle and bellowed as he turned, "I am Jotehba Mokk! I am the boss of the Steel Glove! If you oppose me, you die like Damid Ahtib died!" He ended his turn by looking at me with a big grin.

The crowd was quiet and I called out, "Did anyone see this man kill Damid Ahtib?"

"You do not believe me?" shouted the monster.

I shook my head wondering why prisons ever allowed weight-lifting programs. I mean, why not get it over with, teach them karate and issue guns and knives?

"Did anyone see this man kill Damid Ahtib?" I repeated.

There were several mumbled affirmatives. One fellow who stood right across the circle from the yard monster looked particularly angry. I pointed at him.

"Who are you?"

He looked surprised for a moment, then he pushed his hair out of his eyes and folded his arms. "Tensin Beyrak."

"Beyrak, can you describe to me the death of Damid Ahtib?"

"Yes I can. Once through the hatch, Damid said, 'We can at least be grateful that the terror of the Steel Glove is at an end.'"

There were murmurs of agreement. One look from Jotehba Mokk and the murmurs silenced. "Go on," I said.

"After Damid said that, a minute later Mokk comes up and

says, 'I will kill you.' Damid backed away, but the thing there put his big hands on Damid and crushed his throat."

I nodded and looked at Jotehba Mokk. "Did this fellow describe what happened accurately?"

The yard monster put his fists on his hips and roared out a laugh. He spat on the sand and held up his right hand. "His account is all wrong! I only used one hand to crush his throat!"

A number of nearby toadys laughed at Mokk's joke, then the yard monster stepped over the ring of fire cubes toward me and said, "So what are you going to do?"

"My job," I answered. "Payback for Damid Ahtib."

I let the muzzle of my rifle fall and fired it point-blank into the yard monster's face. I don't know if he was surprised or not. There wasn't enough left of his face to tell.

He fell backwards onto one of the fire cubes, and my imagination made it sound as though he were sizzling like a piece of bacon. Now there would be one more ghost in my dreams at night. There would be another figure in that pale parade who couldn't understand why he was dead. He had followed the rules, hadn't he? He had done the yard smarts, right? I already began whispering to the ghosts that this was not the yard. This is Tartaros.

If the monster didn't look surprised, the faces in the circle looked shocked. Some of them looked skeptical, however. They really couldn't believe that Jotehba Mokk was dead. And if he was indeed dead, what horror would step into his recently vacated place?

I levered a fresh round into my rifle and rested the stock against my thigh, the muzzle pointed up at the belly of the Spider.

"Murder is a crime in the Razai. The payback for murder is death. You have just seen one of our trials." I took a deep breath and spoke as loudly as I could.

"It is cold now. It will get colder before the night is over. Those lights and sounds from the ship will draw scavengers from all over the Forever Sand right here to steal your clothes, your food, and to enslave you for work and for sex, if you're lucky. If you're not so lucky, they'll just kill you. If you live through the night, there will be tomorrow.

"Tomorrow, just before the sun shows itself, the sky will be a beautiful blue. That will change. In minutes it will be too hot to breathe. Getting out of the desert is all that you will be able to think about. You will see some green mountains, and you will head for them, even though they are thousands of miles away, you are on foot, and your water will run out in less than a week. But you will keep going in that direction, because it is the only green thing you will see.

"By then, the gangs that miss you tonight will probably follow your tracks and catch up with you. If you belong to a small group, you will be eaten. If your group is large like mine was, perhaps you can turn the tables on them and fight back.

"But there are important issues you will need to settle. Who will boss the gang? How will you decide who will boss the gang? What about the races? What about the sexes?" There was a lewd giggle in the crowd.

"You women, and a lot of you men, know what it's like to be raped—to be treated like a piece of meat. There was part of a gang on the dunes who specialized in doing just that. They held women as servants and slaves and to provide them with sex on demand. The reluctant were beaten to death. The gang's name was the Hand."

I slung my rifle. "I belong to the Razai. We wiped out that finger of the Hand."

I turned around and waited for one of Stays's fireworks displays. While I waited, the crowd mumbled among itself. One fellow yelled, "Do you mean we have to join the Razai?"

Alna answered. "No. You're free to join whoever you want or join no one at all."

"I see a chili pepper and two maus. Is your gang brown, black, white, yellow, red, or what?"

"We are the Razai!" Alna hissed. "We are human beings! If you are human beings, you are welcome."

"You're lyin' about them mountains, ain't you, man?"

"No," answered Nkuma. "I started in that direction with three hundred men and women. I was very lucky. I managed to make it back with seventeen left alive."

In the south I saw a white streak rise above the horizon. The sharks hushed as they saw it. I looked at them and pointed back over my shoulder. "Just to the right of that light is south. Unless you can get additional supplies somewhere, that is the only way out of this desert. If you go far enough in that direction, you'll run into the Big Grass and a very powerful armed gang bossed by a killer named Kegel.

"Or, if you want, you can join the Razai. That's who's sending up that white streak every hour or so. That streak seems to be moving more and more east every time I see it, so I guess that means we are going to the Sunrise Mountains to take on the rest of the Hand. The Hand holds slaves and looks upon rape as a pastime, like a lot of gangs on Tartaros. We're opposed to that."

"How long have you been here?" shouted a voice.

I thought about it—thought about lying. But decided to tell the truth. The truth seemed very strange, however.

"This is our eighth day."

There were a great many laughs, and it did sound silly. I mean, it was like that old joke about the protomos in the issue line saying to the one standing just behind in line, "You're new."

Well, they all were new. We had aged fast on Tartaros. After all, Tartaros had longer days. I nodded at them.

"We've managed to cram enough experience into those eight days to fill a couple of lifetimes. You're welcome to follow me and my friends back to the Razai, or go ahead and form up your own gangs and do your own research. Here on Tartaros, you are free to either change your luck or rebuild your own Hell right smack down to the last splinter. It's your choice."

I clucked at my critter and Nkuma and I swung around to the south.

"Hey," yelled a voice, "what's the Razai got to offer that's any better than the other gangs?"

I turned around and looked past Alna. I grinned and reached into my shirt pocket. I pulled out Martin Stays's silver star and pinned it to the outside of my sheet so that they all could see it.

"We have law, Brother Crowbar. We have law."

The three of us rode toward the white streak that night, and when we made camp before the sunrise, we had sixteen thousand new brothers and sisters for company.

Thus endeth the lesson.